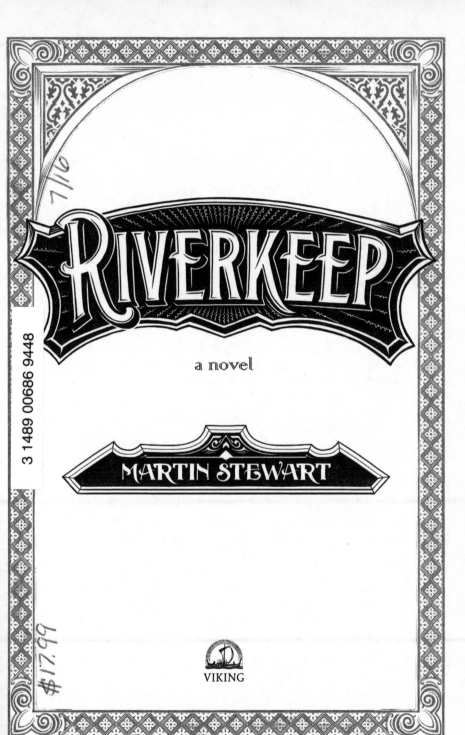

RIVERKEEP

a novel

MARTIN STEWART

VIKING

VIKING

An imprint of Penguin Random House LLC

375 Hudson Street

New York, New York 10014

First published simultaneously in the United States of America by Viking,
an imprint of Penguin Random House LLC, and in Great Britain by Puffin Books, 2016

LIBRARY OF CONGRESS CATALOGING-IN-PUBLICATION DATA

Names: Stewart, Martin J., author. Title: Riverkeep : a novel / Martin Stewart.
Description: New York, New York : Viking, an imprint of Penguin Random House LLC,
2016. | Summary: "When 15-year-old Wulliam's father is possessed by a dark spirit,
Wull must care for him and take on his family's mantle of Riverkeep, tending the
Danek"—Provided by publisher.
Identifiers: LCCN 2015028442 | ISBN 9781101998298 (hardcover)
Subjects: | CYAC: Fantasy. Classification: LCC PZ7.1.S746 Riv 2016 | DDC [Fic]—dc23
LC record available at http://lccn.loc.gov/2015028442

Manufactured in U.S.A.

Printed in Goudy Oldstyle

10   9   8   7   6   5   4   3   2   1

For Ellice and James,

my beloved grandparents

★ *Aldoë*

★ *Rathelow*

★ *Canna Bay*

Holy Isle

Breakwater

★ *Boddin Monastery*

★ *Wellcrow*

★ *Gidlaw*

★ *Decatur House (Clutterbuck)*

Overlee

The Deadmoor

★ *Inveroip*

Ironba

Grassmarket ★

CITY of ORACCO

★ *Danbank*

Keppul Sound

★ *Glyne*

King's foot

★ *Kinmun*

★ *Ciarnton*

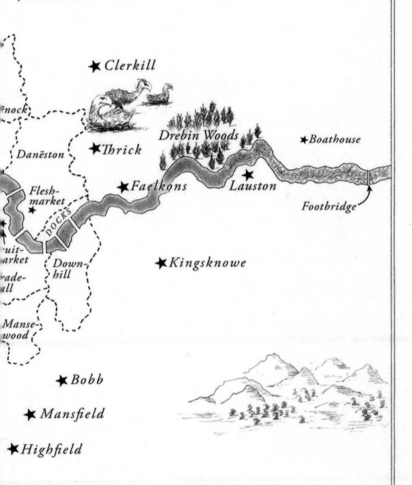

★*Oathlaw*

★ *Hallnock*

★ *Clerkill*

Drebin Woods

★*Boathouse*

Danēston

★*Thrick*

*Flesh-
market*

★*Faelkons*

★ *Lauston*

DOCKS

Footbridge

nock

*uit-
arket*

*Down-
hill*

★ *Kingsknowe*

*rade-
ll*

*Manse-
wood*

★ *Bobb*

★ *Mansfield*

★*Highfield*

Rivermen who tire of the watterscape fynd that lyfe on the land is grim as death benneath it.

—R. J. Fobisher
Proverb, *Riverkeep Ledgers*, Vol. 1, p. 4

The Keep

To keepe the Danék.
To presserve lyfe and to retreeve those claymed by its watters.
To reckord the happnings in the river's oan voyce.
To ackt with dignittie.

—Riverkeep Ledgers, *Vol. 1, p. 1*

"Yer hands are shakin', Wulliam."

Wull shrugged and shifted his hands on the mug.

"It's cold."

Pappa laughed, releasing a stinging breeze of lakoris tobacco.

"That's no' cold. Cold is when yer eyeballs scratch when ye blink, when it hurts to breathe. Ye'll be Riverkeep soon. Ye'll get used to that quick enough."

"I'm no' Riverkeep yet," said Wull. *Never,* he thought.

Pappa secured a knot and sat back on his haunches. "But a week'll no' be long passin', my boy," he said. "Time feels long for the young, but don't worry—ye'll no' be young for long."

He grinned and went to get the boat ready, ruffling Wull's hair as he passed. The deep creak of his rubber boots faded into the gloom beyond the lamp.

Wull put down the mug and looked at his hands, already thickly scarred with the burns of rope and snow. Over the voice of the river—sucking knocks and shifting wood—he felt the needles of sound as the new ice along the banks of the Danék cracked.

Ice meant winter and darkness, and for waterfolk a new kind of danger. Pappa saw it as a great enemy to be feared and defeated with flames and rods. But it brought Wull respite from the river's black void, its thick scum and little puddles of treacherous clarity, and the huge sharp rocks fringed with weed that swirled like a corpse's hair.

In the heat of summer, perfumed wildflowers grew along the banks, insects skittered on the leaf-padded surface, and silvery clouds of fish burst through the water—chased by the seulas whose wet little heads dotted the surface like stepping stones, their golden summer eyes glowing in the sunlight.

But Wull could never think of the river as something living. He had seen what happened on the rocks: the floating bodies, arms raised and mouths howling against the surface as though restrained by thick glass.

It was the Riverkeep's job to push his arms through that barrier to embrace the dead, to lower his face close to theirs and taste the bilge-stink of their breath before lifting them from the water. Pappa did so with a martyr's grace, blind to gangland markings and forgiving of sinners who took their own lives. Wull had watched them since he could remember: propped in a grotesque parody of sleep, as though they were snatching a nap in the back of the little bäta.

Now he sat *with* them. Sometimes the bodies were old, and the flesh slid from their shining bones like the skin of a poached fish.

Wull did not want this wilderness life. With Pappa's help he had read the ledgers in their entirety, right through the ninth volume in Pappa's own careful hand. The ledgers didn't just list the dates; they told the stories, detailed bodies' decomposition, and kept the words of the rescued and their reasons for jumping: sweethearts, fear, sicknesses of the mind, and often, so often, "coin." At first Wull had taken this literally, as though they were jumping into a wishing fountain to fish for pennies. Then he had realized and felt like a foolish child.

Every entry was the same. To Pappa this was priceless—a means of creating something that would stand forever as a monument of pride and respectability. To Wull it was a prison of words—repetitive, rotting words.

He reached over and touched the ledger that sat open on the desk. Their last discovery had been just over a week ago: 3,101, a widow, faceup and floating, her breasts rot-swollen, her cheek cut with a debtor's mark. But as always the most recent entry was the next number—3,102—offered with the prayer of the Riverkeep: that the number might be never filled.

He closed the ledger. The mold-edged pages, heavy with moisture, fell with a report that bounced round the boathouse like the slamming of an enormous door. Wull heard the creak of Pappa's boots in the darkness.

"Yer coming tonight."

Wull shook his head. "It's too cold."

"Ah've told ye, that's—"

"I know, it's just . . . Not tonight, Pappa, please."

Pappa regarded him a moment, shifting the wad of lakoris leaf around in his mouth. Then he shook his head.

"Yer nearly sixteen" was all he said.

The air was sharp and hard in Wull's lungs. Even wrapped in layers of seula gut, he felt the chill on the exposed flesh inside his boots and around his waist like the cut of wire. The white, still world communicated itself as a sharp whine outside of his hearing, and he stamped his feet on the bäta's exposed ribs and buried his face in his elk-fur collar, peeping over when his eyes could stand the cold.

The lanterns, staked in the riverbed where the currents met and the flotsam gathered in eddied clumps, made glowing islands in the velvety darkness, their flames fuzzed in the fog like dandelions. The industrial might of Oracco was silent, the howls of its foundries and smithies carried away on the east wind. The only sound in the smothered world was the rhythmic clicking of the oars and the soft noise of the blades moving through the water.

By the fifth lantern, they had discovered a graygull, torn open by a seula—"Not much else left for them," Pappa said—and the broken spokes of a carriage wheel. The gull was flapping limply, trying to fly on shattered wings while it bled onto the ice. Pappa reached down and gently snapped its neck between his thumb and forefinger. Wull watched him ease the body into the water on scar-twisted palms.

As far out as the edge, at lantern twenty-two, they still had found nothing more than knots of weed and grass clinging to the ice rods. Wull peered into the unseen and untended wilderness beyond the last outpost of the keep's realm, in the depths of which lurked the bustle of Oracco's ports, the flashing steel of bandits, and, past a scattering of hamlets, the Danék's estuary and the wider sea.

He trailed his glove tips in the water and flicked droplets out toward the beyond. Pappa saw him, tut-tutted, then—as he turned the bäta toward the boathouse and its warmth—they found 3,102.

It was male, fat-backed and facedown, white flesh streaked with a pattern of cuts and bruises Wull knew came from the fierce, swirling currents near the footbridge where Mamma had drowned. It had been wearing a uniform that still clung to it in scraps, and there were murky tattoos spilled along its visible skin. Pieces of its scalp were missing, and leaks of blood and fluid colored the wafer of snow-dusted ice that had crept around it.

Pappa looked at Wull.

"The footbridge," said Wull.

Pappa nodded solemnly. The flames cut his face into slices of light and dark, one eye hidden in the black wedge behind his nose. "May Lavernes keep thee," he muttered, lifting the oars from the water. "Here, Wulliam—row."

Wull took the oars, turned the bäta, and heaved it forward. Even now, its great weight pulled at him as though it might shatter his wrists. He looked down at the floating form of 3,102. It looked bunched, not loose, and sat tightly in the water.

The ice must be holding it steady, he thought, dropping the oars and stilling the bäta.

He stood as Pappa stood. The painted eyes on the bäta's prow faced stoically forward. Half-shut and focused, they peered into a darkness that, beyond the reach of the lantern, was absolute. Wull turned from them to the reassurance of the flames. Without the movement of the boat, the silence was so empty he felt the weight shift in his stomach and the hair creep on his back.

"Pappa," he said.

"Ssh, Wulliam, a minute."

Pappa tipped back his hat and muttered the Riverkeep's prayer, then, broad back braced and legs wide, he reached down for that hug to pull the wretched lump into their boat.

3,102 hugged back.

In a flurry of movement that lasted no more than a gasp, the two figures disappeared beneath the surface, and Wull stood rigid, his breath billowing and his skin tight. In the instant his pappa had vanished, he'd seen a brown mouth, opened wide like a snake, and two eyes that glittered like razors.

The eyes had met Wull's. The water was still. There weren't even bubbles.

Fighting the sudden lightness in his skull and with a kick of painful nausea taking his wind, Wull began to sweat, feeling panic speed his heart. He stood still for a timeless age, unable to move, listening to the silence and staring at the space in the water through which Pappa had vanished, trying to force his lips to form Pappa's name and sending only the tiniest wisps of breath into the freezing air.

It was the cold that brought him back to himself, needling wakefulness into his muscles. For the first time in his life he was aware of the thinness of the planks that separated him from the black void beneath, and he felt the emptiness of the world like a fist in his gut—felt the distance of other people as he never had before.

Wull heaved the oars into place and sat in the keep's chair, tears freezing on his cheeks, his gaze locked on the spot where Pappa had vanished. Pappa had shown him how to row—then made him practice until his knuckles bled—but his return journey took an age, weakened by terror and blind to his destination, branches scraping the prow behind him.

A seula broke the water beside the boat, its golden summer eyes now a piercing winter's blue, and Wull dropped the oars in fright. The grabbing shadows of the banks reached across the white water, and beneath him the river moved unusually, each swell and press of current renewing the feeling of the razor eyes slicing into his, and he prepared himself for the water to rise up and take him.

3,102 was waiting for him on the sand.

Faceup, the sight was no better: the face was fish-picked and rotten, the guts torn by an adventurous seula so that its stomach hung open like a bag of wet coal. Its uniform was that of a seafarer, and a broken musket still hung from its belt. It wasn't moving, and seemed to be quite dead. With a huge effort of courage, Wull threw a stone at it. The pebble bounced harmlessly off the hollow body as though it were nothing more than a sponge. Fearing to expose himself to the thing unguarded, he backed into the boathouse and closed the door.

By the time he reached the window, it was gone.

Wull stood at the window for as long as he could before releasing his breath and clouding the glass. Then he went and made himself tea, focusing on the loose leaf and the water and the stove's flame to ground him, to bring him back to normality; in a world of tea and unreliable matches there could not also exist corpses that moved. There could not exist an absence of Pappa, as there could not be an absence of sky or air or water.

He pictured Pappa, thought of his voice.

The ledger, Pappa would say. *It's the record of the Riverkeep. Of* us.

Wull drew the book to him and lifted the enormous cover. As it fell open he thought of the movements that might be hidden by the sound, and he glanced around him, into the corners left by the flickering lamps.

The bodie of a mann found by lanttern twennty-two, he wrote carefully, elbow pointed, *swolen and white haveing been tampered with by the rockes and fishes and a seula. Stomack open and black.*

He paused.

Unabel to returne bodie. Gonne.

Wull lifted his tea, then lowered the mug without drinking. He raised the pen again and wrote the next number—3,103—then sat back, tears creeping onto his face. He felt that his blood, rather than ink, had stained the parchment.

"May this number be never filled," he whispered, eyes closed in prayer.

The timbers of the jetty creaked, steadily, and the sound grew larger until the footsteps reached the sand and ceased.

"May the waters spare whomsoever a-crosses their path from here unto eternity. . . ."

There came a new sound, of creaking rubber boots. They reached the door of the boathouse, and Wull could sense the angry weight on the other side, a plank's thickness away, and he knew it was his pappa as he had always known him—heavy with lakoris and slow of movement—but there was something else there now too. Wull began to sob, forcing his eyes to remain closed.

The handle turned.

"And bless the Riverkeep on his journeys," said Wull, fighting his fear as the smell of the river filled the air and the weight of the thing moved toward him, "as he endeavors to keep thy waters safe from causing harm or from being themselves a-harmed."

The movement behind him stopped.

"Amen," said Wull.

2

Canna Bay

And so by these humble means was the Canna Bay breakwater made, as generations stood and stooped to-gether. Smashed stone gathered, rock reclaimed from the sea, rising in defense of the town. Though uneven and rugged, it served its purpose well, as behind its shield the fruits of the sea were harvested. And so a statue was built in salute to those who had toiled: a totem known as Mother Demlass—more commonly, simply the Mother. Alongside the lighthouse she stands barefoot: symbol and guardian of the catch, her strong arms clutching a basket of pickerel in hopeful prophecy of the town's survival. The people kneel at her feet, hands upon them in prayer: let the catch be as fruitful as the day's past— and tomorrow's even more. In the face of danger—high winds or worse—legend says the Mother's feet find firmer footing. She is ever vital and protective.

–Julyus Agges, Hillfolk and Coast-Dwellers: An Oral History

The fishing village of Canna Bay sat in the Danék estuary between a mountain and the sea: a glistening lump of white houses, lanterns, and shining cobbles that rang with midnight voices and through which the stink of fish guts and sea rot moved like sharp fog. Its buildings were tin and split wood, held together with struts and nets and oil-stained ropes. Between them ran lanes carpeted by the leavings of the markets and the gulls, weeds and grasses pushing through the fish heads and bracelets of scales into the woodsmoked air.

A few hundred yards from the line of the pebbled beach, in the depths of water that was as black as tar and tossed ragged by the wind, the mormorach emerged.

It fought through the seabed with the violent wriggle of a birthing snake and then, freed from the slumber of eons, let its momentum carry it upward, its sensory system taking stock of its changed environment. Along its great length, tiny hairs and vessels tested the newly freezing water, and the big heart behind the first row of pectoral fins quickened at the shock. It flexed its jaw, testing the silt and champing once, twice, feeling tusks clasp against its face.

It called out, a low, sonorous boom that shook the water around it and made the blind darkness come alive. The mormorach saw everything in its phosphorescent glow: small fish, the rugged topography of the seabed, thick tangles of weed, and the hulls of craft. There was landmass, too, with channels of open water ahead and behind.

The creature rotated slowly in the water, letting the current guide its path. As it moved, the hairs on the tip of its beakish face sensed distant fish, the crackle of their oily skin sending a command that passed through the brain to the tip of the enormous tail, which thudded once, like a whip, and drove the mormorach into the dark.

In the village, the gloom of the clouded night matched the water's murk. Emory Blummells slipped out the front door of his cottage, clipping the handle back into place with practiced ease. He pressed some lakoris leaf into his top lip, looked around, and sniffed the air—the salt of the water and the sourness of landed seaweed. The clouds were thick, and the roaring wind meant he could hide behind a cloak of noise.

Conditions were perfect. He grinned to himself, teeth lost behind his wispy beard, as he hurried through the closed market with the quick steps of a fat-legged man.

His wife would be annoyed if she woke and found him missing, but she'd be pleased with the big pearl trout they'd have tomorrow. Emory remembered the days when she would come with him on his nighttime journeys: sneaking around together in the shadows, finding each other's hands, and stifling their laughter. That was a long time ago—before their children, when they'd been young together.

As he reached Main Street he ducked into the tree line, his nostrils filling with the smell of earth. The line of the hilltops and mountain was a smudge against the night sky, above the glow of the lanterns in the center of the village. The fish factories were still awake, laughter and song ringing tin walls seamed by slits of lamplight as the women and men stripped and cooked and packed the day's catch in boil jars to feed Oracco's fat stomach.

Emory moved silently along the seafront in the bushes, parting the damp leaves with his fingers.

A packer stepped out from a glowing doorway, steam rising from his naked torso, then turned and urinated against the factory's wall. Emory looked up to the moon, glowing like a silver coin behind the clouds, then eased himself into a deeper shadow, crouched low in a flower bed beneath the window of a sleeping cottage, absently turning his green-stoned wedding ring as he waited for the hot stream's thrum to stop.

He was good at waiting invisibly. Once, when he'd been after fowl in the Rydberg Woods, a red balgair had peed on his boot. He'd worn the stain on the leather like a badge of honor, but had to endure the frustration of keeping its origin secret. Emory could keep secrets; like everyone else in Canna Bay, his bones shook with them.

As the beat of the packer's water was replaced by the crash of waves, Emory sucked on his lakoris and spat noiselessly into the tin-smelling earth between his boots, neck wound into the high collar of his coat and his hands elbow-deep in the pockets. He counted to sixty, then he spat again and moved forward.

When he reached the harbor, he used the moon's weak glow to light the ground, picking his way delicately between the weed-filled cracks, coils of rope, and rusting chains. Bleached-looking buoys were bundled together like giant grapes against a crumbling wall, and the hulking shadows of landed craft loomed comfortingly over him. As the gray-gulls padded on the masts, Emory caught his breath beside an ancient anchor, then began to cross the reams of spongy, crackling seaweed on the beach.

The water, when it came, was cold enough to bite through the thick rubber of his wading boots, and Emory shivered happily as he hobbled into his skiff.

"Come on, ol' girl," he said to the boat. "We won't be long in the catchin'."

His thick, sure fingers loosed the line that bound it to the jetty and found the oars by touch; then he pushed off, dipping the oars' blades silently into the water.

Far out to sea, the mormorach swung its head around.

The motion of the skiff reached its senses as tingles and echoes that shivered along its body. It switched its focus from the shrill anxiety of the shoal it had been tormenting. The mormorach's brain recognized food in the patterned sequence of the distant splashes and, with another whip of its tail that scattered the fish like dandelion seeds, it thrust itself toward shore.

Emory looked back at Canna Bay through his own panted fog. The water was choppy, but he was an experienced rower, and his rhythmic strokes allowed him to settle once again into his reflective mood, the wind tugging at his thin mustache and pulling drops of water from his eyes.

The bustle of the village could be sensed even at such a distance and such an hour, the murmur of voices in the shrinking specks of light thrown into the air with the smoke and the steam.

The breakwater reached out alongside him, a broken finger of piled stone, the silhouette of the Mother's statue at its tip. The village's houses were mostly in shadow, lit at intervals by the lighthouse's sweeping beam. His own house was among them, and he thought of his wife sleeping there, snoring gently, pictured the familiar things of his ember-lit bedroom around her, and shivered again to think of its warmth finding its way back into his frozen toes when he returned.

He passed a few moments spotting the roofs of the other Blummells in Canna Bay: so many that an intricate system of bynames had sprung up over the centuries. His own family were the Blueloon Blummells, named for the color of woolen stockings his great-grandfather had worn to sea; next door were the Cutblade Blummells and, three cottages seaward, the Corry Blummells.

Emory paused in his rowing for a moment to hoist his own blue stockings to his knees.

By the time he had reached the open pen of the trout farm, he had been rowing for more than twenty minutes and his elbows had begun to ache. He fixed the skiff to the pen and let it drift a moment. It was even colder so far out on the water, and he fancied that his mustache had begun to crisp in his mouth's fog. He pulled a few fresh strands from the lakoris pouch and pressed them between his lip and gum.

Forty yards below, the mormorach circled on the seabed. The oils of the fish behind the net were thick in the water, clouding its senses. The splashes above had stopped, and it could not yet see the skiff. Instinct told it that a roar could drive away its prey, and so it waited, moving patiently, its every fiber delicately triggered for a sign of movement on the surface.

Emory cracked his knuckles one by one, then lifted his net. It was about the size of a cooking pan, with a long, flowing mesh. It hardly needed its size—there were thousands of fish in the pen and they were all as greedy as they were stupid—but it made a straightforward task simpler still. He crumbled some meal between his fingers and sprinkled it on the surface. Any minute now he would see their pale shapes, then all he had to do was extend the net and let the fish swim into it. It always seemed strange to him that a pearl trout, so delicious and strong, could be so blind—so unknowing of its fate.

The mormorach began to drift toward the surface.

A thin line of silver flashed across Emory's vision.

"There ye are," he whispered. "Come on—we need only the one o' you . . . wi' butter 'n' beans. Come on now. . . ."

A sudden wave made the skiff lurch, and Emory staggered back, righting himself on the seat.

"What in gods' was—"

The mormorach's senses were now brightly alert, and it dipped a pectoral fin to align its vision with the wide shape on the surface. It darted quickly forward.

Another wave sent the lakoris pouch from Emory's pocket and through the air. It landed with a tiny splash, barely rippling the water.

It was enough.

The mormorach thudded its tail and rose like a meteor, smashing its face through the frail hull of the skiff and clamping its jaws around the soft thing it found there, a roar of satisfaction trembling through its muscles. It sailed through the air, twisting for joy through the beam of the lighthouse before crashing back into the water and whipping its tail to drive toward the seabed.

Emory felt only the heat of his blood surrounding him, the pain in his guts throwing the rest of his senses around in confusion. As the mormorach drove him through the freezing dark and the pressure began to pound his skull into unconsciousness, he reached down instinctively, touched scales and bone, and his hands filled with a warm, slippery mess.

Just before Emory's heart stopped beating, he had time to understand that he was holding his own guts—that the creature had bitten him open.

And, unbidden, from a flash of light in his brain, the word *intestine* came. . . . Then he was a young man again, holding hands with his wife in the Rydberg Woods and kissing her for the first time.

3

The Keep

Ursa: literally, "running death." A large, houndlike, nocturnal carnivoran (they will hunt only once the moon has left the sky), the ursa can grow up to sixteen feet in height (when reared on hindquarters) and can reach great speeds on its short, thick legs. Equally at home in water or on land, it can outpace both a seula and a horse with ease, and its six unretractile claws help it climb with unexpected dexterity. This dexterity is crudely mechanical, even allowing for the opening of doors or windows. Completely hairless, it has a dense layer of blubber beneath its brilliant white skin. This insulates the animal perfectly, regulating blood temperature in even the harshest conditions as well as providing protection from attack—even from the bullets of the most powerful rifle. Ursa hides, teeth, and bones are highly valued by traders, but the animals' strength, ferocity, and resistance to gunfire make them rare game, and their habit of eating fermented sunberries (the ingestion of which fuels aggression) means even well-armed huntsmen shy from their pursuit.

–Encyclopedia Grandalia, *University of Oracco Print House*

The boards were foot-slipping glass, slicked with invisible slime from the kiss of dew and the frozen moisture in the air. Around him the snow swallowed nature's sounds, and the world was still and calm, the midafternoon sun white and heatless behind the clouds. The fog of the day had mixed with tendrils of smog from the far-off city, and through it the bäta's painted eyes, heavy and staring, watched Wull at his task.

He drove his boot edge into the slats and heaved again at the ice rod. But the force of his strength, though it brought pain into his neck and spots to his vision, set only the bäta to rocking, the rod unyielding in the crag of white that covered its bottom half. He cursed himself for leaving it so long—and for letting the lantern burn out. Without the flame to warm the iron, the ice climbed freely and choked *the river an' the traffic an' the creatures what lives in it.*

Wull heard Pappa's voice in his memory, and pulled his hat tighter about his ears.

One winter they had found a body stuck headfirst in the

frozen ground beside a burned-out lantern. The ice had covered it to the waist so that the torso and head were preserved as though the man was holding his breath; but he had been picked clean from hip to toe by the insects and the birds and the elements, so his skeleton was shining and bare. When they'd lifted him, the legs had collapsed, all the connectiveness taken by the mouths of hungry things.

That was why the lanterns were lit, Wull knew: so water flowed and the fallen stood a chance.

And he had let lantern one extinguish. Of the remaining twenty-one there would be more gone cold, their wicks frozen into black stumps and their rods locked into immovable, glistening rock.

His second day as Riverkeep, and already the threads of it had slipped from his grasp, pulled away like weeds in the current. He stilled his movements and felt the surge of the river beneath him, its constancy and strength pushing against his fumbled knots; never waiting, never resting, the splintered ice—shot through with scattered-seed bubbles—closing round the bäta like a fist.

What had seemed in Pappa's keep a peaceable realm—where the bäta moved on rails and the lamps were a ceaseless barrier of heat and light—now seemed a frozen chaos. The lanterns' placement, catching the swirls of current for centuries, now seemed foolish; reaching number one meant he'd had to row *against* the flow at its strongest until the sinews of his back felt they might snap. And when he'd made it, sweat frozen to frost on his skin and his lungs reduced to stinging, flapping bags, he found the replacement whale oil (*Reekin' liquid gold, this*, Pappa whispered in his mind) was near empty and he would have to return to the boathouse, top up the fish-stinking bottle, repeat the whole journey, and *then* find his way backward through the fog and the rocks and the trees to the next silent, frozen pole, turning every few seconds to check his course and losing what tiny momentum he'd achieved.

He'd never seen his pappa refilling the whale oil. It was always full.

Riverkeep. He felt the idea of it sitting on him, like a coat of paint that wouldn't dry. In his two days, he had been sent for to clear the Oracco Road of andal-geese who had honked and hissed and bitten chunks from his trousers. The guardsman had asked where his father was, and Wull hadn't known what to say for such a long time that the man filled the tortured silence by burping and swearing at the weather. In the time he'd been on the river he had recovered: another pair of dead gulls; the skull of some flat-toothed animal, bulbous and thin where the brains had sat; a grass-sewn cloak; the wrought-iron door of a city furnace stuck to a raft of plants, hinges burst out by some explosion; all manner of foodstuffs whitened to crisps in the winter air. And the most recent find: a decent coat that would be dried and cleaned and hung alongside the vacant jackets and feetless boots in the dry room kept for the unrotten clothes of the dead.

But he had found no bodies. Not yet. When he had spied the coat his heart had stopped in his chest and he'd moved toward it with leaden arms, the pressure of his blood bringing color to his face and floating his head. But he'd found it mercifully unoccupied—just the current pushing its empty sleeves into arms and stretching the trunk of it as though there was a man inside.

He looked at it now, lying on what *had* been his seat, frosting in the chill, yawning its torn lining into the air. He flicked it closed with his boot and pushed off from the lantern, the weight of the oars hot against the bruises they'd drawn already on his palms as he sculled into the river's still-flowing center.

Wull rowed, looking around his world. The banks slid past in their slow, distant way, wedges of icy sand and white banks met by woods filled with the unexpected and terrifying blackness of unwintered bark. From inside came the chirrups and cracks of forest life, but Wull—safe in the knowledge that the ursas would be sleeping—paid them little heed. A recent landslide had taken a bite from the riverbank, and fresh, crumbly soil still tumbled down its brown surface, exposing the nostril of a rodent's burrow.

Even in a year the river altered unimaginably, the shape of his boundary always shifting, falling to the snap of winter or the lash of summer's heat. Last spring a flash storm had taken a grove of trees in the night, and the absence of their shadows on the horizon had been alarming and lasting, like the vacant space of a missing tooth.

And then, in the manner of things, it became the way it had always been, and when Wull stood back and watched, his world seemed to stand still.

In the far distance Oracco's smoldering furnaces could be glimpsed as an orange glow beneath the clouds, like a buttercup tickled under a chin. But as ever its voice was silenced by the east wind, taking the beat of industry out to sea. Wull closed his eyes and pictured it: endless streets of carriages and towers, ever changing, always pushing up— higher and bolder and grander, its masses warming their feet by the fires of industry.

He glanced over his shoulder to correct his course. In the split second before he met them, he could have sworn the bäta's eyes flicked away.

"I'm sorry, all right?" he said aloud, startling himself with the sound of his own voice. "I won't let it happen again."

He rowed another few strokes. The river bubbled pleasantly, shards of ice knocking lightly against the hull.

"An' I'm sorry about the nets. At least it's only the one torn—there were plenty o' things in the others. They're workin' fine."

The answering silence was solid; his was the only voice

for miles around. Instead of replying—and he was glad it could not, for he imagined what it might say, this boat worn smooth by generations of better men—the bäta stared forward, the weary eyes of its high prow nodding with the river toward the boathouse.

Wull's home sat on the bank, the jetty stretching for him like an accusatory finger, eyelike windows gazing out. He could feel the weight of the place in his mind like a stone on a stretched sheet, dragging everything else toward it.

He tethered the bäta to the jetty. It should go inside now, he knew, behind the big doors, but he would have to go out again so soon, carrying a full bottle of whale oil that could blow him to red scraps should it catch the wrong side of a flame. The bäta's eyes were like steel in his back as he plodded across the few feet of beach that led to the front door.

He felt better once he'd closed the door. With hours until real darkness, the ursa bars didn't need to come down yet, but even without them, the thick varnished wood was as hard as iron. He leaned his forehead on it, drawing the smell into his nose. The fire was almost out, but a tiny heat still glowed in its heart—a solitary ember amidst the wreck of his day. Alongside the aroma of the coals were the other smells of the boathouse: whale oil, tar, salt, the sweet rot of vegetables, and the pungent, damp smell of drying fungus;

the dangerous smell of the smoker and the sharpness of Pappa's lakoris; the odor of cooked fish and stewed, piled tea leaves; the cold, oily smell of iron tools; the smell of rubber boots and the polish for leather ones; the sour smell of woolen clothes drying and the clean, tinny smell of worms jarred for bait; the smell of wood and the dust of wood beside the high pitch of varnish; and the warm, sweet smell of mice that could not be caught or driven away. The river entered the house under the big doors and the thick bars of the ursa cage, and everything else was smothered by the green, head-filling stink of it.

And now, he thought, to add to all that was the smell of Pappa, mulching in the spare chair.

The water washed in with a little wave that slapped gently on the wood. Its bobbling sounds kept the feeling of movement in Wull's guts and bones so that he never sat truly still. Even on land he swayed a little, and it was Pappa's custom to walk with a roll in his shoulders, the way deep sailors did after years on the ocean.

Wull filled the big copper kettle and carried it with two hands over to the range in an awkward waddle. The kettle had dulled already, and the reflection that peered back at him was indistinct and faceless, just the vague haze of his nut-brown skin and his tight-cropped black hair.

Which is no bad thing, he thought, knowing how gaunt

and bruised his face would be after two nights of fitful, twitch-waking sleep.

There was a shake in his hands he hadn't noticed—the match hopped on the strip and took four strikes before it caught. He watched the glow of the gas ring until the water began to bubble with heat, then turned to the lamps.

He had cut one of the wicks the day before, and it burned now with an uneven, smoky glow. He'd seen Pappa do it, little scissors in his big hands neatly smoothing frayed edges into perfect, tapered nubs, their flames rising halfway up the globe. When all four lamps were lit it was close to daylight inside.

Wull looked at his own attempt—sliced into threads as though rhat-picked. By the time the last of Pappa's wicks had spoiled, he'd be scrabbling in the gloom and spending matches to avoid bumping into walls. But he had to try to mend them—he could hardly buy new wicks every time they needed trimming—and besides, maintenance of the boathouse was one of the Riverkeep's duties—he'd seen it on the list in the first ledger. There were amendments on extra parchments wedged in between the pages. It was a long list.

He worked on. Just as he finished his first straight cut, Pappa spoke.

"Where is it?" he said in that new voice.

Wull swallowed and turned to face the parlor door.

"Where's what?"

"It, it. It that speaks."

"You mean me? Wulliam?"

"It dun't matter's name. Need to eat."

Eating, thought Wull, remembering breakfast.

"I'm trimmin' the lamps," he said. "You can eat when I'm done."

"Lamps! Light's no good. Darkness good."

"You like the light. You say it's everythin' we need out here."

"Never did," the voice rasped, dry as dead leaves. Somehow it dripped too, choked with fluid.

"You did," said Wull. "'Safety an' heat on the water and in the house,' you said."

"Never did."

"You did so. Why don't I light this one jus' now? It'd be nice. . . ."

"No! Darkness!"

Wull leaned away from the door. Pappa's shape was just visible in the murk of the room, hunched, hair across his face, wrists bound to the arms of the chair. Wull could hear bubbles in his throat.

"That's fine," said Wull. "Does it hurt your eyes?"

Pappa, sagging like wet cloth against the seat back, peered at him. His eyes were hidden behind the hang of his hair, but Wull felt their force. They were not Pappa's eyes, nor had they been for two days; their calm, solid brown had gone milky and gray, set deep in a face that had already passed into slackness. And there was something else in them: a fug that bled into his pupils and clouded them against seeing.

"Doesn't *hurt* eyes . . . darkness," Pappa whispered. Then: "Eat."

"Just let me finish this lamp," said Wull, but as he lifted the scissors again they shook in his grip and he dropped them without cutting.

"Eat," said Pappa.

"All right," said Wull. "What will you have?"

"Same as again."

"You can't just eat that every time."

"Same as again!" shouted Pappa.

"But they're *fish heads*—"

"The same!"

Pappa's voice was enormous. Wull jumped back from the crouching shadow.

"All right," Wull said again. "Please calm down and don't shout. You've never shouted at me, even when you were angry, even that time I set fire to your hair. Remember that?"

"No. Calm. Eat."

His shape settled into itself, and Wull knew he'd get nothing more until he brought the food. The fish heads were kept to feed seulas and gulls struggling to hunt in the frozen wasteland, but Pappa had refused to eat anything else since Wull had restrained him and tied him to the chair. He was pleased the knots on Pappa's wrists were holding—he had only really mastered a few simple loops and never once managed the moncad's fist, the king of the waterfolk's bindings.

Wull had learned the keep's knots under Pappa's watchful shadow—tiny fingers shredding as he bound and unbound his little cutting of hemp—and always, after hours of fumbled labor that strained his patience to a taut cord, the big hands would flash over his head with invisible swiftness and drop into his lap a perfect kellick hitch, sheepshank, double-overhand . . . whatever had just bested Wull and stripped the flesh from his hands.

Then Wull would be scooped and carried upside down round the boathouse over Pappa's laughing shoulders, all the blood running to his head.

He looked now at the big hands, held by the knots they'd taught. If the bindings Wull had tied—simple bowlines—yielded or slipped then Pappa would escape, as he seemed intent on doing.

Or he might not escape. Wull didn't know what that would mean, but the thought of Pappa wandering loose in the boathouse while Wull slept beneath the glass buoys and the ropes filled him with a profound, stomach-chilling dread.

So different to how it had been before, when Pappa's

steady movements in the small hours—mending and readying the bäta—had acted as a balm for his childish night terrors.

He went out to the storeroom and lifted one of the buckets of fish scraps, silver scales glinting green and blue and yellow in the fading light of the afternoon, dozens of gray, puddly eyes slack-staring at the ceiling. Wull's nose no longer registered their presence, so he felt the stink only as an invisible press around his face as he lugged the bucket through and dropped it on the floor in front of Pappa's chair.

"Eat!" said Pappa, sitting up. "It that speaks brings the food."

"My name is Wulliam—Wulliam Braid Fobisher. You named me that: Braid for your pappa, my gran'pappa."

"It dun't matter's name. Eat."

Wull lifted a breamcod's head—it was heavy and cold, its drying skin tacky against his fingertips. They had eaten breamcod filets for supper the night Pappa had disappeared under the ice, bickering quietly about a deliberate nothing, leaving the understanding of Wulliam's reluctant ascension hanging unspoken above them in the web-hung rafters.

He held the head out to Pappa, who lunged at it. Wull could see the bonds cutting into his wrists as he stretched, pulling the skin like it might peel off.

"Untie the arms," said Pappa.

"No," said Wull. "We've talked about this. You'll just run off. We need to get you some help."

"No help. Free. Now eat."

Wull held the head, mouth first, to Pappa's face, and kept it there while he grabbed and pulled at it with lips and teeth. When it was gone, Pappa, in a choked and swollen version of his new voice, gurgled, "Again," and Wull held up another head and another, until the bucket was nearly empty and the slack face was glistening with lost spit, scales, and skin scraps. There was part of a tail in his beard, Wull saw, and he reached to clean around Pappa's mouth with a dampened cloth.

"Enough!" said Pappa, head shaking to avoid the wipes. "Too hard!"

"You can't sit there with that all over you. You'll end up stinking, and then I won't come near you at all."

"Good, it that speaks."

"You don't mean that," said Wull. "And my name is Wulliam."

He cleaned Pappa's face and beard as gently as he could, holding the back of his head in his hand. Pappa relaxed slowly, the muscles of his neck softening against Wull's palm.

"Wulliam," said Pappa, and his own voice was in the echo of the sound, quietly, like a word shouted from a great distance.

"Wulliam," said Wull. He smiled, then cried on his knees as his pappa drifted into a fitful sleep.

Eventually, joints stiff from the floor, Wull went and made tea, letting the leaves stew in the undrunk cup as he sat in his own chair, Pappa's empty and brooding beside him, looking at the Danék while the night broke over its surface and turned the narrowing ribbon of still-flowing water to rapid ink.

The hand that held his mug shook slightly as night filled the boathouse, the lamps untrimmed and unlit, and Wull watched darkness spill over the books through which he had pored these last two days, the encyclopedias and the almanacs and the ledgers themselves: all the tomes in which Pappa had prided and which laid out the facts of the world in such detail. There were facts about plants, sun times, tide patterns, crop rotation, wine making, embalming, needlework, folklore, and the forensic history of wars fought so far in the dusty past that the names of the places and soldiers were built with strangely shaped and unpronounceable letters.

But he found nothing that gave a name to Pappa's condition, to the hollow looseness of his skin or the change in his voice. Wull had read until his head ached, and had woken, curled and solid, with his face on the page, the ink running in the water from his open mouth.

Now, in the silence of night, he fancied he could hear the wicks of the lanterns sputtering and freezing in the face of winter's elemental force, their rods surrendering to the ice as it swept its glittering malice across the world, and he held his cold tea and waited for the spark of courage that would propel him to rise up and face the world outside. *His* world.

An ocean barge puttered past, lantern bright on deck, the captain looking agitatedly at the river's locked-in whiteness. Wull watched him raise his eyes to the lampless boathouse and shake his head.

"I bloody can," said Wull aloud, feeling color in his cheeks. "It's my bloody river."

He stood then, collecting himself, feeling the balance of his feet on the boards and the strength of his muscles inside his clothes. He heaved a big, whooping sigh that became a defiant growl, and reached for his hat.

Then Pappa woke up.

4

Oracco

Hanged men are valueable lumps inddeed, and can be myned thusly: bones ground for the tamperring of bred and the enrichment of soyl; teeth for the prodduction of false dentures; fat for the mannufacture of tallow and greese of all sorts; offal and other fleshily mass for the feeding of cattle and furthering of annatomollogy. The seed, eyes, heart, and brayn go for the growth of plants assosiated with magick and the occult; an long list of shrooms and fungi, webseeds, and mandrakes—this last an most valuable and cursedd thing, for it carrys a poysoned soul. The city sells these prodducts for hannsome reward, and returns to the bereeved a seeled casket weyted with turrf. A curssory glance at the ballance sheets of the municipal treashury will show exaktly where there also occurs a sharp ryse in the hangmans productivitty, and the administtering of capytal judgment for such crimes as petty larsenny and the befiddlement of lyvestock in the throws of economic crysis is common.

—From "Upton Died on Us," the unpublished autobiography
of Upton Dempsey, chief undertaker to the city of Oracco

"And why should I, Mr. Tillinghast? Why *should* I let you live?" Rattell skipped a little, his voice shrill. "You steal from me—I kill you."

Tillinghast hung between two bulbous men, arms clamped firmly in their grips. In the lamplight of the cellar, his pale, blue skin—cut in places on his face—glowed greenly under a tinkling neckful of silver charms. His jacket and shirt lay on the floor. But he had held on to his wide-brimmed hat, and it sat low over his eyes.

"'S not really up to you, that," he said, and sniffed. The air was old and powdery. It smelled of things from under the ground and the cold dampness of the earth that pressed against the brickwork. Lopsided towers of crates were stacked in a rough circle around them, buried beneath ghostly sheets.

Rattell looked at him, his good eye twitching. "What?" he said.

"Lettin' me live an' that, 's not really up to you, sir." Tillinghast rolled in his captors' grips. He decided the man on his left, the rose-lakoris chewer, was stronger, and leaned in that direction. "I's not *technic'ly* alive right now, Mr. Rattell."

"You can yet be made to suffer," said Rattell, smiling. Dabbing water from the corner of his eye, he lifted Tillinghast's chin with the point of his cane. "All things can be made to suffer, in time. Is that not so, Mr. Rigby?"

"Right, Misser Rattell," the egg-smelling blob on Tillinghast's right-hand side rumbled, then made a wheezing sound like a blocked drain.

"What in gods' was that, Mr. Rigby?" said Tillinghast. "That your first time laughin'?"

"I suppose there is little point in asking for your opinion, Mr. Pent?" said Rattell, addressing the mountain holding Tillinghast's left arm.

Pent squeezed Tillinghast's wrist.

"Aargh! I reckon he agrees, Mr. Rattell," said Tillinghast. "What a shame we can't hear from Mr. Pent—I imagine he's got a wonderful singin' voice. High an' flutey, I shouldn't wonder—like them fellas with no plums."

Pent squeezed his wrist again.

"Aargh! All right, Mr. Pent, I takes it back—you've a nice deep voice! *And* plums!"

Rattell hunkered down before him.

"Mr. Pent stole from my employers and me a number of years ago. Some money, a small amount. For this petty act, Mr. Tillinghast, he lost his tongue. In contrast, *you* have tried to steal the last mandrake grown from the seed of the hanged man Garswood Fenn, a man more beloved of my employer than his own children. The mandrake is the last scrap of this dear man in existence; it is therefore an item of immense value and one which—happily, thanks to your clumsy attempts at burglary—remains safely ensconced in my study."

"You've a study, Mr. Rattell? Tha's grand, sir. I din't know you could read."

Rattell smiled, his eye twitching. "I should like to take that slippery tongue of yours to silence your . . . *wit*, but it would deny my lumbering companions the joy of your suffering, and since I pay them so poorly, this is the sole treat that keeps them loyally in my employ. Having said that," drawled Rattell, warming to his theme, "I've seen Pent and Rigby's work in the past, and I rather imagine they'd carry out these little chores for free. Mr. Pent in particular seems to have used his enforced silence to channel his energies into . . . *creative* ways of inflicting pain."

"'S very impressive, Mr. Pent. Give us a song, will you? I's always had a soft spot for 'Pickle the One-Eyed Sailor.' . . ."

Pent hissed.

"Stop antagonizing my associates, Mr. Tillinghast. Your focus should be on making the short remainder of your life as bearable as possible."

Rattell wiped some sweat from his top lip. Tillinghast relaxed and straightened his back.

"I 'in't got a life right now, Mr. Rattell. You keeps forgettin' that. What you plannin' on takin' away from me? My breath? My heartbeat? You take all the time you need to find 'em, and good luck, 'cause I never has and I've had plenty time to rummage about, believe me. Some days when there's not much else to do, I rummage with my bits for hours, and I'm gettin' plenty good at it an' all."

Rattell sighed, then dabbed at his narrow face with a handkerchief. "Do you believe in the theory of nominative determinism, Mr. Tillinghast?" he said at length.

"I's never had a head for mathematics, sir."

"Oh, it's not mathematics; it's the notion that the name a person is given at birth determines much of their path through life—their successes and character traits and so on. My mother was a believer, hence my given name, Lucian. It means 'light,' which I take to mean cleverness—and *that* I certainly possess."

Rattell spread his arms wide and gave a half twirl, as though his skinny frame were produce on display.

"Cleverness, eh?" said Tillinghast. "D'you save it for special occasions?"

"Nominative determinism is a fascinating idea," Rattell continued, ignoring him. "I've swindled fishermen whose names came from the sea, professors named for their areas of expertise, farmers named for produce or livestock. I even encountered a woman who made fabrics—her given middle name was Threadcount. Isn't that extraordinary?"

"Extraordinary. Borin' as all hells, but sure, extraordinary."

"Mr. Pent, for example," said Rattell, "is a . . . ball of stored aggression and anger—just waiting to explode."

"In a cascade o' glorious song?"

Rattell wiped his top lip again. Pent hissed a threatening sound.

"Misser Pent says he's got a 'pecific plan for Misser Tillinghast," said Rigby.

"You hear that, Mr. Tillinghast? *If* you tell us who sent you for the mandrake, then I'm sure Rigby and Pent will be more merciful in their interrogation. . . ."

"I highly doubts that, Mr. Rattell," said Tillinghast as the men rumbled. "I can sense the tension betwixt 'em. Prob'ly on account of Mr. Rigby's jealousy at the sheer beauty of Mr. Pent's singin' voice."

"Will you S-STOP! ANTAGONIZING! M-MY!! ASSOCIATES!?!" shouted Rattell, lashing at Tillinghast with his cane.

Tillinghast absorbed the blows without flinching, gazing blankly at the veins of his right hand—smaller than his left and twice as pale.

"You done now, Mr. Rattell?" he said, once the greasy little man had staggered backward, his round hat askew. Neither Pent nor Rigby had moved.

"Yes . . . yes," said Rattell. He reset his wardrobe and

smoothed his hair. A dew of sweat glistened on his thin mustache. "It's time for you to be taken away from me now, Mr. Tillinghast—I must to my mi-milk bath. Good-bye. And may you know the price of stealing from Lucian Rattell."

"Right you are, sir," said Tillinghast. "Then I'd best be off."

He lunged forward as though barging through a door, tearing his left arm off at the shoulder and leaving the whole limb in Pent's astonished grasp. One-armed and freed, he spun quickly and butted Rigby on the bridge of his nose, crumpling the big man into a dust-throwing heap on the cellar floor.

Tillinghast looked at Pent, who dropped the arm and rushed forward. A short, grubby knife appeared in his hand and he sank it into Tillinghast's stomach.

Tillinghast punched him twice, quickly, in the solar plexus, then reached into his belt and popped a yellow capsule into Pent's open, tongueless mouth.

Pent's eyes rolled back in his head, and he fell beside Rigby, arm thrown over his fellow henchman's body as though they were snatching a romantic nap.

Tillinghast brushed Pent's knife onto the floor, picked up his left arm, and poked Rattell in the eyes with the outstretched fingers. The little man squealed, grabbed his face, and ran with quick steps toward the staircase at the end of the low, gloomy room.

"So, Mr. Rattell, which one's your study?" said Tillinghast, grinning. "I wasn't sure the mandrake was even here, see, an' it was just as easy to let your goons get ahold o' me as it was to creep around all stealthy like. Easier, actually," he added, scratching his back with his severed arm.

Rattell spun around, backing away slowly. His face was nearly as white as his suit, and his pockmarked skin trembled.

"How . . . how?" he stammered.

"I's not bloody alive, sir, as I've told you on sev'ral occasions. See?"

Tillinghast pointed to the burst of straw, sand, and herb fronds in the open wound of his shoulder.

"But . . . but . . ."

Tillinghast slapped Rattell using his left hand as a bat.

"That's gettin' a sight annoyin' now, sir, if you don't mind. So: which one's your study?"

Rattell's gaze flicked to the top of the staircase.

"Lovely, I thought it might be. Well, you jus' stay there if you likes. I'll pick the little bugger up an' be on my way. Your pets'll be all right, I shouldn't wonder. Mr. Rigby's pretty face might be a bit bruised for a few days, right enough—I caught him a fair crack on the nose. Mr. Pent's had a sleepin' draft I picked up in Whilsall Market. He should wake up by . . . what day's it today?"

"Suh-Suh—"

Tillinghast slapped Rattell again.

"Sunday!" wailed the little man.

"Tuesday then, maybe even tomorrow—he's a big lad after all. Jus' keep an eye on 'im, make sure he doesn't dirty 'is kecks."

Tillinghast jogged up the remaining stairs and opened the door to the study.

The dark, pokey little room was filled with bric-a-brac: yellowed, torn books lay open on shelves and piled flat on tables; scrolls of parchment littered the floor; and a shuffle of paintings wrapped in stiff-looking brown paper was stacked against the far wall. The only light in the windowless space came from two dust-blanked globes that burned dully with fish-smelling whale oil. Rattell at least understood the importance of atmosphere: the study dripped with promising antiquity, and—although most of the items would have been made in the last month by craftsmen lurking in Oracco's seedy underbelly—the thick age of the place would convince many an impressionable buyer to part with more money than they'd intended.

It was a while since he'd been to the seedy underbelly, Tillinghast reflected as he rummaged for the mandrake, using his left arm as a tool. He should make a point of going soon—his favorite pub, the Haha, was there. Tillinghast had spent many nights at its bar, happily dousing his insides in fiery potœm that made no dent in his sobriety, soaked up as it was by his sand and straw. But it passed the time, and there was usually a fight, which he enjoyed.

A small drawer was filled with banknotes and coins, maybe fifty or so ducats; Tillinghast pocketed everything but the ha'pennies and pennies. After another minute and another drawer of wadded ten-ducat notes, he found—stuffed down the side of a bookcase—a hessian sack that bulged with the shape of a small person.

"There you are, my lovely," he whispered, and sniffed. There was a dark lump huddled in the depths of the bag, from which poured odors of cinnamon and woodsmoke and blood. He rifled through the clutter of amulets and charms that hung about his chest, selected a small black stone, and placed it carefully onto the shape in the sack.

Its odor lightened, as though a fresh breeze had been released through an open window.

Tillinghast tucked his left arm under his right, hefted the sack carefully, and made for the stairs, knocking a small brass figurine into his pocket as he passed another object-laden surface.

As the study door swung closed behind him, he dropped his arm and turned to grab it, hoisting it just before the door slammed on his prone bicep and catching the mandrake sack on his foot. He held the arm aloft and chuckled.

"Close one there, Mr. Rattell!" he said, trotting down

the stairs past the little fraudster. "Need to look after me bits an' bobs."

Rattell hadn't moved—his eyes, both the twitching and the still, were fixed on the slumbering forms of Rigby and Pent.

"They'll be fine, sir. By an' by, you was wond'rin' who sent me for the mandrake. Nobody, as a matter of fact—I came into an awareness of its hereabouts an' thought it'd be a wonderful thing to plant it an' make it mine, rather than have it suffer at your hands. I'm reckonin', though, that the employers you was holdin' it for might want it back fair sore, an' that its pendin' disappearance is the reason you've a streak o' wee on your nicely pressed inseam."

Tillinghast nodded at the yellow stain on Rattell's white suit.

"Rosie . . . Rosie . . ." muttered the little man. He appeared completely unaware now of Tillinghast's presence—staring through the walls of the cellar into another place, where unspeakable things were already happening to him.

"Well, don't you worry none 'bout that. Jus' tell them that I's got it, an' I likes drinkin' in the inn at Lauston—you gets a fine clear potœm there, an' there's hair on the pork scratchings. They can come an' fetch the mandrake if they fancies. Ta-ta."

Tillinghast dressed, tucked his neck-silver inside his shirt, then sauntered out the cellar, whistling happily. He stepped over the unconscious lumps of Rigby and Pent, tucked the mandrake under his elbow, and, holding his severed arm by the hand as though it were an infant child, disappeared into the freezing city night.

Rattell whimpered softly for a few minutes, until his sniffling was interrupted by the handclap fanfare of Mr. Rigby's unconscious fart, at which point he began to sob.

5

The Keep

*It is a sight to truly gladden the heart when one
sees a bäta break through a river's foggy shroud.
The bright colors in which they are traditionally painted
stand in stark contrast to the murk on which they sit
and the earthen tones of the surrounding land. Their
brightness is for visibility: that they may act as beacons
of fortitude and hope in the darkest places of the
waterfolk's world.*

*But it is perhaps the eyes painted on their ornate prow
that remain uppermost in one's mind when their form has
once again been subsumed by the clouds: heavy-lidded and
wide, they are for the warding off of evil spirits and the
guidance of the tillerman's hand. Yet they convey something
that is deeper and more human than should emanate from
a smear of pigment, and there is no doubt that the beholder
reads often into that stare the contents of his own soul.*

–Wheeldon Garfill, A Path Trod Well: Journeys of My Life

"Untie the arms!" shouted Pappa.

Wull leaned on his shoulders, pressing him into the seat. Pappa writhed and fought him, the sinews of his neck straining and pressing inside the quick skin like fish in a sack.

"Sit down!" said Wull, teeth clenched.

"No! Untie!"

"*Please*, Pappa . . ." said Wull.

"Stinking boy! Stinking!" shouted Pappa, the rasp of his voice rising to a wet gurgle again until he spluttered and choked. "Stink! Stink! Stink!"

"*Pappa* . . ." said Wull again, and he leaned on the shoulders until his bruises from the oars began to ache.

"The river," said Pappa urgently, and there again was the sound of his own voice, whipped by the storm that raged inside him.

"The river?" said Wull. "What about the river?" He spoke quickly, trying to hold on to the wet, slippery rope of Pappa's real self. "Pappa? The river?"

"Keep it," whispered Pappa. "Keep it . . . keep it, keep it, keep it . . . stinking, stinking it that speaks!"

Wull slumped to the ground and watched as the angry, violent face took over Pappa's expression once again. Pappa seethed at him, glowering through his brows, his muscles shaking.

Behind Wull, the Danék moved along as it always

had—relentless and solid. Over Pappa's straining he heard again with his mind the sputter of lanterns in the cold and he felt the weight of it all, the insides of him stewing in the bile of his fear, burning and wasting like a salted slug until he was nothing but the dull ache of Pappa's anger and the river's constant strength.

He checked the bonds on Pappa's wrists—they would hold. Fat, dirty fingers grabbed at his.

Pappa met his eyes as he stood, but they were *not* Pappa's eyes; clouded by milk and fury, they belonged to some hunted thing, not the man who had bounced Wull on his knee and whispered stories to him in bed.

Wull took his hat from the floor, wedged it on, and shrugged himself inside the clammy, seula-gut shift and the deerskin coat (first skin-raisingly cold and then prickly with heat), heaved up the replenished bottle of whale oil, and went out into the frozen night, leaving Pappa tied to the spare chair.

The wind had picked up, and the black surface of the moving water rippled and shimmered. A manic twitch moved the skeletal branches of the trees along the bank, shaking the stark, dead whiteness of the world.

The bäta glared at him from under a soft layer of windblown white; it shouldn't have been out for this time, he knew—the paint would flake down to the wood in the wet wind.

"I'm sorry, all right?" he said, climbing gingerly aboard.

The bäta nodded in the water, moved, he knew, by the river, not as an act of forgiveness.

Wull pushed off into the current and let the boat drift. Even through his glove he felt the smoothness of the wood on Pappa's seat . . . the Riverkeep's seat. His seat.

In the center of the night's star-scattered black, the moon beamed down, half covered by scraps of cloud. If it was high that meant there were no ursas around; only when it dipped below the tree line would he have to worry about them, and by then he would be long gone. He *should* be all right, so long as he was careful. Only once on his keep had Pappa encountered an ursa: an adolescent cub, still twice the size of a man, disorientated by the effect of fermented sunberries. The animal had snapped one of the oars like a twig before Pappa had smashed his lamp on the ground and it fled in a shower of flame.

Pappa had been lucky. "An ursa," he had said, "will run an' climb an' swim an' fight better than you—better than ten o' ye, twenty o' ye."

"What about twenty o' *you*, Pappa?" Wull replied.

Pappa had laughed. "They'd make a big, long scarf out of twenty o' me!" he'd said, and mussed Wull's hair.

Wull laughed, but Pappa had taken his shoulders and knelt beside him.

"Ye can't be out past the dippin' moon, all right? 'Cause the moment you see the flash o' their skin it's already too late;

they're on ye! An' ye'd be just a scrap in their teeth."

"All right, Pappa," Wull had said, and then he'd gone to bed and dreamed fearless, childish dreams.

And now he was here and they were all around him, hidden in dens covered by snow-drenched branches, caged behind only the thin barrier of sleep.

Sometimes, *sometimes*, if they came at you, it worked to play dead. But you could never be sure. Wull looked at the shadows moving in the woods and wondered how much courage it would take to remain still and silent while an ursa snuffled about your skin and gave your flesh an experimental tug.

In the distance, the ocean barge's soft putter was fading, and the captain's light had already been taken by the fog. The bäta's nods felt impatient to Wull, and he sensed the eyes on him again.

"Fine, fine," he said. "Let's get it done. It's all well an' good for you—you don't have blisters on your hands."

He began to row, ghostly bubbles spinning from the blades, the muscles of his back stretching painful and tight across his shoulder blades. The bäta was heavily built, its frame wide with thick-hewn beams.

"It's easy for you right enough," he muttered to it. "You get crafted an' varnished an' painted up all pretty, an' then you get steered around an' looked after—someone else takin' care o' you. Fine, fine. Tradition, isn't it? Tradition."

The bäta, nodding in the swell, looked hard at the river before them. Puffs of snow burst soundlessly in the thick heights of the forest, and Wull watched a family of red skirrils flying from branch to branch, their rosy fur monochrome in the pale light.

Gradually, lantern one—whiter and thicker down the wind side—came into view.

"Gods," said Wull, planting his right oar and letting the bäta ease in alongside. "Look at the state of this now."

He lifted the whale oil bottle, supporting the porcelain bulb from below with a cupped hand. It was immensely heavy, and he cursed himself for filling it to such a level.

Even Pappa might have struggled to lift this, he thought, hoisting the bottle onto his shoulder. The water clonked against the bottom of the bäta as it rocked back and forth.

The whale oil stank even in the cold, and Wull held his face back from the glugging sloop of it as it filled the reservoir. A few drops spilled down the side and he straightened the bottle immediately—every drop of the oil had to be used, for its cost was steep, and Pappa . . . He heard what Pappa always said whenever he gave Wull a lesson or a chiding about the river: *An' for Lavernes's sake, don't spill a drop o' that bloody whale oil; it's worth more'n you an' me put together—liquid gold that stuff.*

Wull filled the reservoir without spilling another drop, stoppered the bottle with its rubber cork, and returned it to the floor of the bäta. Then he worked at the ice around the wick and the rod with his bone-handled knife, stabbing hard at the chunks of it that clung to their surfaces, knocking a spray of white into the air.

A noise from the forest interrupted him.

He froze, looking immediately at the moon. It was still high, far higher than the tree line. There was no sign of movement, no falling snow from the canopy. In the strain to hear more, Wull found his ears filling with the sounds of his own body until listening became useless and he began to feel dizzy.

There was nothing. Just a red balgair, perhaps, or a hare scrattling through a bush.

He resumed his knife work more slowly, keeping half his attention on the forest, which seemed now ever bigger and blacker in its depths.

Soon the wick was freed and Wull gave a small cry of triumph. He struck a match, holding it behind his glove to let the flame swell into life, and held it to the fabric stump. The fire burned against it flatly, as though it were stone. Wull held the match until it winked out in the grip of his fingers and lit another, then another.

"Come on . . ." he whispered. "Light! Light!"

Five matches were spent. He flicked the last black stump into the Danék and sat down in the back of the bäta, in his old seat, looking at the smooth wood of Pappa's bench.

"Now what in hells am I s'posed to do?" he asked the bäta.

The boat moved with the water.

"I'll need to come back tomorrow an' hope a bit of day-light's made the difference. Even if it is still freezin' all bloody day. An' there's no point in gettin' irked, 'cause there's nothin' else I c'n do, is there?"

He moved over and into the keep's seat once again, wiped his damp nose, smelling the fish of whale oil on his gloves. He spat the taste of it over the side.

"Disgustin'," he muttered. "Look, you wouldn't like it much better if I used all the matches an' it still didn't take, so I need to just stick on an' see if the next one does. Right?"

The bäta bobbed into the current as he turned the oars. After working the knife, his fingers had lost all feeling, and the pain from the grips on his hands ached through his wrists and into his elbows.

"I'm glad you thinks so too," muttered Wull. He shot an-other look into the unmoving forest, felt its energy looking back, and sculled more quickly into the middle of the Danék.

Lantern two, tucked into a pocket of current beside a grove of trees that had grown in a low sweep over the riv-er's surface, was also iced solid. The trees around it were un-commonly white, accustomed as they were to the heat of the lantern, and the scabs of moss and lichen were crusted with blown snow. Across the grove hung, like strings of pearls, the frozen ropes of weed and parasitic roots that clung to the trunks and branches of all the riverside trees. Wull wondered how long the lantern had been out—the whole space had an air of unmoving timelessness, and the ice around the rod was far thicker than on lantern one.

He guided the bäta alongside, took up his knife, started to chip away at the prison of ice, the blade bouncing back at him from its unbreaking face. The cold in his hands began to burn, first with a curious warmth, then with a growing and painful fire that ripped at his skin.

He continued to stab until the wick was freed, the closeness of the reaching tree boughs bringing the forest's grasp near to him even as he stood in the wobbling bäta.

"Oh, there you are," he whispered, brushing the black lump with a thumb that was a wedge of sharp pain. He allowed himself a smile, felt the freezing air grip his teeth, then filled the reservoir with the same fragile care as before, spilling nothing of the precious oil.

By the time he'd thrown the twelfth unsuccessful match into the Danék, he was already sitting in his seat in the back of the boat with his eyes closed.

"What would Pappa have done?" he said to the bäta. "If the fire won't take, then the fire won't take! There's no magic to it. I can't spell flames onto the damn thing! I'm just as well going back in 'cause I'm gettin' nowhere here."

He glanced at the boat's eyes, and it was then he noticed

it had turned gently to point toward lantern three.

Wull dropped his scarf for a second to spit over the side.

"One more," he muttered. "Though I don't see the bloody point—I might as well stand by the fire at home an' throw matches out the window for all the good I'm doin'."

A few minutes of sore rowing took Wull to lantern three, positioned on a straight bank that ran for a few hundred yards. Although burned-out and frozen, its empty reservoir and wick were more clearly visible through the ice.

That looks better, thought Wull, easing the bäta alongside.

He chipped at the ice, gratified by how rapidly it yielded, coiling lengths of it peeling from the rod like bark shavings. Then he lifted the whale oil. Even with two reservoirs' worth gone it seemed far heavier to hands that were sapped of strength by the knife and the oars. The porcelain slipped against his glove.

"So. This is the keep's role," he said, "heavin' this bottle of fish slime around forever. I shouldn't even be here. . . ."

He stood, hefted the bottle, and went to lean toward the empty, frosted reservoir.

His feet slipped, the slick wood of the bottom boards taking his balance, sending him flying forward and throwing the whale oil from him—over the side.

"No!" shouted Wull, stretching for it in midair, his hands short of the spinning handle and fingers clawing nothing as he fell. His chin burst on the gunwale, filling his mouth with numb heat and the thin copper of blood.

Wull's eyes rolled as he fell, crashing onto the floor of the boat.

There was a moment, lying flat and being rocked by the floor of the bäta, when the pain and the cold vanished and the only things that existed were the patient stars glimmering behind the torn cotton of the winter clouds; then the agony returned, the cold flared in his joints, and the sounds of wood knocking against his ears pulled him back into reality.

"Oh gods!" said Wull, spraying blood. He pulled himself upright and leaned out, expecting to see the whale oil slip into the Danék.

The bottle sat on the ice, unbroken, between the lantern and the bank.

"Oh, thank the gods—don't move!" he shouted to the bottle. It rolled a little toward the water. "Don't move!" Wull shouted again, wiping blood from his chin. There was a tug of raised flesh against his glove.

It could wait. He pulled the bäta tight against the lantern and fumbled at the rope with fingers that were now little more than agonized lead stumps. He dropped the rope once, then twice, shooting panicked glances at the bottle. At last he managed a rough bowline and gave it a gentle, experimental tug, hardly daring to pull firmly lest it be unraveled into a tangled mess. Then he lifted his foot over the gunwale and onto the ice.

He stopped, heard Pappa's voice: *Never get oot the bäta, Wulliam—the minute ye get oot that boat, ye're lost—ye can't be rescuin' folk if ye need rescuing yersel'.*

The ice creaked under his heel. He lifted it back, slightly, bracing himself against the wood. Then he remembered once more the other thing Pappa had said: *An' don't spill a drop o' that bloody whale oil. . . . Liquid gold that stuff.*

Wull leaned his weight onto the ice. He felt it move, settle, the studded soles of his boots locking on to its surface.

So, he thought. *This is fine. It's not far. Just a few paces.* He looked at the bäta's eyes. "Those might be painted on," he muttered, "but you're doing a bloody good job o' lookin' annoyed. Lump o' firewood that you are."

He lifted over his other leg.

Standing on the ice, he realized how little time he'd spent walking around the river. Apart from playing in the trees beside the boathouse when he was very young, he'd hardly ever taken walks or run around, because there had been no other children for miles. *And even if there had been,* he thought bitterly, *they'd never have played with the keep's son. They think we eat the bodies.*

Walking the river gave the whole world a different sense, even less secure than with the bäta beneath him—and with the sharp awareness of the short distance that now separated him from the ursas. A cough might bring them running.

He took a step forward.

The ice lurched, a tabletop rolling with his feet and trembling with the river. The bottle rolled again toward the water.

"No, no, no, no, no . . ." whispered Wull, stepping backward. A groan came from the ice, like cattle under strain. In his mind Wull saw the moment of it cracking, sending him into the current and the weed beds to freeze there, floating to the surface in the summer as sun-melted flesh to be found by . . . no one. To be picked apart by birds and flies.

And Pappa, tied to a chair, wasting to yellow bones just yards from buckets of stinking fish heads.

That could not happen.

"Aaaaaarrrghhh!" he shouted, running at the whale oil as though trapping a wild animal. The ice leaned wildly as he leaped, but he grabbed the rolling bottle beneath his body and dug the stud of his toe into the ice.

"Yes!" he said, flushed. "Oh yes! Ha! Oh, I've got you. Oh, thank gods."

He hugged the bottle, heard the thick gloop of oil, stood—then fell instantly, feet splayed out in front of him, the thud of his backside on the ice shaking his teeth and flashing fresh pain into his bleeding chin.

As he watched the bottle fall he had time only to gasp before it broke with a deep round split and showered him in fish-stinking, flammable liquid gold.

"Oh . . ." he said, glistening under its coating. "Oh . . . oh . . . gods . . ."

The bäta nodded, and a noise like a splitting branch told Wull the ice was breaking beneath him.

Subconscious animal instinct lifted him to his feet and propelled him forward, almost without touching the surface. He launched himself into the bäta as the tabletop of ice split in two and the larger chunk, speckled merrily with shards of the porcelain bottle, drifted into the current.

Wull sat in the back of the boat, in his old seat, watching half a winter's worth of oil reflect the moonlight on its way downriver.

"Oh gods," said Wull. "There's not the coin to replace that. Oh gods, gods . . ."

He looked around at the white world, unchanged and uncaring in the face of this fearful loss. A night lark released a burst of song.

"How can birds sing in the middle o' this?" he said aloud. He found he was, again, addressing the bäta.

From the back of the boat he couldn't see its eyes, but they arrived without effort in his mind: hard and forward-looking.

He returned to the Riverkeep's seat and hefted the

oars again, rowing to nowhere, oblivious to the pain in his hands and shoulders and the throb of his bloodied mouth and chin.

"Why do I have to do this?" he asked the bäta. "What difference would it make if the river locked? People could just drag their boats along the ice like sleds, couldn't they?"

He wondered why this had never occurred to him before.

"Couldn't they?" he said again. His voice seemed to travel no farther than his lips; the oppression of the freezing air was like being locked in a cupboard. The bäta lurched through the little islands of ice with his jerky, uneven strokes. The only other sound was the grinding of the oars in their rowlocks.

"Some seulas'll die," Wull carried on, fighting for breath. "There's bloody hundreds of 'em: rhats wi' flippers, Pappa calls 'em. So why should we care? An' why do we feed 'em? No wonder they hang about the boathouse. An' if Pappa keeps eatin' like he is, there'll be nothin' for 'em to eat anyway. So why bother? An' why, when everyone else just carries on with themselves and their own lives, should I be out here in the freezing bloody cold, tryin' to stop ice from freezin' and talkin' to a bloody boat?"

The tiniest echo of his last shout sang across the water and was snuffed out by the heavy, winter silence, through which the bäta bobbled sternly.

"An' without the oil, what am I to do anyways?" said Wull. "Use these things?"

He released an oar, lifted an ice rod from beneath the bottom boards.

"On ice like this these'll be worse'n useless. I might as well hit it wi' grass."

Wull stood holding the rod, letting the oars drift in their rowlocks, turning the bäta against the current.

"So is this what I mus' do?" he shouted, stabbing tentatively, then harder, thrusting the point of the rod more sharply on the surface of the ice until it began to chip and flake. "An' how long mus' I do it?"

His voice rose as he began to thrash with the rod.

"To make such tiny dents in so big a thing"—he struck harder, the thud of connection jarring his bones—"I might hit its white face forever"—he struck again, still harder, with blows that bounced into his spine—"and forever and still never crack . . . a bloody . . . piece of it!"

The ice split with a surprisingly gentle sound, parting with a break that was almost perfect. Wull straightened his back and let the rod clatter at his feet. Hands on his knees, he filled his lungs with stabbing air to release a long and bitter laugh.

Then he saw the face peering back at him from below the ice, and the breath stopped in his throat.

Canna Bay

Scores of them came in the night, slices of a deeper black on the horizon: strange craft under strange flags, crewed by the salt-cut and the sea-hardened, seeking the bounty of the mormorach's flesh. The people of Canna Bay watched them anchor, blaze up their lamps, and dot the harbor with light.

The lamps glowed faintly blue—magic had come with the mormorach, and the air in the village had changed. There was a smell—of burnt things and hot metal—that had begun to inhabit everything: clothes, skin, hair, bread. The people went to their burnt-smelling beds and held each other and whispered prayers of fortune that the harpoons of the morning would find their mark.

In sleep, the village—fishless now for days—was silent: the night packers' heat and laughter snared with the fishermen's empty nets.

One ship arrived after all the others, once the people of Canna Bay had taken their bed leave. Although wide-hulled and misshapen, the *Hellsong* was faster than the rest, and its prow and flanks were studded with rows of teeth that caught the moonlight and shone. Its bowsprit was the pearlescent spike of a great narwhal; its terrible figurehead the skull of a huge cragolodon. And fixed to its rails were the skulls of game fish: mairlan, shark, and greenfin. Damage to its mast and deck was splinted by enormous bones and trussed with rope, a skeletal patchwork that gave the vessel the look of a wounded and rotting animal. But underneath this projection of decay, the impression was of tenacity.

In the guts of the *Hellsong* sat its captain, Gilt Murdagh, turning a lump of ivory in hands that were three fingers short and thick with dirt. Five of his crew were cramped beside him, awaiting his word; in the doorway lurked the wide-eyed cabin boy, Samjon, snatching conversation beyond the table's kicking feet.

The hatches had been battened somewhere over the Keppul Sound in the face of a storm that dropped the barometer's quicksilver almost out of sight, and the galley's air had grown sour in the hours since. A tang of sweat, fish, and false, itch-making heat crawled on the skin of the crew and into their mouths and noses.

Murdagh was unaware of the stifling atmosphere; decades at sea had chewed him to a strip of teak-strong gristle, and he no longer tasted the well-lived air. He had about his face a thick clod of beard, lumped by tangles and tar and livened by the bright flash of scar tissue. Beneath a curtain of once-injured flesh glowed his bloodstained left eye; his right, deep-set in sunbrowned skin, was gray and hard. From the floor came the scrape of his whalebone leg against the deck's grain, and he bumped the sharp point of his iron crutch in a distracted rhythm.

Murdagh lifted his long nose and opened his mouth, tasting the air. He turned the piece of ivory again, knocked it on the table, then smiled at the men and women before him, running his tongue over teeth that were ribbed with grime.

"We's here," he said quietly. "Let's hunt."

6

The Boathouse

When I have done the work o' day,
An' aw the dead are tucked away,
I sit, bankside, an' breathe my whiff,
An' munch the skin from off the stiff.
When I have tucked away the dead,
An' aw my seula friends have fled,
I sit bankside, upon my heels,
An' out my teeth I pick the eels.
When fled have aw my seula friends,
An' aw Dan-ey-ék's water scends,
I sit, bankside, upon my rear,
An' chew the wax from out my ear.

—Oraccan children's song about the Riverkeep

Morning found Wull, undrunk tea cold in his hand, perched opposite a fragment of skull as though he had arranged for it to enjoy a formal breakfast. He sat, still tight with cold, slow-blinking in the glare: the morning had arrived without cloud, and the small window was filled with the dazzle of sunlight on snow. It illuminated a woodcut darkened by soot and time: a man, barrel-chested and thickly bearded, standing proudly in a bäta with a modestly wrapped corpse elegant in the stern. The sky was a sweep of cloud with a fat, benevolent sun beaming down.

Wull looked at it a while, then turned to the inelegant lump on the cadaver slab: the arrow-shaped piece of skull and its strip of face—comprising the eyes, most of the nose, and a corner of the mouth—that had peered at him from beneath the ice. Once he had realized it wasn't attached to a body, he had stretched out an oar to lift it into the bäta. Snagged in a drift of net and weed of the type that often clung to the hulls of ocean barges, it must have come up from the coast on the back of the head-shaking captain's boat.

As first recoveries went, it wasn't especially unpleasant. It certainly hadn't taken much lifting, and with his hands, shoulders, and tailbone in a grim state following the disaster at lantern three, he was glad of that at least.

He had recorded the skull in the ledger as soon as feeling returned to his fingers:

The partskulle of a mann discoverd under the ice neer lantern three. Some face remayns and also bothe eyes, returnd to boathuse.

He remembered the story of Pappa's first recovery: a guardsman whose strangled corpse had settled in the bottom weed. Before he could float to the surface, an ocean barge anchored directly above him, and stayed for the summer months while the captain gambled away winter's money. As the water fell, the barge settled deeper in the river atop the corpse, so that when eventually the captain returned to his winter trading, Pappa—then a gangling boy of sixteen—found the guardsman on the bank, pressed as thin as paper, looking like nothing more than a discarded floor mat.

Wull wondered if Pappa had ever failed to light the lantern wicks. Or dropped a whole bottle of whale oil. It didn't seem likely.

His recovery was now sat in the mortuary at the head end of the cadaver slab. At first he'd set it in the middle, as he'd seen Pappa do with torsos, but the head section had a small, raised pillow in the stone. And it *was* a head after all.

He could have set it to face the other way, but somehow that seemed worse: he imagined the swollen eyes pulsing into life and flicking around the walls. So he had sat in the clay-smelling room opposite its slack gaze, fighting the needles of his slow-thawing flesh and his trembling hands, waiting for Mrs. Wurth the undertaker to make her weekly appearance.

And now the maddening woman was here, keeping perfect time as ever. From the parlor, behind the closed door, came the urgent silence of Pappa straining against the bonds on his wrists and the cloth wrapped across his mouth. Wull was certain only he could hear it.

He sighed, and felt his wind throb in the struggle to control himself. The constant, dull ache was back: the acid boil of tension and worry that filled him from his guts through his muscles to the tips of his fingers. He ignored it.

"An' whair'd ye say ye found this?" said Mrs. Wurth.

Wull looked at her gray face. Mrs. Wurth had shown no sign of surprise or disgust or humor on seeing the face peeking up at her from the slab; just turned it over to inspect the mottled insides and nodded.

"It was under the ice by lantern three," said Wull. "There was weed all round it, like when they gets caught under barges."

Mrs. Wurth nodded again. "Whut's happened to yer chin?"

Wull put his hand to the torn flesh of his fall. "I slipped," he said.

Mrs. Wurth nodded. "Ice is slippy. Sure this is *all* ye've come across since last I was here? I din't manage last Monday, mind—there was a fire in one o' the mills, an' me an' the boy spent all day shuttlin' crisps back to the mortuary."

Wull stared at her. Mrs. Wurth was from somewhere up north and had a peculiar singsong accent—"morch-oo-airy"—that meant Wull could focus only on the sound of her voice and not her actual words.

"What?" said Wull.

"A mill fire," said Mrs. Wurth, without irritation. "A fair pile o' crisps. No' a pleasant job, but we saw a grand juggler in the square. Chap was throwin' up knives an' burnin' torches. . . ."

"Right," said Wull. "The face, Mrs. Wurth."

Mrs. Wurth lifted the skull fragment in a gloved hand.

"Aye," she said, "this piece of face is right familiar. O' course, faces are faces, an' much like backsides an' elbows in that respect."

Wull laughed, saw that Mrs. Wurth hadn't been joking, and turned the chuckle into a cough.

"Sorry," he mumbled, "I choked on my tea."

He and Mrs. Wurth looked at the undrunk tea in silence.

"Whair's your faither, did you say?"

"He'd to go into the town," said Wull.

"Oracco?"

"Aye."

"On whut business?"

Wull shrugged. "He doesn't always tell me, ma'am. His own, I s'pose."

Mrs. Wurth held the skull-piece by its chinless point a few inches from her own, peering into the eyes.

"As I understan' it the city has plenty scope for the pursuit of merriment, fur those inclined to that sort of thing. It ne'er struck me as your faither's line of interest, I must say."

"What, merriment?"

Mrs. Wurth nodded. "Just so," she said. "That considered, there's plenty who have gone the way o' happiness in the past, an' I can't say I saw that comin' either. It often strikes when ye least expect it. Like food pois'nin'. I mind the last time I'd pois'nin'. Both ends, it was, an' such a spectrum o' colors as you've never seen brighten a privy floor. . . ."

"Right," said Wull, who was at a complete loss. When the mortuary was empty Pappa brought Mrs. Wurth into the parlor and gave her root tea and biscuits and the two of them shared unlistenable, looping conversations. It occurred to him that, despite all the hardship the Riverkeep endured in his stand against the elements—all the cold and damp and corpses made runny by water—weekly conversations with Mrs. Wurth might be the grimmest task of all. Talking to her was like trying to nail smoke to the wall. "The face, Mrs. Wurth."

Mrs. Wurth tapped the skull's forehead thoughtfully. "Aye," she said. "I reckon I knows where I's seen this afore, right enough. This could be right int'restin'," she added, placing the fragment respectfully on the cadaver slab and wrapping her face on her way out the door.

Wull listened for noises from Pappa. There were none, not even the little movements of his feet on the boards.

He placed his mug beside the face and, using one of the body-washing rags that littered the floor, lifted it up.

It was completely clean at the point of injury, with no ragged flesh or torn skin. The skin itself was thick and pale from its time in the river, making the hairs of the thin mustache darker still; and the whites of the eyes—open the tiniest crack—were gray.

It had never occurred to Wull that it might be possible to recognize a person who came out of the river. He didn't really know anyone apart from Pappa and Mrs. Wurth.

The undertaker's footsteps approached the door.

Startled, Wull tried to replace the face, but fumbled, dropping it mouth-first into his mug.

"Oh no, no . . ." he said.

The handle turned.

Mrs. Wurth stamped the snow from her boots.

"I'm fair convinced aboot this," she said, holding a news-paper out in front of her. "On the second page ther's . . ."

She looked at Wull, who was clutching a mug of tea that held a piece of human face.

"What are ye doin' with that, lad?" she said slowly.

"It fell in," said Wull.

"It's mibbe best ye take the deid man's head oot yer tea. O' course, folk make tea oot all kinds o' things—there's a brew made frae the soil o' beavers is meant to be right bracin'. I like root tea mysel', pref'rably wi'oot bits o' cadavers in, though I will admit to likin' it sugared."

"Right," said Wull. He took the skull fragment out of the mug and shook away the liquid. There were some tea leaves in the mustache.

Mrs. Wurth looked at him a long moment. "When's it goin' to be you as keep?" she said.

"Oh," said Wull, "a few days. I'll be sixteen on Thursday."

Mrs. Wurth looked at him another long moment. "A lot can change in even a few days, I've always found. Things're always changin'—'cept deid folk. They're always the same, 'cept when they're diff'rent, an' they can be, dependin' on circumstances, which can vary to a fair degree."

"Right," said Wull. "What was in the newspaper?"

"Aye," said Mrs. Wurth, brushing some of the tea from the dead man's face. "It's on the second page there, sketch of a gennulman lost in the waters oot in the estuary. Look at the 'tache there an' tell me that's not the same one ye jus' dipped in yer cup."

Wull looked at the sketch, looked at the section of face, then back again. Although puffed and creased by its time in the water, there was a definite resemblance, especially in the shape of the round, squashed nose.

"It does a bit," he admitted.

"An' there's plenty bits o' him missin', says the paper," said Mrs. Wurth. "Bits, I shouldn't wonder, like parts o' his face, such as ye was jus' dippin' in yer tea."

"I wasn't . . ." said Wull. "You know I'm not plannin' on drinkin' the tea now, Mrs. Wurth? It was an accident it fell in my mug."

"'S up to you what you do, Masser Keep. I ain't never had an interest in either the contents of another's larder nor any food whut has a flavor. I mind o' a time I tried this pickled thing—they said it was a farmyard oyster, but I foun' out that meant—"

"What does it say under the sketch, Mrs. Wurth?" said Wull, rubbing his eyes. "What happened to the man?"

"Aye, seems he was killed by a creature, an' quite a big one," said Mrs. Wurth. She smiled with the lower half of her face, her eyes remaining expressionless and dull. "There's spec'lation it could be a mormorach, if they even exists anymore."

"What's a mormorach?"

"Well, it's a big long eel sort of a thing, but they've no' existed for thousan's o' years. 'S a story, really, now, an' I don't hold with stories much mysel'—not in favor o' things ye can't

75

put yer hands on. If I can't see it, I don't want it. 'S why I got rid o' my sense o' smell. Made that decision aroun' the same time as the food pois'nin' which, come to think of it, was shortly after I ate those farmer's oysters—"

"Mrs. Wurth! If they don't exist anymore, why do they think it might be one?"

Mrs. Wurth scanned the article. "Fisherwoman found a hand in an empty net—green-stoned ring on it identified this fella Blummells. Found another few parts after that, but not much, an' it seems all the parts were bit clean off, not like they was torn by a mairlan or even a cragolodon . . . like this bit o' face, right enough—look how it's sliced apart, all neat like—it'll be fair valuable if that's what it is, a mormorach. 'S no tellin' when magic like that's goin' to strike, an' it's no' happened fur so long, folk hardly believe in 'em anymore."

"Like you? You don't believe in them?"

"'S right."

"Even though it says here there's one on the coast? An' they definitely used to exist?"

"'S right."

Wull rubbed his eyes.

Mrs. Wurth scanned farther down the article, tracing the words with her fingers and lip-wetting absently with her gray tongue.

"Apparently there's a *man* says he saw a big giant eel of a thing jumpin' up oot the water on the night this Blummells went missin'. But there's not to be much in that—whut's the word o' a man when all's said an' done?"

Wull looked at the sketch, then back at Mrs. Wurth's blank face.

"I'm a man," he said.

"Not yet, bless you."

"An' what about Mr. Wurth?" said Wull. "Doesn't his word count for anything?"

"Nope," said Mrs. Wurth, "that gudgeon's a head full o' magic an' no mistake. I can't make head nor tail o' whut he's sayin' half the time. Exhaustin' fellow—I hardly lets him oot the house."

Wull rubbed his eyes again. "So what does this mean?" he said.

"It means I's goin' to take this piece o' Mr. Blummells to the newspaper people to see about exchangin' money for the story o' his face," said Mrs. Wurth, smiling with her eyes this time. "Splittin' it halfways wi' yer faither, o' course," she added quickly.

Wull glanced over his shoulder at the closed door. "O' course," he said. "I'll let him know when he gets back."

Mrs. Wurth picked up the fragment of Emory Blummells's skull, wrapped it in the newspaper, and tucked it under her arm.

"I'll be seein' ye nex' Monday, if you's around, an' I'll be prayin' yer faither's back from whatever ill-begotten pursuit he's got himself engaged in. I'd hate to see a good man like he lost in the pursuit of enjoyment."

"Thank you, Mrs. Wurth," said Wull. "I'll be sure to keep clear of it myself."

"Ye'll be the keep by then, man or no' man. Good luck." Mrs. Wurth tipped her cap, wrapped her face in her scarf, and went out, a blast of cold darting in around her through the open door.

Wull stood in the mortuary until the rattle of the horses' halters had faded into the distance. Silence returned to the boathouse.

A mormorach. Something about it stirred his blood.

He opened the parlor door and peeked in. With the shutters blocking the morning's sun, the room was a sour-stinking gloom of tight, lived-in airdust swirls dancing in the tiny slivers of light. Pappa was rolling in sleep, grease-matted head swinging over protrusions of collarbone, and his feet had begun once more to move on the boards.

Wull went to him, knelt at his feet, touched his face. "Pappa," he said quietly. "Are you all right?"

Pappa's eyes burped open: vacant and fogged and deeply ringed with the bruises of restlessness.

"Sleep," he whispered. "Sleep . . . sleep . . . sleep . . ."

"You can sleep," said Wull, pushing the hair from his face. As Pappa drifted, Wull held his ankles, absorbing their quick twitches in the aching muscles of his arms. Slowly, Pappa's head ceased its deep-chested swing and the small movements of his wiry frame calmed to a frightening stillness. His big head hung forward, bristled mouth gaping, a thin rope of saliva connecting mouth to knee.

There was something under Pappa's skin, a looseness, as though the muscles were untethering from the bones.

Wull continued to hold the thin legs after sleep had come, his kneeling feet bloodless and sore, watching the movement in the wasted face and drifting into reverie and daydream, overwhelmed by the sense of lost happiness, his wishful memory restoring the flesh to Pappa's bones and the warmth to his eyes.

Eventually he stood and looked at the clock. Even if he meant to return before nightfall, there was at least an hour before he would have to launch the bäta.

He thought of the black-frozen wicks, impervious to the licks of the matches' fire, and the iron rods of the lanterns iced into ever-thickening whiteness. He thought of the mormorach, swimming now out in the estuary, flying—terrifying and powerful—through the depths. That such a beast could be in these very waters filled him with . . . something. A quake that was not dissimilar to the last days' fearful tremors, but also caused his muscles to tingle with excitement and desire.

The books through which he had pored in search of a solution to Pappa's ailments were still spread across the ledger desk. In habit, he returned to the mortuary to lift his mug, decided instead to hurl it in the river, then went to find mention of the great creature in the pages of his grandfathers' vast, ancient tomes.

Canna Bay

*Mormorach: literally, "big, big, terror." Presumed
extinct—with no confirmed sighting in over a
thousand years (see also Bohdan, Greenteeth,
and Suire)—a creature of semi-myth possessed
of incredible strength. Estimates put its length at
anything up to fifty-five feet, with the breadth of its
trunk around six or seven feet. Its mouth, certainly,
was filled with tusks the length of a man's forearm,
and it is the ornate carvings of these ivory pieces
(along with its teeth—razorlike shards of translucent
enamel more precious than diamonds) that comprise
the bulk of its present-day remains. Strongly linked
to the occult, the mormorach contained all manner
of valuable substances, from the juices of its eyes
(said to be curative of blindness); powder of its bones
(relief from rheumatic and arthritic pains); and—
most valuable of all—the dark, viscous secretions of
its brain glands (curative of dead sleeps, paralysis,*

possessions, sicknesses of the mind, and even, it is much rumored, capable of granting eternal life).

–Encyclopedia Grandalia, *University of Oracco Print House*

Weeds brushed the mormorach's flanks as it slipped with stately calm through the trench. Several days of hunting had left the waters almost empty of life, and, having finally found something to arouse its interest, it had been following a few ink-spurting squid for more than an hour, moving above them as they scuttled into caves and hollows in the rock. It banked, dipping a slow fin to alter its trajectory, then, as the squid darted back on themselves in a cloud of frightened ink, it twisted in the water, head brushing its tail fin as it whipped its body and dove, mouth wide, taking the squid into its gullet without movement. It bit at the ink, tusks clamping on its face as it sought more prey in the confusing cloud.

Finally the sensory tips of its mucus membranes stopped their signals of food and it drifted in the current once more, shifting its attention to the large shapes on the surface. The slapped contact of hulls on the water arrived as both food source and warning, and the mormorach continued to drift, bellowing, spinning through the silt in the light of its sonar voice. The surface was crowded, and it allowed itself to rise, settling under a large shape and resting against its bulk, champing its tusks and waiting for the guidance of instinct to shape its course.

Above it, aboard the *Flikka*, the crew ran to their positions at the gunwale, harpoons and ropes hoisted in firm hands that dripped with sweat even in the teeth of the icy sea wind.

The captain, an ageless salt known as Doc Fletcher, stood on the bridge with his fist on the tiller, eyes wide in spite of the constant spray. Flocks of graygulls, frenzied by the catchless days, whirled around him, wailing and keening and launching themselves at the tossing surface.

"The first sight, lads!" Doc shouted. "Launch those bloody darts into his hide! If we lose him to another boat I'll lash the skin from ye! Come on now, eyes to the water—he's right under us, and he'll surely take a look out and see what we're about. An' what are we about?"

"The hunt!" came the response, the deep resonance of many voices shouting as one.

Doc showed his teeth. The boards of his deck were stained a deep crimson, the wood having soaked in blood beyond imagining each time a whale or mairlan or shark was hauled aboard to have its skin and blubber flensed: the termite-scurry of the crew stripping the fleshy giants to the bone within hours, the meat and fat rendered in stinking fires on deck, skeletons smashed with hammers for corsetry and medicine. The *Flikka* was a ceaseless engine of death, harvesting the lives of the sea with merciless and relentless efficiency. Doc had stolen the wind of the other ships to beat them to this stretch of the water—a creature so large would hunt in the Rosa Trench, and he meant to be first at the harpoons.

A mormorach would be a fine addition to his long list of kills, and would finance the purchase of another boat. Perhaps two. Doc had always seen himself at the head of a fleet, a position that would qualify him as gentry. As the arms of his crew bulged with the tension of their lofted weapons, he pictured the house that might be secured on a purseful of mormorach tusks and began shouting again, senseless exhortations of violence and purpose that came through gritted teeth and fell on the hard ears of sailors for whom death meant money and whose blood had already boiled to the point of fury.

Beneath the *Flikka*, the mormorach floated happily in the current, mouthing the pieces of drifting weed and sea scraps that passed. Another echo told it that even the squid were gone, and the waters of the bay were entirely without fish. The constant impulse to eat meant the empty water was transmitted as threat, and it allowed itself to drift sideways, senses working to find another meal.

"There it is!" cried a steward, pointing.

The rest of the crew rushed about, following the direction of his steady hand and peering through the brightness of the sky glare on the waves. Doc rushed to the bridge's edge.

"Throw!" he yelled, spotting the creature's gliding shadow.

A flurry of harpoons speared the water.

"I hit it!" shouted one man, pulling on the rope that fixed his harpoon to the gunwale. It came up too easily, the point of the blade loose in the water. "But no spike!" he cried. "I've winged it only!"

"Keep throwin'!" shouted Doc. "It'll sound if ye keeps missin' it!"

The harpoons were recovered, thrown again, the lurking shape of the mormorach shrinking as it allowed itself to sink away from the confusing bubbles.

One of the hissing columns had grazed its side with a sharp sting. The shape on the surface was hostile, and with so little food in the water a competitor could not be tolerated.

"It's comin' back!" shouted Doc. He looked at the speed of the moving shadow and grabbed ahold of the tiller. "Lavernes's name," he whispered.

The mormorach broke the surface and kept rising, clearing the height of the ship and scooping two harpoonists in its jaws before smashing through the edge of the deck in a shower of broken wood and crashing back into the waves. It threw its head from side to side, serrating the sailors' bodies and sending their limbs drifting, then it passed its mouth through the blood cloud around their corpses, sifting for flesh, biting at clothing and hair and bone. Then it sounded, turning against the seabed before whipping its tail and roaring again.

"To me!" shouted Doc, grabbing a fallen harpoon and mounting the gunwale, rolling with unconscious balance on the swell of the sea against the frozen wind. "When he comes back you stick him with all you've got!"

The mormorach soared past Doc, its massive head knocking him into his crew and shattering the central mast as it broke once more through the deck and—Doc saw with a constriction of his guts—the hull. With majestic slowness, the sail began to topple into the water, and the *Flikka* split in two.

The sea rose in an instant to Doc's feet.

"The ship!" he shouted. "She's breached! She's sinking! Abandon . . . abandon ship!"

But his crew had already begun to flee, throwing themselves from the sinking vessel and swimming for the shore or the boats that surrounded them.

Only Doc remained, scrabbling at the red deck that, now sharply inclined, tipped him into the sea's turbulence. He fought for purchase, the toes of his boots fast on sodden boards now slick with blood, its iron smell filling his nose over the water's salt. As the deck passed below the surface, Doc felt himself come loose, his flailing, heavy legs exposed to the black depths, a million icy needles stabbing his skin, and he looked around desperately for a sign of the mormorach's silver shadow.

"Help!" he shouted, waving frantically at the other hunting boats. "For the sake of . . . Help!"

The boats, faceless under sails he did not recognize, rolled in the current.

As his thick layers of clothing saturated, Doc sank, his face splashing through the waves, spray filling his mouth as he gulped in a final, desperate breath.

On board the *Hellsong*, far off in the safety of the harbor and leaning on his crutch, Gilt Murdagh snapped closed his telescope between wide leather-skinned palms.

"Mormorach right enough, Cap'n?" asked Ormidale, the first mate, his wide, dark face scrunched in the light.

Murdagh nodded, a grin splitting his beard. "That fat sod Fletcher jus' lost his boat. Himself too, it seems. Went after it wi' harpoons like it was a reg'lar game fish." He snorted and laughed, shaking his head.

"'In't we usin' harpoons, Cap'n?" said Samjon.

Murdagh glanced at the wind-pinked cabin boy, then shifted his weight to the whalebone stump below his left knee. "There's a reason this ol' tub's still floatin' while others've made their way to gatherin' hermits an' coral on the seabed."

"What's the reason, Cap'n? Ow!" said Samjon as Ormidale kicked his ankle.

"Patience," said Murdagh. He opened the telescope again, pressed it to his good eye, and smiled. "We'll wait till folks around here get nervous—money moves quick on clammy palms. Let's see how the next lot gets on. . . ."

The Keep

Wull read the passage again.

It was real. And what a beast! If he could get his hands on such an animal, he could buy all the whale oil in the world. And imagine how much the oil of a mormorach would be worth! What would the wealthy lords and ladies in the city pay to have their ballrooms lit by a creature of myth?

He read it again.

For all the wealth in its tusks and teeth, it was the secrets of its glands that stirred him most powerfully: the adventurous capture of treasure was dismissible fancy, but the properties described in the juices of its eyes and the liquids in its brain meant something altogether more urgent.

Wull looked across at Pappa, at the cloudy strip of pale yellow that bled out below his half-open eyelid; the red-veined looseness of the skin on his face and neck; the hang of his strong head, from which came an almost audible buzzing of mania and pain.

What might the juices of a mormorach's eyes do for Pappa's? And if the ooze of its brain could cure paralysis and sickness of the mind, could it release Pappa from the rotting cage of his body?

Wull looked out the ice-patterned window. The river, closing under slabs of foot-thick ice, had reduced to a narrow channel of still-flowing water. He would need to light the lanterns soon, all of them, to stand a chance of breaking some of the locks of winter.

He read the passage again, and this time searched out the cross-references, starting with the bohdan.

His eyes flew along the tiny print, barely taking it in. He tore both pages from the encyclopedia and pushed the closed book to the back of the desk. Then he read them both again.

He felt faint and short of air, his skin flushing with heat in the cold room. A bohdan—that was what had taken Pappa. Wull saw in his mind the brown mouth and the flash of the eyes, and vomited onto the floorboards between his feet.

Wiping his mouth, gripping the arm of the chair, Wull glanced again at Pappa, saw the shrinkage in his body, fat and muscle having run off him like water from a drying corpse.

He read again. There was still time, a few days at least.

So it was settled: he could go or he could stay. If he took the few days' journey to Canna Bay, he would need to go now and the river would freeze for certain, casting a pall of shame on the house of the Riverkeep. But if he remained and was unable to light the lanterns, he would be facing a winter locked inside the stinking boathouse with Pappa barking and shouting and angrily dying away from the light and the sky, the pall of shame cast regardless as the thing consumed him.

And the river would cope. The river always coped, and whether or not he failed to light the fires or abandoned it to the creep of winter, it would thaw and rise and teem come the spring as it always did. By which point Pappa would be in the ground.

"It that speaks . . . stinking boy . . . it . . . stinking it . . ."

Wull looked at the furrow of Pappa's brows in his muttering sleep and felt once more the acid wrench of it all, the weight of everything pressing on him, Pappa and the river and his closed-off future tightening around him, stabbing and knotting his guts until his fear throbbed in his skin.

He shook himself, read once more about the mormorach: *curative of possessions*. This monster was the answer.

There was a drawing of it, a sketch of what the creature might look like from the guesswork of an artist too fond of flowing lines: the animal in the picture was an elegant ribbon of shining skin, tusks little more than decorative ornaments at the corners of a mouth that was coquettishly closed, like the pursed lips of a porcelain doll. Wull imagined the real thing would be more lumpen and raw.

Whatever it looked like, inside it ran medicines that could save Pappa. He thought of the first page of the ledgers: *to ackt with dignittie*. Even though Pappa was still the Danék Riverkeep for the next three days, his dignity had been taken by the river—and by the thing inside him.

But he was still there. There was still time. And that meant Wull had no choice to make.

He moved aside the ropes and oilskins and fishing lines that hung in front of the harpoons stacked neatly along the riverside wall. They had never been used in Wull's lifetime; Pappa had often boasted that they were sharp and heavy and made of good iron.

He lifted one free and tried it in his hand. Although well balanced it was immensely heavy, and as he raised it to shoulder height the barb dipped and crashed onto the floor.

"There must be a knack to this, right enough," he muttered, trying again. His long arm quivered under the weight, and the barb fell once more, the clang stirring Pappa into a cursing sleep-mutter.

Wull lowered the harpoon to the floorboards and freed the three others from the wall. Then he extinguished the fires in the grates, placed salted trout and hard biscuits in a canvas knapsack, and began laboriously dressing Pappa's shouting, struggling body in the seula-gut and fur-lined clothes he would need on their journey to the coast, feeling all the while the torn pages of the encyclopedia burning like hot coals in his pocket.

8

The Danék Wilds

*Bohdan: literally, "skin-changer." A creature of semi-myth
(see also Greenteeth, Mormorach, and Suire), so named
for its habit of wearing the skins of its victims. Details
of reported sightings vary dramatically, but the alleged
capture of a live specimen in the Splendic Ocean revealed
that the creature is itself largely formless, consisting
of little more than a tentacled mass of skull-less head,
spinal column, and countless nerve endings. The bohdan
achieves form by inhabiting the body and shape of its
victims, a process that takes anything from three to
seven days (depending on the victim's size and species)
and is outwardly symptomized through dramatic weight
loss and clouding in the host's eyes. Once the creature
takes occupancy of a new body, the skin it has most
recently vacated is almost always consumed completely
by the bohdan in its new form. This would account
for eyewitness reportage that describe the creature as
goatlike, houndlike, and humanoid, and perhaps accounts
for a great many unexplained disappearances. There is*

no known cure for attack by a bohdan, although various
magics and mythical treatments are suggested in ancient
literature (see Mormorach).

—Encyclopedia Grandalia, *University of Oracco Print House*

The bäta sat low in the water, heavy with the blankets and food that Wull had piled wherever he could find space: into the pointed nose of the bow, below the bottom boards, and under the stern thwart. Beneath the bucket of salted trout was a paper-wrapped bag: nearly forty ducats, every penny they had.

Wull felt the bäta sulking like an unwilling dog. It seemed when its eyes sat in the periphery of his vision that they were cast away from him, unwilling or unable to look in his direction.

"Can't go!" Pappa was shouting. "Sleep only!"

"You c'n sleep when we're in the bäta—you jus' need to get yourself in there for me, please," said Wull. He was alarmed by the support Pappa needed to walk the jetty, but even more so by the ease with which he was able to carry him. Pappa's whole frame was loose, bones knocking together in the absence of muscle and flesh, a few days having shorn off more than half his body weight. With his head pressed against Pappa's shoulder, Wull's ear felt the breath-heat of

94

muttered insults and protestations, Pappa's mouth rank and rotten with fish, their gleaming scales clumped on his unshaved face like the slobbers of frog spawn that bordered the riverbank in spring.

Wull had tried over and again to wipe Pappa's mouth clean, but had retreated from the biting teeth.

"Sleep now, stinking boy it!" said Pappa, going limp in Wull's arms.

"Come *on!*" said Wull. "It's for your own good we're doing this."

"No good!" said Pappa, digging his heels into the jetty.

Several minutes of balancing and cajoling and gentle pushing passed, Pappa's anger rising steadily to a shout that was smothered by the river's freezing air. Eventually he was slumped in Wull's old seat on the stern thwart, limp with exhaustion, fresh spit glistening in the corners of his lips.

"Take this blanket," said Wull. "You'll need it. It's freezing."

"Heavy," said Pappa, wriggling away from it.

"You have to take it—you'll freeze to death without it. Come on, please."

He tucked the blanket around and under Pappa's spindle legs, checked the bonds on his hands and the knot of his scarf.

In the bäta for the first time since he'd been taken into the river, Pappa looked even smaller, and Wull realized just how much of him had been shrunk and whittled away.

The river was closing in front of Wull, the untamed ice reaching remorselessly inward to the boat-width channel that still flowed in its center.

"We need to be going, Pappa," he said. "I'm sorry the river's like this. . . . I tried, honest. There's no lighting the lanterns—they wouldn't take the flame. But we need to get you proper help. That's all that really matters."

He took a quick drink from his elkskin water pouch, then sat in the Riverkeep's seat and hefted the oars, palms burning under tender skin as he rowed steadily away. In a silence filled only by the sound of the oars' blades and the bäta nudging chunks of ice, he watched the unlit lump of the boathouse shrink, the closed eyes of its black windows reflecting a threatening sky from which daylight was rapidly ebbing, cloud cover speeding the approach of night.

A grandfather (Wull was unsure how many *greats* were involved) named Wilcy had explored the river as a boy, and kept a journal, all the way to its mouth and the beginnings of the wider sea. There was an inn at the hamlet of Lauston that had a jetty and cheap rooms where Wilcy had spent the night and *enjoyd fyne ales in such qwantittys as put me in a plais of fair disposytion.*

Ale tasted like old dishwater to Wull, but *fair disposytion* sounded good, he had to admit. From Wilcy's meandering descriptions and the maps, he reckoned Lauston was close—two hours rowing, all with the current, away from the keep's domain and toward the rest of the world. He rowed lightly, the water urging the bäta forward.

Pappa would have known where Lauston was, would have known the names of the townsfolk, the traders, and the guards. He always knew the world of the river. Wull watched Pappa's face as he sculled into the current's center, willing him to lean forward and laugh with him, chide him and breathe lakoris at him for fun.

"Are you comfortable, Pappa?" he said after he had rowed far beyond the sight of the boathouse, past twenty burned-out lanterns: silent sentinels in the full grip of winter.

Pappa said nothing—merely glowered through the grime of his hair and chewed on his lips.

"I couldn't tame the ice," Wull carried on. "You never had time to show me how to get the wicks lit; the flames jus' bounced off. But I broke a big floe with a rod an' found that face. My first recovery, an' it put me onto this mormorach thing that's down in Canna Bay."

Night had fallen. They were passing close to lantern twenty-one, and Wull shuddered at the shadowed berg it had become. With the fire of the lanterns dead, the river's darkness was breathtaking, lit by just the thin moonlight that struggled through the clouds.

He looked over his shoulder, corrected his course, and carried on rowing as steadily as he could without his shoulders screaming their resistance.

Lantern twenty-two—frontier of the Riverkeep's world and near to where Pappa had been taken—slid into view. Wull's chest skipped as he saw that, alone of all the lanterns, it remained lit, a tiny, wobbling flame dancing on the tip of its wick casting a fragile glow into the black.

He had never been past this point. The Riverkeep's domain was a blockage in the artery of the river, a clutch of islands and whirls of current that slowed the water and made it solid and immovable.

Beyond it the river widened and quickened, a clear strip of it flowing all winter without a keep's hand. Even unlanterned, the ice reached barely halfway into the center, leaving a channel through which to pass.

A storm had been raging the first time he'd come out here in the bäta, and he'd trembled, huddling close to Pappa's bulk as thunder rolled across the sky, so far from home and with the pull of the river so close to his feet. But when an ocean barge puttered past and Pappa waved to the captain, Wull's chest had swelled—proud of Pappa's being known, recognized.

"What's past here?" he'd asked.

Pappa had chuckled. "In the Danék Wilds? Ev'rythin'. All the noise an' danger ye'd never wish for. An' beyond that, war."

"Isn't there magic?" Wull had asked, thinking of his bed-side stories.

"Oh, aye, if ye can find it."

"Then why don't we use magic to keep the river?"

Pappa had lifted him onto the center thwart, onto the keep's seat, held him in under his big arm, and pointed to the vein-bursts of pink lightning flashing on the horizon.

"'Cause magic's like that. Jus' as pretty an' jus' as dangerous, an' it comes to us the way lightnin' strikes the ground. So once ye can bottle up lightnin', wee man o' mine, ye let me know an' we'll use it for the keep. All right?"

Wull had laughed, thinking of a bottle of lightning, and they'd turned back home.

Now, the oars in *his* hands, he looked at Pappa's face, gaunt and loose, eyes once more closed in sleep. Fighting it, Wull knew—fighting for his own skin.

There was a small bottle of whale oil in the bow, packed out of grim duty; taking the bäta on the river without it would have made the abandonment of his keep seem even more cowardly. Wull dropped the oars in their locks and pulled close to the lantern, feeling the warmth of the fire in the iron rod, and, removing his gloves for a second to loose the cork, tipped the whole, stinking bottle into the reservoir. He shut the cap and watched as the oil soaked into the supple wick, swelling the flame to a bold finger of white against its globe. In the absence of the other lanterns, its light was impossibly bright: a beacon at the edge of the world.

Holding his hand on the warm iron a moment longer, Wull looked back into the dark cave of the Riverkeep's world, then sat and rowed on, past that final barrier of light into new, unknown waters.

Scribbled in the margins of Wilcy's journal were the details of currents and whirlpools, along with the names of towns and villages speckling the boundaries of Oracco, the great city, through which spilled people in numbers Wull could not imagine.

And between these outposts of bustling civilization were miles and miles of inhospitable wilderness and threatening badlands—the banks of which heaved with all manner of animal and human danger.

"There's meanin' in this when you think about it," he said after another silent time. "There's got to be a reason for the one recognizable bit o' that Blummells man to land on our doorstep, an' for it to be the thing that brings this animal to us. If we get ahold o' this mormorach, we'll be rich forever, Pappa, but first we'll be able to make you better."

Pappa, who Wull had thought asleep, gurgled loudly—a wet, bubbling croak. Thinking he was choking, Wull went to thump his back, when he realized that the gurgling sound was laughter.

"Better . . ." said Pappa, leering horribly. "No *better* . . . all fine. Strong. Fine."

"What do you mean?" said Wull. "You're ill. You're not well." He jumped as a seula popped up beside the boat, nosing at the smell of fish heads. It blinked its glassy blue eyes at him, then flicked its whiskers and slid beneath the surface once again.

"Am fine, it that speaks," said Pappa, looking directly, properly at Wull for the first time since he disappeared. "Failure boy, stinking *failure* boy . . ."

"Why are you saying that?" said Wull. His hands began to slow on the oars as the needle of pain in his guts pushed vomit into the back of his throat. The light of the final lantern was a speck in the distance now.

"Ice river," said Pappa. "Ice, ice, ice, all the river."

"I tried!" said Wull, rowing again, harder. "I did my best, but it can't be done—not without you to show me how! This winter's worse than any I c'n remember. I can't keep it back on my own!"

Pappa shrugged, a one-shouldered hunch that nearly toppled him on his side. "Failure, it that speaks," he said. "Eat now."

"Don't say that about me," said Wull, raising his voice. "I've done my best! An' I'll make you better when we get there, you'll see!"

"Eat! Now!"

"No! We're hardly even away—there's days to go an' there's not many fish heads left as it is. You c'n eat once we get to the inn. They've a jetty we can tie up to for the night."

"Eat! Now!" shouted Pappa, straining against his bonds.

Wull's head throbbed, a little speck of pain deep in the center of his skull.

"No!" he shouted back. "I've told you, we're goin' to . . ."

His words stopped in his throat: the figure of a man, shoulders bristling with the fronds of a bank fern, was silhouetted against the lantern's pinprick of light.

"Oh gods," said Wull. "Bradai."

The figure dropped out of sight. Wull saw the dot of the low black bandit craft racing toward them—a little dart in the water, the shoulders of its occupants just visible, wafting with feathers and plants.

"Eat! Now! Now!" said Pappa.

"Not now—we're in trouble!" said Wull, digging into the river as hard as he could, lifting himself off the seat with the weight of the water. The bäta leaped forward, but it was nowhere near enough, he could see: already the bradai's skiff had closed a boat length or more on them, and he could see the thin shadows of their black-painted oars working rapidly in the locks.

"No use! Eat!" shouted Pappa. He pushed and heaved against the knots on his wrists.

"I can't!" said Wull. "You said yourself you can't trust the bradai! If I can stay far enough in front of 'em, they might give up and we'll make it to Lauston!"

"Eat!"

"I can't talk an' row! I'm not you!"

"Stinking it that speaks!"

Wull heaved again, palms and shoulders screaming—and this time felt an extra swell of current against his left hand. He drove the oar beneath the surface, turning the nose of the bäta toward it, letting it sniff out the extra power; pulled again on the oars, felt the boat lurch forward, quicker, saw the gap between him and the bradai even out.

"Can't go forever," said Pappa.

"Be quiet," said Wull between his teeth. His lungs were bursting, the frozen air fire in his chest.

To his horror, he saw the skiff's oars quicken: six of them. Six to his two, driving a thin-hulled boat that weighed half the bäta's bulk. There was no hope, no chance of escape. Even if he banked and fled, Pappa could barely walk and the bradai would simply run him down—scurrying through the trees and the gnarled roots of the forest floor like skirrils.

Wull focused on the tiny star of the final lantern and rowed through pain and fatigue and the tearing of muscles. Wind whipped the backs of his ears as the flame's star winked out until eventually, in the darkness of a fireless night that seemed to hold the world in its fist, the bäta rocked and a feather-cloaked figure said:

"Slow *down*, li'l man. We's a-caught you."

9

Those who travel know that bandits are chief of all dangers, accounting for many more deaths per annum than collision-induced trauma, hypothermic complications, or loss of direction combined. The roads leading to and from Oracco are dangerous at night, and there can be few coachmen who travel without the company of a loaded barrel; but the shorelines of the Danék positively bristle with soot-blackened steel, and the bradai who stalk them are fearless in their disregard of both animal predation and the elements. They will strike at any time, night or day, as like from beneath the current as from the great swinging boughs of the oaks that line the banks. Some wear the skins of animals they have slain; others cloaks sewn with grasses and leaves. In all cases their victims' last sound is one of surprise.

–Wheeldon Garfill, A Path Trod Well: Journeys of My Life

Wull's chest was heaving. He stopped the oars' movement but kept them high in the water.

"That was quite a turn o' speed, li'l man," said the bradai. "We's nearly puffed out us-selves. It's rude to run, though—an' you knows we's goin' to catch you eventually."

He stood and stretched, the feathers on his cloak fluttering. Beneath it he wore black clothes that were invisible in the darkness and belts from which Wull heard the light chime of weaponry: blades, Pappa had told him, blackened with soot. Wull said nothing, allowed his breathing to return.

"Where's you goin' in such a mad hurry?" said the man. "Don't you know it's bad manners to run from the gentlemen o' the river?"

"That's herons," said Wull. "Herons are the gentlemen o' the river. You're jus' thievin' scum."

The bradai turned his head to one side and raised an eyebrow.

"People who says a thing like that is usu'lly bold or daft. Which are you, long boy?"

"Neither," said Wull. "I'm jus' not interested in talkin' to you while I'm waitin' for you to rob me."

"An' ain't that a fine way to talk. What's the hurry?"

"That's my business," said Wull. He looked at Pappa, the big head lolling.

The bradai laughed. "What's your name, boldly-daft-hurrying-long-boy?"

"What's yours?" said Wull, meeting the black-painted stare.

The man laughed. "Hear this?" he shouted to his companions. "He wants to know our names! Well, I'm Kenesaw—on the skiff there's Garnet an' Happy. Now, what's yours?"

"Wulliam," said Wull.

"Uh-huh, an' who's your silent friend here?"

"That's my pappa," said Wull. "He's the Danék Riverkeep."

"No, he ain't," said Kenesaw. "I saw the keep ten days ago—he's a fat lump with a neck like a log. Why would you need to be pretendin' to be someone else? You on the lam?"

"He is the Riverkeep," said Wull hotly. "Look at his face! An' I'm nearly sixteen. I'll be the keep in a few days!"

"Good for you," said Kenesaw, "an' happy birthday when it comes, but you ain't puttin' nothin' over on us. The keep does us plenty favors, breakin' up the ice an' all, but this winter's beaten him an' that ain't him anyhow. This looks like his boat, right enough, so I guess you've stole it an' that's why you's in such a hurry. Where's the money?"

"This is *my* boat!"

Pappa stirred. "Eat!" he said.

"Pappa," said Wull, "tell them who you are! Tell them you're the Riverkeep!"

Kenesaw silently drew a foot-long knife from his waistband.

"Eat, it that speaks! Eat! Now!"

"I can see you two must share some riveting conversation," said Kenesaw languidly. "The money?"

"There's no money," said Wull, forcing his eyes not to flick to the cache of ducats in the bow.

Kenesaw sighed. "Now that's jus' silly, ain't it?" he said wearily. "Little runt like you, off in a big, stolen boat like this, maybe you's done in the owners. That's fine—we ain't got no room to judge what a man mus' do. But you ain't goin' to steal somethin' like this without findin' a li'l money, an' you ain't goin' to get far anyways without it, so why not jus' tell us where it is, Wulliam, an' this can be as easy as you like?"

The other bradai emerged from the shadow of their skiff and clambered aboard the bäta. Both had the fronds of bank fern sewn countlessly into their cloaks. Both carried short, darkened blades.

"Thievin' scum," said Wull, dropping the oars.

An arm flashed toward him. At first Wull thought the man had slapped him, then he felt the wet spill of blood on his cheek. He bit off his glove and raised his hand—felt the heat of blood patter on the tips of his fingers.

"Why'd you do that?" he said. The pain was starting to blossom.

"No way we's gettin' cheeked by a stripling like you," said Kenesaw, who hadn't moved. "Reputations are what counts, an' that's ours."

"Aaargh . . . a-attacking defenseless children?" said Wull. He felt his cheek swelling in a bright flash across his face, pulling the rest of his body toward it: hot and tight and hard.

"You's no child if you's stealin' a boat, long boy, an' with a quick mouth like that, you's not defenseless anyhow. Callin' us scum! We's all cut by yer remark, ain't we, fellas?"

The other bradai, smells of dampness and bark pouring from their cloaks, were rummaging around the bäta, under the boards and stern, shifting Pappa's legs around. Wull pulled at their fern fronds and tried to stand.

"Leave him alone!" he shouted.

"It that speaks!"

"I told you," said Wull, reaching for Pappa, the pain in his face almost blinding him, "we don't have any money. . . ."

Behind him came the heavy sound of bagged coins on wood.

Kenesaw's face lit up. "*I* told *you*," he said.

"You can't," said Wull, trying to push past them. "It's all we have. . . ."

"You'll jus' have to steal more from someone else, long boy."

Kenesaw pushed Wull into his seat as he stood, rocking the bäta and following the other bradai into the skiff.

"I didn't steal it! It's ours!"

"It's ours now," said Kenesaw. He tipped his cap. "Take care on your thievin' journey. Gentlemen o' the river, see?"

The skiff shot forward on its black oars, slicing its way into the night. Wull sat as it vanished, listening to the swell smack on the bäta's hull and trying to push away the pain from his slashed face.

"It that speaks! Eat now!"

Wull sighed and tightened his jaw. The blood from his cheek had run under his collar and was gathering in a sticky heat on his neck.

"All right, Pappa. Here."

He dropped to his knees and held up a fish head. Pappa took it like a horse after hay, lips pulling at air and scale.

"Same as again," said Pappa.

"They left some of the salted trout, proper fish—why don't you try that?"

"Same as again!"

"You love salted trout," said Wull quietly, passing him another fish head.

As Pappa ate, Wull looked toward the boathouse. He could go back, forget this ever happened. Lantern twenty-two would be burning still—he could uproot it, take its flame to thaw the others, bring the river back under his control, and fight the ice, as Pappa would have done.

"It that speaks," said Pappa, voice garbled by the white meat of the fish.

Wull looked at his milky pupils.

Once Wull had accidentally cornered a red balgair—boxing it in against the hedgerows. The beast had gathered itself, peering hard at him, all its animal instinct swirling in its glare.

"Cannae be doin' that," Pappa had said when he'd run into the boathouse, shaking. "Ye're lucky it din't have its babbies on its back—would have had yer throat out for comin' near 'em."

"I din't mean to," Wull had said, trying not to cry. "It was an accident."

Pappa had ruffled his hair and made him cocoa.

"I know," he'd said, "but they'd fight an ursa for their babbies. Be mindful o' that. Needs respect, does that."

Wull had nodded and drunk his cocoa and gone to bed to wait for his story.

Now, knees hard on the bottom boards, his cut skin shrieking in the cold, that safe life seemed to have happened to someone else.

And, looking at Pappa's eyes, he saw the same swirl of instinct—the same animal tension.

Wull lifted his water pouch to his lips and took the torn pages from his pocket. He read again about the bohdan. He had to go on—there was nothing here for him. Not without Pappa.

He gathered the oars.

"Eat more!" said Pappa.

"Soon," said Wull. "I don't want to stay here. We need to get to the inn and try to find some more food. And something for my face, I need to cover it—a bandage or something."

"There's a bandage in here," said a small voice from the bow.

Wull dropped the oars and the pages. He looked over his shoulder. For the briefest moment he thought the bäta itself—its eyes as judging as ever—had spoken, then a pile of blankets shifted and a girl about his own age emerged, stretching, thick scarecrowed black hair and a high fur-lined collar around her head. She was chewing a blade of grass and smiling sleepily, her face dented by dimples. As well as a thick woolen coat, she wore heavy-soled boots and thin cotton gloves.

"What in hells!" said Wull, mouth open and head spinning. "Where did you come from?"

"I was on their boat," said the girl, climbing onto the bow thwart. "Smelled awful, though. What's that?" she added, seeing Wull stuffing the dropped pages into his pocket.

"Never you mind! And don't sit down, get out! Are you a bradai? Are you goin' to rob me an' all?"

She tilted her head and looked at him. "Do I look like a bradai?"

"I don't know," said Wull, who'd never met a girl before.

"Well, I'm not. I'm . . . Mix. I was jus' hidin'."

"You c'n hide on the bank then—you're not stayin'!" Wull turned the bäta away from the current and started to row for shore. "How *dare* you sneak on here! An' with them! Maybe I should shout them back? I bet they'd like to find out what you were doin' on their boat!"

"Ah, come on, you wouldn't do that," said Mix, holding out the roll of bandages. "I'm on my own. You wouldn't abandon me."

Wull grabbed the bandages and threw them to the floor.

"You've snuck onto my boat with the bandits that stole my money an' cut my face," he said, rowing faster. "Why wouldn't I?"

"'S not decent," said Mix.

"Girl it!" said Pappa.

"Hullo, Wulliam's paps. C'n I interest you in a fish head?" said Mix. She tried to clamber over Wull to get to Pappa.

"Don't! What are you—stay there!" shouted Wull. "An' how'd you know my name?"

"You told the bradai," said Mix, raising an eyebrow. "Wasn't much of a puzzle."

"Well, don't spy on me! You shouldn't be here!"

"I'll give your paps a fish head while you's rowin'," said Mix.

"Don't talk to him, jus' stay there!"

"I thought you wanted me to leave?"

"I do! I mean, don't move the bäta—you're slowing me down!"

"What's a bäta?"

"This boat, it's what you call—"

"So don't move it like this?" said Mix, rocking the bäta from side to side.

"No!" said Pappa. "Eat!"

"Stop it," said Wull. "You're upsetting him."

"I'm sorry," said Mix. "Why don't you let me help him eat, then you c'n keep rowin' at the same time an' drop me off in a minute?"

"Eat!" said Pappa.

Wull looked back down the river. A few days ago he'd been sleepwalking toward becoming the keep and dreaming of an escape from the stagnancy of the boathouse.

"Fine," he said, moving to the side, "but then you're goin', all right?"

"Not a bother," said Mix, sliding past. As she hovered above him and rearranged her feet, her collar slipped, and Wull saw her neck was marked with delicate white patterns that swirled like a dusting of frost.

"What's that on your skin?" he said.

"Nothin'," said Mix, shrugging into her coat and holding up a fish head for Pappa.

"It's not nothin'. Is it a tattoo?"

"Do I look like I'd have a tattoo?"

"I don't know," said Wull.

"Same as again," said Pappa, chewing the fish head in slobbering bites. Mix hadn't seemed to notice the dribble of scales on her hand.

"So what are they?" he said. "The white marks, I mean."

"A childhood thing."

Wull watched her passing Pappa another fish head, felt the flames of pain on his cheek.

"What's wrong with your paps?" asked Mix.

Wull rowed a few strokes, thought of the bohdan.

"He's jus' not himself," he said. "Something took him under the water a few days ago. When he came back, he was different, aggressive, didn't know who I was. I had to tie him to a chair to stop him hurtin' me. Now he barely knows my name, doesn't remember anythin' 'bout who he was." He gripped the oars tighter. "But he'll be fine."

Mix reached across the bäta and patted Wull's boot. Wull looked at her wrist: the same white patterns disappeared into her sleeve.

"That's horrible," she said. "What did the doctor say?"

"We've no money for doctors," said Wull. "Whenever I've been ill, Pappa's mixed me a poultice from one o' the keep's books. Doctorin' means the city anyway; none'll come out to the boathouse."

"I's right thirsty," said Mix. "How come the doctors won't come see you?"

Wull paused, nodded at the water pouch, slowed the oars.

"I don't know. They jus' don't. It's how things are—we live out on the edge o' things, an' we get along by ourselves. I need to get him help, an' I've only days to do it, so I'm takin' him to the coast—there's somethin' there. It's the only thing that can help him now."

Mix grabbed the pouch. "The mormorach?" she said, drinking deeply.

Wull stopped moving and looked down at her. "How'd you know that?"

Mix shrugged, wiping her mouth, then rummaged for a good-size fish head and held it up. Pappa tore into it ravenously.

"I think anyone'd have guessed. It's in all the newspapers— the bradai were talkin' about it an' all. Mormorach this an' mormorach that. Everyone with a gun's headin' down there to have a shot at it. Worth a fortune, apparently."

"Oh gods . . . I need to get there! If someone else kills it then there's no way we'll be able to afford the stuff Pappa needs. . . . I'll have done all this for nothin'!"

"You don't think *you* can kill it, do you?" said Mix. She laughed, then stopped when she saw Wull's face. "I'm sorry, it's jus' that . . . I mean, the papers are sayin' the place is full o' whalin' ships now—big boats what're made for huntin', with sailors an' things. All *you've* got is a rowin' boat. How're you even goin' to get there in time?"

"I'll manage!" said Wull. "I have to get there. The current'll help us."

"Some current," said Mix. "It'll take you days, at least. An' it'd be suicide to hunt this thing. I mean, it can't be your fault what happened to him. . . ."

"What do you know of it?" said Wull, rounding on her, his eyes burning. "What do you know 'bout my life?"

"Nothin', I s'pose. I reckon I know a bit 'bout your paps, though. He jus' needs takin' care of."

"An' what do you know o' that?"

"Nothin'. Jus' that I've cared for sick people before. Sometimes they jus' need lookin' after an' bein' made comfortable."

Wull looked away from her, his eyes shining.

"I'll help look after him if you like," said Mix, "if you can stand to let me stay here."

"It from boat," muttered Pappa.

"See?" Mix leaned across and wiped some fish-scaled dribble from the corner of Pappa's mouth. "Your paps likes me well enough."

Wull looked at Pappa's face, felt the fevered pulsing heat of the bradai's cut draining him.

He turned the bäta back to the current.

"Sit still an' don't make any loud noises," he said. "We're goin' to the inn at Lauston. The plan *was* to tie up behind the ursa bars, but now they've stolen my money, so I'm goin' to have to try an' get somethin' to eat."

"Don't mind me on that score," said Mix. "I's not hungry at all."

"Well, I am, rowin' this damn thing. You c'n stay and look after Pappa."

"No bother at all," said Mix. She wiped another trickle of drool from Pappa's chin.

"Why would you even want to come with me?" said Wull, watching her.

"Oh, I've nowhere else to go. I'm jus' wanderin'. Or runnin' away, really. Might as well run that way as any other."

"Why are you runnin'?" said Wull.

Mix said nothing, but smiled at him.

"You're a criminal, aren't you?" said Wull wearily. "Brilliant, now I'm an accessory to crime."

"No!" She laughed. "O' course not. I mean, *technically*, I stole somethin'. . . ."

"Oh gods . . ."

"Wait, though—d'you think it's possible to steal somethin' by accident?"

"Yes, def'nitely. Def'nitely."

"Then I stole somethin'."

"Somethin' valuable?"

"Oh, beyond value, really. Priceless."

"Perfect," said Wull. "What was it?"

Mix shook her head. "Another time, maybe."

"Fine. Jus' don't steal my mormorach. I really need it."

"I'm tellin' you, it'll be long gone by the time you get there," said Mix, holding another fish head for Pappa. "An' if it's still there, it'll kill you."

"Shut up."

"I'm just *sayin'* . . ."

"Don't."

The *Hellsong*

Deep in the fetid heat of the *Hellsong*'s armory, Samjon blinked sweat from his eyes and stuck to his task. The ship's great ribs swung with the waves, and he shifted his feet to catch his balance, leaning toward the single lamp, away from the swoops of sharpened steel around him.

After hours below, the paraffin smell was beginning to lighten his head. He blinked again, fluttering his eyes to keep his focus.

"'In't you done?" said Ormidale, his broad face looming at the doorway.

"I's goin' as fast as I can," said Samjon, sliding a flensing saw the size of his leg into a leather scabbard.

"Well, go quicker: we's needin' these oiled and stored an hour ago an' you's barely halfway done! Here . . ." Ormidale hefted a harpoon the thickness of an eel, spinning it as though it were made of paper. He snatched the rag Samjon was holding and swirled it along the metal's length, then slid it inside the calfskin wrap, alongside the others. "See? Don't go as fast as *you* can—go as fast as *I* can."

Samjon sighed. "Why we even puttin' all these away? How we goin' to kill anythin' with no weapons?"

"You jus' button your yap an' keep workin'," said Ormidale, giving Samjon a soft kick on the rump as he left. "'S not for cabin boys to ask questions, least not if they don't want to stay cabin boys forever."

Samjon gripped the cloth, lifted another flensing saw, and dribbled oil on its surface. The liquid rainbowed in the flickering lamplight and rolled from the shimmering blade as the waves battered the *Hellsong*'s keel.

"No weapons," he muttered, sheathing the saw and stacking it in the hold. "An' how d'you catch a fish wi' no bait, I wonder?"

Lauston

Slumped in the dimness of an animal-fat candle, Tillinghast watched the groups of drinkers. The floor of the inn was like a poorly coordinated folk dance: people moving in wavering lines, bumping together, shouting, and throwing up their hands.

Tillinghast remembered such occasions. Somewhere in him slumbered that feeling, a tapeworm in his soul that spoke to him of noise-soaked evenings and riotous fun. Of the company of other people.

After drinking volumes of potœm that would have killed a horse, he had retired to a quiet table at the back of the inn. There, in his roaring, unconquerable sobriety, he picked through the entertainments left to him, his fists itching.

He scanned the faces of the men.

They had to be bigger than him—no crowds like to see small men being picked on—a little battle hardened (facial scars were always a bonus), slightly lumbering, transparently obnoxious, and accompanied by enough friends to make it interesting, but not so many that he might lose. Tillinghast liked winning.

He sipped his water. The candle died above his head,

and he watched happily from the shadows, enjoying playing out each contest in his imagination.

Just as he reached the point of giving up, a boulder-headed lump was revealed by the parting of a group in the middle of the room. The man was gigantic and had a face that dripped aggression.

"Hello," said Tillinghast, "dun't you look unpleasant?"

As he spoke, the man stuck out a leg and tripped the barkeep, who was passing with a stacked tray of empty glasses. He didn't even laugh, just carried on drinking his ale while his friends exploded in laughter. The barkeep was left sprawling in the broken glass, a silent crowd watching him collect scattered shards from the flagstone floor.

"Oh! That's jus' lovely, super," said Tillinghast, chuckling. Rifling through the list of provocations in his head, he toyed with pretending to be the barkeep's brother, but settled instead on a reliable staple: the indignation of having been looked at funny.

He rose, finishing his water and testing the new stitching on his shoulder.

But as he was about to cross the room and unleash the full force of his boredom, he saw a tall, lean boy moving among the tables, lifting food from half-finished plates and scraping it into a canvas bag.

Tillinghast laughed at the brazen lack of guile. There

was no misdirection or subterfuge—the grubby boy, his chestnut-colored face crudely bandaged, was simply scooping up crusts and veg and the remnants of meat cuts as though performing a service. Occasionally he would tip the last inch or so of a tankard into a wide-necked bottle, mixing beer and wine and water.

"What are you doin', little man?" muttered Tillinghast to himself.

The boy was nearly at his target's table.

Tillinghast moved through the crowds just as the boy's wrist was grabbed in the act of lifting bread.

"Tha's my dinner," said the boulder-headed man. "Whatchoo doin' with my dinner? I ain't finished tha'."

"Never mind that," said Tillinghast, emerging and placing clenched fists on his hips. "You, thick neck, were lookin' at me funny."

"'Ere, Ruby, he called you thick neck," said one of the big man's friends.

"Why you takin' my dinner?" said Ruby, unwilling to be swayed.

"I work here," said the boy, trying to pull his wrist free.

"No, you don't. I's here all the time, an' I ain't never seen you afore, an' if you did work here, you'd take my whole plate."

"I must insist you acknowledge the funny look you jus' gave me. . . ."

"It's a new way of doing things," said the boy. "Saves money."

Ruby's brows knotted. "How?" he said.

"Smack 'im, Ruby," said one of the men gathered round the table.

"You, fat guts, *looked* at me funny!" said Tillinghast, who felt that matters were leaving him behind.

"I gather the food, an' someone else gathers the plates," said the boy. "Makes sense, when you think about it."

Ruby's brows knotted tighter. "No . . . no, it doesn't," he rumbled. "I think I will hit you now . . . you little worm! Tha's *stealin'* from *me*! I's the one norm'ly does the stealin'. Ain't nobody stealin' nuffin' from me!"

". . . sad times indeed if a man thinks 'e can go around lookin' at folk funny an' nothin'll come of it. . . ."

"'Oo's this?" said Ruby to the boy. "Your dad?"

"Heavens no!" said Tillinghast. "I's jus' an innocent by-stander who's been wronged by the funny looks what you's been shootin' around this here inn, an' let me tell you, big face, that—"

"Hit 'em both, Ruby," said a voice from the table.

"It makes perfect sense," said the boy. "This way, the person gatherin' the plates won't have to waste time takin' the bread off them. Let me help you with that last bit o' beer you've got there. . . ."

As the boy reached for the tankard, Ruby's pupils narrowed to dots and the sinews of his broad neck seized.

"Oh, I wun't do that. . . ." said Tillinghast.

The boy lifted Ruby's beer, Ruby's hand caught him a huge blow across the face, and Tillinghast sighed happily.

"That's my son, you blaggard!" he cried, and head-butted Ruby on the nose.

10

Oathlaw

One does not have to believe in magic any more than one does the weather! For while the tornado and sand wind are rare, they exist; and just as these tempests remain outwith our control, so too does magic. It will erupt in unpredictable bursts within nature, manifest in its growths and beasts, as untamed and potent as the sun, as far and unknowable as the cosmos. Magic is like the weather in so many ways—and sometimes there are storms.

—*Emmeline Porter*, Observed Phenomena in Nature

Remedie dug with her bare hands, as fast as she could, ripping and tugging at the turf until it yielded in crumbling chunks. The soil, odorless in the freezing air, was agony on her hands, hardened to razors that sliced her skin and pulled at the seams of her fingernails until they split and bled. Still she dug, faster, the calls of the dogs and their men growing closer and closer.

Sweat frosted on her face, wrapping her in a skin of cold before it could drip into her eyes. Finding the first thin roots of the tree, her heart rate quickened.

"Soon you'll be in my arms, my love," she whispered, cutting away a root that blocked her path and throwing it into the basket at her side.

She dug past worms and beetles and the white root buds of grasses, stubbing her numbed fingertips on the stones that riddled the layers of earth, pushed her blood into the soil, ignored the baying and the shouting that had now passed the dyke and was closing on her.

A year had passed since she had last turned over this mud; a year to the day since misery had fallen like a blanket, suffocating her and blocking the world's light and sound.

A dog barked—closer than she'd thought. Remedie recognized in its deep timbre the growl of Masler, Pastor Dybilt's slavering ridgeback.

I have not lived as I have this past year to be taken into the judgment of that whip-necked oaf, she thought.

A thicket of roots appeared. She scrabbled ever more desperately, feeling her fingernails flake away like fish scales.

"And there you are," she whispered, pulling aside the last thin tangle of wood to reveal the object of her search. She lifted it, slick with earth-water and crumbed thickly with mud, and held it to her breast. Far in that moment from the world of gods and judgment and the pain in her cold-lashed body, she brushed its face clean, planted a kiss on its nose, and smiled.

"It's all afoot, my love," she whispered. "Just as I told you. And now here you are, after a year in that cold ground— ready to be born again."

She swaddled it in her shawl, placed it in the basket, and stood. Then she ran, faster than men, faster than dogs, faster than rumor, letting the wind guide her and carry her scent toward the sea and the hills, so that when the pastor and his men arrived they found no sign of their quarry: only a wet hole in the earth filled with broken roots, a scatter of torn fingernails, and a vacant space the size and shape of a newborn child.

Lauston

"Oh, that was fair good fun, wun't it? There was six of 'em tryin' to get me at one point, I reckon. Fat bloke tried stabbin' me an' all—put a hole right through my shirt."

Tillinghast was leaning on the inn's fence, idly chewing a piece of frozen grass as he examined the torn material. "Did you see when I swapped their hats around? You're welcome, by the way."

"For what?" said Wull. He paused in collecting the food scraps and smashed a rotten cabbage against the ground. "Interruptin' me an' ruinin' everythin'? You got us thrown out the only inn in the village! Now what am I goin' to do?"

Tillinghast appeared not to hear him. "Payment's not *strictly* necessary," he said, watching the stars peek through the cloud cover, "but if you've a few spare coins I'd not say no to 'em."

"You know, a person doesn't have to be bright to figure that if I'm *stealin'* food from tables, I prob'ly don't have spare coin," said Wull, his voice rising. "If I did, I'd have *bought* food rather'n lift scraps off other folks' plates, an' they wouldn't be spare coins then—'cause I'd need 'em!"

Tillinghast looked at him. "Need what?" he said, fussing with his neck-silver.

Wull gritted his teeth and tossed the last few crusts into the bag. "I already had nothin', an' now you've ruined that! What am I meant to do?"

"What d'you mean 'ruined'? I saved you from that big lump—he wouldn't've stopped at a punch, y'know. You'd've been in all kinds o' trouble. Could you have done what I done?"

"Could I have beaten up six grown men on my own? No, no I couldn't," said Wull. "That's why I was talkin' my way out of it when you swanned over with your 'funny looks.'"

"They were *his* funny looks, that was the point," said Tillinghast. "He was lookin' at me funny."

"Oh, really? You were actin' like a right nugget. I was givin' you a funny look myself. You goin' to beat me up too?"

"No. Well . . . no. Why are you bein' so ungrateful?"

"Because you haven't *helped* me! I was goin' to get some food then tie up for the night behind the ursa bars, an' now I need to go back on the river!"

"Why you on the river? An' what happened to your face?" said Tillinghast.

"The man you were windin' up punched me in the mouth," said Wull. "You must've seen it, since it was your fault. Burst my lip an' gave me a bloody nose."

"He din't hit you 'cause I was windin' 'im up—he hit you 'cause you lifted 'is beer. That was a bad move, was that."

"I'd have been fine wi'out you."

"You wouldn't," said Tillinghast, lifting half an apple into Wull's bag, "but that's not what I was meanin'. What's under the bandage?"

Wull's hand went to his right cheek.

"Some bradai took my money. One o' them cut my face."

Tillinghast furrowed his brow. "If they took your money, why'd they cut you? Wun't normally hurt kids. You din't try fightin' 'em, did you?"

"I'm not a kid," said Wull, "and no. I . . . I called them thievin' scum."

Tillinghast laughed. "That'll do it! Oh, you's a stubborn one; mouth like yours'll get you in plenty trouble an' find you plenty fun."

"Sure," said Wull, "my life's a real carnival. Now, if you don't mind, I'm goin' to leave—seein' as I'll be spendin' the night on the river I might as well get goin'. Thanks for all your help, ruinin' my dinner an' all."

"Why you on the river?" said Tillinghast, walking alongside him.

"I'm goin' down the coast, not that it's any o' your business," said Wull.

"I's from down that way. Whereabouts on the coast?"

"Canna Bay, an' that's none o' your business either."

"Place I's from is no more'n a two-day walk from there! I knows the land well, or I used to at any rate. 'In't been back in, oh, twenty years. How come you's headed that way? 'S a fishin' town, 'in't it?"

Wull sighed. "I need to get somethin' for my pappa. He needs help."

"Is that your boat?"

"Yes. Good-bye."

"An' is that your pappa?"

"Yes, please go now."

"Who's the girl?"

"She's a stowaway," said Wull. "Please go away."

"It's a fancy boat," said Tillinghast, running his hand along the gunwale. "'In't it painted all pretty?"

"It's called a bäta."

"Who's this?" said Mix. She was sitting beside Pappa in the stern, propping the thin, sleeping body against her shoulder.

"He jumped in an' ruined me gettin' some food," said Wull.

"We've been over this," said Tillinghast, holding up a warning finger. "How come the boat's got eyes?"

"It's got eyes?" said Mix. She leaned Pappa against the transom and climbed into the prow.

"To guide the tiller," said Wull, sighing, "an' they keep evil spirits away. It's traditional, for protection, I don't know."

"Makes sense," said Tillinghast, nodding. "Most boats should have eyes on 'em, I reckon. Seems like some folk should have an extra pair on their foreheads for jus' the same reason. Right, well, I likes this boat well enough, you seem like a solid, if ungrateful, young man, an' the kid with the thick hair seems harmless enough. I reckon I will come with you after all."

Wull paused in climbing into the bäta.

"What?" said he and Mix in unison.

"I's decided to come with you," said Tillinghast, climbing over behind Wull and settling in the stern. "Though you'll need to do somethin' about these seats, they's terrible un-comfortable. Evenin', fella, how's you?" he added, nodding at Pappa.

"Get out!" said Wull. "You can't jus' decide to come into this boat—it's mine! An' don't talk to him; he doesn't understand."

"Oh? What's wrong with 'im? Deaf?"

Wull saw Pappa's head swing round, felt panic grip him.

"No, I . . . look, jus' go away!"

"That's my seat!" said Mix.

"It's my seat now, little miss, an' I will not go away. You might think I's done nothin' to help you, but you was doin' a terrible job o' stealin' that food—you was gonna get caught at some point an' slung out on your ear, or worse. If you'd touched that Ruby's beer when I wasn't there, who knows what might've happened? Could be your old man would've seen your sliced-up body washin' past him on the river there."

"Nobody had said anythin' to me until then," said Wull sullenly.

"Ha! I'd been watchin' you, an' that means someone else was too."

Tillinghast tilted his hat forward, put his hands behind his head, and closed his eyes. His hessian sack was on his lap, his ankles crossed under the center thwart, and he looked completely at peace.

"Blue man," said Pappa.

"Pleased to make your acquaintance," said Tillinghast.

"Please get out," said Wull. "I don't have any room for passengers, an' I'm in a hurry."

"First, you's lyin'—this is a right big boat, an' you's already got two passengers. Second, you's gettin' nowhere in any kind o' hurry wi'out money or decent food. Din't you at least pack somethin' to eat between you?"

"I told you, she's a stowaway—an' yes, I did!"

"*Stowaway's* harsh," said Mix. "You said I could come."

Tillinghast shrugged. "Well?" he said.

"I had salt fish an' biscuits," said Wull. "The bradai took most of that an' all."

"They did a right number on you," said Tillinghast, chuckling. "What's your big rush for?"

"Pappa," said Wull, "he needs . . . help. Soon. I've only got a few days to get there."

"A few days, eh? So it seems you's in a pickle, an' for the second time in quick succession I's here to solve your problems. Aren't you lucky?"

"An' how's that?" said Wull. Tillinghast was as insistent as the current, and he felt his tiredness yielding.

"'Cause I's got plenty coin, an' no fear o' bradai. I'll give you enough for now to get somethin' out that inn, then we can be off. It fair suits me to take the load off my wand'rin' legs for a bit, an' this pretty boat o' yours shall make for a fine means of conveyance."

"They won't let me back in there, an' I don't fancy seein' those men again," said Wull. "That doesn't help me at all."

Tillinghast tossed him a ha'penny coin. "Slip that to the cook at the kitchen door. She'll see you right. I shall wait here for you. An' might I say one more time that you are very welcome."

Wull stood, climbed reluctantly onto the jetty, looking at Tillinghast's weight dragging the stern low in the water. Mix shrugged when he caught her eye, and in that moment he realized he'd never seen another living person in the bäta before. Except Pappa.

"Might be a good thing, I suppose," he said, looking at the coin, then at Pappa. "You can give me a bit o' help wi' rowin'."

"Oh, I's not plannin' on helpin' *row* the damn thing, lad," said Tillinghast, settling back farther into the seat. "I's a payin' customer. Hurry on now. I's anxious to be off."

Oracco

Rattell, hopping on his cushion in the cobble-bounced coach, was sweating. He had bathed in unchanged milk, and its sour green aroma filled the small space. Rigby and Pent, too heavy to bounce, sat opposite, watching their employer and sweating under their greatcoats.

The air was dust-thick and sharp, coal-heated to prick-liness before the coach was sent into the night. Already the men were uncomfortable. Only the light floral note of Pent's tobacco pierced the foul air.

"Rosie . . . I mean, Colonel Fettiplace, is not pleased!" said Rattell, shouting over the thudding clack of wheels and hooves. "He's furious. He wants the mandrake. It's his, and it's all that's left of his beloved lieutenant. There's no limit to what he'll do to get it . . . remember your tongue, Mr. Pent?"

Pent nodded and opened his vacant mouth.

"It was Rosie who did that—did it himself!" Rattell dabbed at his lips with his own dry tongue. "Now he wants us to destroy Tillinghast and k-kill anyone who's helped him. 'I don't care how you do it,' he said. 'I don't care how much of your ill-got money it costs you, and I don't care if you or any of your thick-skulled trolls die trying: get me that mandrake or I'll break you apart and bury you while you're still breath-ing!' He'll bury us alive! N-now, you two, remember we're not chasing a rational person, or even a *real* person; Tillinghast is a damned ho-homunculus—you remember the arm?"

"We knows, Misser Rattell," said Rigby sullenly. Both his eyes were swollen, deep-bruised with round, purple lumps that spread across the bridge of his nose. Pent nodded mutely beside him.

"You know what that means? A homunculus? It means

he's not even a r-real man. He's made of straw! Straw! Like a scarecrow! R-Rosie—I mean, Colonel Fettiplace—he gave me this dossier, Tillinghast's whole history: where he was made, where he's been. . . . Rosie knows everything! Everything! He's been watching *us* too, and he *knows*. . . . If we don't bring this damn mandrake back, he's going to have us killed and buried in the city. He has spies everywhere . . . be careful to whom you speak. Be careful. . . . Rosie is watching everything. Everything!"

Rattell's eye was twitching, and his gaping pupils seemed to be focused somewhere behind Rigby and Pent, outside of the coach.

"Like a scarecrow!" he said again.

Rigby and Pent looked at each other.

"We knows, Misser Rattell," said Rigby again. "You said you had stuff what would help us kill 'im."

A glint came into Rattell's eye. "I do, I do!" he said. He lifted a small painted box from the coach's rattling floor and opened it in his lap. "You'll need these," he whispered. "These will do the job fine and well, and then Rosie will be pleased and he won't kill us or bury us in the city."

"But what is they?" said Rigby.

Rattell looked at him with his twitching eye. "He can't be killed by conventional weapons," he said quickly.

"We *knows*, Misser Rattell," said Rigby. Pent clenched his fists.

"This," said Rattell, lifting a velvet sleeve from the box, "is a rare and expensive p-piece. I sourced this through a contact in the Central Museum. It should be part of the collection of p-preindustrial occult weaponry, but she owed me a favor. They all do, eventually." He withdrew a short dagger of dull metal and held it aloft.

Pent made a disjointed sound.

"Misser Pent says it's a hay dagger, Misser Rattell," said Rigby.

"And he's quite right, named for the shape of the hilt, I'm told, like a hay bale. Doesn't that seem apt, given our quarry? Of course, a normal dagger would simply slip through his skin and tickle his straw. He's a homunculus, remember, like a scare—a scarecrow. . . ." Rigby and Pent looked at each other again. "B-but it's the *material* of this blade that makes the difference. . . ." Rattell slipped subconsciously into his sales voice, holding the dagger up on display. "This is made from a hundred coffin nails, each of which has soaked in the ground for a hun-hundred years before being exhumed and recast with essence of hawthorn. The homunculus is full of herbs and ma-magic and potions—this beautiful knife will put a stop to all their little workings and unravel him completely."

"Sounds good, Misser Rattell."

"Doesn't it? It must be driven between his shoulder blades—there is a seam there in his straw—the knife will reach right into his middle. There's only one bl-blade, sadly, but I have other little treats for you."

Rattell handed the dagger to Rigby, reached into the box, and withdrew three dark prickly lumps.

"These are witch balls," he said.

Pent made a noise.

"Misser Pent says he din't think witches had balls," said Rigby.

Rattell flicked them a twitching eye. "They're for cursing and be-bespoiling, designed for throwing. Cat fur, mostly, boiled up with animal bl-blood and hooves to make them set. But the most important inclusion is an item of the witch's own personal lo-loathing, and it is this that gives them their cursing power. Rare things, these. They can be made only once a year in the nineteen days prior to the Night of the Hungry Ghosts. My associate managed to find a witch whose personal lo-loathing is for homunculi, so these will melt the skin from Mr. Tillinghast's body."

Rattell rolled the witch balls in his palm.

"They were purchased for a very steep price," he said. "Each cost me a gold bar from my vault, so throw them with care." He passed them to Rigby, who dropped them into his waistcoat pocket.

"Finally," said Rattell, "this clutch of herbaceous plants contains every growth that has gone into our straw friend's manufacture. Burn this as you approach him—the aroma will weaken and disorient him. I'm told he'll feel like he's on fire."

Rattell passed the herbs to Pent, who sniffed them, then muttered noises in Rigby's ear.

"Misser Pent says they smells like old milk, Misser Rattell."

Rattell looked at Pent, who spat on the floor of the coach.

"Yes . . . yes, perhaps," said Rattell, sniffing the air. "Be mindful of this item—it cost me some further portion of my gold and the promise of a returned fa-favor. And be careful of its vapors; they'll disorient the scarecrow, but they affect real people too. I'm told the hallucinations can be quite ho-horrific."

They lurched round a corner, through the city gates, and into the farmland beyond. Potholed and scattered with stones, the countryside was rougher even than the city cobbles, and Rattell hopped from his seat with each shuddering crash. He parted the curtains and peered out.

"How I hate the countryside," he said. "It's brown and damp and it smells, but Tillinghast mentioned Lauston. R-Rosie's spies saw him scurry that way too, and so we must scurry after him."

The coach rumbled on. A few miles outside the city, the driver was halted by a trio of highwaymen, flashing short pistols and gold-capped smiles.

The lead highwayman, a pale, rake-thin lip chewer named Greely the Nip, rapped on Rattell's window and leered at him through the glass. While Rattell nodded stiffly back, Pent and Rigby exited the coach's other door.

Greely wiggled his toes as he eyed up the coach's contents, already shuffling through his mental list of fences and traders.

The last thing he remembered was a tap on his shoulder and the unlanguaged whisper of Mr. Pent's fury.

The Danék Wilds

The oars waggled as Wull, belly warmed by a thick meat stew, tried to recapture the current's thread. Tillinghast, lounging contentedly beside Pappa on the stern thwart, trailed his fingers in the bäta's wake.

"You shouldn't do that," said Wull, between gasps for breath. The bäta, already heavy and slow to turn with Pappa and Mix on board, was immeasurably more so with Tillinghast's bulk gleaming in the back.

"An' how's that?" said Tillinghast.

"You'll freeze your fingers, or a seula'll come and nip them off for you."

Tillinghast laughed. "I reckons I'll be fine, thanks all the same," he said, and began making little splashes.

"I'd rather you didn't, is all."

"I heard you," said Tillinghast, patting his huge, open palm on the water.

"All right, Paps?" said Mix from over Wull's shoulder.

Pappa glowered through his brows.

Wull spat over the side. The lights of Lauston had long faded into the distance, and the pain in his shoulders had resumed its droning throb. The wintered riverscape ranged up around him in jagged and unexpected ways, every inch of it unknown and unknowable. He checked over his shoulder every few strokes; the way ahead was strewn with the trunks of fallen trees and the constant turns of the river's meandering way, throwing up new barriers of land whenever his back was turned.

"Are you all right, Pappa?" he said.

"It that speaks," said Pappa, "no more eating."

"There's more if you want it," said Wull. It was true—the cook at the inn had been happy to get rid of fish heads and tails, and a bucket of them was stinking at his feet.

"Why's your old man call you 'it that speaks'?" said Tillinghast. "I thought you said your name was Wulliam?"

"It is. He's . . . not himself. He gets confused easily."

"'S that why he eats fish heads like they's toffees?"

Wull said nothing. He waggled the oars and searched for the current as his stomach boiled.

"I's not meanin' to give offense, like, jus' wond'rin'. Never much fancied 'em myself."

"It's jus' what the . . . what he likes to eat," said Wull.

"No more eating," said Pappa.

"That's fine," said Wull. He rowed a few silent strokes. "'In't you pair hungry? Why didn't you eat anythin' from the inn?"

Tillinghast lifted his hand from the water and slumped back into his seat.

"I'm not hungry at all," said Mix.

"An' it's fair to say I's rarely hungry," said Tillinghast.

"Jus' thirsty?"

"Is that you judgin' me, little master? I drinks, true. An' what of it?"

Wull shrugged. "Why are you wantin' to go downriver?"

"Oh, I's not, really. Jus' you happened to be there with your boat an' found yoursel' indebted to me. I's jus' movin' away from the city, doin' my business. It doesn't really matter where I ends up, so long as it's not there."

"What is your business?" said Mix.

"It's mine," said Tillinghast.

"You know we're headin' back to Oracco now?" said Wull.

"Dun't matter if we's jus' passin' through. Might even be a good idea, come to think of it."

Tillinghast folded his hands on his stomach.

"What're those things round your neck?" said Mix.

"Trinkets of which I's fond. Very useful in the right situation."

"An' what's in the bag?" said Mix.

Tillinghast tucked the sack farther under his legs without opening his eyes. "Nothin' that should bother you, little miss—jus' my pers'nal effects."

Wull said nothing. A few minutes passed in silence. Oracco's still-distant furnaces glowed against the sky, their orange clouds moving steadily above him as the city bled its energy into the surrounding countryside. The perfect soundlessness was broken only by his own gentle movements and the light chuckle of the river moving over rock and sand.

"'S nice not walkin' an' all, but hell's bells, this is right borin'," said Tillinghast.

"Feel free to get off. I'll even drop you on the bank."

"Then I'll get my seat back," said Mix.

"No, I's not meanin' that. Jus' the silence is killin' me. What is it you does with yourself, Mr. Pappa?"

"Not Mr. Pappa," said Pappa, glaring at Tillinghast through his curtain of hair.

"Don't talk to him! I told you, he doesn't understand."

"No shame in not workin'," said Tillinghast cheerfully, still addressing Pappa. "Are you an' your boy crooks?"

"No!" said Wull hotly. "Why would you say that?"

"You was stealin' food when I saw you. . . ."

"He's got a point there," said Mix.

"Right. What is your business then?"

Wull sighed. He felt the current swell on his right oar, and turned the nose of the bäta into it. The boat surged forward, and he started to row with deeper, longer strokes.

"We're the Riverkeep, farther upstream," he said.

"An' what's that?"

"We . . . keep the river. Tend it: cuttin' weeds an' so on in summer, clearin' up mudslides—breakin' up the ice when it's frozen like this."

"I heard you talkin' about bein' Riverkeep—wondered what you meant," said Mix.

"How d'you break up ice then?" said Tillinghast.

"Keepin' the lanterns lit," said Wull, looking down. "The fire heats the iron rods to stop the ice gatherin'. . . . Without it, we can rescue people who've fallen in an' recover them when they're past rescuin'."

"Past rescuin'?" said Tillinghast. "You mean pullin' folks what's dead out the river?"

Wull nodded. "Somebody has to."

"That's an occupation, is it? Is the pay fair?"

"There's no pay, as such," said Wull. "We get donations from the city. It's a noble calling."

"I's heard a noble callin' a few times," said Tillinghast, "but I never listen. So you both does this?" Tillinghast looked at Pappa, withdrawn and jumbled in the bäta's corner.

Wull cleared his throat. "Pappa's the keep for another few days, then I take over when I'm sixteen."

"An' what does you do with bodies once you pull 'em out?"

"We take them to the boathouse. We've got a mortuary, an' they stay there until the undertaker comes from the city to take them away."

Tillinghast nodded, dipped his fingertips in the river again.

"You ever find anythin' gruesome?" said Mix.

"You mean when I've been pullin' on corpses that've rotted in water? What d'you think?"

"I don't know," she said. "I've never seen a body what's been left to rot. What's it like?"

"It's not pleasant," said Wull reluctantly. "But it needs to be done. Who else is goin' to look for these poor souls?"

"Nobody, I s'pose," said Mix. She thought for a moment. "That's a fine thing to do."

"Sure, real fine," said Wull.

And wasn't it fine waiting upstairs for the corpses to be taken away before I could eat my supper? he thought.

"You ever hear of a thing called normative determined?" said Tillinghast.

Wull sighed. "Can't say I have."

"You don't know what it is?"

"Not if I've not heard of it," said Wull, in the stoic voice he used on Mrs. Wurth.

"What about you, little miss?"

"Nope," said Mix.

"'S about your name an' what it means—tells you 'bout what kind o' person you's goin' to be. What's Wulliam mean?"

"'Protector,' somethin' like that," said Wull. "Guardian."

"Oh," said Tillinghast, making circles with his fingers in the water. "Makes sense. What 'bout Mix?"

"It's not complicated," said Mix. "It means 'mix,' as in to mix things together."

"What's Tillinghast mean?" said Wull.

"I's got no idea," said Tillinghast.

"Why've you got blue skin?" said Mix.

"I don't know. 'S jus' the color it is."

"Never seen a person with blue skin before," said Mix, "an' I used to live in the city. You get all sorts there. Once, we saw one o' the pierced folk with all spines in their face. 'Nother time we saw a woman with a feurhund on a leash. A feurhund, mossy as you like, all dribblin'. So how come your skin's blue?"

"It's jus' my skin," said Tillinghast, puffing his cheeks. "I din't choose it 'cause it matched my eyes or anythin'."

"What color eyes you got?"

"Brown. No, green. Why you askin' me so many questions?"

Mix shrugged. "I like askin' questions," she said. "It passes the time and hell's bells, this is right borin'."

"Is you bein' funny? 'Cause I doesn't think . . . Ow! You little bugger!"

Tillinghast swiped at the wet, vanishing head of a gray seula, rocking the bäta as he lunged.

"I told you," said Wull. "Take your fingers off, they will. They've got some teeth."

"He's got nothin' from me. Gave my knuckle a right tug, though," muttered Tillinghast, rubbing his fist. "Why they followin' the boat?"

"It's called a bäta, an' it's 'cause we give them scraps an' fish heads an' such in winter."

"But your pap's eatin' those. You can't be givin' away your old man's dinner to swimmin' vermin."

The clouds parted above them, bathing the spindly bankside thickets in moonlight. In its bright glow the Danék's blackness became a strip of rippling silver.

"Moon's still high enough," said Wull. "There's a few hours till the ursas wake up, but we'd best find someplace we c'n settle for the night."

Tillinghast wrinkled his nose. "Why?" he said. "If we keep rowin', we'll be through the city by mornin'. I thought you was in a hurry?"

Wull glanced at Pappa, sleeping again.

"I am," he said, "but that's not enough to give me cause for suicide. Once the ursas are out, I want to be somewhere with stone at my back an' fire at my front."

"I had fire at my front once," said Tillinghast. "Flared up after I lay with a farm girl in Nantwick—doctor told me to dip my lad in yogurt for a week—cleared it right up."

Mix laughed.

Wull stared blankly at him. "What?" he said.

"Never mind," said Tillinghast, grinning and shifting his hessian sack with his heels. "Nothin' for you to worry about. But why's we got to stop?"

"Because otherwise ursas will find us an' rip us apart, that's why," said Wull.

"Ursas 'in't so tough," said Tillinghast.

"That's not even a little bit true," said Mix.

"Ursas aren't tough?" said Wull. "Then why are there bars an' cages on every buildin' an' jetty the whole length o' this river? Explain that to me." He quickened his stroke and began to scan the banks with subconscious darting glances.

"People are scared of 'em. I dun't know why—I ran into a few of 'em when I went after the Mad Monk o' Boddin. That Holy island's teemin' wi' them."

"Well, let me tell you why people're scared o' them," said Wull. "Pappa an' me have found plenty folks what've come to grief on an ursa's claws, an' there 'in't much left of 'em to find. One man we found was broken in half across his middle with little pulls on his skin, like torn parchment. His guts'd been taken from inside him, the way you an' I would eat a whelk."

"*You* might eat a whelk. . . ." said Tillinghast.

Wull ignored him.

"Other time we foun' bits o' six people scattered like seeds across a fair distance beside a fallen tree. There were fingernails studded into the bark: seems the ursa wanted to get at them so badly, it jus' ripped the tree down. This wasn't a sapling neither; it was a big thick oak. Sometimes we find ursa footprints when we're out in the mornin', an' there's been the odd time you c'n see they were runnin' after somethin'— that means paw prints four times the size o' your head with a stride five times the length o' you—"

"Oh, I's plenty long, be assured about—"

"*They c'n swim faster* than ten men can row, so it does us no good to stay out here an' watch 'em. If we want to get through tonight, we need to find a cave, light a bloody big fire, an' pray to all the gods we know there's somethin' else for 'em to hunt, because if they're hungry enough they'll come right through the fire an' even your smart mouth won't stop them tearin' you apart."

The bäta carried on in silence. Pappa began snoring, his mouth glistening with scales.

"You enjoyed that, din't you?" said Tillinghast eventually, yawning.

"I made my point," said Wull.

"It was good," said Mix, grinning at him. "I liked the bit about the smart mouth."

Tillinghast narrowed his eyes at her. "An' well made your point was, but I doesn't fancy stoppin' jus' yet. Let's stay on as long as we can."

"So you mean you're wanting a turn at the oars. . . ." Wull started.

Tillinghast held up a hand. "I's a payin' customer. You doesn't see coach passengers gettin' out an' givin' the horses a break now, does you?"

Wull gritted his teeth. "I am *not* a horse, an' you shouldn't—"

"Oh, untwist your kecks, I was kiddin'. But I ain't rowin'. The whole point o' me bein' here is to get a rest, so I's not goin' to find restfulness by heavin' away at a dirty big corpse boat for hours on end. I've been watchin' you doin' it an' it looks exhaustin'."

"I was *supposed* to be on my own—not burdened by strangers," said Wull. "An' if I was, I could set my own schedule an' stop when I pleased—now my boat's gettin' pulled down by the weight of a stowaway and an unwelcome lump who's forced his way on here by flashin' some money!"

"Bought his way on here, if you please," said Tillinghast. "Fine, fine, fine. Let's jus' bank it now an' see what we can get."

Wull turned the bäta on a planted blade and guided it to the southern shore.

"I still think *stowaway*'s harsh," muttered Mix. "I was invited, eventually."

Pappa roused, his eyes rolling as he took stock of his surroundings. "Where?" he said.

"We're goin' to find somewhere to spend the night, an' the Drebin Woods is as good as anywhere now that we're past the village," said Wull.

"It that speaks," said Pappa. "What's ursas?"

Tillinghast shot a glance at Wull, who felt his face flush.

"Ursas are dangerous animals. They're very strong. You told me all about them, remember?" said Wull. "You said they would always win, so I wasn't to be out past the dippin' moon."

"Never did," said Pappa.

"Set it down there, Master Keep," said Tillinghast.

"Never did," said Pappa again.

"All right," said Wull, "all right."

He followed Tillinghast's hand and drove the bäta's nose into the pebbled bank under a low-slung branch. Panes of ice split apart under the hull, and Tillinghast hopped overboard, pulling the boat farther onto the ground with a force that rocked Wull's balance and sent Mix tumbling from the prow.

"Hey!" she said, crashing onto the bottom boards.

Wull helped her up and looked at Tillinghast.

"That's some strength you've got to pull a weight like that," he said warily.

"You've no idea," said Tillinghast, grinning. He produced a small lantern, lit the wick with a match struck on the bäta's edge, and set off into the forest.

From a frost-crusted bank shrub ten yards away, mud-splattered eyes watched. Quick words were whispered and a dry, bite-scarred tongue ran over lips pitted by the sores of winter. The shrub trembled with excitement.

"Stand up, Pappa," said Wull. He looked at the woods around them, new and fierce with their hidden spaces, the skeletal spikes of broken trunks poking through the ground like shattered bone. "I don't know about this spot," he called to Tillinghast. "It seems too hemmed in. Maybe we should row farther downriver."

Tillinghast, already too distant to hear, carried on walking, his lantern casting stark light onto the trunks that shot up around him.

"Come on, Paps," said Mix, reaching for Pappa's other elbow.

"No! Leave in boat!" said Pappa.

"We can't," said Wull. "We said we'd camp here for the—"

He stood still, balanced Pappa's weight on the gunwale, and looked at the water, still moving, ever flowing toward the wider sea.

"Wull?" said Mix.

Wull stood still.

We could leave now, he thought, *row off and leave the big lump to walk the woods and force himself on someone else.*

But the idea was impossible. Leaving Tillinghast behind would just mean banking with only Mix for company elsewhere, and Wull had the feeling that the blue-skinned giant would find them anyway. Besides, he realized as his cut cheek flashed again with pain, he needed Tillinghast's money.

"There we go," he said, helping Pappa land ungainly on the frozen bank.

"Untie the arms!" said Pappa.

"I can't," said Wull.

"Even for a bit?" said Mix. "I'll help you keep an eye on him."

"No, he can't be trusted. He doesn't even know what he might do."

"Do know," said Pappa darkly.

"Well, that's something, at least," said Wull. Checking that the moon was still above the tree line, he reached into the bäta, lifted the blankets and the bucket of fish heads, and, with Mix on Pappa's other side, held the frail body by the crook of the arm. Slowly, they followed the light of

Tillinghast's lantern, finding space for their feet and for Pappa's in the root-tangled mesh of the forest floor.

As they disappeared, the muddied eyes vanished in a whispering scuttle of leaves, the tramping feet obscured by Wull's gentle words of encouragement.

11

Canna Bay

Flow on, sweet Danék, through glens green an' deep,
Disturb not the slumbering dead in thy keep;
Thy waters flow fast, quick, and strong evermore,
An' gold-crested boat swell break white on thy shore.
Flow on, sweet Danék, 'neath threat'ning black cloud,
Disturb not the soft-padding ursas aloud;
Thy silent crew's secrets be e'er unclaimed,
An' pray let thy treach'rous current be tamed.
Flow on, sweet Danék, away to the west,
Disturb not the pure, precious life in thy chest;
We pray that thy larder be e'er overfilled,
An' beats o' thy great heart will ne'er be stilled.

—Traditional riverfolk song

A hundred feet below the slow-sinking wreckage of its latest victim, the mormorach spun. Its movements were erratic and painful; days of bountiful food had built a tight pressure inside it like a pot at the boil. Its skin was stretched. Fissures began to appear on its flanks, widening to slashes that ran its length and split to reveal new, tender flesh beneath.

It roared in pain.

In the midst of drowned sailors and wrapped in the ghosts of sails, it writhed, tearing against itself, champing its jaws and screaming, its gray-green skin flaking away. It wriggled harder, peeling the skin away until in a moment of stretching freedom, it was renewed, the shreds of its old self washed away in the dawn tide, the empty skin twirling like silken weed into the depths.

Half again as large and happily coiled with new muscle, the mormorach roared. It thundered gracefully through the deep trenches of the bay, tearing at kelp and rock, its new body—all but invisible in the dark water—hardening again to a rough husk, ready for its next contact with the shapes above.

Clerkhill

Remedie trod carefully, placing her feet between knuckles of root and grass that pulled on her ankles. The cold was now absolute, a bright force on her skin even through the sweat-damped shawls. Moonlight, slivered by the canopy's winter-stripped treetops, made ghosts of the trees, and running shadows of the gaps between, while white drifts burst on her boots, filling the world with the hiss of falling snow. She pressed her bundle to her breast and slowed her pace.

"We're in no hurry, my love," she whispered. "You've waited all this time; there's surely no sense in rushing now."

All around were the telltale lumps of ursa dens, their gathered branches like warts on the earth. Although the moon was still just high enough to keep them pressed into sleep, a stumble in the wrong direction would send her tumbling into their clutches like a doll.

She had stopped only twice to make water since fleeing the pastor and his men. Now, beyond their reach and with her scent hidden on the wind, she could afford to rest.

But in resting she was wrapped too tightly by the forest's silence: an ominous, threatening quiet. Her only companionship was the sound of her own feet—without it, the woods filled with tiny noises that mimicked the footsteps of a stranger, and that was infinitely worse. And so she walked, blind with fatigue, pained by skin-split heels and dead-aching muscles.

A branch tipped snow down her back as she passed.

"Are you all right, my love?" she said, wrapping her bundle still more tightly against the cold. Pushing through a growth of ferns and bracken, she shushed her soundless bundle and began to sing a ditty her sailor father had sung to her as a little girl.

> Oh, *the beast leaps free of the endless sea,*
> *the prison that caged him within.*
> *He's had his rest on the ocean's breast,*
> *and longs for the sun on his skin. . . .*

From below a stack of branches came a belch and a sighing cloud of snuffling breaths, as of a dog searching the ground.

Remedie quickened her step.

> *The howling gale, as it fills the sail,*
> *is music to lull him to sleep,*
> *and he scatters the spray in his boisterous play,*
> *as he dashes—the king of the deep!*
> Oh, *the beast leaps free of the endless sea,*
> *the prison that's caged him within. . . .*

She carried on, nudging through the woods, certain death slumbering inches from her feet, her muscles seizing with every grunted movement from below.

By the time she'd sung a hundred songs, she was hoarse with the cold. Stopping for only the third time, she squatted on the frozen ground, feeling the heat of her water under her skirts.

A candle of hope flickered: a wild-swinging lantern in the distant black.

"Look, my love!" said Remedie, rising and picking up her pace.

Light meant people, food, heat! She focused on it, heedless of the branch tugs and thorn scratches . . . then heard something that smothered hope's flame in terror.

The sound of far-off, heavy, rapid footsteps.

Drebin Woods

"Why didn't you wait for us?" said Wull. Sweat gleamed on his forehead; after heaving at the oars, he had virtually carried Pappa through the forest to catch Tillinghast's dome of light.

Tillinghast frowned. "Whyn't you use your own lantern?"

"I don't have one," said Wull. "We use the moon an' the lanterns on the river."

"Well, I can't see as it's my fault you's unprepared. An' you're here now, so you's no cause to be moanin'."

Wull shifted Pappa's weight on his shoulder.

"Untie the arms," said Pappa.

"You know I can't," said Wull. "So, where are we going to go? There doesn't look like bein' anything around here. We need a cave."

"Oh, I knows that, you's been most emphatic 'bout that: 'wall at your back an' fire at your front,' I know. So what's wrong with that one there?"

"I don't see anythin'," said Mix.

Tillinghast pointed to a drop of branches and foliage hanging from a rocky mound, a snow-thick tumble from which the bony fingers of frost-furred twigs scratched the air.

"What are we lookin' at?" said Wull.

"There's a cave under that, young 'uns. By all the gods, yous really does need me wi' you. Come on. Let's get inside an' build that fire you's so keen on. . . ."

The muddied eyes had been watching them from behind a tree, following their conversation with darting glances. Now they leaped skyward as Tillinghast made for the cave mouth. Face wide, thick-haired, and painted with mud; mouth open and black; arms waving; thick, whooping lines of spit swinging from a tongue that was yellow and furred.

As Tillinghast shot out an arm and grabbed the apparition by the throat, Wull jumped back, Mix and Pappa clasped behind him.

"Whoa!" said Tillinghast. "'In't no need to be rushin' about all shouty—you jus' stay there now."

In his fist was a young man—a matted cloud of dark, ragged hair ringing a face that was streaked with earth. His eyes were pink, and he beat against Tillinghast's wrist.

"Let me go! Let me go, I say!"

"*You* was the one runnin' at us!" said Tillinghast, releasing him.

"Was I?" said the young man, rubbing his neck. "I'm so *frightfully* sorry. I get carried away sometimes—I was merely trying to ask if I could help carry anything."

"Untie the arms!" said Pappa.

"Not jus' now," said Wull, eyeing the man warily. "You gave us a real start. What are you doin' out here?"

"Out here? Oh, out *here*? You mean *here*?"

Wull, Mix, and Tillinghast shared a look.

"He means here," said Tillinghast, "as in the dead middle of a forest what's nearby to bugger-all."

"The same thing as you fine people, I'd wager," said the man.

"You mean you's takin' your sick father on a mission o' mercy to the coast?"

"Well, no . . ."

"So you's makin' your aimless way across the country for no good reason?"

"Oh, certainly not . . ."

"Then are you . . . what're you doin', little miss?"

"Runnin' away from scary people," said Mix cheerfully.

"Well?" said Tillinghast.

The man pulled on his leaf-tangled, wispy beard. "Well . . . p'raps not, p'raps what I should've said is that I live here, and you are, in fact, in my front garden. In fact, you're standing in my shrubbery. You, sir, the blue man. My shrubbery, yes."

Wull looked at Tillinghast's feet. They were planted, as were his, on frozen, shrubless, rooty ground.

Tillinghast said nothing.

"But no matter," said the man. "Come inside, come inside, there's tea for all who require tea! Root tea with the roots left in as the gods intended, absolutely, yes."

Wull looked at Tillinghast as the man bustled off toward the cave, raised his eyebrows, and mouthed, *What do we do?*

We go for tea, mouthed Tillinghast, exaggeratedly. "You don't mind me askin' you's name?" he called.

"I don't in the least mind, sport," said the young man. He hopped across a fallen tree, his skinny legs sprightly and quick, and lifted the hanging plants aside. Warm air drifted out and kissed their skin. "Come along, come along now!"

Wull and Mix helped Pappa in struggling protest over the log and across icy soil, holding the hanging leaves away from his face. Through Pappa's sleeve, Wull felt again the slippery looseness of his muscles, and felt his own guts tighten.

What am I really holding? he thought.

Inside, the cave's walls were decorated with formless shapes and crude paintings of wild animals. Deep in the far gloom of its bowels, a large fire glowed. The cave was eye-nippingly acrid with its smoke, but its strong heat surrounded them.

Wull hadn't noticed until the warmth tickled his skin how cold he was in the bones of his fingers and toes, and he flexed them gratefully.

He had never imagined there could be another person living near the bankside, only a few hours' row from the boat-house.

"So what is your name?" Tillinghast was saying.

The man's eyes twinkled as he passed them steaming tin mugs.

"Now *that's* what you meant to ask me the first time. I know, oh, I know—many a man's taken me for a confusion, but it is I who listens! My *name* is Myron Rushworth, though I use it so little now. As a man of the forest I respond only to the trees, who call me Hhhhhgggnnnnnggghhnn."

Tillinghast choked on his tea. "Beg pardon, lad, it sounded like you was in the throes o' some stubborn digestive transit there. What'd you say the trees called you?"

"It's quite all right," said Rushworth. "To the untutored, tree-speak does sound a little odd—my tree name is Hhhhhgggnnnnnggghhnn."

"I see," said Tillinghast. "What a lucky break you's already wearin' brown trousers."

Wull, holding the mug to Pappa's mouth, thought carefully.

"Rushworth, as in the 'Intrepid Rushworth'?" he said.

Rushworth bowed. "At your service, sah!" he shouted, clicking his heels.

"You're the Bootmunch," said Wull. "Pappa told me that story: you got lost an' ate your boots."

The Bootmunch paused in the act of gathering herbs from a shelf cut into the wall. "I most certainly did not get lost, and a gentleman would never eat his boots," he whispered.

"What?" said Mix.

"I *said* that I most certainly did not get lost, and that a gentleman would never eat his boots!" repeated the Bootmunch.

"No, no, I heard that an' all," said Tillinghast, sipping his tea. "You was tryin' to sail round the northern point of Curralinn, an' your ship got stuck. All the supplies ran out an' a few o' the crew died, but you refused to eat 'em an' got wired into your boots instead."

"That's not true," said the Bootmunch, who had become very still.

"That's what I heard too," said Mix.

"An' what was in the papers," said Wull.

"The papers lie!"

Tillinghast sipped his tea again.

"I don't know if I'd be so hasty denyin' it," he said thought-fully. "I think it's fair play not munchin' the dead punters my-self, an' if you don't own up to eatin' your shoes, folks might reckon that's jus' what you did. Seems to me eatin' footwear's a lot more easily forgiven than slicin' bits off a dead man's bahookie."

"You mustn't speak ill of the dead, blue man," said the Bootmunch. He lifted another jar of herbs and wound a long string of green around the bunch he'd already formed.

"Tillinghast," said Tillinghast, "and this here's Wulliam an' his pap, an' Mix what's stowed away on Wulliam's boat."

"I was *invited*. . . ." said Mix under her breath.

"He doesn't mean any rudeness," said Wull.

"I find that hard to believe, Wulliam," said the Boot-munch, glowering at Tillinghast.

"No, it's true. I didn't even want him to come with me, but he did anyway—he's jus' generally rude an' unpleasant. It's not personal."

"*That* was personal," said Tillinghast.

"But it's right you're the missin' explorer?" said Wull.

"Yes," said the Bootmunch, sitting beside them on the log, "though I must quibble at 'missing,' for I'm certainly not missing. I have been here, that is to say *here*, for a number of years. If I must be known in such crude terms, I'd much rather be the 'Hiding Explorer'!"

"What do boots taste like?" said Mix.

The Bootmunch shot her a look. "As I *said*, a *gentleman* would never *eat—his—boots*," he hissed.

"What age were you when you ate them?" said Mix. "You're still quite young even if you talks like an old fella— must've been dead wee when you was doin' that."

"I cling yet to my salad days," said the Bootmunch. Blank eyes blinked at him. "I'm nineteen," he added, "but I was only twelve when I was given my first captaincy, a recognition of my unique qualities of leadership!" He clicked his heels again.

"I heard it that your daddy owned the ship an' gave it to you as a birthday present," said Mix, slurping her tea.

"An' what else was it they called you? The Sucklin' Adventurer?" said Tillinghast.

"No, no," said Mix. "It was Captain Cute Face."

"I've got a beard now!" said the Bootmunch, tugging the tuft on his chin. "I hate those names!"

He's looking even wilder, thought Wull, shifting slightly in front of Pappa. The other two didn't seem to have noticed.

"They're not *bad* names," said Mix, "an' they do say there's only one thing worse than being talked about."

"Gettin' stabbed in the face?" said Tillinghast.

"She means *not* being talked about, you silly fool!" shouted the Bootmunch. "And she's wrong!"

"Why is it you're hidin'?" said Wull quickly.

"Because I am good at it," growled the Bootmunch.

"We found you easily enough," said Tillinghast. "Hey! What you standin' on my toe for? Wull stood on my toe there for no reason, d'you see that?"

"An' what is it you're hidin' from, sir?" said Wull, ignoring Tillinghast.

"There is a simple answer to that," replied the Bootmunch. He was wearing, Wull saw, a torn military jacket, civilian trousers that were several sizes too small, and a shirt that looked, in its fabric and cut, to be that of a woman. "I am hiding from a world that understands me as little as I understand it. I've no wish to be part of it—especially that rhat's nest of a city, with its rumor and filth—when I can be here, safe and happy among my tree friends, living off the river."

"How's you live off o' the river?" said Tillinghast. "'S good tea this, by the way."

"Thank you," said the Bootmunch. "It really is hard to beat fresh roots from my shrubbery." He wound another strip of green around his bunch of herbs. "I live off the river in the sense that everything I need flows in its waters. Of course, the flow is reduced in winter—half of it is frozen over—but it still provides me with seulas and fish and clothing."

Tillinghast raised an eyebrow. "You mean those are clothes out the river?" he said.

"Oh, absolutely. I've found quite a wardrobe in my time here. It's rare a month passes without some worthwhile garb floating past."

"Does *you* wear the clothes you pulls?" said Tillinghast, looking at Wull.

"No!" said Wull, looking at the Bootmunch. "Once we take them in we clean the clothes that c'n be saved an' they go to workhouses an' shelters for the needy. We only take some pennies for 'em so we c'n eat an' light the river!"

"I'm needy enough out here—there's no shame in it," said the Bootmunch. "And what does a river need light for, might I ask?"

Wull's mind flashed to the clothes hanging clean of the river's muck, filling the boathouse with emptiness. And he remembered Pappa rowing shirtless corpses, gleaming and soft, toward the jetty while he played on the little beach.

"We often find bodies missin' some part o' their clothes," he said. "You mean it's 'cause *you've* taken 'em an' put the bodies back in the water?"

The Bootmunch looked perplexed. "Well, yes," he said, holding his finished herb bunch at arm's length and looking at it critically. "You can't wear a corpse."

Wull stood, feeling sick. "We treat the bodies with dignity! Folks taken by the water need their dignity restored to 'em, but you sit here, *usin'* them for this . . . grim life. . . ."

"Here, Master Keep," said Tillinghast, pulling on his arm.

"Pappa an' I work hard in what we do! Everythin's in service o' the water an' its poor drowned souls, an' you would *wear* their clothes without offerin' them any kind o' peace? You put them *back* in the water?"

Tillinghast pulled his arm again, harder.

"Oh, it's not a bad life," said the Bootmunch. "I've re-learned all sorts of useful skills I'd forgotten when I'd footmen and servants. I can gut a fish—flense blubber from a seula before it spoils. I can see and feel things in ways ordinary people cannot: rain before the first drop, lightning before the flash. . . ." Eyes bright, he flicked the herbs and struck a match on the stone floor of the cave. "Even acts of magic. Magic beings in numbers one can't imagine wander the hidden spaces of the world, mostly at night, mostly . . . but often in the brightest day without the least shame. Skills such as these are how I've thrived all these years. To return to your point, Mr. Tillinghast, that you found me so easily . . ."

"'S right, we was headin' right into your cave here."

Applying the flame to the herbs, the Bootmunch cupped them and encouraged their quick glow with a puff from his cracked lips.

"I rather think I found you," he said. "I'd been watching you for quite some time, you know, hiding in the bushes, listening to the trees whisper your passing. *They* know what you are too. Trees are of nature, not of magic—of nature. But it's absolutely all right, everything is going to be all right, because you see, Mr. Tillinghast, one of the magical beings I've learned to spot in my time here"—his eyes met Tillinghast's—"is the man of straw."

"Oh, wait . . ." said Tillinghast.

"HOMUNCULUS! HOMUNCULUS! STRAW MAN! DEMON! DEVIL!" shouted the Bootmunch, thrusting the burning bundle in Tillinghast's face.

Wull took the smoke burst in his eyes and staggered back, spluttering, knives in his throat and flames in his nose. He tripped over the log and continued to spin backward, his mind tipping round and round, an unliftable weight at the back of his skull, pulling the darkness behind his lids in looping, sick-making turns that rolled as he stood, his stone head dropping forward, his open eyes flooding with waves of color and light that wracked him with nausea and hurt his skin.

He saw Tillinghast run from the cave, the Bootmunch roaring in pursuit, and reached a hand for Pappa but found only empty space where he should be.

"Pappa?" he said. "Pappa? Pappa? Where are you? Mix? Are you there?"

He looked around. The grays and oranges and browns

and reds of the empty cave smeared against his eyes like oil, mixing and blurring in a dreadful light—acid that burned from within, dripping out in tears of molten lead that burned his cheeks and bled upward into his brain.

Wull pressed his hands to his skull and closed his eyes.

With a huge effort he grabbed Tillinghast's lantern and fled into the blissful, ice-dripping cool of the forest. Out here all was still, and the muted colors of nature stayed where they were, glowing in the starlight and guiding his path.

"Pappa?" he said again. "Pappa?"

The trees leaned over him, their cold, faceless bark peering with timeless patience. Wull walked, directionless and slow.

In the moonlit glow of winter, the forest pressed in on him—ranked trunks as far as he could see, twisting above his head and shrinking the world around him like a boiled skin. His ears filled with the sound of his own breath and the cacophonic crunch of his boots as they ground snow and slipped on the exposed ribs of black roots.

He walked for a minute, then a minute more and a minute more, the forest unchanging, empty, and still—its bough-rustling wind and animal chitter silenced by the hermetic calm that surrounded him like unseen mist.

"Pappa?" he shouted, desperation on the edge of his voice. "Pappa?"

"Ah'm here, Wulliam," said Pappa, stepping out from behind a tree. "C'mere to me, son."

Wull ran, the ground unfelt beneath his feet, and threw himself into Pappa's arms. He allowed himself to be held, gripped against the round muscle of Pappa's chest, the weight of the thick arms on his back, and felt tears, cool and salty, leak from his eyes.

"Pappa, I thought you'd gone. I thought that thing had taken you over," he said. "I didn't think I'd see you again."

"Gone! Ah've been here all along—we're rowin' the Danék, aren't we? An' if there's anythin' in this world that's mine besides my big strip of a boy, it's this river. Ah'm still the keep; these're my waters. I *am* these waters. There's not a chance ah'll be goin' anywhere until this ol' thing dries up for good. Let's walk awhile."

"I couldn't light the lanterns," said Wull, hurrying after him. He craned to see the broad, jowly face, but Pappa turned his head.

"It's all right," said Pappa. "The river survives all, an' it always will. It changes all the time, but it's constant, too. It's a special thing, that."

"I know, but it's locked up for winter now. I didn't know what else to do. The river'll survive, but you might not. I had to try an' fix you."

"To keep the keep?" said Pappa, chuckling.

As Wull moved to see his face, Pappa turned again, big hand clasped on the trunk of a tree to spin away, deeper into the woods.

"I suppose," said Wull.

"An' a fine job yer doin'. 'S not easy lookin' after someone who doesn't want it. I know. My dad didn't know me from a stranger by the end, but I still tended his bedside an' kept him safe. An' yer doin' the same. Yer a good boy, an' ye'll make a fine Riverkeep once yer back home."

Wull trotted a little to keep up. He stumbled, reached for Pappa's hand, and found only cold air.

"Pappa?" he said. "How do I light the lanterns? You have to tell me. The wicks are all black and useless—how do I do it?"

Pappa kept walking, face turned away.

"Ye'll manage," he said. "We all manage, the keeps, once it's our turn at the oars. By gods, they're heavy at first! But the river'll speak to ye when she's ready, whisper her secrets, give ye her strength, an' when it's time ye'll feel it an' know it's yers, my boy . . . my boy . . . stinking, my stinking, stinking, it that speaks, it that speaks!"

Pappa spun to face him, his flesh melting away, eyes clouding, milk-filled and unseeing. The sharp-lipped mouth was sunk with drawn cheeks, their thin skin ribbed by the teeth inside.

Wull felt the world fall away from him, and the cold rush back to his feet and hands.

"It that speaks!" shouted Pappa. "Untie the arms! Untie the arms!"

"Pappa?" said Wull. "What happened to you? What . . . where did you go?"

"Stinking boy it!" shouted Pappa, lunging at him, teeth bared.

Wull dodged, tripped on a mound of earth, and fell to the ground. He looked up to see Pappa running into the distance, hair flying around his head.

Wull shook himself against his skull's rolling weight. The colors of the woods were still glowing faintly, a false glimmer of starlight from the fog in his head. His limbs felt heavy, reluctant, his boots an inch short of where he needed them to be.

He tried to gather himself, move forward, waving the lantern with exaggerated swings to guide his missing feet.

Footsteps snapped ahead of him, and a figure swam in the cloud of his breath, darting through the trees.

"Pappa?" he said. "Pappa? Is that you? Why are you trying to get away from me?"

Wull felt his head lighten, his vision clear with an almost audible crack of released pressure.

"Mix? Tillinghast?"

The figure came into focus: a woman running toward him. Fast.

The weight of the ground returned against his feet, pulling him back to himself, lifting the fog, and as his head cleared, Wull saw the light was different—darker, gloomier. He looked around at the trees, a cage of ghostly, inhospitable pillars, then up at the sky.

There was no moon.

12

Oh, the beast leaps free of the endless sea,
The prison that's caged him within;
He's had his rest on the ocean's breast,
And longs for the sun on his skin!
The howling gale, as it fills the sail,
Is music to lull him to sleep,
And he scatters the spray in his boisterous play,
As he dashes—the king of the deep!

—Traditional deep-sea hunting song

Wull's heart hammered: they'd hardly been in the Boot-munch's cave ten minutes. Where had the time gone?

The running woman burst through the trees, skirts billowing behind her, infant bundle on her chest, and a broad stick in her spare hand.

"Run, boy!" she shouted. "Ursa!"

A roar filled the woods. The sound was louder than anything Wull had ever heard, a force that was both deep and high, vibrating his guts and buckling his knees.

"Where?" he said, pointlessly.

The woman ran past him, striking his shoulder with her stick.

"*Behind me!*" she shouted. "Run!"

The ursa roared again, and this time Wull saw it: bigger than sense, bigger than bone and blood could ever be, the size of three horses, four, five; long and broad and bulging with ropes of muscle that were threaded by nets of coiled veins. Its skin, shimmering sheets of wet leather, shone white in the dark. It was all the pain and fury in the world, and as it roared again, Wull saw the rows of shining teeth in its huge, spit-hung mouth, the loose pink flesh of its lips shaking with the force of its breath.

He felt himself turn to water, naked against the power of the animal.

"Run!" shouted the woman again.

Instinct battered aside his fear, and Wull ran to the sound of trees smashing behind him, all the fog of confusion gone in a rush of terrible clarity.

"Did you see a man?" he shouted, catching her. "A thin man?"

"I've seen no one." She gasped. "Don't talk. Run."

The ursa roared again, closer, and Wull felt the sound like wind at his back, stripping away his defenses. They ran, the woman bashing aside leaves and low-hanging branches with her stick, the light of Wull's lantern throwing the shadows around in flashing bursts as it swung madly in his hand. He ran faster than he knew how, legs flailing, cold whistling in his ears.

The river came into view—the bäta at its edge, nudged into the bank, stern shifting gently in the swell.

"Get into that boat!" he shouted.

"They can swim!" said the woman.

"It gives us a chance! What else can we do?"

"Some chance," she said, but she ran along the bank, her boots throwing up chunks of white turf.

"Push off once you get there!" shouted Wull. "Don't wait for me. I'm right with you!"

The woman tripped as she reached the bäta—her swaddled infant falling, rolling noiselessly on the frozen grass. She caught her step, stumbled, and landed with her hands on the gunwale—six paces away.

The ursa broke the forest's edge behind them, the trunk of a small tree exploding out and landing on the ice at the bank's edge. Its great head swung from side to side; then, picking up their scent, it dug the ground, ripping at the skin of the earth with its claws.

"My baby!" the woman shouted.

Wull darted past her.

"Get into the boat," he said, grabbing an oar from its rowlock, heaving against its awkward weight. He slung it across his chest and ran back to the baby.

The ursa covered the ground with impossible speed, each enormous stride three times the length of the bäta. Wull had barely made two steps before it had reached him and reared up on its back legs: covering the moonless sky, filling the world.

"Get back!" he shouted, hoisting the oar and jabbing at its chest.

It roared again. Wull quaked deep in his belly but jabbed and stepped forward, the oar a blade of grass against the animal's bulk.

Wull connected with flesh, pushed, drew a confused growl. He pushed forward again, taking a step toward the baby.

The ursa roared.

Summoning every ounce of strength he had, all the despair he'd felt since Pappa had been taken by the river, all the bile that stewed in him, all the frustration—Wull roared back, a howl of blind rage that brought pain to his eyes and strength to his arms. He pushed with all his anger.

The ursa, unbalanced, dropped onto all fours, its head still high above Wull's. It regarded him, its bristled, orange eyes tight.

Then it *screamed*.

The wall of it hit Wull: breath and spit and the rotten, meat smell of its stomach, noise that was formless white deafness in his ears. It pounced, splintering the oar in his hand, twisting his wrist, and knocking him to the ground.

"Boy!" shouted the woman.

Wull scrambled backward, moving his legs just as a paw the size of his torso smashed down.

"Here!" she said, throwing the other oar.

The ursa batted it from the air, sending it twirling into the Danék, then turned and advanced on her.

"No!" shouted Wull. "Here!"

He kicked its leg.

As it turned on him, Wull watched its bulk move in slow motion, the full, round swing of its paw starting far out on the end of its vast arm, needle claws clenched against the starlight, the tendons and sinews of the great limb tensing as they made to strike.

He closed his eyes and waited for the impact.

"You dirty big lump!" shouted Tillinghast.

Wull opened his eyes as Tillinghast jumped over his shoulders, catching the huge paw on his elbow and kicking the ursa's other leg from under it. He caught its head—half the size of his entire body—head-butted its nose, then punched its chest and throat with blows that Wull felt through the ground.

"Bugger off! Pickin' on little boys! Pick on me! Pick on me!"

The ursa stepped back, screamed again in confusion and anger.

"Gods, your breath *reeks*!" said Tillinghast.

He reached in and grabbed its tongue. The ursa clamped its jaws shut.

Tillinghast pulled his arm away and looked at the stump of his wrist, bits of straw and leaf sprouting from the handless wound.

"You rotten *blaggard*!" he said, and punched it again. "My bloody hand! That's my good bloody hand what I uses for recreation, an' now you've bit it off! Give it back! C'mere, you white turd, give me my bloody hand!"

The ursa began to back away. Then it turned and ran.

"Oh no, you don't!" said Tillinghast, grabbing the short stump of its tail with his remaining hand and pulling himself onto its back. Wull darted forward to grab the baby as the ursa sprinted, Tillinghast swinging from its loose skin, into the forest.

"Be careful with my baby!" said the woman. "Is he hurt?"

"He's . . ." Wull lifted the infant and opened the swaddling. The baby, from its pristine bud-shaped mouth to its immaculate little fingernails, was perfectly white, still, and made of wood.

"Oh, thank heavens," said the woman, scooping it from

Wull's arms. "He's unharmed—the gods are truly merciful in their wisdom."

She knelt on the grass, the wooden baby held tightly against her bosom, her lips moving in prayer. She looked at Wull.

"And you, brave young man, are you hurt? What's your name? Let me see you."

"I'm Wulliam, an' I'm fine," said Wull. He took in the baby's still face again. "Is . . . he . . . all right then?"

"Thanks to the gods." She smiled, checking Wull's face and body for injury. "And you. And your friend! Isn't he wonderfully strong?"

"I'll say," said Wull, eyes wide. "That's Tillinghast. The ursa should have torn him apart."

"He gave it a real hiding! But it's taken his poor hand, that's for certain. I do hope he's safe. He's saved all our lives this night, hasn't he, my little treasure?" She kissed the wooden baby on the nose. "What's this wound on your face?"

"Oh," said Wull. His hand went to his bandage: one side had come loose, and the slash from the bradai's dirk was exposed. "It's jus' a cut, it's fine."

"That's more than a cut—that's a nasty one." The woman touched her fingers to Wull's cheek. "It's so deep! Whatever were you doing to sustain such an injury?"

"Rowing," said Wull. He reaffixed the bandage to his face, its fabric like sandpaper. The cut was hot and itchy, and he felt the layers of it—the sharp scab on the surface and its deeper, heat-filled center—distorting and pulling the rest of his face.

"I'd like to clean that injury if I may. I'd worry you might lose an eye if it turns on you. The ursa didn't hurt you?"

"Jus' my wrist," said Wull, moving it gingerly. "When it knocked the oar out my hand, it got my arm an' all. It's fine, though, I think."

She had wide, slightly maddened eyes, thought Wull. He thought of Pappa, running unseeing through the woods.

"I need to go back for my pappa," he said. "He got lost."

The woman took his hand in hers and squinted. She massaged the wrist's round bones and watched Wull biting back a reaction.

"It's a bad sprain, I should think, but not broken. It must be very painful—you'll need to rest it a few days."

"Well, that 'in't happenin'," said Wull. "I'm gettin' down the coast in this boat an' it's not gettin' there by itself. . . ."

"You're going to the coast?" she said. "Oh, how wonderful. I'm also on my way to the seafront—we can travel together! How the gods provide!"

"Oh, wait, now, I didn't—"

"I's got it!" Tillinghast emerged from the tree line, holding his hand above his head, his face split by an enormous grin. "Dirty big blaggard was startin' to chew on it, would you believe, but I's jus' wedged his mouth open an' kicked his unmentionables to send him on his way. An' let me tell you, young Master Keep, these unmentionables is the size o' your head."

"Thank you, sir, for your help—you've saved us all," said the woman.

Tillinghast smiled and dropped his eyelids. "Oh, you's quite welcome, Mrs.—"

"It's Miss . . ." she began.

"How splendid . . ." said Tillinghast in tones of honey.

"Miss Remedie Cantwell. Is your hand badly hurt?" she said.

"Oh, it's severed, Miss Cantwell, torn clean off. It'll be quite all right, let me assure you. Remedie's a right lovely name. What's it mean?"

"Oh, I . . . Thank you. I was named for my grandmother. It means 'a cure,' or 'a solution,' I believe."

"'In't that somethin'?" said Tillinghast. "An' here's me, nursin' a broken heart. . . ."

"Right," said Wull, "what was all that about? How were you able to do that? An' what's a homunculus?"

"You're a *homunculus?*" said Remedie. She looked properly at Tillinghast's hand for the first time, at the straw leaking from the stump.

"O' course," said Tillinghast. He smiled at her again. "I's made from the parts of several men, Miss Cantwell. The *best* parts, let me assure you . . ."

"What?" said Wull. "You're made from bits of other people?"

"You's mibbe not as bright as I'd given you credit," said Tillinghast. "I's got scars on all my major joints. Did you think I was jus' clumsy?"

"I didn't really think about it. There could be lots o' folk with scars like that. It's jus' that none o' them drowned in my river."

"It makes sense, of course," said Remedie. "A real man would never have withstood—"

"Whoa!" said Tillinghast. "Enough with the 'real man' talk, please. I's a real man an' quite a man an' quite well made, see, an' I'll show you right now if it pleases you. . . ."

"Absolutely not!" said Remedie, clutching her blouse around her collar. "A real *gentleman* would never suggest such a thing!"

"Oh, you's quite right about that," said Tillinghast, winking.

"So, you're a homunculus?" said Wull.

"I feel like we's established that already," said Tillinghast, "an' I's proud of it an' all. Made o' the best—"

"Please don't say it again," said Wull.

Tillinghast coughed, then added quickly, "Parts."

"Yes, I think we all get it," said Wull as Remedie clucked with disgust.

"How could you *not?*" said Mix, emerging from the forest's

edge, rubbing her eyes as though having woken from a nap.

"Are you degradin' my humor, little miss?" said Tillinghast, trying to force his severed hand back on.

"You've done most o' that legwork," said Mix.

"What's your name, child? Are you hurt?" said Remedie.

"Mix," said the girl, "an' no, I'm all right. Bit of a headache though—that smoke! Who're you?"

"I'm Remedie Cantwell. Wulliam and . . . Mr. Tillinghast saved me from an ursa."

"'S impressive stuff," said Mix, sharing a look with Wull. She turned to Tillinghast. "Homunculus, eh? *That* explains the blue skin."

"Does it?" said Tillinghast. "I wouldn't know."

"Whose heart've you got?"

"Boxer," said Tillinghast proudly, "fittest man there ever was."

"An' whose blood? The boxer's?"

"I . . . 'in't got blood, really. . . ."

"That doesn't make sense. Why've you got a heart if you got no blood?"

"Well, shall we get goin' then?" said Tillinghast, turning away. "Let me help you aboard, Miss Cantwell. . . ."

"Don't touch me, you rude man!" said Remedie, shaking off his hand.

"No, wait! Get out!" said Wull. "I'm not runnin' a bloody passenger service! I'm in a hurry, an' Pappa's missin'! Mix, you snuck on an' even if you's helpin' with Pappa I need to move faster, so you might as well get out here. An', Miss Cantwell, I'm right glad I was able to help you out an' all, but I'm in a hurry an' can't be slowed down with the extra weight. I can't help that I needs *your* money," he said, turning on Tillinghast, "so *we* are goin' nowhere till I find Pappa! He's still wanderin' around those woods, an' who knows what's happened to him? That ursa might still be around, so you've got to help me before we get on our way."

"Well, that's rude," said Mix.

"Wulliam," said Tillinghast, "I'll help you find your old man, course I will. But d'you mean to say that you, protector o' this river, is goin' to leave a couple o' young women—one with a tiny little baby—here alone? It's the kind o' thing *I* would do, but—"

"The baby's not . . . it's not real," said Wull. "It's made o' wood."

"What?" said Tillinghast, looking at Remedie, who held the baby closer to her. "You mean we's been nearly killed an' had our hands bit off so's we could nobly protect a paperweight?"

"That's even ruder," said Mix.

"His name is Bonn, and I don't care for him to be spoken about in that manner," said Remedie.

Tillinghast rubbed his eyes. "Mibbe you's right," he said, looking at Wull. "That's nutty."

"Seems a bit rich comin' from a homunculus what's carryin' a mandrake in a sack," said Mix.

"*Who's* carryin' a mandrake," said Tillinghast, rounding on her. "An' I'll give you a right smack for lookin' through my pers'nal belongin's!"

"You've got a mandrake?" said Remedie. "Then what can you possibly have against my Bonn? Why, he's no different from a mandrake or even you, sir, when all's said and done."

"It's not *my* mandrake! An' I's nothin' like that! I's quite the—"

"Will you all shut up?" shouted Wull. "I don't know what a mandrake is, an' I'm not askin'. I need to find Pappa now, so stop wastin' my time!"

He stormed off into the closed silence of the forest, stepping over the wrecked splinter of the one remaining oar, and walked for quite a long way through the unseeing fog of his anger before he realized he was completely, hopelessly lost.

Lauston

"So, Mr. Ruby—"

"'S jus' Ruby," said Ruby, his battered face white-wrapped with bandages. "Here—c'n you smell sour milk?"

"No, I can't," said Rattell. He blinked away some water from the corners of his eyes. "Ruby, you believe that Mr. Tillinghast was in here tonight—with his *son*?"

Ruby nodded.

"'S what he said jus' before he nutted me. He said, 'Tha's my son, you blaggard.' Din't he say that, Errol?"

A small man with a face like a boiled beet nodded. "Aye, 'e said that, Ruby."

"He called me a blaggard an' everythin', an' that's mean," said Ruby.

"It sure is, Ruby," said Errol.

Rattell dabbed at his eyes with a handkerchief. There *was* a smell of cheese, now he came to think about it. It seemed to have followed him from the coach.

"It seems very unlikely that this was Mr. Ti-Tillinghast's son, Ruby," he said, "but it matters only that he was here." He dabbed at his eyes again and took a deep breath. "Could you describe him to us?"

"Oh, sure, he was big, nearly big's me, an' well built, like, strong lookin'. He'd a stupid hat an' . . . an' . . . what else, Errol?"

"He carried 'n air o' wistful melancholy, Ruby," said Errol, finishing his drink.

"Yeah," said Ruby, "that."

"I see," said Rattell. He turned to Rigby.

"What color skin'd 'e have?" said Rigby.

"I dunno," said Ruby.

"Azure," said Errol. "No, more like . . . duck egg. Can I 'ave another drink?"

"Of course," said Rattell. "Mr. Pent, if you wouldn't mind?"

Pent, his craggy face impassive as ever, grunted and walked to the bar. Errol beamed on his stool.

"Ruby," said Rattell, "how would you like to see Mr. Tillinghast again?"

"I'd like it a lot," said Ruby. "If I'd seen 'im comin', he'd never've got the better o' me. If I sees 'im again, I'll be ready an' I'll give 'im a proper kickin'."

"Wonderful," said Rattell. "It just so happens that m-my associates and I are looking for Mr. Tillinghast as well. Was he carrying anything with him? A bag of any kind?"

"I dunno," said Ruby.

Rattell looked at Errol.

"He'd an 'essian sack o'er his shoulder when 'e left," said Errol.

"He still has that which we seek!" said Rattell, shooting a glance at Rigby. "Ruby, I'd like for you to try and find Mr. Tillinghast. Ask around, prod into the dreary little co-corners of your world, and when you do find him, you can hurt him as much as you like. But don't kill him; it is for me to kill him! And you must ensure that his sack is returned to me, do you understand?"

"No," said Ruby.

Rattell looked at Errol.

"Kick 'is head in, don't kill 'im, cut 'is knackers off, an' post 'em to Mr. Rattell 'ere," said Errol.

"N-no!" said Rattell, wringing his hands. "Not his . . . the sack over his shoulder! It contains something of great va-value."

"Oh," said Ruby and Errol together.

Pent returned with two tankards of ale, which he placed on the table. The men lifted them and drank with grim, seasoned swiftness.

"Can you do that, Mr. Ruby?"

Ruby finished the ale, wiped his mouth, and nodded. "Sure," he said. "C'n I get some money now?"

Rattell took out his purse, counted five coins into Ruby's palm.

"There's five ducats to start you off—if you do as I've asked, there'll be ten times that for you."

"Oh," said Ruby.

"'S another fifty ducats," said Errol.

"*Oh*," said Ruby. "Right then. Said he was goin' down the coast, I heard."

"Then that is where *we* shall go—I need *you* to ensure this is not a ruse on his part. You should go into the hills—start in the villages on the Crissle Road, ask for him there. He'll leave a trace wherever he's been; he won't be hard to track."

Ruby held his coins tightly in his fist. His eyes gleamed. "What's 'e got in that bag? 'S it worth more'n fifty ducats?"

Rattell leaned toward him.

"It is a mandrake. Do you know what that is?"

Ruby looked at Errol, who shrugged.

"It's a magical plant grown from a hanged man's seed," said Rattell. "Mandrakes are rumored to carry their . . . father's . . . person, or soul. Mr. Ti-Tillinghast has the last remaining mandrake grown from the spillage of a notorious criminal much beloved of my employer. That means the most d-dangerous people in the land are now bent on its recovery, making it perhaps the most valuable item currently in existence, if one measures value in the lives it may ultimately c-cost. Should you so much as *breathe* on it, Ruby, these people will obliterate you utterly—so I suggest you leave it to us."

Ruby looked at Errol.

"Means they's scary sods an' they'll kill you, Ruby," said Errol.

"Right," said Ruby, then left the inn, Errol sloping at his heels.

"Nothin'll come of them lookin', Misser Rattell," said Rigby.

"I know, but it can hardly hurt, can it? Another person looking for that sc-scarecrow is another chance we've got of finding him. If it only costs me five ducats, I'm happy. Yes, I'm happy!"

Pent made a noise.

"Misser Pent says that'll be the last you see of your ducats, Misser Rattell."

"And so what if it is?" shouted Rattell, striding past his looming henchmen and back toward the coach. "If he's going to the coast"—he flicked through the dossier of Tillinghast's history—"aha! Look, there, this ruin of a house is where he was born. . . . Not born—made! Gathered from the fields and knitted like a sock! He thinks he's being so clever, leading us here—but we're one step ahead of him now!"

"What about this boy 'e was with? 'Is son?"

"He has no son, you fool. He's got no . . . none of the . . . It doesn't matter what! If he escapes us, then Rosie will find out and I'll be buried in the foundations of some horrid building with you two lumps in the pillars beside me, dribbling in that *infuriating* manner for the rest of time!"

"Now, Misser Rattell," said Rigby, looking at the shining black strip of the Danék, "you mustn't worry 'bout that. I reckon Misser Fettiplace changed his mind 'bout all that already."

"And how would *you* know what 'Mr. Fettiplace' is thinki—No!"

But Rigby's knife was already in Rattell's neck, sawing at

the back of his windpipe in patient strokes until, in a shower of crimson and torn flesh, his throat tore open.

The little man fell, crawling in agony, holding his neck together to snatch a desperate gasp with trapped, animal squeaks. Pent stood on Rattell's hands, watched the bubbles pop in his open wound, and waited until the breath left him completely.

"Sorry, Misser Rattell, 's jus' that ev'ry man's got 'is price, an' yours's been paid by Misser Fettiplace. I hopes it's a comfort to know it was more'n five ducats," said Rigby, flipping Rattell's body over with the toe of his boot. He laughed and wiped the dagger on his greatcoat. "Right, let's get his—"

Pent made a noise in his ear. Rigby's eyes widened.

"Gods, don't . . ." he began, but Pent's knife was already hilt deep in Rigby's skull. The big man's eyes rolled upward into whiteness, water pouring unchecked down his cheeks, pooling in the bags of his eyes, and mixing with blood from his nose. He gasped, a thin wheeze that wound to nothing as his heart stopped beating and he slumped, lifeless, in Pent's hands.

Pent pulled back his dagger, the blade moving through bone with the shrill jerk of scraped cutlery, a whistle of purple blood following it into the freezing air. Rigby's body fell to the ground.

Pent removed the coffin-nail dagger and the witch balls

from Rigby's pockets, along with the money and the sharp little trinkets that were the tools of a henchman's trade, slipped the dossier of Tillinghast's life from Rattell's coat, and emptied the little man's wallet into his own.

He stood, swept the blood from his flat cheeks.

First, Ruby. With a few tugs of leather, he uncoupled Colonel Fettiplace's prize stallion from the coach and hopped into the saddle, his blade-lined coat tinkling softly.

Half an hour later came the rattle of five ducats hitting the coins in his pocket, and Pent was riding for the coast.

13

Drebin Woods

Seula: literally, "water dog." An omnivorous, semi-aquatic, snub-snouted, fin-footed mammal common in all regions of the world. Hunted for their fur and blubber, they are considered vermin in townships dependent on the fish that even a small hurtle (defined as five or more seulas) can consume by the hundredweight, and so these peaceful creatures are often poisoned or shot on sight. Elsewhere, they are frequently woven into myth as water-dwellers who were once human; this is most likely due to their eyes, which change from gold in summer to pale blue in winter, and their immensely tactile and sensory whiskers, which give them a pleasant and anthropic face. Although they lack external ears, their other senses are acute—both on land and in water. And though largely docile, competing males use their advanced upper incisors in mating season to battle for rights to females.

–Encyclopedia Grandalia, *University of Oracco Print House*

Wull was surprised by how quickly his eyes had grown accustomed to the moonless gloom. In the hours he'd been walking—dragging his stumped feet over frozen ground and pushing aside thickets of green ice with his bruised wrist—he'd thought back to the days and nights in the bäta's stern, watching Pappa row, hot-wrapped with shirts of gut, tight in the skins of seula and elk, thinking himself cold.

Pappa was right—it hurt to breathe now. The cold was an iron clamp on his head, needling through his teeth into his gums, its agony buzzing around him like a fly swarm, an insistent haze in his face wherever he turned.

He had called to Pappa at first, then thought better of it. There could be scores of ursas around, and only one would be freshly wounded by Tillinghast's blows—the others would pounce on him without hesitation, and he wouldn't have an oar to buy himself time. So he'd walked and kept as keen an eye as the cold would allow, blinking through the ice crystals.

As he'd blundered away, he'd heard Tillinghast, Remedie, and Mix shouting his name, but he'd ignored them and plowed on through his rage. By the time the tempest of his mood had calmed, they were gone and he was lost, with no way of knowing even where the river was, no way of finding his way back to the bäta, and no moon to guide him.

And even if he *did* somehow find the bäta, he had no way of getting it moving with the ursa having shattered the oars, no way of getting home, and no chance of making it to Canna Bay in time to save Pappa.

And Pappa was gone.

Could it really be just that morning that Mrs. Wurth had come to the boathouse?

Wull heaved his breath into the fabric of his collar and closed his eyes, walked without seeing, hands out, stump fingers grasping at the trees, his feet finding their own way through the roots.

He should have stayed at home. Choosing to abandon the river had been madness; he had let it freeze solid for the first time in more than a hundred years, and for what? So he could hand all their money to bradai, lose Pappa in the ursa-filled forest, and set the bäta to ruin on the riverbank?

Even in the cold, he felt the swollen heat of the bradai's cut, felt his heart beating through the meat of his face, fingers of pain spreading out into his body like the roots of a weed.

He had ruined everything.

Never get out the bäta, Wull thought. *And what have I done? Got out and kept going, that's what.*

Through the trees he spotted a frozen puddle, huge, nearly a lake, its white surface ringed with pearlescent swoops of ice, its banks tufted by spiky shoots of winter grass. A heron picked its way across, pin legs flapping on the surface, wings tucked against its body.

"Gentlemen o' the river," said Wull to himself.

The heron, hearing his muttered voice, darted its head and leaped into the air, a tangle of wing and limb that fumbled upward, leaving in its wake an emptiness that was more impenetrably silent and still than before.

Wull stumbled on, his boots falling sullenly forward, catching his body with each step. The weight in his head returned, his skull wobbling. He felt so heavy, every part of him slipping: flesh from bone, bone from joint, his eyes cold pebbles in his head.

He slumped to his knees.

Cold like this didn't kill painfully, he knew; it came as sleep, as a soft whisper that lulled you in peace. If he took off a layer and lay down he would feel the chill, but it would be quickly swaddled by a wave of comfort, of calm. . . .

He pawed at the fastenings of his coat, tugging at the buttons with fingers that could no longer move.

Then he spotted movement ahead, struggled upright—fell.

"Pappa?" he said. "Pappa, I'm sorry."

The shape blurred—legs and feet.

"I'm sorry," he said again.

Boots appeared before him. He stared at the detail in the leather and slow-blinked, eyes flickering.

"It's you," he said.

"It's me," said Mix, kneeling in front of him. "Oh, you don't look good, do you?"

Wull sighed. "How did you find me?" he said eventually.

She smiled. "We've been lookin' for you. Even after you told us to bugger off."

"Thank you," said Wull.

"Not a bother. C'mon. Let's head back."

"I jus' need to find Pappa. He's been alone out here for hours. He'll freeze to death."

"You're not goin' to find him lyin' on the deck then, are you?" said Mix, hoisting him to his feet. Wull caught his weight on his heels and blundered forward. "Are you hurt?"

"I'm fine, just achin' from the rowin'. . . . No wonder the damn thing was that heavy with four people in it. Nearly popped out my shoulders."

"Be five people once Remedie comes on too," said Mix, grinning. "A merry troop we'll make."

"I can't . . . I can't take everyone," said Wull. "I don't mean to leave anyone, but there's no room, an' I need to get to the coast as quick as I can."

Mix turned. In the gloom of the woods, the white markings on her skin glowed faintly in the shadows of her collar: thin, elegant, repetitious lines—like the rings of a tree or the patterns of blown snow.

"What are they?" said Wull, pointing.

"Never you mind," said Mix. She raised an eyebrow. "There's no way you'll leave us here."

"An' how d'you know that?" said Wull. He coughed, tasted coppery blood.

"'Cause I've been out in cold like this before; it'll kill you so quietly you don't even know. Besides, you said I could come with you, an' that's final. Even the homunculus agrees—said you were even rubbish at stealin' food 'cause you were too decent an' honest. I don't think he meant it as a compliment, mind you."

"Right," said Wull, "so along with my other faults, I'm too honest. Great. An' his name's Tillinghast."

"I know. I jus' like the word: *ho-mun-cu-lus*. An' I din't think you'd stick up for him. He your friend now? Is that it?"

"Hardly," said Wull. "I don't have friends—I've got passengers."

Mix jogged up alongside him, hopped over a log, and pointed. "An' no wonder, if you—Look, there he is!"

"Pappa!" shouted Wull. He ran forward, fell, and slid over the wet ground toward Pappa—slouched into the open trunk of a fallen tree, totally still, his skin bloodless with cold. Before him lay a red balgair, its neck broken and twisted, a thin, painful whine rasping from its bloodied mouth. Pappa was watching it dispassionately, his face empty and blank.

Wull looked at him, felt his stomach sink, and reached for the animal—gave its neck the final snap it needed to end its pain.

"Pappa! Sit up! Can you hear me? Can you hear me, Pappa?"

He lifted Pappa's wasted spindle body, felt with the memory of his skin the bulk he'd held in the forest outside the Bootmunch's cave, and let go a deep, painful sob.

"It that speaks," said Pappa, his voice a whisper. "It that speaks . . ."

Wull almost laughed. "I'm here, Pappa! It's all right now. Here, have my coat."

He fumbled at his buttons, then bit off his gloves, throwing them to the ground and wriggling free of his coat. Without it, the cold came as an assault, scalding him, but he wrapped Pappa tightly, leaned in close to the big, sunken face.

"It that speaks," said Pappa again, and this time there was a note of weary affection in the voice, a recognition that lasted half a heartbeat, and Wull knelt before him and took his hand. Behind him, Mix picked up Wull's gloves and stood back.

"Pappa, do you know me?" said Wull, tears at the edges of his eyes. "Pappa, it's me, Wulliam. Wulliam. You named me that, do you remember? Pappa, it's me! Look at me! Please look at me!"

Pappa's eyes rolled in his head, untethered, like a doll's eyes. Wull shook him, tipped him forward.

"Pappa! Do you know it's me? Wulliam? I'm sorry

I've ruined everything. I'm so sorry. . . . The bäta and everything—I was trying to help you. . . ." Wull pressed his hands into the thin arms, pulling the frail threads of Pappa back to him. "I didn't know what else to do! I'm sorry, Pappa, please stay here with me!"

Pappa's head fell onto Wull's shoulder, and Wull held it there as the cold wrapped them both, his mind lost in a safe place where they'd been happy together, safe in the boathouse, safe in the bäta; when they laughed and floated on the summer currents and when Pappa would hold him tight in his safe bed.

"Wulliam," whispered Pappa, soft as the wind, soft as a thought.

"Yes," said Wull, holding him tighter, "I've got you here. I've got you. It's goin' to be all right. We can go home, I'll stay with you there, I'll stay with you always. I'm sorry. . . ."

Pappa went limp. Wull felt carefully for the rising of the thin rib cage, waited to feel Pappa's breath.

Pappa sighed.

"You've got no idea what happened to him?" said Mix softly.

A bohdan took him, thought Wull. *It's living inside him and killing him slowly and I can see it happening.*

"No," he said aloud after a moment. "He jus' wasn't the same once he came out the water."

He put his arm around Pappa's waist and lifted him from the ground. Mix hurried forward, took Pappa's other arm, and turned him slightly.

"It's this way," she said. "You keep goin' the way you were an' you'll end up hittin' the wrong coast."

"Thank you," said Wull again. They walked together, lifting Pappa over glassy pools of ice. "How scary are these people you're runnin' from?"

"Oh, proper scary. Like, glowin' eyes an' shadows scary."

"Why did you steal from 'em then?"

"I told you!" said Mix, sliding over a smashed trunk and reaching back for Pappa's elbow. "I didn't mean to! It is possible to steal by accident, y'know. You never made a mistake in your life?"

Wull thought of the smashed shards of the whale oil bottle drifting downriver, of the oar that lay in ruined splinters on the bankside, and of the impossible distance that separated him from the safety of the boathouse.

"Yes," he said.

"Well, then," said Mix, "that was my mistake. One of 'em, anyway."

"One of 'em?"

"Yup. We's all made a few, I reckon. 'S jus' livin', 'in't it?"

"I need to get to Canna Bay, Mix. I need the mormorach, for Pappa—look at him."

"I know, but I'm tellin' you, even if you get there—"

"Don't tell me that. I don't need to hear it. I jus' need to get there, all right?"

"Sure. An' don't worry, I'll go with you."

"But the extra weight . . ."

"An' what do I weigh?" said Mix. "Hardly a thing! I's not worried anyway—you're too good to leave us here, right out in the far end of nowhere."

Wull sighed, a lump of air that stuck in his throat as he helped Pappa over a frozen puddle.

"I know," he said.

Canna Bay

Dawn shone pink against the sky, the furrowed clouds stretching out from the horizon, talons grabbing at Canna Bay, boiled purple in their troughs and black where they met the sea. Balanced silently at their focus on the horizon's edge raged a speck of shattering drama as the matchstick of another splintered mast tumbled into the brine.

Gilt Murdagh was perched languorously on the statue of Mother Demlass, his eyeglass resting on her basket of pickerel. At the base of the statue's marble plinth were strewn bow-tied pieces of wicker and seaflowers. To his left stood the white tower of the lighthouse, its beam left to die as the fish crews had deserted the port, its guidance no longer required.

Murdagh's tongue worked over his teeth as he watched how the mormorach swirled, how it tore its way through the sail. He watched as it rose, leading with its buttressed face to smash through the hull, the seas around it threshed into foam by the sinking ship and the frantic strokes of men and women swimming for safety. The shining tip of his whale-bone leg tapped idly on the stone of the Mother's bared feet.

"It's a fair morning," said a voice behind him.

Murdagh continued to watch the mormorach.

"I's quite aware o' the weather, an' not one for interruptions," he said. "Also, you's wrong—it's bloody perishin' *and* it's no' quite mornin' yet."

"I'm sorry, Captain Murdagh," said the voice. "I was told you would be here, and I don't mean to interrupt—"

"Now if tha' was true you wouldn't have interrupted me, would you?" said Murdagh, snapping his eyeglass closed and turning to face the speaker.

A fat man in a fussy wig was knitting his fingers and chewing his lips. His startled owlish face, propped on his collar like a target at a fairground booth, was flushed with cold and confrontation. His clothes, brightly hued and lace-trimmed, were layered velvet, and his shoes gleamed.

"I'm sorry," he said again, "but I must speak with you."

"So speak," said Murdagh. He looked evenly at the man, blinking slowly, allowing the skin of his eyelid to linger on the raised red meat of his injured eye.

"Yes, yes, of course. I am Dayl Seamer. I'm the—"

"You's the mayor of this town—I knows who you are. What c'n I do for you, Mr. Mayor?"

"Yes," said Seamer, satisfaction glazing his round face. "I am the mayor, and I . . . I wish to speak with you regarding the creature known as the mormorach."

Murdagh raised an eyebrow, deepening the lines of grime on his forehead. "'Known as'?" he said, laughing. "It's not a crook, Mr. Mayor; beast 'in't got an alias. It's known as nothin' 'cept what it is—a dirty big mormorach, an' it's doin' a grand job on all these boats what've gone after it."

"It is that grim fact that has compelled me to seek your counsel," said Seamer, nodding. He took a step forward, hesitated, and stepped back. "The mormorach killed Blueloons Emory, our most senior magistrate, and the people of the town are in a panic: this is the longest they've ever been without fish, and they're desperate. The town is built on fishing, Captain Murdagh, and completely dependent on the fruits of the sea for survival. Should this continue, people will have to leave to find work elsewhere to support their families. That means Oracco, and the gods only know what kind of work awaits them there. These are *fishing* people—generations of them. We have to do something to save the town."

Murdagh had been motionless throughout Seamer's speech. Now he spat on the ground.

"*We* does? Where does I fit into this?" he said. He slow-blinked at Seamer again and suppressed a snort as all color drained from the mayor's face.

Seamer was sweating. "The word of the people is that you are the only man capable of catching this leviathan," he said.

Murdagh nodded slowly. "That might be," he said. "I takes it you've been watchin' the others take their try?"

"I have, of course. I've never had sea legs, but I've watched this coastline my whole life, and I've never seen aught like it; the fiercest machines of war could not do to a ship what that animal has done. Tonight's is the third of them to fall. If these hunters are destroyed and you fail to act, the town is finished."

Murdagh dragged a slow lump of spit round his mouth and let it fall onto the ground.

"'Fail to act'?" he said. "You'd best watch the tone you's takin' with me, Mr. Seamer. There 'in't no supposin' I'd manage any better. 'S an awful lot o' risk for me, takin' the *Hellsong* out into these waters wi' that thing swimmin' around. 'In't like my boat's made o' rock, an' even if it were, I don't reckon it'd make much o' a difference. What call has you to be tellin' me I's *got* to be actin'?"

Seamer wrung his hands. Desperation moved his feet and he came toward Murdagh, beseeching, his palms and face open and pleading. "But, Captain—"

Murdagh stood and drew his dirk, held it loosely in the air between them. "You jus' stay right where you is, Mr. Mayor. I din't get this pretty by lettin' strangers rush me unchecked."

Seamer looked perplexed. "You can't think I meant to . . . Captain Murdagh, I'm here to beg for your *help*! I don't wish to quarrel with you."

"You 'in't begged yet, son," said Murdagh. He lifted his head and gave Seamer the full benefit of his scarred, passionless face, his bone leg and bludgeoned eye, and watched the mayor wilt under their terrible heat.

Seamer forced his eyes from the ground. Behind the old sailor, the sky had darkened to a violent red, the cloud furrows clenched to a fist.

"I'm begging now," said Seamer, his voice wobbling. "Please, Captain, help us. People are terrified. There's talk of evil magic spreading: families have come to blows; there are outbreaks of violence every day. Last night a rider brought word of a trio of highwaymen torn apart, their body parts nailed to a dozen trees—this sort of thing does not normally happen outside of the city. The creature's magic is poisoning the air—two days ago a dog was crushed dead under a cart and started barking on the slab. When the dead start walking, talk of heavenly judgment inevitably follows; some think we are being punished for our centuries' feeding on the sea, that the mormorach is an agent of the water gods' vengeance. You sit here on the statue of the Mother, surrounded by offerings, pleas for help; people are desperate! They look to me, as their mayor, and I find myself powerless—powerless unless you help me."

Murdagh spat again. "I 'in't runnin' a charity, sailin' around bailin' out every little town what's in trouble. I got no claim on your people, an' they got none on me—seems that if the gods've chosen to send this thing forth maybe it *is* a sign folk should stop plund'rin' the waters. An' what's the trouble if there's a trout farm? Why can't they farm their fishes an' leave the big beasts to Gilt an' his crew?"

"The trout farm belongs to one man and is not well loved. These are fishing people, Captain—they want to catch their quarry, not have it penned like cattle. Surely you understand that?"

Murdagh nodded. "I do. So they move themselves on to someplace else."

"And to where would they move? There are no other fishing grounds on this coast that would support such a settlement of—"

"Then maybe they's meant to start up again in Oracco!" shouted Murdagh. "An' maybe I's meant to be practical an' take my little tub farther up the coast to spike myself a big whale or two or three, live on their oil, an' drink myself into gin-soaked safety for the next year. But still," he added, "you speak well. I like words—reckon I'd vote for you meself if I heard somethin' like that comin' from a soapbox."

Seamer smiled sheepishly. "You're most kind," he said, "but I rarely speak publicly. The mayor isn't elected in Canna Bay; it's a hereditary position."

"That so?" said Murdagh. He sheathed his dirk. "A gentleman, then?"

"I try to be, sir," said Seamer, clasping his lapels.

"I imagine that comes with a tract o' land, that title. Puttin' you to livin' in rarefied strata, so to speak." Murdagh's voice had softened. He cocked an eyebrow.

Seamer felt the tug on the line, and his smile began to fall. "I have some land, a few acres only, but—"

"It's a common misconception 'bout sailin' men that they only has love for the sea," said Murdagh, turning his back on the mayor and looking out to the wrecked speck of the mormorach's most recent victim. "I, f'r instance, *loves* land, 'specially valuable land. There's no tellin' what I might do for a good bit o' land." He turned and grinned at Seamer. "Needs a sea view, mind."

Seamer, colorless and clammy, swallowed. "I . . . I don't . . ." he began.

"I'll catch this little thing for you, Mr. Mayor, an' all this freedom'll cost is that pretty land o' yours," said Murdagh, stomping off toward the village, his terrible crutch ringing on the stone. "We'll let the others have their try, an' then I'll go huntin'. Doesn't do Gilt any harm to watch the competition bein' smashed to splinters—more whale meat for the *Hellsong* when all this is over!"

The mormorach, far out to sea and flushed with triumph, leaped high in the air and roared before crashing back in a shower of spray into the water.

Seamer leaned on the statue of the Mother, hand on his chest, watching the pigment bleed from the sky as Murdagh's whalebone leg clicked to silence in the distance.

As the light pierced the clouds, the breakwater became an uneven net of shadows. Seamer looked at the Mother's basket, and saw it filled with only the cold black of the dwindling night.

14

Drebin Woods

*Faelkon: literally, "rot wing." Hunting primarily using
long talons, the faelkon has an average wingspan of
fourteen feet. It is the largest of a family of giant, pred-
atory ground-nesters (including gyræptors and kierks;
collectively, the accibidae genus: see Dale, K.), feared
for their beakless faces; their large, flat, equine teeth;
and the protrusions of wood that appear as extracuta-
neous bones. Uniquely, this genus does not shed dead
skin cells, meaning a thick layer collects under the dark
plumage. Rigorous scratching of this on trees gathers the wood, which is then gradually internalized by
freshly formed crust. Despite the faelkon's frightening
appearance, most who encounter it remark first upon its
smell: an intense odor caused by bacterial activity in the
permanently rotting crust. This is also manifest in its
decayed face, and so has given rise to the faelkon's long-
used hunters' sobriquet, "the flying corpse."*

—Encyclopedia Grandalia, University of Oracco Print House

Tillinghast was leaning on the bäta, picking under the fingernails of his severed hand with a pocketknife. He peered intently at his work, the hand held close to his face.

"You found 'im then?" he said, spotting Wull and Mix emerging with Pappa. "That's good, 'in't it?"

"No thanks to you," said Wull, settling Pappa on the ground. "I thought you might come an' help me."

"I did," said Tillinghast, "then I came back. Wasn't much point in all of us wand'rin' in the woods, was there? An' besides, makes sense to have someone here when you come back." Satisfied with his fingernails, he folded his knife away and regarded his hand.

"So you've left Remedie alone?" said Wull.

"Too right. I tried followin' her, an' she told me where to go. Right sour woman, she is, unfriendly an' sour."

"I think she seems nice," said Mix, selecting a stalk of frozen grass to chew.

"Nobody asked you, little miss."

Mix stuck out her tongue.

Wull touched Pappa's face. He wasn't asleep, but was emptied completely, his mind wandering far away. *Fine,* thought Wull. *Anywhere's better than here now.*

"What a nightmare is this thing," said Tillinghast, waggling his loose hand. "I's no trouble gettin' this fixed in the city when there's plenty o' seamstresses about, but what am I to do out here?"

Wull took the hand and looked at the stitching.

"I reckon I could fix that," he said. "Needle wouldn't hurt you?"

Tillinghast narrowed his eyes. "You c'n sew? How's that?"

"I mend the nets, fix the ropes, sew up clothin'. Seen Pappa stitchin' up bodies an' all, never done it myself, mind."

"What's he stitchin' bodies for?" said Mix.

"The ones that get cut up," said Wull, "when we rescue them or pull them in the bäta, they . . . burst a bit. Sometimes they need puttin' back together so's they stay on the slab."

"Lovely," said Mix.

"You were the one asked about gruesome things," said Wull.

Tillinghast furrowed his brow. "I dun't know," he said. "If you've never really done it—"

"What's the harm if it doesn't hurt?" said Wull. "Worst thing that can happen is it just keeps it in place until you can get it fixed properly, right?"

"I s'pose," said Tillinghast reluctantly. "I's still not sure 'bout it though. What you goin' to use?"

"Stringed gut," said Wull, "tough as you like. I've got a ball of it in the bäta, here." He swung over the gunwale, reached into the prow. There was a hollow in the blankets where Mix had sat, and a space where the money tin had been. He flashed his hand around, seeing through the tips of his fingers.

"It's not there," he said.

Mix coughed and held up a ball wound of dull, waxy string. "Is this it?" she said.

Wull ran over and grabbed the ball from her hand. "You *stole* it?" he said, checking the needle was still in place.

"I'm sorry. I was just . . . bored, curled up there. It passed the time."

"An' how much time did robbin' it pass?" said Wull, turning the gutstring, checking for damage. "Five seconds?"

"Well, two or three," said Mix, "and, to be fair, the thirty or so we've been discussin' it now."

"Let me see that," said Tillinghast. He took the ball from Wull and examined it, tested the end between his teeth. "That's pretty sturdy," he said. "All right. Do your worst."

"How'd you get that?" said Mix. "I thought you'd no money."

"We have some money," said Wull quickly. "It's jus' that it all goes on the river. But we don't buy this—Pappa makes it with seulas' guts."

Mix leaned away from the ball in Tillinghast's hand.

"How d'you do that exactly?" she said.

"You need to gut the seulas an' pile up their intestines, then you clean them, strip off the fat, soak them for a couple o' days in river water, scrape off the outside skin bit, an' soak them in lye for another week or so. You end up with a pile of skinny wee bits, an' you wind those into strings. I can do that part. Pappa always let me help."

"What a treat," said Mix, wrinkling her nose. "I bet you're sorry you put it in your gob now, Till."

"I's tasted worse," said Tillinghast, thoughtfully tweezing the string in his lips.

Wull looked at Mix pulling grass from the bank. "What else did you take?" he said.

She grinned, held up a rubber hat and a wooden mallet. "An' that's it, I swear."

"She's got a glass thing an' all," said Tillinghast.

"Come *on*," said Wull, rolling his eyes.

Mix scowled at Tillinghast and handed it over.

"It's for whale oil, is this," said Wull. "It was my gran'pappa's. Don't take nothin' else, all right?" He tucked it carefully beside the oilskins.

"What's happ'nin' with my hand then?" said Tillinghast.

"Give it here," said Wull. He sat down and lifted the skin's edge from Tillinghast's wrist. "That doesn't hurt?" he said again.

Tillinghast chuckled. "No, lad, look at my arm."

Wull, with Mix peering over his shoulder, lifted the skin higher and peered inside: Tillinghast's arm was a damp pleat of muscle and straw, ropes of fiber and flesh that were threaded with little fronds of herbs. The ropes moved as

Tillinghast breathed, the whole mass pulsing gently with a wet, fabric sound. Wull moved the skin between the tips of his finger and thumb, felt its cold, parchment thinness.

"See?" said Tillinghast. "You jus' get that needle in there."

"Right," said Wull. The skin yielded immediately to the needle's point. "It's like leather," he whispered.

"Whose skin was it?" said Mix.

"I dun't know," said Tillinghast.

"It's a good skin," said Mix. "Big."

Tillinghast laughed. "Jus' the right size for me, anyway. Any bigger an' I'd be trippin' over my own bum cheeks."

"Sit still," said Wull. He had pulled three stitches tightly along the top of the wrist, his face close in and focused on the tiny movements of the gut as it worked its way through, feeling the friction in his fingers. "It doesn't hurt?"

"No!" said Tillinghast again. "If it din't hurt when that big blaggard bit it off, you ticklin' me with tha' little thing's not goin' to be much of a problem."

"Right," said Wull, making another stitch, his arm reaching out as he pulled the length of gut through, making another solid bind.

"I never much cared for this hand," said Tillinghast. "See how it's different to the rest o' my skin? A bit smaller, even, an' more pale."

"I hadn't noticed," said Wull.

"Why's that then?" said Mix.

"I's no clue. You'd have to ask the man what made me."

"How come it doesn't hurt gettin' stitched?" said Mix.

"I's straw, mainly," said Tillinghast. "'In't no nerves to give me pain."

"Do you have a brain?"

"What kind o' question's that?"

"Sensible one," said Mix. "Life works into funny places sometimes; 'in't always a need for a brain."

Wull, Tillinghast's hand twitching to life in his, worked his patient way around the torn seam, binding it more strongly with each solid loop. The filling in Tillinghast's hand stirred in the thin skin, and his fingers began to move.

"Stay still," whispered Wull.

"I'm tryin'! It always does this. It's jus' what happens when I gets reconnected, is all."

Wull glanced up at him. "How many times you lost bits o' yourself?"

"Oh, plenty. Even meant some of 'em. You wun't reckon on how much folks can be frightened by such a thing."

Wull felt Tillinghast's insides turning under his palm like insects through soil. "Right," he said.

"I's never lost the *best* bit, mind," said Tillinghast.

"Remedie's not here," said Wull, beginning his final few loops, adding, "I hope she's all right."

"Oh, she'll be fine. Face like that'll keep most things at bay I shouldn't wonder."

"You've no cause to be so rude to her," said Wull.

"She's rude to me! I dun't know why I should be expected to chin-wag with so rude a woman."

"You always start it."

"I do not!"

"You do, and it's needless."

"So?" said Mix, who'd been waiting.

"So what?"

"*Do* you have a brain?"

"Oh gods, yes, of course I do. How'd you think I'm talkin' and walkin'?"

"Whose is it?"

"Clever fella, schoolmaster," said Tillinghast promptly. "I used to be able to speak the old tongues, but I forgot 'em, not findin' many on the roads who shared 'em. Shared my own plenty, mind you."

"Where's your straw come from?" said Mix.

"Eh? I dun't know. Farm, I s'pose."

"But isn't your straw jus' as important as your muscle? Like, your muscles come from these men, an' your straw is part o' that. Like havin' a mam and a pap."

"I don't bloody know. . . . Are you nearly finished, Wull?"

"Almost," said Wull, turning the needle again.

"Do you dream?" said Mix.

"In the name of . . . yes, I bloody dream."

"When you dream, are you a man or, y'know . . . not a man?"

Tillinghast's brows knitted. "You mean a woman?" he said.

"No! Like straw. Do you dream you're, I don't know, straw, grass—part o' the land?"

Tillinghast sniffed and squinted at her. "Are you bein' funny?" he said.

Mix shook her head, ran her fingers around the line of her collar. "Course not," she said.

"I dream I'm a man, all right? I am a bloody man, an' that's what I dream. Dreams comes from brains, an' straw dun't have brains, does it?"

"I don't know," said Mix. "There must be all kind o' memories in the land—all the rain and sweat and blood that've landed on it. I jus' wondered."

"Well, stop wonderin'. Gods only know, I's never heard so many questions in my life."

"Do you like bein' made of straw?"

Tillinghast sighed, then thought for a moment. "I s'pose. There's plenty not to miss 'bout flesh an' blood. But I do miss the farts. Such farts I made as would cause corpses to roll over and fan where their noses should be."

"There," said Wull, cutting the gutstring and binding the final stitch. "How's that?"

Tillinghast tried his hand, flexed his fingers. "Oh, tha' feels great, so it does." He shook his arm violently and grinned. "I got my arm put back in the city the other day, an' I thought they did a good job, but, oh, I couldn't pull that wrist apart no matter how lonely I got. You'll need to do me other bits like this—I'd be invincible."

Wull looked at Tillinghast's enormous body and suppressed a shudder.

"Maybe later," he said. He looked along the frozen bank and saw, sprawled at the base of an oak tree, the ursa-twisted oar. It was torn almost in half and split from the blade, pale, new wood shining through. His hand went to the bandage on his cheek, pressing the swelling of his cut. "But now what do we do?" he said. "We can't get anywhere jus' driftin', an' that'll take forever."

"Oh, 's easy, that," said Tillinghast, still swinging his hands around. "That Bootmunch fella had all kinds o' stuff in that cave—I'll bet he'd some oars an' all."

"The Bootmunch!" said Wull, looking at the tree line. "I'd forgotten all about him! What happened?"

"He was tryin' to bloody kill me. Decent effort, I has to say, but I should've been prepared. When he was puttin' those herbs together, I jus' watched him, like he was preppin' dinner or somethin'. Daft, daft, daft."

"It made me hallucinate," said Wull, remembering.

He looked at Pappa on the ground, frail and bundled like kindling.

"Really? I'd been wond'rin' why you hadn't jumped in to help me, I has to say. Guess that explains it." Tillinghast grabbed hold of a tree and pulled on his wrist.

"What happened? What did you see?" said Mix.

"I don't know," said Wull guardedly. "What about you? Where did you go?"

Mix's eyes shone. "I had a vision too. There were ships all around, comin' for me an' for us, then I was all tangled in roots an' the smell of mud, an' when I got free, I tried eatin' somethin' I *thought* was bread, but it was a lump o' dry earth full o' dead things. It was weird. So, what *did* you see?"

Wull tossed the oar into the long grass and shrugged. "Things. Impossible things."

"That's the point of 'em, isn't it?" she said. "Did you enjoy it?"

Wull thought back to the weight pulling his head around, to the melding, burning colors, and the feeling of Pappa's fat weight against him.

"Aye," he said, taking a long drink from his water pouch. "I s'pose I did."

Mix laughed. "You'll be addicted next thing you know— bunches o' herbs stickin' out your pockets, rowin' in circles."

Wull, despite himself, despite all the pain in his body,

laughed, then laughed again to find himself laughing.

"What's funny?" said Remedie, climbing through the riverside brambles, Bonn wrapped tightly on her front. "I'm there worried I'll be lost, and I come back to find you all having a lively chuckle. Hello, Wulliam, I'm glad to see you've found your . . . father."

"I know," said Wull, smiling. He knelt beside Pappa and tousled his hair. "I'm glad to see you. Mix an' me found Pappa. Thanks for goin' lookin'," he added, looking at Tillinghast.

Tillinghast's eyes bulged. "I told you I went lookin' an' all, only this one sent me back!"

"I did no such thing!" said Remedie. "I merely asked you to stay farther away from *me*—not to stop looking for Wulliam and his father."

"You said I was repellent!" said Tillinghast indignantly.

"You are! I've never heard so many libidinous comments in my life!"

"You might if you fixed that bird's nest you's passin' off as hair!"

"See?" said Remedie. "This from a man of straw who hasn't a scrap of hair. Here, Wulliam, hold my Bonn for a moment while I empty the stones out my boots."

"I's proud o' my baldness," said Tillinghast. "It's manly to be without hair."

"And so you wear a hat because . . ." said Mix, grinning.

Tillinghast opened his mouth, then closed it. "It's winter," he said lamely. "I dun't need to be standin' here debating the merits o' hair with you people." He straightened his hat.

Wull took Bonn from Remedie. She kept her hand on the baby's head until Wull had cupped it in his own palm and begun to move his arms as she did, in shushing, gentle rocking motions that felt sharp and clumsy. She smiled fondly at him.

"Your baby's made of wood, miss?" said Mix, her voice innocent and light.

"That's right," said Remedie, balanced on a fallen tree, shaking one boot at the ground.

"How's that work, then?" said Mix.

"This one and her questions," muttered Tillinghast, rubbing his hand over his face.

"Well, he's my baby, and I love him," said Remedie. "There's not much else that needs work."

"But how did, I mean . . . Where'd you get him?"

Remedie smiled sadly, heaved a deep breath.

"I had a son a year ago, the natural way, the blood and skin way, but he died. He was Bonn too." She put her boot back on, swapped hands on the tree trunk, and shook the other boot. "He was a strong lump of a boy, then one morning after a few weeks he wouldn't wake. I found him in his cradle, all cold, all heavy. So I kissed him and cleaned him and buried him."

She sat down, folded her hands in her lap. The others were silent. Wull kept moving Bonn's fixed little body, watching Remedie's face. Beside him, Pappa let go a sharp snore and whispered unintelligible words.

"And that's that," said Remedie.

"Wait a minute," said Tillinghast. "Where'd this thing come from then?"

"This *thing*, Mr. Tillinghast? You mean my son?"

"Whatever, the wooden kid," said Tillinghast. "D'you win it in a raffle?"

Remedie drew her face in against him. "From a homunculus with a mandrake," she muttered. "I buried Bonn beneath a yew tree and made sure certain . . . conditions were met. A year to the day I dug down, and there he was, waiting for me."

The three looked at Bonn, still and white in Wull's arms, perfect as a marble cherub.

"You mean . . . you didn't carve him?" said Wull.

"Carve him?" said Remedie, laughing. "Gods, no, he was there, waiting. This *is* Bonn. I dug to where he'd been buried. His flesh was gone, and here he is now, a new body of yew root, with his soul already inside."

"So you did magic?" said Mix.

"I did."

"So you're a witch?"

"Miss Cantwell doesn't need to be asked so many questions," said Wull. He thought for a minute. "So you c'n control magic, then?"

"In a manner of speaking, yes, I can, and I am a witch. But I don't belong to a coven."

"'In't it dangerous?" said Wull. "Like lightnin'?"

"If you don't know what you're doing, it can be, of course."

"So, did you"—Wull paused, looked at Pappa—"did you make the mormorach come here? Is it because of you it's in Canna Bay?"

"Oh heavens, no! I just . . . knew it would be, that's all. There'll be all kinds of other creatures around in the throes of a storm like this, I'm quite sure. Like in the sea, when there's a storm, all the water swirls up and the little beasts of the sand and rock are set in motion. It's amazing what little animals you find that would normally be hidden."

"Right," said Wull. He touched Bonn's cheek.

"So where's the magic come from then?" said Mix.

"In the name of . . ." said Tillinghast.

"It comes from the land," said Remedie, "and my grandmother. She taught me."

"That's int'restin'," said Mix, eyes wide. "So do you need to get naked an' chant beside a fire?"

"No!" said Remedie, laughing despite herself. "Why on earth would one do such a thing?"

"Keep your plums warm," said Tillinghast.

"I saw it in a book once," said Mix. "So you doesn't have to be in a certain place for it to work? Could you do it here?"

"Well, no. It comes from the ground—but from my *own* ground. There my family are all in the soil—here I can't connect to the same energies."

"So do you have to be outside?"

Remedie laughed again. "No. The kitchen's just as good."

"The parlor?"

"Yes, the parlor's fine."

"The bedroom?"

"No," said Remedie. "It's upstairs, too far from the soil. There's no magic in the bedroom."

"Tha's a shame," said Tillinghast. "Mibbe it's your squint?"

Remedie turned her shoulders so she couldn't see Tillinghast's face. "The point is that Bonn's ready to be reborn now with a new skin and a new body. A stronger one."

"A wooden one?" said Mix.

Wull felt Bonn's weight on his palms and examined the ornate little face. The baby's surface—skin—was faintly iridescent, the sparkle of his fibers lit by the stars so that he appeared bathed in pale, glowing light. He seemed, without moving a fiber, to respond to the pressure of Wull's hands, shifting in the same position: arms half raised, legs bent so that the heels almost touched, mouth slightly opened, as though searching for the teat.

Wull lowered his cheek to the little mouth. The wood was cold, but he hovered, expecting to feel a bloom of breath.

"Exactly," said Remedie, "and when we get to Canna Bay and we're close enough to this creature—"

"Hey!" said Wull. "You're going after the mormorach too?"

"Of course," said Remedie. "Is that your plan also?"

"For Pappa," said Wull. "It has stuff inside it that'll cure him."

"It has a body of magic and wonderful power," said Remedie seriously. "I'm sure it holds the answer for your father's ills too. The mormorach will give Bonn *true* life once again, and then I will live with him in happiness."

She lifted Bonn from Wull, kissed his nose, and strapped him into the sling on her body.

"Here," she said, snapping off the bandage and striking a line of mud across Wull's cheek. "I made this for you while I was wandering in the forest."

Wull touched his cut. The mud—tingly and at once hot and cold—had filled it like grout.

"Thank you, miss," he said.

"You're quite welcome. It's burdock, mainly, with a few other things. It should clean up that nasty cut of yours."

"Brilliant," said Tillinghast. "So we're all on missions o' mercy an' helpin' each other out, 'in't that jus' peachy? Now let's get some oars an' get the hells out o' here."

"And where are we going to find oars in the middle of the forest?" said Remedie as Wull rose and stretched. "Is there a ship broker up a tree?"

Tillinghast relished the chance to be insufferable. "No, Miss Cantwell, we's already sourced the supplies we needs, thank you," he said, striding back toward the cave.

"Or we think we might have," said Wull.

"From the Bootmunch," said Mix.

"We bloody has!" said Tillinghast. "Don't tell her . . . that . . . Jus' come on. There might be other things as worth takin'."

"Who's the Bootmunch?" said Remedie.

"A missing explorer—he tried to kill us," said Mix. "Well, tried to kill Till, and got me an' Wull at the same time. Doesn't like homunculuses, apparently."

"Homunculi, if you please," said Tillinghast. "Let's jus' go."

"What happened to him anyway? The Bootmunch?" said Wull, hobbling after Tillinghast, Pappa grumbling on his shoulder.

"Oh, by the time he'd caught me, my eyes had fair cleared up. It din't go the way he was expectin', I'd say."

Decatur House

Numberless legs clacked and creaked through the ruin's untended wilderness. The wind blew across the garden, pulling the tops of the uncut, dying plants and bending the bare treetops toward the ground.

The wicker Things ran sightlessly and without aim, cracking their restless legs and changing direction in rapid swoops, responding to the slope of the ground and the air's patterned energies, their bodies channeling the magnetism and magic that flowed through the evening sky like the currents of the tide.

Something about the sky's energy had changed.

There was a sharpness and a focus that unsettled them. It jittered their limbs and whipped them into a swarm, like birds panicked in the gaze of a predator.

The wind swelled again, sending loose stone tumbling down the front of the wrecked building and into the long grass.

The man watched the Things from the window, chuckling at their wildness and speed. Then he let the curtain fall and sat inside, listening to the thud of their feet, bathed in the silent hiss of flame on glass while the air filled with the flutter of thick-stitched wings.

The Drebin Woods

The Bootmunch blinked at them. He was hanging by his heels from the cave's roof, trussed up by whip-thin branches and swinging gently. Tillinghast had wound some herb knives into his beard so that he tinkled as he swung, like a bulbous, hairy wind chime.

"And who is this lovely lady?" said the Bootmunch, spotting Remedie. "Could I be more charmed? I do not think so. How would it be possible? What a vision of loveliness! I would kiss you on the hands and face, but alas this devil of straw has seen fit to suspend me from my own ceiling—"

"You tried to kill me," said Tillinghast, rummaging through the Bootmunch's belongings.

"Even if that were possible, straw devil, you have in return dangled me here like a Newsun decoration. So I must therefore apologize, madam, and leave my hands where they are, which is to say, tied completely behind my back."

He smiled. Mix patted him on the cheek.

"Nothin' here's worth takin'," said Tillinghast.

"We're not *takin'* anything anyway," said Wull. "We're payin' for whatever we get."

"*Payin'?*" said Tillinghast, scandalized. "I's got a reputation, you know."

"I can imagine," muttered Remedie.

"Mr. Bootmunch . . ." started Wull.

"Rushworth, remember?" said the Bootmunch quickly. "The Hiding Explorer?"

"Mr. Bootmunch," said Wull again, "when you tried to kill Tillinghast, here—"

"That's impossible, he's a—"

"*When you tried to kill him,* you gave me a mighty strong hallucination that damn near got me and this lady here killed by an ursa. . . ."

"What about the little one?" said the Bootmunch.

"I was miles away, eatin' mud," said Mix.

"Top work, that girl," said the Bootmunch, grinning. "Yes, I'm awfully sorry about that. Sorry, sorry, everyone, frightfully sorry"—he tried to swivel round to include Tillinghast—"but he's a straw devil. I mixed the herbs wrong—I'd have bloody got him if I'd remembered the fennel. You should always remember the fennel."

"We need supplies, Mr. Bootmunch," said Wull.

"I've got stacks of fennel," said the Bootmunch, "on

account of forgettin' to burn it at the straw devil."

"If he calls me that one more time . . ." said Tillinghast.

Wull put his hand on Tillinghast's shoulder. "We don't need fennel," said Wull. "We need—"

"Fennel," said the Bootmunch, "fennel, fennel, fennel. Help yourself to my fennel. Isn't it a funny word? *Fennel. Fennel.*"

"Stop saying *fennel!*" said Tillinghast.

"I'm awfully sorry, straw devil, sorry—sorry, everyone, sorry! It's just that you've tied me upside down, and all the blood's rather rushed into my fennel."

"We need oars," said Wull firmly, "and enough food for a few days."

"Oh, I have oars. *Plenty* of oars," replied the Bootmunch. "By which I mean two. Two's enough."

"We'll take those, please," said Wull.

"Fine, fine. Let's say six ducats the pair."

"*Six ducats!*" said Tillinghast.

"A reasonable price. As a boatless man, I never use them, but they're made of fine wood. Considered making them into stilts once so I could talk to my tree friends on their own level. But I'd have been too short, anyway; they laughed at me: 'Hhhhhgggnnnnnggghhnn,' they said, 'you're just a little mite next to our stately—'"

"Shut up now," said Wull. "Where are they?"

The Bootmunch waggled his eyebrows. "Money, money, money," he said, then added, "fennel."

Tillinghast grabbed Wull's arm. "An' where're these ducats comin' from?" he hissed.

"Where else?" said Wull wearily. "I'd have used my own money but the bradai stole it, an' you said you'd give me money as trade for comin' with me. I can pay you back."

"I'm not payin' *him!*" said Tillinghast. "He tried to kill me! What's he need money for anyway, livin' out here in a bloody cave?"

"Principle of the thing," said the Bootmunch, swinging jauntily.

"It's only right and proper, Mr. Tillinghast," said Remedie, "and you're . . . mercifully unharmed, after all."

"You button your lip, toots," said Tillinghast.

"Are you goin' to let him speak to you like that?" said Mix as Remedie drew her breath.

The Bootmunch giggled happily.

"I fixed your hand," said Wull, standing between Tillinghast and Remedie. "You said if you came downriver you'd help me."

"Wi' food an' so on—basic needs."

"What's more basic than oars for a boat?" said Mix.

"You stay out o' this, little miss!" said Tillinghast sharply.

"We need these, or we can't go anywhere," said Wull.

"So take 'em!"

"I need to pay," said Wull, looking at Pappa. "There's no discussin' it."

"Then shall we say ten?" said the Bootmunch, swinging his head back and forth and sending the knives in his hair to a melodic ting.

"You'll say six an' be glad to get it," said Wull. His eyes met Tillinghast's and held his stare.

"Fine, fine," said Tillinghast, "but we's takin' other provision for that an' all—'in't no way under the gods I's payin' for your breakfast after this."

"Thank you," said Wull.

"Wonderful news!" said the Bootmunch. "In the spirit of friendship, would you mind awfully cutting me down? The straw devil has rather fixed me to the roof here and I've been hearing the call of nature for some time now."

Mix laughed, and was shushed by Remedie.

Wull looked hard at the young explorer. "We'll let you down only if you apologize for callin' Mr. Tillinghast that name. His name's Mr. Tillinghast, an' it doesn't do for you to be callin' him anythin' else, understand?"

"Of course, old boy, of course. Dreadfully sorry, straw Tillinghast, sorry!"

Tillinghast glowered but said nothing as he cut the Bootmunch down.

Wull respectfully lifted six ducat coins from Tillinghast's money-pouch and handed them to the Bootmunch, who held them to the firelight.

"Seems to be in order," he said, and cackled. "The oars're up the back of the cave, sport, beside all the other rubbish."

"*Other* rubbish?" said Wull, watching the coins vanish about the Bootmunch's person.

The Bootmunch looked at him from the side of his eye. "Figure of speech, sport!" he said, grinning and moving over to Remedie. "Is that a baby, too? How marvelous! Aren't babies wonderful? I miss my infancy: it's to my immense sadness I lost the knack of passing wind and drinking simultaneously once I mastered walking. A shame, a great shame."

Mix laughed while Remedie pursed her lips.

"This is Bonn," she said. "He's sleeping."

"They love their sleep, don't they, the little ones? I'm so very charmed, madam, but equal to my charmedness is confusion at your choice of coterie. Tell me," said the Bootmunch, kissing Remedie on the hand, "how has such a lovely flower found such boorish company?"

"It's jus' bad luck," said Mix. "Wait, you mean the boys, right?"

There came a series of clattering noises, the flat bang of heavy wood falling, and after some muttered curses and slow dragging, Wull emerged into the firelight pulling two long, wide oars, their blades marked with the stamp of an ocean-going trade company. His hands were unable to meet around their width, and they were more than twice his height in length.

"What in gods' are these?" he said, throwing them to the ground. "An' where'd you get all that stuff?"

"These are *o-a-r-s*. You put the flat bit in the water and pull," said the Bootmunch, ignoring the second question. "I thought you knew about boats?"

"I know they're oars, Bootmunch," said Wull, "but they're bloody massive!"

"Are they?" said the Bootmunch. "I always had other chaps for the rowin', I must say. Looked awfully hard work, too! Well, good luck, mustn't detain you."

"I can't use these!" said Wull as Remedie lifted one of the handles and dropped it with a loud report onto the cave floor. "You could row a battleship with these. How am I meant to use them on a bäta?"

"As I said, I always had other chaps for the rowin'. Couldn't give you any advice there, what! Indeed, no! Right, lovely having you visit. Ladies, a pleasure. Straw devil—I'll get you next time! Ha-ha! Fennel! Yes! Friends for now though, the boy insists, friends!"

Tillinghast straightened up, a canvas bag filled with food gripped in his fist beside his hessian sack. "Let's go," he said to Wull.

"I can't even lift these!" said Wull. "This isn't a solution!"

"Best we're gettin' here," said Tillinghast, without turning round, "an' it was you that wanted 'em."

"We should go, Wulliam," said Remedie. "Thank you, Mr. Rushworth." She bobbed a curtsey.

"Such manners!" said the Bootmunch. He looked expectantly at Mix, who squinted at him.

"You've got the worst breath I've ever smelled," she said.

"Beg pardon?" said the Bootmunch.

"Fine," said Wull. "So I've to drag these to the bäta myself, is that it?"

He realized he was talking to no one, and that he was alone in the cave with the Bootmunch, who was giving him an inquisitive, *hungry* look.

"You could stay if you like, squire," said the Bootmunch. He ran his tongue over his lips.

Wull heaved at the handles and dragged the oars into the freezing air, where the milk of dawn was spreading a watery light through the treetops.

15

The *Hellsong*

Of all the seafolk I met, it was a Watchkeep named Ambergris who expressed most succinctly why people choose to put themselves in harm's way on voyages that can last for years at a time: "Whale oil's just about the biggest treasure available," he said (I am, of course, paraphrasing the rough coastal dialect!). "You can make soap and perfumes and clothing and grease for factories and machines, and clothes and corsets and obviously candles and lamps. Folk used to carry it around to keep themselves from plague. It's worth more than gold. If it didn't stink of fish, posh ladies would dangle it from their ears." In this assessment Ambergris was right in every respect but one: whale oil is not "just about" the greatest treasure; it is, for all the reasons detailed above, without question the world's preeminent treasure!

–Gentling Norbury, The People's Sea

"What're these, First Mate?" said Samjon. The morning's low sun caught him through the porthole, and he screwed up his face.

Ormidale glanced at the cabin boy and then continued unpacking the crate.

"I shudn't be surprised you dun't know," he said. "Where's you from again? Coll?"

"Clell," said Samjon, indignant. "I'd rather drown meself than be a Collander."

Ormidale gave him a sideways glance. "Clell and Coll are less'n a mile apart. They's almost the same place."

"Heavens above, that ain't so! We's goat farmers in Clell. In Coll they farm *sheep*," said Samjon, shuddering.

"I'm sure they's both the same at nighttime," said Ormidale. "Leastways, it's no kind o' fishin' life. 'S a wonder then you ended up on a whaler an' no wonder you 'in't seen these afore. Mind you, 's only the cap'n uses these. It's a secret o' his—'e had 'em made special."

"So what is they?"

"Gongs," said Ormidale, running his hand over the huge brass disk. "You puts them in the water an' pull the rope—see how the beater's hinged there?—an' the gong bangs under the water. There's six of 'em all round the ship."

"Why?" said Samjon. "So's the whale thinks it's dinner an' comes lookin' for the bait?"

"Not *quite*," said Ormidale. "They finds the noise confusin', like the cap'n's talkin' to 'em. With this mormorach thing, he reckons it'll cause it all manner o' problems—might even kill it."

"How's he know that?" said Samjon, eyes wide.

"I dun't know. It's the cap'n, 'in't it? He jus' knows things. He's been listenin' to it shoutin' an' reckons these're the way to go. He's a genius. Mind you," Ormidale added, looking about the hold, "if you asks me, he's—"

"He's what?" said Murdagh, stepping around the galley.

"Too handsome for his own good," finished Ormidale. "C'mon now, cabin boy. Help me up on deck with these."

"Too handsome?" said Samjon, confused. "You know, by the tone o' your voice, I thought you was goin' to say something more negati—"

"There we go, lad!" shouted Ormidale, heaving the first gong onto the pulley's platform. "You jus' pull on that rope there, an' I'll be off upstairs to load it overboard. Aye, Cap'n, aye," he added, saluting Murdagh as he passed, pressing against the wall and sliding onto the main deck.

"We's goin' to talk to the mormorach, Cap'n?" said Samjon.

"In a manner o' speakin'," said Murdagh, flashing a brown smile and running his stump-fingered hands over the gong's surface. "We'll be givin' it some noise to deal wi' anyway. When these gets in the water and sets to ringin' you'll feel it in your sheep farmer's bones."

"Goat farmer's," said Samjon.

"Same thing," said Murdagh, stamping off into his quarters and slamming the door.

"'In't the same thing at all," muttered Samjon, "lest a pickerel's the same as a gutback, an' I don't think *that's* true. . . ." He rapped the gong with his knuckle. Its *bong* resounded in the hold, deep and long and inside everything—wood, men, and metal—so that it rang through his bones and quivered the eyes in his head.

It's the sound a god would make, thought Samjon, and flicked its surface again.

The gong lifted in steady bursts, chiming as the swell moved its hammer, ringing like approaching thunder as the hatches opened and the rain dappled its polished surface.

"Send the next one, lad!" shouted Ormidale once it had been unloaded, his face a black dot against the brilliant, pouring square of sky.

"I can't. . . ." started Samjon, looking at the other gongs. Each weighed several times more than he did. "I—"

"Hurry up, cabin boy!" shouted Trehv, the bo'sun.

"But I can't. . . ." Samjon glanced at the captain's quarters. "Hang on!"

He took a few steps and opened Murdagh's door.

"Cap'n, I can't load up the—"

"What business has ye bargin' into my quarters?" roared Murdagh, naked but for his johns.

"I'm sorry!" said Samjon. "Oh, Cap'n, I'm sorry!"

"Take yer hands from yer face, boy," said Murdagh.

Samjon did so. Murdagh stood very still, his weathered skin bathed in the thin light of the cabin, his damaged, ruined eyes burning into Samjon's.

The captain's body was decimated, cut and withered like a steak left to sun, its internal threading pressed to the surface in purple tangles of thick veins. His back, crooked and pained-looking, was caged by pale baleen struts, sagged through by loose skin like trussed putty. Below the waist, emerging with a frightening round tightness, was Murdagh's half leg, a thin finger of grubby, ribbed skin.

"Take a look at the sea's price, lad, if that's what ye've come to gawp at," said Murdagh quietly, holding his arms to his sides.

"Cap'n, I'm sorry," said Samjon, feeling tears in his eyes. "I's jus' lookin' for help with the gongs. It was the gongs was all."

Murdagh snorted and sat on his bed. The small, gloomy cabin smelled of peppermint and lakoris, and, more overwhelming still, of stasis—the ingrained grime of decades lived in a narrow rhythm.

"Gilt's not to be gettin' his nap time, it seems," he muttered. He lifted his terrifying, pale bone leg, its tip ground by wood and stone, and began to strap it to his stump.

"You's not a whaler at heart, boy. It's there in the swing o' yer legs an' the pallor o' yer face. Most men who find themsel's aboard a ship like this is runnin' from somethin' on land: coin, crime, disgrace—maybe you's touched up the wrong sheep? Ye'll find no judgment here on . . ."

"They're *goats*," said Samjon before he could stop himself.

"It's the same thing, lad, an' ye'll be served well by no' interruptin' yer captain. The point is"—Murdagh stood, tested the false leg, began to wrap the joint in thick linen—"there's another group who's been called to the sea from the moment they wriggled out their mammies' trenches, an' the longer the first group sails, the more they realize they's always been part o' the second. All of us are called to sea; jus' some of us has better hearin'. You miss the land, but you's not yet realized what it means to live on the water.

"Think on the respectful, dignified, *hidden* violence o' the sea, all its monsters floating, graceful as angels, all those masses o' death-bringin' teeth and tusk as smooth in that world as heavenly bodies in the sky. Think about the messy predation o' the land, all its beasts chargin' an soilin' an' matin' in noisome lumps."

Murdagh hefted a flat strip of bone and pointed it at Samjon before splinting his right forearm.

"Think on the beautiful tints of the sea, the loveliest tints of azure an' emerald, as rich a spectrum as sky could muster an' such as could never be glimpsed in a precious stone dug out the ground. Think on the sea's livin', glitterin' body, then think o' the mud o' the docile soil, an' tell me ye don't feel like spittin'. Why did the old tribes o' the north or the Sadani or the ancient Poogs hold the sea to be holy? Why are there gods in their hundreds for its care an' worship but only a han'ful for the land? Think o' your reflection in the surface o' water: only the sea can show ye to yersel' an' tell ye who ye really are. The land shows naught but its own muck."

A tear escaped and ran down Samjon's cheek. Murdagh shifted the baleen on his ribs with a grunt, then started to wind the linen over his waist and onto his torso.

"An' think on the whale," he said. "The thing about a whale is, he knows when ye moves alongside him, he *knows* ye're goin' to try an' spear him, an' he challenges ye to kill him. He looks at ye, an' if a shark's got lifeless, black eyes, a whale's got warm eyes, warmer'n cragolodon or mairlan or anythin' else. He looks at ye with eyes as deep as yer own soul, an' he *chooses* to fight ye. There's dignity in that fight, that desire to fight, an' you's not goin' to find that on the land. I'm not sayin' your sheep don't struggle—"

"They're *goats*, Cap'n, an' we don't . . ." said Samjon, his words out between his tears before he knew it.

"Sheep, goats, rhats, cats—whatever they are, they're land animals, an' they'll never have the *dignity* o' the whale," said Murdagh, dressing in his trousers and boots and coat, growing bigger and more fierce in his wardrobe, the vulnerability of the thin man Samjon had found vanished by the fabric.

"Yes, Cap'n," said Samjon.

"An' sure," said Murdagh, dropping his hat onto his head, "it's whales've done this to me. They's taken bits o' me as they could, an' they's broken me down, but I've taken 'em in their thousands onto this ship, an' I'll take this damn mormorach if it's the last o' me that's needed for it. When I have that beast's skin, I'll make myself such a cloak. . . . I'll feast on his meat and throw bits o' him to the birds. I don't need his bounty—I want his *title*. I want to face the sea's champion an' crush him till he bursts. If it ends not here I'll follow him thrice an' more round the world to hold his dead heart in my hands, an' you's signed up to go too, young Samjon, until either me or him is dead by the other."

Samjon nodded. He hadn't moved since entering the cabin and now stood in the open doorway, a fully dressed Murdagh before him, his dreadful crutch tucked into his arm, the familiar leer on his face.

"You get on deck an' send the bo'sun an' his mate to get the gongs," said Murdagh. "An', cabin boy," he added as Samjon fled to the stairs, his voice softer, quiet, "tell them I gave you three lashes for the delay."

Samjon smiled gratefully. "Thank you, Cap'n," he said, then scrambled up into the light.

Behind him, Murdagh glowered, ran his hands over his back, then closed the cabin door.

The Danék Wilds

Wull woke, drifting, dusted by a puff of fresh snow—little towers of it on his sleeves and head. He brushed himself off, compacting the powder into a smear. The seized claws of his hands held the Bootmunch's gigantic oars tight to his chest, but without guidance the bäta was twirling through the floes across the river's breadth, accompanied by the quietly slipping blues and grays of seulas. The banks were lined heavily by white trees, invisible against the white cloud, the land almost disappearing around them.

He looked at Tillinghast sleeping under his hat, the gray strip of Pappa beside him—head heavy on his stringy neck, hung forward, drooling. Wull reached out, took the spit string on his glove, then looked over his shoulder, saw Mix and Remedie sleeping too, Mix tucked into Remedie's chest, Bonn, his unmoving face puckered upward, clutched in Remedie's arms.

Wull took in the growing brightness of the sky, felt in its light the new day's imperceptible warmth, and stretched the pain from his spine. High against the clouds spun the unmoving silhouettes of birds gliding on unseen thermals.

His wrist was locked to stone. He tried to move it gently, pushing against the steel of his tendons as much as he dared, feeling it close to snapping. His face, too, burned painfully— less so now that Remedie's smear of mud had worked into it, but still enough to pull the rest of his face in a permanent rictus of discomfort. Added to the ache of his shoulders and arms, he felt the fraying of the thin fabrics that held him to- gether, every tiny strand of tissue that kept him from bursting apart screaming under the strain: a tension that started in his acid-boiled guts and moved out through his bones and his muscles into the innermost coils of his mind.

He sometimes reflected that it was not, perhaps, a good thing to be so intimate with the tightly packed wonder of slippery mass that was the human body: it didn't help his headache that he could picture exactly the brain's jellied lump pulsing inside his skull, or know, when they screeched fire at him in the night, the miracle of compression that pressed the slick guts inside a human torso.

Better to live in ignorance and deal with the outside, he thought as he drank from his pouch, looking at Tillinghast. *An' the gods know that's bad enough anyway.*

The water was ice-crisp in the pouch's skin. It hurt his teeth.

He began to row with the ton-weight oars, found the current by instinct, turned the bäta's nose into it and felt it kick gratefully ahead, like a horse loosed for play. He kicked the sole of Tillinghast's boot.

"Wake up, Till," he said. "It's mornin'."

"Hmm? What? Oh . . . what?" Tillinghast lifted his hat from his face and squinted at him.

"We all fell asleep," said Wull. "It's a fair, bright, clear day. There's seulas with us, an' birds—look like faelkons."

Tillinghast shuffled uncomfortably. "Where are they? In the trees?"

"No," said Wull, "the sky. They're miles away—nothin' to worry about." He laughed. "Faelkons nest on the ground anyways. You wouldn't likely find 'em in trees."

Tillinghast peered at the sky until he found the faelkons' shadows. "'S long as they stay there," he muttered. "Dun't like birds."

"What's wrong wi' birds?"

"They's dirty: horrible feathers, flapping noise, ticks on

'em. . . ." said Tillinghast. "I dun't like the way they moves. It's their bobbin' heads when they gets close to you with their ugly feet. Faelkons is the worst an' all—ugly blaggards: no beaks, dirty big teeth, bits o' wood." He shuddered.

"I like birds," said Wull. "Look at how free they are." He watched the birds' swoops for a moment, graceful specks whirlpooling like flotsam through an eddy's funnel.

"Free to mess on my hat, more like," said Tillinghast. "You ever seen a faelkon's mess? 'S like a bloody omelet, so it is."

"I wish we hadn't slept," said Wull. He puffed out his cheeks. "I don't know how much time we've lost, but I'd rather have it back. This is why we should take turns rowin'."

Tillinghast dropped his hat back onto his face, snorted, and muttered something unintelligible.

"What was that?" said Wull. "If you jus' said the words *payin' customer*, I swear . . ."

"Well, I am a payin' customer!" said Tillinghast, reappearing from under his hat. "Paid for those bloody oars, didn't I?"

"Untie the arms!" said Pappa, spluttering into life. "Untie the arms!"

"I can't!" said Wull. "And, sure, thanks, heaviest oars in the damn world—you could row a warship with these! If my wrist wasn't sore before . . ."

"Good morning, gentlemen," said Remedie. She yawned

and stretched, then flicked the swaddling from Bonn's face and smiled at him. "Let's not bicker like children, shall we? There can't be far to go now, and it befits no one to debase themselves with gutter talk."

"Who's got gutter talk?" said Tillinghast. "'In't nobody had any gutter talk—jus' *him* moanin' again."

"I wouldn't moan if you would jus' bloody well row," said Wull. He started the blades in the water again, his body popping under the renewed strain.

"You know, it's real funny how you's been complainin' about havin' me an' the ladies here with you, an' yet you'd still rather I take a turn an' help out. If you wants to do it all yourself, then do so an' don't be bringin' me this rot all the time."

"I wouldn't even *need* you to take a turn if the bäta wasn't so damn full! I could row Pappa an' me to the North End!" said Wull.

"Well, we are here now, and we're very grateful, Wulliam," said Remedie. "Aren't we, my love?" She ran a finger over Bonn's cheek. "After all that running through the woods I'm just so happy to be safe here, having a gentle journey downstream, without having to worry about any of the dangers of the road. And Mix is too," she added.

"Oh, sure," said Mix grumpily, her face still sewn tight with sleep stitches. "Delighted. What a lovely snooze I had on the wooden boards, an' bein' woken by fightin' is the most cheerful welcome." She held out her hand for the water.

"I don't want gratitude," said Wull. "I'm glad to help—I am—even if you just snuck onto my boat—it's what Pappa would have wanted me to do."

"Good man," said Tillinghast.

"I wasn't talkin' to you," said Wull, heaving against the water. A seula broke the surface and blinked at him, twitching its whiskers at the smell of fish heads.

"Now, boys," said Remedie, "you're narking for the sake of it. I'm quite sure you wouldn't even be able to tell me what started all this, would you?"

"Wull's annoyed Till won't row, and Till's annoyed Wull doesn't appreciate his contribution," said Mix without opening her eyes.

Remedie sighed. "Thank you, Mix."

"That's jus' it!" said Tillinghast triumphantly. "My *contribution*! Money and strength is what I brings, an' is it appreciated? Is it, hell!"

"What about *my* contribution? I sewed on your damn hand!"

"Which got bitten off by that ursa when I was savin' you, wasn't I?"

"You only did that 'cause you like fightin'—an' I've rowed you this whole way since! An' I reckon we'd already be there if—"

"Don't," said Tillinghast.

"Don't what? What's that mean? 'Don't.' That doesn't mean anythin'."

"Don't," said Tillinghast quietly.

"Don't bloody well what?" shouted Wull.

They stared at each other while Wull rowed a few strokes.

"He means don't ask him to take a turn rowin'," said Mix. "Right, Till?"

"*Thank* you, Mix," said Remedie.

"So, will nobody help me for a bit?" said Wull. "Mix?"

"I'm a tiny little girl," said Mix. "When it suits me, like."

"And I'm afraid I must tend to Bonn," said Remedie, rocking the baby against her breast. "But in fact, Wulliam, would you hold on to him for just a minute, please?"

"I . . . Well, I need to row now," said Wull.

"It'll only take a moment—I'm afraid my garments have twisted in the night, and I must rearrange my underskirts. . . . I trust you'll avert your eyes like a gentleman, Mr. Tillinghast?"

"It's that or lose 'em," said Tillinghast. "Reckon I'd turn to stone if I clapped eyes on that."

"And wouldn't we miss you terribly?" said Remedie. "I think I'd stand you in my garden to keep pests from the vegetables." She placed Bonn in Wull's arms, supporting the baby's head until the last second, stepping back with her eyes on his delicate face.

"Nothin' spoils a romance quicker'n a woman with a

sense of humor," said Tillinghast, trailing his fingers over the side, flicking away a seula's questing nose.

"Then let me ensure I'm at my wittiest, Mr. Tillinghast, so I might spoil your pickle in its jar."

Mix and Wull laughed. Tillinghast grumbled wordlessly into the water.

"Good one, miss," said Mix.

"Thank you," said Remedie, rummaging with her voluminous skirts. "I rather thought so."

Wull, holding Bonn high on his chest, his face close to the baby's, felt again the strength inside the inanimate shape, the energy that seemed to somehow press back against his hands. Bonn, weighted by some internal mass, was heavier than seemed possible. Wull watched the bank, looking for movement, and found his eyes pulled to the sky. "They faelkons are gettin' right close," he said. "Look at the size o' them."

"Here, Wulliam," said Remedie. "I'll take him back now."

"Right," said Wull. "Is he . . . Is he all right? In the bäta, I mean?"

"He's quite well, and thank you for asking," said Remedie, smiling. "He knows it'll not be long until we're there."

"It's not goin' to be that soon, miss," said Wull. "We've not even passed through the city, an' from there there's plenty miles left. We won't be there till night comes."

"Then it'll be a day of no walking and good company," said Remedie.

"Ha!" said Tillinghast.

Wull touched Bonn's nose. "I'm glad he's all right," he said, turning in his seat and holding Bonn up to be taken.

As Remedie leaned down, arms outstretched, a shadow crossed her face and all color drained from her skin.

"Gods, no!" she screamed, throwing herself forward.

Wull turned, too late, into the talons of a gigantic faelkon: a fist of black glass, long grasping blades curved and terrible and bigger than his head. They spread out, the fist opening inches from his eyes—talons stuck with foulness, clinging blood, and tiny feathers, the ruts of the huge palm map-lined with flaky dirt.

As Wull's mouth filled with the decaying whoosh of its wings, he moved instinctively and saw the faelkon's dreadful claws piercing Bonn's white tummy, lifting the baby from Remedie's scrambling reach, vanishing in a burst of shrill, grating noise as time caught up with his horror and left Wull on the bäta's bottom boards, heart leaping at the walls of his chest.

"BONN! BONN!" screamed Remedie, veins sticking from her neck, her eyes wide with fury. "YOU CURSED PIGEONS! I'LL RIP YOUR GODS-DAMNED HEARTS OUT!!"

The faelkon beat quickly into the sky, Bonn slack in its

grip, his swaddling cloth hanging loose beneath him.

Tillinghast hadn't moved. "It's got my hat," he said as the waters around them thrashed with diving birds snatching seulas whole and squealing from the river.

"BONN!" screamed Remedie. "Get to shore, get to shore now! Row, row, Wulliam!"

Wull gathered himself, climbed into the keep's seat.

"Pappa," he said, turning the bäta for shore. "Are you all right? Pappa?"

Pappa's eyes swirled in his head. "Untie the arms?" he said.

Wull almost laughed with relief, rowed harder.

"Hurry!" said Remedie. "Hurry, Wulliam, we're losing sight of them!"

"Watch out!" said Mix.

The bäta hammered into the bank, sending Remedie over the side and facefirst onto the frozen ground. She rose without pausing, blood streaming from her mouth as she ran at the faelkons' fading shadows, skirts gathered in her fist.

Wull jumped after her, grabbing a harpoon. "Mix, look after Pappa—Till, come on!"

Tillinghast hadn't moved.

"It took my hat," he said. "It nearly *touched* me."

"Are you joking?" said Wull. "It's taken Bonn. Remedie's gone after it on her own. Come with me, for gods' sakes!"

"I can't," said Tillinghast, shaking his head and crouching farther into his seat. "I can't be dealin' with birds. I can't."

"We need you! I'm nowhere near as strong as you—we need you to help us!"

"Not a chance! But listen, Wull?"

"Yes?"

"Keep an eye out for my hat, eh?"

"You . . . gudgeon!" said Wull, blank faced. "What about Bonn?"

"A wooden doll?" said Tillinghast. "You 'spect me to go after those things to save a doll? It's not even a real baby!"

"And you're not a real man!" said Wull. He spat on the ground and sprinted after Remedie, leaving Tillinghast silent and furious in the swaying bäta.

16

Decatur House

Bash the river! Pour hate on its wretchedness! Well may it be wretched, but so might be we, were we to be beneath the split pink faces of ten thousand privies, content to hold open our mouths for the patter of their brown tongues! We, the populace, stuff the river's throat with the guts of hogs and the dung of cattle, the sweepings of tanneries and butchers and halls of slaughter—and complain its breath is foul! We, the populace, are content for it to carry, like the sailboats of grim children, an endless pageant of dead dogs and rhats and cats and fowl, and for this rancid chowder of drownèd beasts (season'd by scabs of lettuce and turnip tops) to heat under the sun till its gases burn the skin—and complain that it tastes sour! When considering the extent of its feculence, ladies and gentlemen, is it any wonder that my daily swims have, of late, been weekly done?

–Transcript of Oceanus Crissenger's "Great River! We Are Sorry!"
Green Hollows Club lecture series

He'd spent over an hour in the chicken coop, twice that patching a rust-eaten gutter, and a painful twenty minutes stretching into the sarcophagus to paint a bald conductor with silver, so by the time he had untangled the tapeworm, salinized the jars of organs, and tended the wicker Things, Clutterbuck was exhausted.

The Things tired him the most: they were growing at different rates, and not evenly. The week before last the Thing on five legs had hobbled back from the frozen lake, swollen down one side and fluffy with damp growths. Even now it walked with a two-legged limp. Their voicelessness was becoming a problem too—without speech, he could never be sure they understood his cautions, and so off they went into the world, ruining themselves.

But then, they were just *Things*, shapes. There was nowhere for the voice to go, but still character was emerging even in silence, each Thing interestingly influenced by its shape and, therefore, its interaction with its environment, the ability to climb stairs, trees, and so on. It was fascinating, no question. . . .

He prepared a simple lunch—salt pork, black bread, tomatoes, and root tea—and sat in his clove-smelling, crackling workshop, listening to the snap of the flames and the thump of cane stem on stone as the Things ran about outside, the stump of his handless right arm resting on his knee.

"Banqueting hall, this was," he said to Mac, the mostly raven.

"Hello," garbled Mac, clawing the red beard that covered the little scientist almost to his eyes.

"Before your time, of course," said Clutterbuck, holding up a piece of pork for the bird. "Mam and Pap would have dances here, with all the village, candles and wine. . . ."

"Hello," garbled Mac again, gobbling the pork in his long black beak.

"All worth it, of course. One cannot place a value on science. Look at you, the Things, all the others. . . ." He cut a tomato into pieces, scooped up the stray seeds, and laid them on the bread. "Science is without price. Gold tarnishes, but knowledge will enrich the whole world. The whole world, my Mac!"

"Again," said Mac, head bouncing. He flapped his párrát's wings—long and tapered and blue—then settled again on his perch.

Clutterbuck held up another piece of pork. Around him, glassware bubbled and steamed, looping cords of filtration dripped into vivid pots, and gears of all sizes clicked and whirred.

"Yes, I know I've told you this before," he said. "It's just when I sit near the portrait of my old pap . . . I can feel him looking at me, wondering what's become of his house."

Mac flapped his wings, throwing dust onto Clutterbuck's lunch and upending a titration flask.

"Mac!" said Clutterbuck, righting the glass and stemming the spill with his sleeve. "That took me a whole . . . oh, never mind. I don't suppose . . . Yes, little one?" he said to a wicker Thing who'd appeared at his side. "You mustn't run like that with the fire so high—running is for summer. Sum-mer."

The Thing pulled at the space where his right hand had been.

"Ow! Oh, do be careful, my angel," said Clutterbuck, rising and allowing himself to be led to the entrance hall.

Another Thing lay still on the carpet, its three legs twisted beneath it.

"What have you been doing?" he said, scooping it into his arms. "What have I told you about that balcony? Dear, oh dear, that's quite a job you've made for me. I don't know. . . ."

The Thing raised an arm and touched his face.

"I know," said Clutterbuck. "I love you too."

As he was heading back to the workshop, there came a rapping at the door, the big brass lapphund's head falling three times, nearly bending the wood.

"Who on earth could this be?" he said, placing the Thing on a chair and holding out his arm for Mac, who flew to his wrist and climbed onto his head. "When was our last visitor, Mac?"

"Hello," said Mac, picking at a scab on Clutterbuck's forehead with his beak.

"You're probably right, you know," said Clutterbuck, turning the handle.

A large man stood in the portico, the rest of the Things gathered around him, tugging his coat and scuttling nervously.

"Hello?" said Clutterbuck. "Don't touch our guest, be off with you!" He waved his empty sleeve at the doorframe. A bell sounded, and the Things scattered. "I'm sorry, sir; they're inquisitive, is all. They wouldn't hurt a fly. Now, yes, off you go. . . . How may I help you, sir?"

The man held up a piece of paper.

"'I am a weary traveller,'" Clutterbuck read aloud. "Well, *traveler* has only one *v*, but still, I assume you're not seeking linguistic advice. How may I help you?"

The man turned the paper to himself, scribbled more words.

"'I am in need of rest and shelter from the cold,'" read Clutterbuck. "'I can pay you for your . . . trouble,' does that say?"

The man nodded.

"Well, there's no payment required, good sir!" said Clutterbuck, spreading his arms and sending Mac onto the antlers of a wall-mounted elk. "You must have traveled through the night, and we're only too happy to have guests. What a treat! Oh yes, a treat, absolutely. Come in, come in. You must be half frozen. Give me your coat, yes, and you can set your boots there. . . ."

Clutterbuck, chatting happily, turned toward the kitchen and the range's heat, the wet, freezing, tinkling coat clutched in his hand.

Behind him, Mr. Pent swapped his paper and quill for a box of matches, dropped them into his trouser pocket, threw a ball of sticky rose tobacco at Mac, and followed the reedy little scientist, smiling.

The wicker Things, dragging the broken, twisted one between them, fled, clacking into the darkness and the corners and the hidden spaces of the attic.

The Thrick

The sharp hands of the forest tore at Wull as he ran, his boots slipping on puddles of ice and snowbursts in the pools of spread roots. The woods were filled with a blindness of white fog that hung like a curtain between the trees, settling on the thornbushes like cobwebs, and through it he saw nothing. He heard only the frantic breath of Remedie ahead, and kept following her as fast as his feet would allow.

The harpoon's weight had almost toppled him more

than once, and he carried it now in both hands, held against his body as he ran.

"Remedie!" he shouted. "Remedie!"

His voice seemed to die on his lips. There was no answer, only her glimpsed breathing and the movement of foliage.

Wull ran on. His pounding heartbeat had spread from his breastbone to his seized back, throbbing wrist, and swollen cheek, until his whole body rang with it. Inside the sharp heat of his seula-gut shift and fur-lined clothes he felt himself boiling even as the exposed skin of his eyes froze solid.

He leaped a stream, landing badly on bare rock and tearing his trousers. Fallen trees loomed around him, the craters beneath the roots' raw fingers deep and white.

"Remedie!" he shouted again, finding his feet and pushing on. "Wait for me! I can't help if I can't catch you!"

"Hurry up!" came the reply, a muffled voice, tiny in the thick distance.

"I'm trying. I'm . . . trying. . . ." he said, and ran on, fording another stream and scurrying over a mossy boulder.

He ran farther, the harpoon slipping in his grip, and then found himself at the edge of a clearing that ran into the far edge of his vision. Remedie stood still at its edge, a heavy stick in her hand, listening.

"Where . . . are—" he started.

"Ssh!" she hissed without turning around. "They're here—you can smell them. And look."

Wull peered into the fog, tumbling in currents from huge dark shapes. The air was rancid with flesh rot and the sourness of mold, a sick-making poison that entered his mouth and nose and filled his stomach with unsettled gas. Peering farther, he saw the seulas: sausages of dark blubber, dead and dying, their mournful bleating audible now in the stillness.

Around him the trees were coated with pale, gray scrapings that were flecked with feathers and spots of dark blood. He looked down. The ground was uneven, lumps of grass and clods of earth under a layer of white frost and snow, between which ran a carpet of small bones—skulls tipped with rodent teeth; rib cages the size of his palm; little legs and plates and joints—all smothered in pellets of murky green fluff, so that the little creatures seemed to have drowned in a thick, intestinal soup.

"They know we're here," whispered Remedie.

"So what do we do?" said Wull.

"We find Bonn, and kill them if they try to stop us," she said simply, and took a careful step onto the nesting grounds.

The faelkons' guttural, scratching shriek went up around them—a sound that started in their bellies and ended in their skulls. As they moved, twenty or more of them, Wull saw their ugly, skin-slack faces leering at him, the cracked plates of their horselike teeth pushed out on long pink gums, wet and glistening between loose lips. Wooden splints stuck out from their wings and backs, as though their skeletons had grown larger than their bodies.

They spread out around Wull and Remedie, moving with burped sounds and clicking teeth. Even grounded and walking on two legs, wings at their sides, they were far bigger than Wull, and close enough that he could see the detail in their furious, yellow, black-lined eyes.

"So what do we *do?*" he said as the faelkons, ranked in solid lines, spread their wings and began to scream in a terrible, pressing rhythm, the flexing of their muscles and skin rippling the hackles of their wooden spines in agitated twitches.

"Hit them and run," Remedie said, and vanished.

The faelkons screamed again and half rose from the ground, their huge wings sending spiraling clouds of stinking fog around him and clearing a brief space through which he saw Remedie running—pursued by a dozen giant birds—turning and battering the closest one about the face with her stick, screaming Bonn's name.

As the fog settled, Wull saw the birds that had stayed for him: eight or nine, all fully grown, all focused on him, clacking their teeth as though conspiring. He hefted the harpoon in his hands.

"All right," he said. "You're jus' birds. Come on then!"

A faelkon stepped beside him, corpse-rotten stench pouring from its body, half his height again, its face sharp and angry, a fat branch leaning from its neck. It howled at him, its long, pitted teeth buried in deep, bright gums, its black tongue whipping like a ribbon.

Wull reached in and grabbed it, pulling his hand back just as the teeth snapped shut. The faelkon looked confused, then howled again—louder—spread its wings, and came at him.

"Aaaaargh!" said Wull, swinging the harpoon with all his strength. The barb caught the bird on the stomach, tearing out feathers and skin, and it squawked backward, scrabbling at the ground.

The weight of the iron pulled Wull almost flat, but he heaved it in a round swing behind him, driving back the feathered wall that had surrounded him in a hail of angry cries.

"Remedie!" he shouted. "Are you all right? Remedie?"

There was no answer, but a faelkon's shriek was cut off with a thump, and Wull smiled to himself as he jabbed the harpoon again. Something crunched under his feet. He looked down into a massive nest filled with fur-smothered bones. Among them were the shells of eggs—as big as a soup pot and pink on the inside.

He looked for Bonn, found nothing, swung the harpoon, and ran into another nest, the faelkons swooping along behind him, the air filled with the rank scent of their feathers.

"Remedie, I can't see him!" he shouted.

"Keep looking!" she replied, her voice a whisper in the clouds, grunting as she swung her stick about.

"I am! There's nothing in the nests but—"

A faelkon grabbed at Wull, its outstretched talon ripping his coat, spilling its fur lining like torn skin. He stumbled back, stabbed the bird's belly with the harpoon, felt the barb sink into the muscular body and stick there. He twisted, roaring, and pushed again, driving farther inside the creature; heard it wail in pain, its cries sending the others into a flapping rage as hot, dark blood poured down the harpoon's length onto his hands.

"Get back!" he shouted. "Get back!"

The faelkon gave a half flap of its wings, fell, then turned, moving into the fog, the harpoon still sticking from its front, wobbling and pouring with blood.

The other birds, their rot-blanched skin close enough to taste, crowded toward him. Wull looked at his empty hands.

"Oh gods," he said, and ran.

He barged through their ranks, feathers snagging on his coat like thorns as the birds grabbed with teeth and talons, half rising like cat-startled crows.

He ran through another nest, found nothing, ran into a faelkon and bounced off, trying desperately to keep his feet, anything to avoid falling.

Another nest: bones, red flesh, eggs—and a white lump wrapped in swaddling.

"Bonn!" he shouted. He tried to turn, but the dead bulk of a seula loomed through the fog, and he tripped on its neck, his ankle turning under him, sending him to the ground.

Reaching over the seula's body, he stretched for Bonn, his fingers nearly touching the white wooden skin, when a huge foot reached down in flight and snatched the baby into the air.

"No!" shouted Wull as Remedie streamed into view and leaped, her stick falling beside him, her hands grabbing the low-hanging piece of swaddling, pulling herself into the air and screaming obscenities as the bird, startled, struggled for height before disappearing into the fog again.

Wull grabbed Remedie's stick, found it was broken, and rolled out of the way of a taloned smash as all the remaining faelkons turned on him.

He ran again, sprinting blindly for the tree line, all his pains forgotten; heard the birds take to the air behind him, ready to swoop and stamp him down. His long, skinny legs kicked with an extra fright of speed, faster even than when the ursa had chased him through the woods, and as the whump of their wings closed on him and their shrieks built to a crescendo, he threw himself into the shadow of a long-limbed tree and scrambled into its branches.

They reared up instantly on every side like dogs after a balgair, burping and squawking and screaming at him, their black tongues and yellow eyes all reaching for him behind the horrible clack of their huge, brown-fractured teeth. He beat down at them with his boots, shouting, catching their faces and sending them back, cracking their bark spikes and making them scream, but each time one fell back it was replaced by another, angrier bird reaching farther into the tree, fluttering and crashing and smashing the boughs in its attempt to get to him.

He saw it then: they would break the branches of his cage and they would get to him.

"Blaggard birds!" he shouted again, slipping as he swung his boots and hugging the trunk. "Blaggard, stinking birds!"

There was a thump on the nesting grounds. The faelkons turned, howling. Then, as Wull gripped the trunk with his legs and his arms, they moved back to the clearing, their wings shifting the fog and sending tendrils of it spinning outward—revealing Remedie beside the body of a dead giant, her foot on its head, Bonn wrapped tightly against her chest.

The other faelkons barked and shrieked but stayed back, panting and heaving their lurid breath as she walked through their ranks, her face smudged with blood, her eyes and hair wild. As she approached Wull in his tree, the birds pounced on the body of their dead comrade and began to tear it apart, turning its richly feathered, powerful bulk into a red mess of torn string, the air filling with the sharp urgency of flesh and death alongside the birds' odor.

Remedie looked up at Wull and smiled serenely.

"Hiding?" she said.

"One of them took my harpoon!" he said, sliding down beside her. "I killed it, I think, an' did my best with a few others."

"You did well," she said, touching his face. "A brave boy. Your pappa would be proud."

Wull looked down, said nothing. Remedie turned to the faelkons, now gorging on the meat of the bird she'd killed.

"Disgusting, isn't it? The way they turn on their own."

Wull watched the faelkons chugging down the pouring meat, their ugly faces already pink with its blood.

"'S just nature, miss," he said. "'S better than buryin' it, in some ways. They've got no shovels in any case."

She laughed, lifted the swaddling from Bonn's face, kissed his nose.

"Is he all right?" said Wull.

"He's . . . fine," said Remedie, "but there's a wound in his side from its claw."

She moved the cloth, and Wull saw it: a round hole three inches across, disappearing into the darkness of Bonn's belly.

"Gods," said Wull, "but he'll be all right?"

Remedie tucked Bonn back inside his swaddling. "He won't be the same," she said, "but he'll live."

Wull sighed. Bonn's face hadn't changed. Of course it hadn't. But it seemed impossible, when Wull had felt the living weight within Bonn's body, that he could have borne such an injury in stoic silence.

"An' are you all right, miss?" he said.

Remedie nodded. "I'm fine, thank you, Wulliam."

"How'd you kill that thing? You'd no weapons!"

"I broke its neck between my boots—the tricky part was trying to land it."

Wull nodded. "Yes, miss," he said.

"There's a lesson for you, young man," she said, strapping Bonn to her chest and stepping forward.

"Yes, miss," said Wull again, understanding nothing.

"And here," said Remedie, producing Tillinghast's hat from a fold of skirt. "*You* can give it to him."

Wull took the hat and nodded, then followed her into the woods, the yelping, screeching convocation of faelkons fading into silence as the trees and the fog closed about them once more.

Despite trying his best to catch up, he walked behind Remedie, her sure, quick steps never failing, keeping her always a few paces ahead. She wore the damp clouds of the forest's mist like a shawl, pushing through sheets of it and finding branches to support her movements by instinct. Wull fell more than once following the same path, finding slick moss where she met solid ground and missing the branches that supported her effortless weight. But as they approached the river and the fog lifted, he caught up, walking alongside her toward the bäta and the water.

"You made it then?" said Tillinghast, opening his eyes at the sound of footsteps.

"Thanks to Wulliam, and no thanks to you," said Remedie, stepping into the boat, her hair screwing outward, her face brown with dry blood.

"Are you all right?" said Mix.

"I'm very well, thank you. But I won't say the same for the bird that took my Bonn away."

Mix whistled. "Good effort there, miss."

"Here," said Wull, tossing Tillinghast's hat across the bäta. "How's Pappa?"

"You got it!" said Tillinghast, delighted. "Stinks o' birds' mess now, but that's all right. I's 'ad it smellin' worse."

"Paps is fine," said Mix. "Ate a bit, then slept." She wiped a thread of Pappa's dribble onto her sleeve.

"Thank you," said Wull. "Have you eaten this morning? Bootmunch gave us some dried meat and fruit." He bit into a stick of dry black elk meat.

Mix shook her head. "I'm fine. I've never liked that stuff anyway. What you call it? Vénnton?"

"You haven't eaten a thing since I've seen you here. Take something."

"All right," said Mix, biting into the vénnton without

enthusiasm. "That was right impressive, miss, you takin' off after that big bird like that."

"'S not as impressive as your cursin'," said Tillinghast, reclining in the stern, a grin peeking from under his hat brim. "I've known sailors would blanch at that kind o' . . . How did you put it this mornin'? Gutter mouth?"

Remedie flushed pink, took a pear from Wull, chewed it, and looked out over the river to where the rue trees' low, thick-leafed branches were locked into the river's white surface.

"Did she kill it?" whispered Mix to Wull.

"Aye," Wull whispered back, "an' she said it was a lesson for me."

Mix looked confused. "What was the lesson?"

"I don't know," said Wull, shrugging. "That she's mental, I suppose."

Remedie finished her pear and threw the core over the side of the boat.

"My appalling blasphemy came in a moment of high emotion, and I must apologize," she said, "to all of you."

"Oh, it's all right, miss," said Mix. "For what it's worth, I reckon Till's talkin' straight about bein' impressed. He was goin' on about it while you was gone."

"And not about my safety?" said Remedie sharply. "Not expressing concern for my baby and me? Or thinking that a person of your prodigious strength might in fact come to help?"

Tillinghast sat up. "First," he said, "I's not a fan o' birds, 'specially big dirty rotten ones with teeth like draft horses. Second, it's not a baby—it's a wooden statue of a baby."

"He's not a statue," said Wull, kneeling in front of Pappa and stroking his hair. "You can feel him living inside. There's somethin' makin' him live."

Remedie stared coldly at Tillinghast. "You are the most selfish person I've ever met," she said. "What makes us human but our compassion for others?"

Tillinghast dropped his hat onto his face and sat back.

"I's always reckoned it was *livin'* that made us human, Miss Cantwell, an' I might not have your compassion, your capacity for prodigious cursin', *or* your ability to delude yourself into thinkin' you's a pure, virtuous soul when you's carried a flesh-got child, but I's livin' now, an' I mean to go on to do more of it."

"You . . . oaf!" said Remedie. "You are the single most obnoxious and despicable creature I have ever encountered. . . ."

"Oh, Miss Cantwell, if you think flattery'll work, then let me—"

"*And* you continue to decry my Bonn's claim to life while lugging around a grubby *mandrake* of all things! A *man plant!* You must know what comes of them, and what on earth have you that thing for if not to grow it?"

"Well, I *is* goin' to—"

"Your disgraceful smarm *will* end now, for your obscene comments are quite beyond the pale! You, sir, are lower than pond scum, lower than field pats, lower than the ticks that *live* in field pats!"

"Is that so?" said Tillinghast.

"That is so," said Remedie, cheeks burning.

"Really? Then let me tell *you* something, Miss Cantwell: many years ago I was lookin' for a banshee down in Ciarnton an' in my huntin' came across a most singular old woman. Her bearded mouth was puckered in the way of a cat's rear end, an' she'd a voice like a goose fartin' in the fog. Her skin was right foul too, hangin' all loose an' sour with sweat from not bathin', an' she used to jab animals an' kids with a pointy stick. She once killed a balgair with a rock for sport. I's always reckoned she was the most repellent character I'd ever met, but let me say now that should I meet her again, I'd be off'rin' a solid apology along with a description of *you*, Miss Cantwell, as confirmation of her havin' been replaced in my inestimation!"

"How wonderful!" said Remedie. "You can't imagine my delight, for that's *exactly* the position I hope to have in your heart!"

"Keep talkin', toots, an' you'll find yourself sore disappointed: every time you speak the prospect of our canoodlin' gets more remote—in fact, that's it! Forget about it altogether!"

Remedie sat down, crossed her arms, and followed the bäta's line downriver, looking away from them all.

"If it's not too much trouble, Wulliam, I would like to be off now. This is an unpleasant place to be."

"Yes, miss," said Wull quickly, taking up the center thwart and guiding the bäta into the current again. He rowed steadily, the adrenaline of the morning and the faelkons' screams still in his blood, and, although time passed like cold mud as Remedie fumed and Tillinghast sulked, it wasn't long before the forest's mist was replaced by the city's smog, and the jagged towers and spires of Oracco, the world's great city, were stabbing at the flame-blushed sky before them.

17

Canna Bay

*More bustling than any road, the Oraccan waters of
the Danék teem with craft of all types and trades: tide-
chasers, pickerel-trawlers, whelk-barges, eel-skiffs, hally-
slips, swart little tugs, and the wide, jostle-bumping
hulls of passenger ferries. From their decks, voices ring
with such coarseness of accent and language as would
curdle milk at the teat! When gentry or royalty sail its
length, social rank is trampled beneath the hooves of the
river's great antiquity: princes barge against ferrymen
and think nothing of the indignity, for the river has a
law of its own, and all men are paupers in the face of
its urgency. The Danék is a place of unimaginable noise:
a more active hive cannot be found anywhere in nature.*

—*Packroyd Bunting*, Fair and Foul: The Black Waters of the Danék

---

The mormorach flew through the trench's thick weed,
maned briefly by sheets of yellow and green as kelp ripped

on its tusks. The tail whipped and the creature dived deeper—farther into the darkness and the cold and away from the waves of sound that beat at its skin like hot sharpened knives.

For hours now the shape above had been following, spearing down stabbing points with strange infrequency.

The mormorach had sensed a new threat, and circled below warily, roaring into the freezing black and writhing with growing anxiety as nothing happened and its instincts began to twitch. The big heart had beaten faster, and it had screamed its fury.

Then the shape had answered with its own noise: huge, booming walls of sound, pushing into the darkness an unfamiliar force that rushed the mormorach's senses in overlapping waves, heating it in panic and turning it miserably like an eel at the spit, blinded and cut by noise, the surface and the seabed a single white space in the walls of sound that seized its muscles and locked it as though frozen in ice.

Far above, one hand on the *Hellsong*'s tiller and the other on his crutch, Murdagh licked his teeth.

He turned the ship a fraction to keep the wind, the filling of the sails as vital as his own breath. The prow smashed into a wall of water, and he felt through the skin of his feet the timbers of the old, bone-trussed tub meeting the waves' force, the masts shaking, the frame rumbling with a shudder that knocked the crew to their knees.

"We'll have to turn back, Cap'n!" shouted Ormidale, clinging to a wet rope.

Murdagh spat. "He needs more!" he shouted back. "This 'in't enough to take him! Keep swingin' the hammers!"

"But the ship—"

"The ship can take it!"

"The quicksilver's all but fallen oot the barometer, Cap'n! We *have* to turn back!"

"Keep on the hammers!" shouted Murdagh over the wind and the gulls. He steadied the tiller, pressing with all his strength against the sea's desire to turn his ship.

Women and men ran about him, falling on the slick, blood-darkened boards as he kept steady, the points of his crutch and leg driven into grooves worn smooth by the action of years. He was as much a part of the ship as the sails and the transom, a growth on its body. His closed eyes saw the movement of water over its every inch, and the heat of his blood—near to the boil—bubbled with the mormorach's pain, feeling the moment of its capture coming to his outstretched hand.

"Hammer!" he shouted again, knowing the moment of nets was close. "Hammer that beast till he dun't know which way's up an' his black heart pops in his ribs!"

He turned the tiller into the wind again—and stopped. Every function of his body clanged shut at the sight of the mormorach's vastness clearing the gunwale and bearing down upon him with its tusks flashing and the great, shining cave of its mouth wide and howling.

Orocco

"So how did you kill it?" said Mix, crouching beside Pappa. Behind her the shadows of the city began to cover the horizon as they neared its stone-lined banks.

"I snapped its neck," said Remedie.

"How'd you manage that?"

"Oh, it was quite easy, really, once I'd found the gaps in the vertebrae."

"The what?" said Tillinghast.

Remedie ignored him. "It wasn't pleasant," she said, "but necessary. He was going to tear Bonn apart. I'd have killed them all if that had happened. And there's a lesson for you."

Wull shared a look with Mix. He turned the oars in his grip, massaging feeling back into his palms.

"What's the lesson?" she said.

"Don't trifle with a mother and child," said Remedie, "because we will destroy you."

"Ha!" said Tillinghast, throwing back his head. "What a pile of tripe is that. Mothers is all thinkin' they's fearsome beasts—jus' 'cause you've managed to push a wailin' lump out your clam doesn't mean you're a bloody warrior. I could take that paperweight off you an' snap it over my knee."

"That paperweight is my son," said Remedie coldly. "If you even move toward me I'll burst your straw and turn you into a bonnet."

Tillinghast laughed again. "A bonnet o' my straw would be too pretty to sit on *that* face," he said.

Mix, her eyes flicking from Remedie to Tillinghast, held a fish head up for Pappa.

Wull, his arms moving in a constant ache, looked at the bloodless, heavy head, the gray mouth opening for the cold silvery lump.

"Eat," said Pappa.

"That's what we're doing," said Mix.

"It from boat," said Pappa.

"That's me," she said, smiling.

Wull found her eyes, held them.

"Untie the arms, it that speaks," said Pappa.

"I can't," said Wull automatically. "You know I can't."

"Are you not tempted to try it?" said Mix. "Untying him, I mean."

Wull shook his head. "He'll try to escape. Or something else. It's for his own good. I jus' need to help him, that's all. An' we're nearly there, Pappa," he added.

"Stinking it that speaks boy," said Pappa, a thick roll of

white fish muscle clutched in his teeth like a cigar. He worked it into his mouth, chewing roughly and mashing it into a paste of tufty lumps.

"What was he like, your paps?" Mix asked.

Wull, caught off guard by the question, took a moment to answer. He rowed while the others waited, the sound of Pappa's chewing filling the boat.

"He still is a great man," said Wull eventually. "He's strong an' brave, an' he loves the river."

"An' what about your mam?"

Remedie glanced at Wull, whose face had deepened to a red that was beyond exertion.

"You ask too many questions, young lady," she said.

"Sorry," said Mix.

"It's all right," said Wull. "Pappa found her near the footbridge. I was too young to remember."

He rowed through the quiet.

"Quite a man, your paps, bringin' you up on his own," said Mix, handing Pappa another fish head.

Wull nodded. "He's my best friend," he said quietly.

He rowed a few minutes more, silence in the bäta but for the wet movements of Pappa's mouth. In the space of a few strokes, they had broken through the skin of smog, under the slime-slicked stonework of the Old Oracco Bridge, and emerged with a noisome burst into a bacterial slurry of shouting, bumping craft. Above them poked the towers of hovels, lodging houses, apothecaries, and mongers that were the life of the famous old bridge, its gibbets filled with fabric corpses in a nod to its grisly history. Wull turned to look over his shoulder and found they were already in the heart of the city itself, leaned over by the steaming lump of its iron body, the air as foul as a blocked drain—feculence and staleness and decay.

He slowed the oars until they moved no faster than the current. The bäta began to drift through the other craft, the multitude of heads before them as teeming as a market square.

"It's so *big*," he said. "I never knew it was as big as this. An' it stinks."

Tillinghast lifted his hat from his face and peered out. "Oh, the docks. They's a fair size, right enough. Most o' the city's behind this, mind, an' the docks go on for a mile or so. These is jus' the shipyards."

Wull's eyes bulged as he took in the industrial might of Oracco. Through fog that was brown and sour, the shipyards' corpulent mass roared above him, a rusting beast skinned with metal and soot-blacked stone. The skeletal legs of cranes spidered across its body, while at its feet huge arterial belches of water and steam sluiced a constant effluence into the Danék. From inside the dock came pulses of sound—ringing hammers and humming flames—and men and women, innumerable and tiny, crawled like fleas on its back, sending bursts of sparks tumbling in such constancy down its great face that they became a waterfall of shining fire.

"How could it be bigger than this?" said Wull. He remembered a time he and Pappa had found a walrös dying on the bank. The little things of the river and soil were already harvesting its flesh; the creature—agonized and bleeding internally from some stone-dashed wound—lying still, puffing helpless, desperate breaths.

Tillinghast laughed. "'S a huge place—you could walk all day an' not cross it. Oracco's like a termite mound, 'cept with more drinkin' an' less work."

"I've heard the city is a place of such foul vice and debauchery it befits no good-thinking person to enter its gates," said Remedie.

"You's absolutely right," said Tillinghast. "I's immensely fond of it."

"Seems like you two don't agree on this issue," said Mix casually, trailing her fingers in the water.

"Don't do that," said Wull, turning to face her.

"What? I'm jus' sayin'."

"No, I mean with your fingers. You'll freeze them off, or the seulas'll have them."

"I think I'll be all right," said Mix.

Wull looked at her. "That's what Till said," he said eventually.

Mix laughed.

"Well, I certainly don't agree with Mr. Tillinghast," said Remedie. "I don't hold with pleasures of the flesh."

Tillinghast lifted his hat and peered at her, a sly grin on his face. He pointed at Bonn, clutched tightly in her arms. "*Somebody* held you," he said.

Remedie flushed and drew herself together, a gathering storm of indignation. "How dare you think to speak to—"

"All right, both of you, drop it," said Wull. "It's gettin' right busy here, an' I don't want you fightin' an' puttin' me off so I crash."

He steered the bäta through the crowded boats on the water, shapes that loomed through the thick fog with suddenness and shouting, with strange voices and foul language rising above the knocking of wood as hulls and oars clacked together in the tangle of craft.

"You, fine people!" shouted a man from a floating platform. He held up a brown, crimson-dripping bag. "You want t' buy some meat? Fresh meat, only two days old! Is usually beef!"

"Say no," muttered Tillinghast from under his hat.

"Yes!" said Mix.

"No, but thank you!" shouted Wull, glaring at her.

The man started to say something else, then switched his attention to a ferryman whose bow was nudging the bäta's stern. Wull saw the bloody bag pass across the gap, the man running on his platform to keep pace and gather his coins. He vanished in the smog and was replaced by a square tug, itself bashing a fish skiff aside.

"This is impossible," said Wull. "Nowhere with this number of people can make sense."

"It's exciting," replied Tillinghast, "an' it works."

A dead dog, split by maggots and rot, twirled past, plated by a droning armor of black insects.

"Does it?" said Wull.

"Oh, sure. More money goes through here 'n a day than you an' I could count in a lifetime."

"And that's how you judge success and virtue, Mr. Tillinghast? By how much money is made?" said Remedie.

"'S as good a way as I's found," said Tillinghast, grinning.

"But the river should flow," said Wull. "There's so many boats here, you could walk across them like a road."

"Handy if you's bein' followed, that," said Tillinghast.

"Followed by who?" said Mix.

"Oh, anyone: guards, crooks—husbands."

"What d'you think o' that, Miss Cantwell?" said Mix, tut-tutting.

"You stop that," said Wull.

"Where?" said Pappa, waking with a splutter. "Untie the arms!"

"Hello, Paps," said Mix.

"We're in Oracco jus' now," said Wull. "We jus' got here, an' we're goin' to row through the docks." A transportee bell sounded above his head as he guided the bäta through a narrow channel. The boat's eyes seemed half shut in a grimace, he thought, like it was unused to sharing its water.

"What's Oracco?" said Pappa.

"The city. You like comin' here, said you'd take me one day when I was the keep."

"Never did."

"You did so," said Wull, struggling to control his voice. "Oracco, the city. Biggest city in the world. Remember?"

"Never did," said Pappa again.

"What's this about rowin' through?" said Tillinghast.

"That's what we're doin' now. Won't take long."

"But I's wantin' to stop now, jus' for a bit. Just a couple o' drinks—come on. You c'n watch me drink potœm."

Wull scanned the bankside buildings, through which scaffolds poked like bone. The huge white names of trade posts were painted on crumbling brick made grimmer still by the fog's wetness, and their feet were greened by the creeping moisture of the river. Their walls hid the city beyond, as impenetrable and dark as a forest's matted face, and with the same seething sense of unseen life within.

"We're not stoppin'," he said.

"We're certainly not!" said Remedie. "I wouldn't soil my-self by setting foot there."

"I sincerely hopes you ain't goin' to soil yourself under any circumstances, Miss Cantwell. . . ."

"You cheeky bugger," said Mix, laughing as Remedie fumed. "Right, Paps, I'm goin' to sit next to Miss Cantwell."

She patted Pappa's cheek and clambered awkwardly over Wull, who had to drop his left oar and lean away.

Tillinghast sat up and wedged his hat on his head. "Look, I's the payin' customer here . . ." he began.

"You told me you wanted to jus' pass through!" said Wull, reclaiming his oar and sculling around a barge. "You said that was a good idea."

"An' now I've decided to go an' see what's what in the city for a bit. Could be there's some excitin' stuff happ'nin'." Tillinghast craned his neck. "See there? That's Slack Jenny's place. I'd only be a minute! You could time me!" He tucked the hessian sack farther beneath the thwart as Remedie shook her head in disgust.

"It's to do with that mandrake, isn't it?" said Wull. "That's why you want to go ashore?"

"Never you bloody mind," said Tillinghast.

"What is it?" said Wull. "Tell me what a mandrake is if it's so important to you."

"You really wants to know?"

"Yes!"

"All right—it's a plant grown from the spilled seed of a hanged man," said Tillinghast. "They's shaped like men too, an' it's growin' well already near the water, jus' soakin' it up. This un's from a very well-known man, an' not a pleasant one. Some even less pleasant people had it, an' I took it off 'em."

Wull's hands slowed. "Why?" he said.

"It's a little life, so it is. Wun't right for folk such as they to have it."

"So you're a thief, too?"

"*Weeell*," said Tillinghast, "I s'pose if you wants to be *technical* about it. . . ."

"I do!" said Wull. "You stole that? From who?"

"*Weeell*," said Tillinghast, "I s'pose you'd *technic'ly* call 'em gangsters. . . ."

"Gangsters!" said Wull. He picked up the oars' pace, speeding blindly and bumping lighter boats aside.

"And do they want it back, these gangsters?" said Remedie.

"Oh, a great deal, I imagine," said Tillinghast.

"And they'll be following you?"

"I very much hopes so," said Tillinghast. "I's not punched anyone for hours."

"So, you've come onto my boat knowin' there's bloody gangsters followin' you?"

"Yup."

"Which means they're followin' me an' Pappa now an' all?"

"'S right," said Tillinghast. "Excitin', 'in't it?"

"What happens if you plant it?" said Mix.

Tillinghast winked at her. "It all depends," he said.

"You wish to grow this thing into a person, yet you sneer at my Bonn?" said Remedie. "You, sir, are the most foul-mannered, selfish—"

"Pipe down, toots," said Tillinghast. "Don't you feel like you could be usin' some fun, Master Keep? It's jus' a quick stop, an' then we can be goin' again."

"This is not a passenger boat!" said Wull. "I'm takin' you because I have to, because some scummy bradai took my money, and because *they*"—he jerked his head back toward Remedie and Mix—"ended up in my bäta through bad luck and sneakin' around . . ."

"Um, Wull . . ." said Mix.

". . . otherwise, I'd be flying all the way down to Canna Bay on my own," Wull carried on, not hearing, "an' a damn sight better for it an' all! I'd still have my own bloody oars, an' I'd be a damn sight happier!"

"You couldn't do this on your own!" said Tillinghast.

"Wull!" said Mix.

"Shouting!" said Pappa. "Untie the arms!"

"I can't!" said Wull, reaching across to press Pappa back into his seat. "Look," he said to Tillinghast, "I can't stop. I know you want to, but—"

"Wulliam!" Mix shouted, kicking the bottom of his seat.

"What?"

He looked around the riverscape. The other craft had vanished, emptying the hull-bumping waters so that the bäta was alone, the river's width suddenly vast, its naked water slicked by the colors of its trade: white flour, black coal, and the red sheen of spilled offal.

"Why's it gone so quiet?" said Remedie.

"I don't know," said Wull. He turned the bäta's nose into the current again, kicked forward.

"Where've the other boats gone?" said Mix.

"I don't know!" said Wull, rowing harder.

Tillinghast turned around. "I dun't know either, but it'd be even easier f'r us to be gettin' across the water now, see down by—"

"Be quiet. Something's happening."

They all looked around at the empty fog. Wull stood, oars gripped on his chest, ready to throw the bäta forward. The Danék pulled on the blades, and he felt the current's edge turn the handles against his skin.

"This can't be good," he said.

"What's all that commotion?" said Remedie.

Wull turned to follow her arm and saw, pointing through the murk, the V-shaped hull of an enormous ship lurching through the doors of a dry dock. The crowd inside the dock was visible only by the faint dots of faces, and the sky-filling grind that replaced the noise of their cheering came as the nose of the ship leaned forward on its slipway and began to drop toward them.

In an instant Wull saw what was going to happen.

"Grab Pappa!" he shouted to Tillinghast, dropping to the keep's seat and pulling as hard as he could on the oars. The bäta shot forward, eyes locked and focused, and Wull found the current instantly, giving the heavy boat another surge of speed.

"What? Why?" said Tillinghast. "Why 'in't we goin' ashore?"

"Will you just grab hold of him? When that ship hits the water we'll be swamped by the wave—you need to hold on to him, or he'll be washed overboard!"

Tillinghast turned to look at the ship, now more than halfway to the river. "It'll be fine, jus'—"

"It won't! We could die—just hold on to him!"

"Untie the arms!" said Pappa.

"I ain't holdin' anyone. We's not goin' to—"

"Hold on to Paps!" said Mix. "I can't reach him from here!"

"I's not holdin' another man," said Tillinghast, shifting on the thwart. "I'll shake 'is hand. . . ."

"You selfish pig!" cried Remedie, Bonn clutched to her neck.

"Will you hold him *please?*" shouted Wull, the veins in his neck bulging with the force of his rowing. He risked a glance over his shoulder, saw a natural breakwater up ahead.

And realized as the ship dipped into the river that there was no hope of making it.

He dropped the oars and leaped across the bäta, pushing Tillinghast aside and grabbing at Pappa, who fought back, howling in protest, kicking him away.

"Hold on!" Wull shouted as a wave the height of a building smashed him into the water, Pappa beyond his reach alongside the flailing lumps of the others, swirling, blind-panicked in foul, silt-clouded water, up and down lost— only the freezing pressure of the river pushing on them with such intensity the air was forced from their lungs.

The cold of the water sliced Wull as he twirled in the spinning thump of the ship's wash. He threw out his arms and legs, tried to steady himself, and forced his eyes open.

At first there was blackness and the needles of cold, then he turned, found light and the surface, and saw Remedie— her skirts huge and billowing around her, kicking for the up-turned bäta, Mix close behind.

He looked for Pappa as the air screamed in his chest and his heartbeat quickened. But he saw nothing, and rushed frantically for a grabbed breath.

He swam down again, the water a thick, impenetrable swirl of silt and the scraps of river life, and held his breath until there were spots on the edges of his vision and the ice of the water had made cold stones of his eyes.

Lungs bursting, he made to kick for the surface—and saw a hand waving above the split gunwale of a wrecked eel-skiff, the shape of Tillinghast's head behind it.

He swam over as hard as he could, his whole body tight with urgency, fighting the pressure in his throat.

Tillinghast held out his hand.

Wull took it and pulled. Tillinghast didn't move. Wull heaved again, but it was like tugging on a rock. Tillinghast's body seemed anchored to the riverbed, his feet barely lifting from the ground, as though Wull were pulling at a boulder.

As his muscles screamed for oxygen, Wull's head began to lighten, his skull losing its tether on his neck and floating, loose in the current's swell. He felt the pressure of the water on his skin and allowed it to hold him, his mind just on the edge of sleep, the freezing cold softening into a welcome, safe warmth that massaged the pain inside him.

Wull began to open his mouth.

There was no fear, he realized, just peace . . . then a call for help interrupted him like a flash of lightning, and Tillinghast's face was in his, shouting unintelligibly.

The currents returned, and this time he felt them inside his body, felt their power and constancy and purpose alongside his own failing strength as he heaved at Tillinghast's hand once more, felt the big body lift free, pulling tight to Wull, and in the space of a few rapid kicks they were on the surface, and Wull was pulling agonized stabs of air into his flattened lungs and leading Tillinghast's hand to the bäta's edge.

"You took your time," said Tillinghast, his voice slow.

"Are you all right?" said Wull to Remedie and Mix, grabbing the bäta for support as he heaved in the frozen air.

They nodded.

"And Bonn?"

He saw Bonn clutched in his swaddling, tight to Remedie's neck.

"Where's Paps?" said Mix. "Is he gone? Where is he?"

"I lost him," said Wull, taking a huge breath, "but I'll find him."

"He's been down so long!" said Mix. "Hurry!"

Wull dived again, his sodden clothes heavy on his limbs, peering into the darkness for a sign of Pappa.

Where are you? he thought, closing his mind to Pappa's bound hands keeping him in the depths, stopping him from swimming, drowning him.

He began to fill with the early pain of airlessness. Pappa had been under the water for too long. Unless you got to someone in less than a minute . . .

But then, Pappa wasn't entirely Pappa, and Wull didn't know what that would mean.

He pushed out the last of his air and sank farther into the riverbed and the clouds of silt. Inside the skeletal wrecks of old barges and fishing craft, the weeds stuck up like an untended garden, and Wull saw in the belly of one shattered ruin, almost invisible in the waving fronds, Pappa—still and calm, his eyes closed.

Wull kicked down to him as hard as he could, fighting his own buoyancy and the lift of the air inside him. He pushed out yet more bubbles, sinking himself deeper still and feeling the rising panic of light-headedness before grabbing Pappa's hand and lifting his almost weightless body toward him, kicking them both to the surface as the need for air became a throb in his head, and his heart started to squeeze.

He burst through in a breathless shout, his lungs rasping and sore, Pappa held firmly to his side.

"It that speaks!" said Pappa, hitting him with bound hands. "Untie the arms, it that speaks!"

"Pappa," said Wull, "you're all right! You're all right!"

"It that speaks!"

"Paps!" said Mix, swimming over. "You found him!"

"Take him, take him, he's fine, he's all right," said Wull, resting his head on Pappa's shoulder and slipping into unconsciousness.

18

Oracco Ironbank

*The estimable Captain Murdagh, when at last we were
introduced, virtually burned with an excess of personality!
The man was like an overstoked furnace, filling the room
with his heat, dripping character wherever he went like
shed clinkers. He seemed not to exist as a person but
as an idea—the whole of his extraordinary energy was
founded on the pursuit of his quarry, and for the outward
appearance of his person he cared little. So it was that
when one looked at him, one did not see a crunched, mal-
formed little man with a shipwrecked body; one saw only
his purpose, and the intensity with which it was pursued!*

—Gentling Norbury, The People's Sea

Wull opened his eyes. He was in the bäta, sitting on the
stern thwart, his back on the transom. Pappa was in the
keep's seat on the center thwart, pulling the boat along with
long, slow rolls of the oars.

Sadness flooded Wull: the slender, light wood of the keep's oars betrayed this instantly as an illusion. The broad, steady man was not really there at all.

"Look who's up," said Pappa. He smiled, and Wull's eyes roamed the fat cheeks and the laugh-creased eyes; the tooth knocked to gray deadness by a childhood tussle; the flat knuckles kneading the grips; and the overall sense of the big body's peaceful strength. These were all the little fibers of the pappa Wull carried with him still . . . except his smell, he noticed—Pappa smelled of lakoris and tallow and the river. Nothing here smelled of anything.

"Sleepin' in the bäta's a kind o' sin, y'know," Pappa said. "Once, I did it mysel' an' your gran'pappa gave me a right smack. Hand like a leather shovel, that man."

"You told me," said Wull.

Pappa nodded. "I remember," he said.

The river they were sculling bore no resemblance to the Danék—there were none of the low-hung trees, crumbling banks, or pale arcs of pebbled sand that made up Wull's childhood. But this *was* their river in a truer sense than the real thing could ever be; this was the space they had shared in their private moments made solid around them, and Wull felt himself settling into it like he was slipping into a familiar boot. He closed his eyes again and found the feeling of belonging to this quieter, hidden seat, free from the weight of the oars, the press of guidance and responsibility—subordinate to Pappa, the *real* keep, rowing with constant, fearless strength.

"What's wrong with you, Pappa?" Wull said quietly. He was tired, more tired than he had ever been in his life, and the pain in his shoulders and wrist and the wound on his face were as present here as they were in his waking world.

Pappa chuckled. "Ye already know. Ye've looked at me enough; ye've seen my eyes an' heard my voice. An' ye've read it in that book! Jus' as well I learned ye how, I'd say. Ye didn't want to read, ever—moaned and wailed about goin' oot huntin' skirrils."

"I remember," said Wull.

"I know," said Pappa.

"I miss you," said Wull, fighting against tears.

Pappa nodded. "I knows that an' all. No parent ever wants to outlive their child, so ye fill 'em up with everythin' ye can give 'em. I hoped I'd see ye as an older man, a grown man. . . ."

"Pappa, you can! You're still with me in the bäta—I said I'd stay with you—"

"But I've seen ye become a man already, a grown man in the body o' this long streak o' hollow legs—brave an' proud an' strong. The river's started talkin' to ye, givin' ye her strength—an' ye can feel it already. Soon ye'll start talkin' back, an' then ye'll be hers yer whole life."

"Pappa, I don't want—"

"Ye'll understand all o' it before the end," said Pappa. "There's no weakness in facin' the truth—or in lettin' me go."

"I can't!" said Wull, sitting forward and placing his hand on Pappa's. There was nothing under his palm, nothing to hold at all but empty space.

"Ye'll have to," said Pappa.

"But I still have time, you're still with me, I can tell it's you in there! It is you! That thing's not taken you yet!"

Pappa smiled at him. "The thing ye'll understand, my beautiful, beautiful boy, is that ye've always thought I was the river's, its servant an' its master—but that's no' who I am."

"It is!" said Wull. "You're the keep; I never wanted to be! I was goin' to run away! I wanted to be somewhere else, away from the boathouse an' the river, even if it meant leavin' you! I'm so sorry, Pappa. I'm sorry. I'll stay now. I do understand, I promise!"

Pappa shook his head and smiled again. "I knows all that, ye daft tumshie. Ye think I didn't see ye, sittin' up in bed an' lookin' oot the window at the light on the clouds?"

"I've been in the city now," said Wull. "I didn't know what it was. It just meant . . . somewhere else. People. More lights than a few lanterns."

"What more light could man need than the fire on the end o' a lantern?" said Pappa. He laughed and started rowing again. "Yer gran'pappa said that to me when I was yer age, an' I thought he'd lost every marble goin'—I know what it's like to want somethin' different, even if ye don't know what it might be. An' what I mean is I never *belonged* to the river, Wulliam—I belonged to ye. The moment ye opened yer eyes, I gave mysel' over to ye. I'd have let the river freeze a thousand times if it meant keepin' you from harm an' helpin' ye become the man ye are now. My beautiful boy. My boy who does the right thing. My boy who puts other folk afore hissel'."

Pappa let the oars slow in their locks again and looked at Wull. "My boy who loves me," he said, "an' who thinks I'm a good man."

Wull fought tears. "I do, Pappa," he managed. "I love you."

"An' I love you, Wulliam. Ye're my boy, an' I'm proud o' ye. I know ye'll do the right thing. But ye'll have to wake up now—there's folk needin' help, an' ye're the Riverkeep, after all."

"Why can't I stay here?" said Wull.

Pappa's fist tightened on his, and this time Wull felt its pressure, felt the strength of Pappa's hand.

"Ye'll find yer way back here," said Pappa. "Don't worry about that. Wake up now, Wull, wake up. Wulliam!"

Wull woke just as Mix was about to slap his face.

"I'm awake!" he spluttered, coughing up river water.

Mix slapped his face.

"Sorry," she said. "I had it all ready to go. It's good to see you. I thought you were dead, then Miss Cantwell said you were still breathin'."

Wull leaned on his side, over the edge of the righted bäta, and fought back the acid of vomit.

"Well, thank you," he said.

"Are you feeling better, Wulliam?" said Remedie.

Wull groaned. He thought his pain had been there all along, but here it was, returned in all its force, shrinking him like a coat of iron.

"I'm fine," he said. "Who righted the bäta?"

"We all did," said Mix, grinning. "Are you impressed?"

Wull looked around. The docks' spires were in the distance across a sea of gray stone buildings and teeming roofs, and the bäta sat in an area of shining jetties at the city's other edge. The jetties were noisy with people, bustling with passenger ships and the black-puffing stovepipes of steam craft.

They were floating motionless at the edge of a broad expanse of sunlit, golden water leading to the wider estuary and, beyond that, the sea and the rest of the world. Seeing the water begin to spread its banks toward the coast gave him a jolt: they were nearly at the brackish straight that led to Canna Bay.

"How long have I been out?" he said.

"An hour or so. Perhaps more," said Remedie.

"But you knew I was all right?"

"Oh yes," said Remedie. "You were even talking. About your father."

Wull flushed. "Then we've been drifting all this time? Why is nobody rowing?" he said.

Remedie and Mix looked embarrassed.

"We can't move the boat," said Remedie. "Even with one of us on each side, we couldn't get it moving much at all. And, well, Bonn," she added, looking at Tillinghast.

"Tiny little girl," said Mix, holding up her hand.

"An' I's dryin' out," said Tillinghast. "Takes a while for my straw to get rid o' all that water once I's had a swim."

"So you knew I was out cold," said Wull, "but waited for me to wake up rather than row for a little while? You still won't help me with the rowin', even when this happens?"

"In my defense," said Tillinghast, "I knew you wasn't dead. Stubborn little bugger like you's not goin' to roll over that easy. Rowin's your job. An' what's the hurry? Be glad I din't row in to shore an' go for a drink."

Wull rubbed his eyes, steadied his breathing. "You are unbelievable," he said. "I could've died savin' you!"

"True," said Tillinghast, "so we's even, I reckon. Remember the ursa?"

"We're not even! You only did that for the fun o' fightin' it!" said Wull. "Draggin' you off the bottom nearly made me lose Pappa! What if I'd lost him to save you?"

"Now, Wulliam," said Remedie, "perhaps we should leave

this conversation a while until you've calmed down. . . ."

"Don't tell me *you're* defendin' him!" said Wull. "He wouldn't have cared if Pappa *had* died!"

"Well, he din't, so there's no use cryin' about it, is there?" said Tillinghast.

"You know there was a moment when I saw you down there," said Wull, "when I thought of leavin' you an' jus' lookin' for Pappa, but that's not what he'd have wanted. He's a good man, an' he'd have wanted me to save you."

"I doesn't actually breathe, you know," said Tillinghast a little sheepishly. "I'd have been all right for the rest o' time. I jus' couldn't get myself off the bottom. Too heavy with all the water, see?"

Wull closed his eyes. "So you let me take you when you could easily have waited?" he said quietly.

"Well, yes. I din't know you'd not found your old man, mind. . . ."

"Get out o' my boat!" said Wull, taking up the oars and turning the bäta for the bank. "You selfish gudgeon! I've never met *anyone* who lives the way you do!"

"That's 'cause you've hardly *met* anyone!"

"That doesn't matter! I know my pappa an' my grandparents: they gave me all I need to know about what's the right thing an' the wrong thing, and you've only ever come down on the wrong side o' that, Till. You've put all of us in danger jus' by bringin' that bloody mandrake with you when there's folk after it who'll kill us jus' for bein' with you! An' instead o' helpin' us, you just keep ahold o' that plant an' your damn hat? An' what d'you even want that thing for? The mischief o' takin' it?"

"No! I wants it for . . . Never mind what I wants it for! It's none o' your damn business!"

"Well, I bet you're lookin' after yourself again, jus' like always. You're a selfish, selfish thing!"

"A thing an' not a man?" said Tillinghast, his eyes narrowing. "I c'n see it in all o' you. None o' you thinks o' me as a real man, even her with that doll."

"Bonn is not a doll!" shouted Wull, pulling harder on the oars. "An' maybe we don't think o' you that way because you act the way you do. You ever think 'bout that? That maybe you're *not* a real man because a real man, a real person, lives a good life by livin' for other people, an' you only live for yourself! You don't appreciate what you've been given! Do you want *pity* for what you are? You've been given what you've got an' you could use it however you like, but you waste it trawlin' round the world's gutters an' pickin' stupid fights!"

"That sounds all right to me," said Mix, rubbing Pappa's back. Remedie shushed her.

Tillinghast's face was impassive. "What I's been given," he said. "An' what is it you think I's been given, young Master Keep who knows everythin' about life now that his voice has broken?"

"You've been given life!" said Wull. "You've been given the thing I'm tryin' to hold on to for Pappa an' the thing Remedie's baby lost! An' what do you do with it?"

"I's not a human bein'!" said Tillinghast, sitting up angrily and leaning toward Wull. "Don't think a *boy* like you can tell me about how I lives! Miss Cantwell, you asked me what makes us human but compassion. Let me tell you: human bein's is *memories*. Once the memories are in there, there's no gettin' 'em out again, an' all the little moments you's lived is everythin' that goes into makin' a whole person, all the little lessons an' feelin's that come with 'em. I 'in't got no memories. I got nothin' but the scraps I's made of, bits o' sinners an' murderers, an' all the time I's fightin' back against little twitches an' horrors o' these blackhearted men screamin' at me. I can't even drink to force their silence. You, Wulliam, who understan's life so well, what do you remember?"

He looked at Wull through his brows, and his voice was toneless.

"What do you mean?" said Wull.

"O' your life. What are your memories?"

"I don't know," said Wull, keeping his attention on the oars' grips. "Everythin', I suppose. Faces, smells, feelings. Pictures of things that've happened, but still . . . like in a woodcut."

"That's good, that is. That makes sense. An' does you

have a look at these woodcuts from time to time? Pickin' through 'em, rememberin' your past?"

Pictures flashed through Wull's mind, a gallery of dim-lit moments: the river, black water, Pappa reading Mamma's letters when he thought Wull was asleep, his clothes and wet hair and cut palm, the spectral gathering of empty boots and hats and cloaks hanging in the empty pantry like so much death, awaiting the city's needy. And at the end of the gallery's dark corridor, unseen but sharp and hot in his mind, the brown, wide mouth and the moment Pappa disappeared.

"No," he said. "No, I don't."

"Then let me call you a liar, 'cause they was crossin' your face this minute. Miss Cantwell an' Mix an' all—even at the mention o' memories, you goes to them, an' don't ye always remember that the sun was shinin'? In rememb'rin' you's fiddlin' the parts of yoursel's what makes you's human, all the little empathies an' struggles an' triumphs. I's not an old *creature*, Wulliam—older than you, mibbe, but still younger than this face would have you think. This face belonged to some-one else, an' these hands an' legs an' the brain that thinks away in my big skull. So I has memories I's made myself, an' I's done some int'restin' things, things would curl the hair on your cocksure little head an' would make for fine tellin' if I thought Miss Cantwell could stand to hear 'em. But my own memories're a fart in the wind next to the mountains what're buried in the meat an' bones o' this body. This body has thoughts lurkin' in it you'd faint to hear, an' I keeps them locked away as best I can.

"But I can't tend locks in sleep. When I dream I's attacked by the memories of my skin and the bloodied mob o' black thoughts. My parts all came from the leavings o' the gibbet; the hanged lumps o' these scoundrels cut down an' sold off, sliced up an' stitched together, an' here I am. Even now when you speak to me as you are, I feel on the edge o' my temper the curlin' fingers o' my murderer's hands, an' the memory o' neck veins bursting under pressure o' stranglin'. I wake most mornin's with these thick legs feelin' they's bein' chased. All the voices of the blaggards what made this body howl at me like monkeys, an' the only time I gets to talk for myself is in wakin' moments like this. But soon I'll sleep again, and they'll all nudge forward again to remind me I's a nobody.

"So you tell me again, Wulliam, that I don't value what I's been given when I's been given this prison to carry around. I's not a real person, an' why should I try to live as a man when I'm nothin' but a cheap trick? Is it a wonder I live as I does when agony lives on the other side o' every thought? I was jus' gettin' to toleratin' havin' company for the first time since I started walkin', but I's better on my own—I c'n live as I please an' have none o' your judgin'. I value life, Wulliam, I value it fine. I jus' hasn't got it. An' by the way—neither has your old man."

"Don't you dare say that!" said Wull, meeting Tillinghast's eyes as the bäta nudged into the bank, knocking them all off-balance.

"I 'in't tellin' you nothin' you doesn't already know! Din't you wonder how he was still livin' when you found him? He'd been down there a long time. Seems there's somethin' else goin' on in there, don't you think?"

Tillinghast heaved a waterlogged foot over the gunwale and onto the grass, toppling under its weight. Mix stepped forward to help him.

"Are you all right, Till?" she whispered.

"I's fine, thank you, little miss," he said, pulling himself fully onto the bank.

"Good. I'm takin' my seat back now then."

"Ha! An' you're welcome to it. Oh, that feels good right enough, solid ground."

Tillinghast tried to take a step, heaving his right foot as though it were a lead weight. Wull, his eyes shining, made to climb from the bäta.

"Don't!" said Tillinghast. "You jus' stay there wi' your pappa an' the ladies. I'll be fine, jus' as I always has been— water'll drain out me in no time. You's not far to go now we's through the city. Shouldn't be more'n—what? Five, six hours down to Canna Bay? Best get goin' now. But by the way, you's not catchin' more'n a pickerel on that stupid boat, an' there's no way you's gettin' on the crew of a proper whaler, so you might as well turn back."

Wull opened his mouth, looked at Pappa, sat down again, and kicked the bottom boards.

"Good-bye, Mr. Tillinghast," said Remedie.

"Cheerio, toots," said Tillinghast without turning round. "Think o' me sometimes, in your lonely, private moments."

He moved his left foot, then his right again, pulling his legs with his hands, gradually achieving something that was almost a shuffle.

By the time he turned to look, Wull had pushed off and was already rowing steadily down the Danék's central current, the bäta a tiny piece of black on the dazzling screen of the sunset's golden water.

The Deadmoor

An hour or so of slow shuffling had passed and the blue light of evening spilled over the sunless sky before Tillinghast felt his limbs lighten, the squash of his insides flushing the last of the river into the earth and returning to their usual sticky lightness.

He felt his strength fill him again and straightened his back, flexing his muscles as they drained, enjoying the sense of his own weight and power.

The words of a child. Nothing more. Since he'd been able to think he'd known his life was a fragile thing, bound up in borrowed skin, a miracle of delicately balanced herbs and chemistry. When his existence could be taken so easily (and the Bootmunch had been closer to taking it than he'd been prepared to admit—he could still feel the effects of that fennel-less smoke in the deepest parts of him), it made sense that he should live as he had. People rejected him—he drew the wrong kind of attention. People had always rejected him. Except Wull.

He shook his head, walked faster.

The forest had started a few paces from the river's edge and thickened steadily into a tangle of branches, thick with roots and foliage and a pervading soggy darkness, a place designed by nature to be hospitable to plants and hostile to people. The green-bloomed bulk of fallen trunks littered the ground, creating impassable barriers connected by gnarled knots of roots and broken branches, and all was wet and slimy and thick with moisture and moss.

Tillinghast stepped in a deep puddle of loose mud that

rose past his knees. When he came to the pool's edge, he hoisted himself from it with one arm and carried on, his stride unbroken. In the slivers of new moonlight that cut through the canopy his cool blue skin gleamed.

The forest was dark, but Tillinghast saw everything, his trapper's eyes effortlessly picking out the detail in the gloom, his footing sure and steady.

Time passed. As he went deeper into the heart of the woods he was aware of a growing sense of familiarity, not conscious recognition of the trees and pools of gathered water—unending in their sameness after so much walking—but of being able to locate himself in the world, feeling the sense of the place coming through his pores, knowing it with his eyes closed.

It was a feeling he hadn't known he'd known: a long-forgotten extra sense of being in the *right* place. This was the place of his creation: the Deadmoor.

And when he realized where he was going, pushed by some interior drive that worked outside of his thoughts, he shook his head.

"Would've been a lot better bein' dropped off a good bit downriver," he muttered. "Save me all this walkin'."

He ambled for hours in a state of happy bewilderment, closing his eyes and taking blind paces with a mouth-open smile, enjoying the forest's spirit, the sighs of its wind-tickled leaves and boughs, the canopy high and unforeign around him. He passed through clearings of borrow-vines and star-flowers and toadstool lanterns that glowed a dull green and spat damp-smelling powder around his feet. He sniffed it, grinning and remembering.

Eventually he broke through the tree line and into a field of untended barley, saw the house, and was so struck by the force of the past's assault, he dropped to a knee as though winded.

"An' there it is," he said to himself.

The house had been built into the hill, perched over what had once been ornately groomed gardens. The gardens, wild now, he saw, made a gap in the trees through which the big, eyelike windows could peek out at the surrounding woods. Tillinghast felt the attention of the place shifting toward him, as though the chattering of a busy room had fallen silent at his approach. A light flared in a downstairs window.

He approached it in a dream, the winding path slippy with unkept plants and years of neglect, the hedges—once immaculate topiaries of animals and fruits—lurking like muggers in the dark.

He remembered the knocker, too—a heavy brass thing cast as a lapphund that shook the door and sent pealing echoes into the house. The portico's stones were crumbling like broken teeth and were shot through with moss. Through a buttress on the front wall lanced the thin, white stem of a sapling.

Tillinghast realized as the door began to open that he had knocked before preparing, before thinking, and that he was not ready to see the face he knew was coming.

"Hello?" said Clutterbuck, peering round the door, Mac stuck to his scalp.

"I . . . I mean, I's . . ." stammered Tillinghast. He took a step back into the light from the window, the shadows cutting him into slabs of light and dark.

"Is that . . . It can't be . . . *Tillinghast?*" said Clutterbuck.

"Sir," said Tillinghast, head down, new-made and shy again.

"Mac! Look who it is!" cried the little scientist, sending the patchwork bird croaking into the air. "Well, come in!" he added, ushering Tillinghast inside, reaching high above his head to clasp his shoulder.

Tillinghast leaned away from Mac's wings, narrowing his eyes. "I saw the house," he said stupidly. He sniffed, smelling something familiar but out of place—a light fragrance that did not belong.

"I always knew you would be back. Yes, indeed, my boy, I did!" said Clutterbuck, walking into the sooty heat of the kitchen.

Tillinghast looked around the hot, domed space, feeling

heavy with recognition, seeing phantoms of himself in corners, his skin firm and clean, bare feet spread on the cracked
flagstones.

"I din't know this was where I was comin'. It's . . . I—"

"And how do you feel now that you're here? After fifteen
years, twenty?" said Clutterbuck with a professorial air.

"I dun't know, sir," said Tillinghast. "Truth is, I's been
havin' a strange time in the run up to my arrivin'. I met some
folk an' spent time with 'em, an' then I left with bad feelin'.
An' I feels wounded by it, quite unexpectedly."

"It happens," said Clutterbuck, one-handedly heaving a
fat kettle onto the stove.

"Not to me," said Tillinghast. "I lives by myself an' away
from pryin' folk."

"But life is a strange thing—it wriggles, like an eel! Just
when you think you've got it pinned down, it changes on you,
shifts, and moves out of reach. And, like an eel, it can be
quite delicious, absolutely—if you're careful. Have you been
careful, my glorious Tillinghast, since I made you and sent
you off into the world?"

Tillinghast looked at Clutterbuck peering over his spec-
tacles, and turned away, unable to meet the inquisition.

"I dun't know, sir," he said again. "I's taken daft risks.
Said hurtful words an' taken things. Many things."

"Ha! That's a lot of people," said Clutterbuck, gesturing

for Mac to land on his forearm. He stroked the bird's patchwork plumage, fanning the feathers in affectionate twirls as Mac gabbled in his ear.

Tillinghast stepped back, away from the bird's twitching.

"Oh!" said Clutterbuck, sending the bird to his perch. "I'm so sorry, my boy, I forgot all about your little—"

"It's not little," said Tillinghast quickly. "That damn bird pecked my eyes out."

"And I got you fresh ones!" said Clutterbuck brightly. "Even better ones, hmm?"

Tillinghast glowered at Mac, who champed his black beak and shuffled on his perch.

"Well," said Clutterbuck, taking Tillinghast's shoulder and leading him away from the mostly raven, "there's not many a person could give a straight answer to that question: have I been careful? Am I living as I should? Most of the time we just blunder about—only at rare moments are we granted a snuck glance into ourselves and the nature of our lives. In my case it happens when I stand up too quickly in the bath. A matter of blood pressure, I'm afraid."

Tillinghast felt himself stepping toward the edge of panic.

"An' what about me?" he said, tugging the silver amulets on his neck. "I 'in't properly got blood to feel pressure! I got goop an' straw, an' you made me like that!"

"Do you think it's a coincidence you found your way back here tonight?" said Clutterbuck. "At the exact moment you were beginning to connect to other people and finding yourself vulnerable for the first time?"

Tillinghast snorted. "I can't make connections wi' other folk, sir—I's made o' dead men who fed the noose. What is I but a plate of leftover meat what's learned to sit up an' talk?"

"But you *did* bond with these people; otherwise, the bad feeling wouldn't have wounded you so! And a plate of leftovers? My boy—you're a work of art!" said Clutterbuck, grabbing Tillinghast's thick arms. "Look at you! I've never managed such beauty before or since. You are unique, my boy, just like the rest of us! But unlike those of us made by the unknowable mess of seed and egg, *you* are *art*! Given to yourself the first time you opened your eyes. You don't *belong* to me any more or less than any son belongs to his father."

"Father?" said Tillinghast. His head spun.

"I created you," said Clutterbuck, smiling. "What else would that make me?"

"But I's made of dead meat! What use am I when—"

"And what am I made from?" said Clutterbuck. "It's true that I could split your seams and make a pile of body parts, all dead and cold. . . ."

"Right," said Tillinghast. "I's not a man, an' I don't know what you even made me for."

"And if you were to take this and split *my* seams?" Clutterbuck lifted a short knife from the kitchen table and cut his forearm, vivid blood springing up around the blade. "What would you be left with then?"

"I dun't—"

"A pile of dead lumps!" said Clutterbuck. "We are all of us just skeletons wrapped in meat, dear, sweet boy—all dead tissue that lives by the grace of the gods. The voice that speaks in your head is *yours*, and it never belonged to anyone else. We are all of us miracles, each with a swirling universe inside his own head. And so it is with you."

Tillinghast took the knife from Clutterbuck, sliced it carefully across his own palm, watched the dark viscosity of his interior bead up around the blade.

Clutterbuck took Tillinghast's hand and clasped it to his own bleeding skin.

"Where do you think this little white hand of yours came from?" he said, raising the stump of his wrist to Tillinghast's face. "Oh, I didn't cut it off! I'd lost it to some bad engineering years ago—a clumsy prototype, youthful foolishness—kept it in a jar, then realized I could give it to you. So you're not simply made of *bad* men—there's quite a few vials of my blood in you too," he said, eyes twinkling. "You are as much mine as any son could have been."

Tillinghast lifted his small hand free and looked at the redness of Clutterbuck's blood on his skin.

"You made me to be like you?" he said.

"I made you to be like *you*!" said Clutterbuck.

"I's myself, an' totally myself?" said Tillinghast.

"Quite so. You are as much your own as I am mine or any other who lives! For you *live*, my boy, yes, indeed!"

Tillinghast's head spun. "So my life's worth livin'?"

Clutterbuck looked horrified. "Of *course* it is!" he said. "Life is always worth living. Always."

"What's my name mean?" said Tillinghast. "What's it determined about me?"

"Your name? It means 'strong one.' And you always were. Think of yourself standing in this room the day you left—full of your own sense of adventure, all that desire to go away from here and see the world!"

Tillinghast saw the moment—saw the sun lancing in through the dirty glass, the tears forming in Clutterbuck's eyes.

"I'm sorry. . . ." he said.

"No! I was delighted! *I've* never seen anything outside the Deadmoor! I didn't put that wanderlust in you—it's yours! Yours, yours, yours! How wonderful to find parts of your nature that have grown contrary to the expectations of parent or breeding! How simply wonderful!"

"I does like to wander," said Tillinghast, laughing as Clutterbuck hopped around the boiling kettle.

"Splendid!" said the little scientist. "Think, my boy, think of these people with whom you connected. We all want to help one another, yes? Human beings are like that. We want to live by each other's happiness—not by each other's misery. We don't want to hate and despise one another. The way of life can be free and beautiful, Tillinghast, and you have the love of humanity in your heart. Don't turn your back on other people, my son. Only the unloved hate; you have always been loved in this house and you have found love now for yourself in the world. It is the rarest of treasures, that moment when people, strangers, reach out to one another— and worth fighting for. Stay tonight, won't you, and then be gone again, living your life and finding love!"

"Maybe I was meant to come back here tonight. Mibbe that's why Wull put me ashore," said Tillinghast, sitting down. "Maybe it was planned for me."

"Of course it wasn't!"

"What?" said Tillinghast, leaning away from Clutter-buck's red-haired face. "But you said—"

"Don't you think it's more likely that *you* meant to come back here? That you ensured you would have to part from these people by deliberately *creating* conflict?"

"Why would I do that?"

"Because you've had someone in your life, just for a short time, and realized what it's worth"—Clutterbuck stepped back and spread his arms—"so you've come home."

"I din't mean I planned it. I meant—"

"There can't ever be a *plan*!" said Clutterbuck, cackling. "We're all just making it up as we go and *you're no different*! Because you are a human being! You'll have to make it up as you go, and hope you can look back and say you made the right choices because that's all any of us will be judged by."

Tillinghast looked at the ground as Clutterbuck poured the tea.

"The right choices," he said quietly, then, quieter still, "the strong one." He looked up. "It's really somethin' bein' in this house again—you can feel how old it is. I can feel the past comin' up through the soles o' my feet."

"It's funny," said Clutterbuck, pouring. "You're not the first person to say so today—a traveler stopped by this afternoon, quite extraordinary—no one visits for months, and then two people in a single day. It's quite broken our solitude in the most wonderful way, Mac, hasn't it? Yes, indeed!"

"We never used to get visitors," said Tillinghast, a needle of unease in his voice.

"And we still don't!" said Clutterbuck, pulling herbs from the wall and arranging them on a wooden block. "I shall freshen you up," he added, showing Tillinghast the herbs. "I can see from your stitches you've been having a time of it. You never did look after yourself. And nor do the Things! Oh, you must meet the Things, let me call them. . . ."

He pushed his empty sleeve at the wall, and the house filled with a low chime.

Tillinghast raised his eyebrows.

"Have you forgotten?" said Clutterbuck, waving his stump and giggling. "Phantom switches for phantom limbs!"

"No," said Tillinghast, "I remember. There was somethin' I think I might have wanted to bring you," he said.

Then he realized why walking had felt so strange as he'd shoved through the forest toward the house: in his rush to leave the bäta, he'd left the mandrake behind.

"Mmm?" said Clutterbuck.

"No, nothing," said Tillinghast. He sat back in his chair, settling his weight, his huge hands wrapped round the mug. As he thought of the mandrake the sense of *himself*, a self-possessed strength he'd never known, grew inside him—and he had the first pangs of something being wrong, of having acted badly.

He sniffed the air again. "Who was the other person?" he said, unease swelling in him while Clutterbuck teased tiny leaves from sticks of thyme.

"You mean *is*," said the little scientist, smiling. "He's still here. Quiet chap, missing a tongue, of all things!"

"Missing his tongue?" said Tillinghast as the floor shifted. He sniffed again, finding the nagging smell from the corridor.

"Oh yes, occupational injury, apparently—writes down everything he has to say."

Tillinghast stood, knocking over his seat and sending his mug clattering onto the floor.

"Big fella?" he said. "Black coat?"

"That's right," said Clutterbuck, blinking at him happily. "You know him?"

Footsteps sounded in the corridor.

"Look—the Things are coming. . . ." said Clutterbuck. "Oh, oh gods, no!"

The wicker Things swarmed into the room in a burst of fire, scampering blindly on thudding legs, black smoke pouring from them in thick, acrid torrents.

"Run!" shouted Tillinghast. The smell he'd wondered at blossomed now, floral and sweet, and through it the sharpness of burning herbs stabbed his nose, its tendrils winding inside him like red-hot blades. As Pent entered at a run—face wrapped in a scarf, eyes staring hatefully through the cloud—Tillinghast fell to his knees and screamed.

19

Canna Bay

Allways the succesive keep has beene the son first born to the incumbent, with the transfrence of tytle being granted 'pon the sixteenth anniversarrie of that son's birth. This continnued uninterrupptd for the first fyve keeps, all of whomm were bore strong Fobisher boys. But it so fell that mine father, Hume, sixth Riverkeep, sired only two girls of which I, Lotte, being the elldest and in any case the most sensibble, took the oars.

On passng my keep this day to mine own son, Braid, I retturn it to the lyne of men. The Fobisher name has been kept, and the keep's dignittie presserved. The latter has come at high pryce, for my tyme on these watters have been a tryal matchless in the histtory of the Danék, and my most wellcome rest is needed fair sore.

—Riverkeep Ledgers, Vol. 7, p. 23

The houses of Canna Bay were ranked like tombstones on the hill, their gull-pebbled roofs barely visible through the mist that clung to the village like its frozen breath. The irregular loops of its sloping streets were discernible by the glow of lanterns, but the tin shells of the packing plants were almost invisible in their silence, their dull gray walls melting in the town's shadow. Even the lighthouse was still, its great flame spent and black.

As his face had continued to throb, Wull's arms had reached the point of agony, the movement of every bone whining in his wrists. He rowed them past the breakwater and through the port with leaden slowness, thinking of the lanterns and picturing the frozen waste outside the boathouse.

"Aren't you goin' to untie Paps's hands now we're here?" said Mix.

Wull looked at Pappa, saw the gray eyes flick back at him, and shook his head. He wondered for the first time what the bohdan, lurking inside, had heard, what its thoughts were.

"I can't," he said. "I need to help him first. He can't look after himself, an' he might do somethin' dangerous."

"Well, the creature's here all right," said Remedie. "Look."

She lifted the cotton from Bonn's face. Wull saw a flush of color on his cheeks—Bonn's hands had curled to fists and his little mouth to a smile. Remedie beamed down at him.

"A mormorach is a magical beast, a touch of the gods on this earth—even the air is changed. Can you taste it?"

Wull mouthed the air. It tasted metallic and hot, like the air of a forge.

Remedie saw his expression and smiled. "That's it," she said. "That's what's giving life to Bonn and what'll help your father. We're here! We made it!"

"I thought this was a fishin' port?" said Mix as Wull sculled past the dark, tethered lumps of fish boats bobbling in the swell, their decks lifeless and dark.

"It is. Not much else happ'nin' but the hunt for the mormorach I suppose," said Wull quietly.

"So now what do we do?" said Mix.

"We find somewhere to sleep," said Wull, "though how we're goin' to manage that with no money, I don't know."

Mix went to her pocket, produced a pile of mixed coins, and smiled sheepishly. "Till's," she said.

"Mix!" said Remedie. "You mustn't steal!"

"We c'n pay him back when we see him! He'd hundreds of ducats, you know. I only took some. An' it's not like he was really good to us."

Remedie sighed and looked troubled. "He did save Bonn and me from that ursa," she said.

"An' me," said Wull, "an' he paid for these oars, even if they do weigh a bloody ton. An' he was funny."

"Well . . . let's not overdo it," said Remedie.

"Right," said Mix. "The thing is, he's left us with that mandrake thing. So we maybe shouldn't feel too bad spendin' his money."

"He what?" said Wull, sitting upright as they beached on the pebbly, weed-stricken shore.

"The mandrake thing. That's it there, behind the oily jacket."

"That gudgeon!" said Wull. He stood up, stumbling across the bäta and lifting the sack, peering in at the rich, blood-smelling lump. "Gudgeon!" he said again. "He *knows* there's folk lookin' for this, an' he's left it with us so he c'n bugger off an' get away with it!"

"We could jus' throw it overboard," said Mix.

"I don't know," said Remedie.

Wull and Mix looked at her.

"Why not? I thought you din't like it?" said Mix.

"I don't—mandrakes can be evil things—but it's started to grow, just like Bonn's waking up. What if throwing it overboard would be like drowning a person, or killing a child? I couldn't do that."

"But it's a plant," said Mix. "We're always cuttin' down trees an' things, for the good of them, trimmin' and prunin' them. I like plants, don't get me wrong, but they are jus' plants."

Wull helped Pappa stand, took his empty frame on his shoulders, and carried him onto the beach.

"It that speaks," said Pappa quietly.

"We're not throwin' it away," said Wull. "There's got to be somethin' we can do with it that's the right thing to do. Mix, you carry it, an' bring that bag o' fruit the Bootmunch gave us an' all."

"You know that mandrake stinks," said Mix. "If there's dogs lookin' for it, they'll find it no bother at all once we're on land again. I'm tellin' you, we should throw it away."

"Nobody's throwin' anythin' away!" said Wull. "Bring it an' don't argue. We've not come here to start hurtin' helpless things."

He reached out a hand to help Remedie over the side, Bonn balanced against her neck.

Mix, grumbling, lifted the sack over her shoulder, ran her hand over the bäta's gunwale, and followed them over the banks of weed, toward the village.

The streets were silent, the smell of the sea moving through them like a ghost, rotting fish lumps and the white mess of gulls spotted like raindrops. The cobblestones, Wull noticed, were run through with the leavings of the fish trade, and the houses patched at their places of failing tin and stone by nets and frayed rope. The whole place seemed to embody its single-minded purpose—the soul of fishing life made solid on land—and Wull sensed in its quiet decay the licking of fatal wounds, as of a great animal settling down for death.

Passing countless dark windows, their breath leaving them in the climb, they eventually came to a low-roofed, shabby dwelling with a hand-painted sign above the door that read MRS. VIHV'S VIVISECTION AND GESTHOUSE. There was a doormat thickly sodden with decades of filth, an odor of working grime, and a lamplit card behind the lace curtains: ROOM.

"I'm not staying here," said Remedie.

"Why not?" said Wull.

"*Look* at it," said Remedie.

"You slept in the bäta last night!" said Wull. "How bad could it be?"

"Well, quite apart from the smell, vivisection is barbaric!" said Remedie.

"What is it?" said Mix.

"It's the practice of cutting animals open and studying their living parts. Frogs and mice and such. While they're still living."

"Yuck . . . What for?"

"*Science,*" said Remedie, with the air of one confiding an unpleasant secret.

"It's the only guesthouse we've found so far," said Wull.

"It smells of ale," said Remedie, shocked. "I won't lay my head where ale has been. And the signage is poorly spelled."

"You'll kill a giant bird with your bare hands, but you won't sleep near beer or have frogs killed in the name o' science?" said Wull. "You're a puzzle right enough, Miss Cantwell. Well, I'm not trampin' through the rest o' this village to end up back here in an hour's time. Mix?"

"Sorry, Miss Cantwell," said Mix.

"Well, really," said Remedie.

Wull rapped on the door, the bubbles of paint flaking on his knuckles followed by the yowl of cat displacement. The handle turned, and a thin brown face peered around the doorjamb, eyes narrowed and brows raised in readiness of judgment.

"Yes," said the woman. "What do you want?"

"We'd like a room, please," said Wull.

The woman took in Pappa's closed eyes, the loose drape of his body. She heard the rasp of his wind and saw the spit gathered in the corners of his mouth.

"Scarred young man an' a drunk old man?" she said, edging the door shut. "Unreliable."

"He's not drunk—he's ill, an' it's not jus' us," said Wull, stepping back so that Remedie and Mix could be seen, "There's—"

"A babby!" said the woman, throwing open the door and smiling, her eyes immediately wide and warm. "Come in, ach, the wee bundle must be frozen to the bone out there. I'm sorry about keepin' you on the stoop but you can't be too careful—so many frightful fish types turn up here, pickled in rum an' without a ha'penny to their name. Hello, young lady," she added as Mix shuffled past her. "Aren't they funny drawings on your neck? Wherever did they come from?"

"They're not drawings, but thanks," said Mix, snatching her coat around her throat. She glanced at Remedie, who appeared not to have noticed.

"You're quite welcome, takes all sorts," said the woman. "Welcome to Mrs. Vihv's Guesthouse. I'm Mrs. Vihv, an' we've plenty room now that damn monster—forgive my cursin'—has smashed up most o' the huntin' boats. We're all dyin' here! So it's a pleasure to have you an' your ducat a head: breakfast an extra crown an' a half, or a crown if you've no taste for eggs."

"What about the vivisection?" said Mix. "Is that included?"

"We do that out back," said Mrs. Vihv.

"So what's that?" said Mix, pointing at a small frog, neatly sliced open and spread-pinned to the dining table like a groundsheet, its insides exposed, the little pink and brown tubings twitching like a ticking clock.

"Oh!" said Remedie, covering her mouth. "Oh, how awful!"

"It's quite unconscious," said Mrs. Vihv. "With no guests, I likes to work in the parlor next to the fire. I'll move it. Don't worry."

"But why would you even . . . What could possibly . . ."

"Oh, I's no guilt—I mean to put something of what I've

learned into medicine that could save hundreds. An' that's worth a few frogs to me, 'specially when they gets into my strawberry patch. I's learned all kinds o' things, findin' out how we lives an' how to keep us livin'. So fascinatin'." Mrs. Vihv leaned in toward the frog. "You find out what it means to live: sometimes it's little chemicals an' muscles, the biology swishin' away. Other times it's somethin' else, some other force—a *will* to keep livin'. If we could harness that! An' sometimes you see the moment they choose to yield. There's a lot in that, too."

Wull fought back the bile in his throat. "People don't choose to die," he said. "They don't. They're taken."

He saw Mrs. Vihv's eyes dart to Pappa.

"Not all the time," she said gently. "Even frogs turn their faces to the wall." Then she reached down and stopped the frog's little heart.

The sudden absence of its busy flutter seemed to Wull an explosion of silence.

"Is that what's for breakfast then?" said Mix.

"Aren't you a cheeky thing?" said Mrs. Vihv. "Not like this precious, quiet wee bundle. What's his, her . . . ?"

"His. Bonn," said Remedie. "He's . . . sleeping just now. Long day traveling."

Mrs. Vihv clasped her hands under her chin.

"I've four myself, not that you'd know it. They only come past here when their bellies are rumblin' or their garments are lousy, the ungrateful cretins—forgive my cursin' again. It's terrible, terrible, an' in front o' the child too."

She ran a fingertip over Bonn's forehead and smiled before turning and stoking the fire.

"That's why we're here, actually," said Wull. "The mormorach."

Mrs. Vihv stopped with the poker in midair.

"An' what are you plannin' to do, a bean pole of a boy, a young girl, an' a new mother? Forgive me, but the beast's already sunk half a dozen o' the best huntin' boats that sail. There's only one left now. It's our only hope. Unless *you've* some grand plan."

"We've got a . . . bäta," said Wull, helping Pappa into a chair.

"A *bäta?*" said Mrs. Vihv, laughing. "What are you plannin' on doin'? Teachin' it to row?"

"I've got harpoons," said Wull defensively.

"An' good for you, but I've been hearin' stories about what this thing does to harpoonists, an' believe you me, I'll not stand by here with four boys o' my own—not that they ever come to kiss their mother's cheek, the swine—forgive me cursin'—an' watch a young man throw himself at the tusks o' this brute in a rowboat. It would tear a wee thing like that apart without noticin'."

Wull knelt down at Pappa's feet, and tucked his hair away from his face.

"I have to go," he said. "I've come all this way."

"Not while you're under my roof," said Mrs. Vihv, gathering a pile of laundered clothes into her broad arms.

"I'm a payin' customer," said Wull, confused.

"An' be that as it may, you're not takin' a wee boat out for that animal. There's one proper huntin' boat left, an' much as I'm loath to even say this I've seen men an' their hothead ideas o' glory, an' I know it's a failed task to change your damn mind—forgive me cursin' again. If you must find a way out there, you'll have to speak to its captain an' get yourself a place on its crew."

"I must," said Wull. "I have to, I *have* to—Pappa needs some o' the medicine inside it."

"An' haven't I been hearin' fine tales o' the treasure in this beast the last week—sailors an' their money! It's worthless if you're dead, young man—corpses can't spend the coins on their eyes."

"I don't want the money," said Wull. "I jus' want to save him."

Mrs. Vihv started arranging tea things on the table. "Am I not glad I let you in here now," she said, "wi' a babby an' a sick man needin' took care of. Why're his hands bound up, if I may ask?"

"He . . . he might hurt himself," said Wull quietly. "He's ill."

Mrs. Vihv tilted her head and gave him a hard look. "Well, there's a tavern called the Brunswick in the market square—all the huntin' folk go there on an evenin' to drink their pay. You'll like as not find this captain in there—Murdagh's his name. But careful, mind: I've heard he's a fearsome type—ran the mayor here for all his land if the tongue waggers have the right of it."

"Thank you," said Wull. "Oh gods, thank you!" He looked at Mix. "Will you look after Pappa?"

"I'm comin' with you," she said. "Don't reckon I want to miss this."

"*I'll* look after your pappa," said Mrs. Vihv, "an' Mrs. . . . ."

"Cantwell," said Remedie. "Miss Cantwell."

"Miss Cantwell an' her babe. There'll be root tea and flat scones when you're back. An' be careful, mind, huntin' folk are not normal folk. . . ."

"Stinking it that speaks!" said Pappa, spluttering awake.

"But you might not be as shocked as I imagined," said Mrs. Vihv without missing a beat. "You can take your things up to your room before you go."

Wull gathered the bags and headed for the thin, warped stairs. Remedie pulled his arm as he passed.

"She *touched* Bonn and thought him flesh!" she whispered. "It's really happening!"

"An' I'm glad, miss," said Wull, smiling.

"I only worry about the wound from that bird." Remedie lifted Bonn's blanket away. The white wood had browned at the puncture's edge, a vein-burst of thin lines spreading from its center like a bruise. "I hope it won't change him too much, or cause him pain."

"I'm sure he'll be fine," said Wull, touching Bonn's palm with his fingertip. "He's a strong one, an' he's—"

Bonn's fist curled around Wull's knuckle.

"Did you see?" said Remedie. "Oh, Wulliam, there's so much *magic* here! And it was you who brought us to it." She beamed up at him.

"I saw," said Wull, squeezing her shoulder. He looked at Bonn's hand on his.

"If you're going out, take the . . . thing, you know—the *mandrake*," said Remedie, mouthing the last word. "I don't want to be alone with it."

"If you like," said Wull. As he climbed the stairs, he looked beyond the curtain and saw a long low-lit room lined with jars of yellow water, all filled with coils of organs and the glutinous lengths of sea creatures, a few dead edges moving delicately against the glass.

He threw the bags into the room, hoisted the heavy mandrake sack over his shoulder, and, squeezing Remedie's shoulder as he passed, followed Mix back into the cold night.

Decatur House

From Pent's open mouth came wordless sounds of fury, uncontrolled spit hanging in strings from his chin.

Tillinghast writhed away from the swinging boots, his insides an expanding agony, the misshapen fires of the wicker Things burning his clothes and singeing his skin as he crawled past them into the corridor.

"How'd you even know to find me here?" said Tillinghast.

Pent held up the dossier, flicked through the pages, and smiled.

"That's about me, is it? 'Bout my life?"

Pent nodded. Then he dropped the book into the pile of burning Things.

"No!" said Tillinghast, reaching for the curling paper.

"Tillinghast!" cried Clutterbuck, pulling on his arm.

"Run!" said Tillinghast. "Get yourself away!"

"I can't! Not without—"

Pent's fist knocked Clutterbuck to the ground, dashing his glasses in a tinkling mess on the flagstones.

"You blaggard!" shouted Tillinghast, rising, swinging madly, fluids bursting from his eyes and nose.

Pent dropped him with a boot to the chest, held him

there. He leaned close in on him, let his spit fall onto Tillinghast's face, then held up a piece of paper.

"The mandrake?" said Tillinghast.

Pent nodded.

"It's no' here! I gave it away . . . sold it! Look, in my money pouch: money, hundreds o' ducats! Take 'em an' go, jus' leave him alone!"

Pent turned his head on one side, his expression inscrutable. He went to his pocket and lifted out a witch ball.

"Whassat?" said Tillinghast, his mind fuzzy.

Pent rolled it between his fingers, smiling, then held up the piece of paper again.

"I told you I dun't have it anymore!"

Clutterbuck pulled himself to his knees.

"The Things!" he said, reaching sightlessly around him. "Why did you burn the Things?"

Pent looked at him crawling on the floor, then back at Tillinghast. He showed him the witch ball again.

"I tol' you, I dun't have it!" shouted Tillinghast, seeing the straw inside the dark lump. This witch ball was made to kill him. He hugged himself to fight his seams bursting, the force inside that would split his skin.

Pent smiled again, spat on the floor, then tore up the piece of paper.

"What's that mean?" said Tillinghast. "Take the money, jus' don't hurt—"

Pent threw the witch ball.

Tillinghast was seized by a pain that seared through him like a terrible white light. He felt his skin break where the ball had landed, melting at its touch, and his ears filled with a high-pitched whine that dizzied his head and brought more fluid into his mouth.

He screamed again, and writhed, gone from time and space to a realm where only agony existed, unconscious of the slabs beneath him or of the burning touch of the Things as they lay dying around him.

When at last he opened his eyes he found himself in the workshop. Pent sat patiently on Clutterbuck's chair, the little man gathered to him, a knife at his throat.

"I'm so sorry, my boy," said Clutterbuck, his mouth smeared red, matting the hair of his beard.

Tillinghast looked at Pent. "Dun't," he managed. "I's goin' to gerrit f'you, the mandrake. I's goin' to . . ."

Pent shook his head and pointed at Tillinghast.

"You want me?"

Pent nodded.

"I thought . . ."

Pent moved the knife to the back of Clutterbuck's head.

"Dun't! I'll tell you—it's on a boat, headin' for the coast . . ."

Pent tilted the knife.

". . . for Canna Bay! The people in the boat din't take it.

They's got nothin' to do with me, but the boy, Wull, he'll give it you if you help 'im catch that mormorach thing. That's why he's goin' there. If you get 'im out after it, on a proper boat, he'll give it you. All right?"

Pent nodded, smiled, and drew back his hand.

"No!" shouted Tillinghast.

"Remember you are yourself," said Clutterbuck quickly. "You are your own—"

The knife drove into his skull with a squeak, making white slits of his eyes and sending blood running from his lips.

"Father!" shouted Tillinghast. "No! You blaggard . . . you . . ."

He dragged himself to his knees, face running wet onto the floor.

Pent tossed Clutterbuck's body aside and stood in front of Tillinghast, a new dagger, dull and misshapen, in his hand. He smiled again.

"Whassat now?" said Tillinghast, loose and beaten. "What you got? A new toy?"

Pent nodded, waggled the blade in front of his eyes. Around him the glass valves of the workshop hissed and popped, and the little gears turned among bottles and tubes of bright liquid.

"So, you's not even after the mandrake now, 's that it?"

Pent shrugged.

"You'll still take it, 's long as you get me, too?"

Another nod, another smile.

Tillinghast stood slowly, his great weight swaying, his skin bulging and straining as he leaned on Clutterbuck's workbench.

"Well," he said as Pent turned the dagger in his hand to make his cut, "'s too bad for you I's my father's son, so I's got a fair idea this is goin' to hurt," and he threw a vial of green liquid in Pent's face.

Pent fell to his knees with a hiss of burning meat, clawing at his eyes. The dagger clanged on the ground, and Tillinghast kicked it away, feeling the sting of it through his boot.

"You blaggard!" he said. "You've come here an' killed my father an' for what? The mandrake? The sport?"

He kicked Pent's stomach and doubled him over.

"How *dare* you?" he said. "Did you think I's goin' to let you get away with it?"

Tillinghast winced, grabbed at his side as his filling lurched through the split in his skin.

"Oh gods . . ." he said, falling to the floor and pulling himself toward Clutterbuck's body.

Pent rose in a tangle of desperate limbs and fled, pressing his hands out in a blind fumble. A moment later there came the sound of horseshoes on stone, and the vanishing drumbeat of a horse at gallop.

"Father," said Tillinghast, pulling Clutterbuck toward him. The body was lifeless and still. Tillinghast threw back his head and howled.

"I's goin' to make the right choice," he said quietly, closing Clutterbuck's eyes and laying him on his back. "An' I's goin' to make you proud o' me."

He stood, tore his shirt into strips, and bound himself together, tying knots with fingers that trembled with a weakness he'd never experienced. Finally, feeling some of his strength returned, he ran into the darkness, the moon gleaming off his pale torso as the woods swallowed him once more, the creatures of the night scattering before him as he thundered on toward morning.

20

Canna Bay

Oh! Canna Bay Sound, we wish ye were potœm!
Canna Bay Sound, oh my,
How nice it would be if the potœm were free
An' we could all drink ye dry!
An' what if the trawlers should tip in a storm
So we in the potœm were drown'd?
How happy we'd be, in the potœmy sea—
Never carin' if we're to be found!

–Traditional Canna Bay fishing/drinking song

The Brunswick Tavern sat glowing in the corner of the market: a square skinned with cobbled scales that shone under the moon, bordered by ranked, silent stalls on which the tarpaulins shimmered like ghosts. The Brunswick peered at them across the emptiness, orange light in its eyes and raucous bellows from its mouth. There came at regular intervals the rumble of upended furniture, of quarrels and falling tankards, and every voice seemed to be raised against the deafness of alcohol—every utterance shouted as though into a storm.

"I'm not in a hurry to get in there," said Mix.

"What choice have we got? Mrs. Vihv said there's only one huntin' ship left, an' the captain's in here," said Wull. He rubbed the top of his belly, pushing his fingers against the pain of his guts.

Inside, the scene was as chaotic as it had sounded. People lay on floors, on tables, in the alcoves of the windows. The floor was sticky with spilled liquor, and the air tasted of yeast and the animal heat of cheap sheep-fat candles. Wull stepped over a thick-bearded man who was asleep with an expression of unfocused bliss, and waved at the barkeep.

"Does I know you?" said the man, setting a ham-sized forearm on the bar.

"I . . . no," said Wull.

"Then why's you wavin' at me?"

"He waves at everyone," said Mix.

"I was jus' tryin' to get your attention," said Wull. "I'm sorry."

"Well, you's got it now. What'd you want?"

"We're lookin' for someone," said Wull.

"'In't tha' super," said the barkeep. "An' what's you drinkin' while you's lookin'?"

"Oh, we don't want a drink. We jus' need to speak to him."

"Well, look, long lad: I sells hard drink in here for those who wants to get drunk fast. We don't need bright-faced younglings like you'selves to give the place atmosphere by makin' merry chatter wi' folk whose only conversation should be wi' the bottom o' a glass an' maybe the gods after they's had one too many. So I'll ask again—what's you drinkin'?"

Wull looked at Mix. "Have you more o' Till's money?" he whispered.

She held up a handful of coins. "Plenty," she said. "I was only kiddin' when I said I din't take much."

"You thievin' sneak," said Wull, smiling. "What can we have?" he asked the barkeep.

The man took his finger from his nose and rolled a sticky lump delicately between his thumb and forefinger.

"A couple o' kids like you's can have milk suds or milk suds, though come to think o' it there is a third option."

"Is it milk suds?" said Wull, standing on Mix's toes.

"'S right. What'll it be?"

"Two milk suds, please," said Wull.

The barkeep turned to the barrel.

"That was cryin' out for a smarter mouth," whispered Mix. "Why din't you ask for some potœm?"

"Because I don't want to get thrown out," hissed Wull. "So don't you say anythin', either."

Two sloppy tankards were placed on the bar, sudsy white bubbles spilling into the puddles that had already gathered.

"Crown an' a half," said the barkeep.

"Thanks," said Wull, counting the money into his palm. "Can I tell you who we're lookin' for now?"

"You c'n try me," said the barkeep, "but most o' these wretches 'in't my customers. People from here's had no coin since that beast showed up—these're mostly the sailors what's come from out o' town, drinkin' away their huntin' money."

"It's a hunter we're lookin' for," said Wull. "Gilt Murdagh."

The barkeep's eyes widened. "You sure 'bout that now?" he said.

Wull nodded. "We were told his was the last ship sailin' for the monster."

"An' you were told the truth, but I's not sure I'd want to be both'rin' the captain this night. He's over by the fireplace, crutch on his shoulder."

Wull followed the barkeep's hand, saw the man slumped in the firelight, alone at his busy table.

"Thank you," said Wull. He lifted his tankard and turned into the tavern, sniffed the cloudy liquid and wet his lips with its foam. "This tastes like sweat," he muttered.

As he stepped through the crowds, someone found most of the piano keys they were looking for, and a thin tune was picked up by the rolling crowds: a song Wull had heard Grandmamma sing about wishing the deep sound of Canna

Bay were made of potœm. He reached Murdagh's shoulder and cleared his throat.

"Captain Murdagh," he said, "I wish to speak with you."

Murdagh made no move, gave no sign of having heard.

"Captain Murdagh?" said Wull again. "Sir, I wish to—"

"I heard ye, lad. Don't go strainin' yourself wi' that stiff-shirt voice," said Murdagh, his face obscured by his hat. "Speak."

Some of the men—Murdagh's crew, Wull supposed—had stopped singing and were listening intently.

"I wish to join your crew as you sail for the mormorach," said Wull. "I've come a long way to kill it, an' I badly need somethin' it has inside it. I can row an' I can mend nets an' . . ."

Murdagh laughed, a wheezing, choking sound.

"An' 'in't they mighty fine, all those little skills?" he said. "You know how many other's've come beggin' me, lookin' for a slice o' Gilt's money?"

"I need none o' its gold, sir, jus' the juice from a small part o' its—"

"Well, you're gettin' none from me," said Murdagh. He drew a knife from his sleeve, lifted a vivid red fruit from the table, and began to peel it in long, slippery ribbons. "My crew is my crew is my crew, an' how d'you think they's goin' to feel about splittin' their haul wi' a cut-cheeked stranger who's no legs for the sea?"

"I've spent all my life on the water," said Wull.

"How many times, I wonder," said Murdagh, lifting a slice of fruit into his mouth, "have I heard that claim, untested against the bright heat o' my work?"

"I've been tested plenty," said Wull coldly.

"Have ye? So, you reckon you's a water man, do you?" said Murdagh. He tilted his head and looked at Wull for the first time, never stopping his blade at the fruit's husk, its juice running clear on his dirt-thick hands. Keeping his attention on Wull's eyes, he kissed pieces of red flesh from his blade with lips that were sun-bleached and cracked.

"Aye," said Wull, looking back. He focused on Murdagh's good eye and set his mouth to stop his own lips trembling. "I'm the Danék Riverkeep."

Murdagh rumbled and looked at his crew. "A squirt like you's keepin' the Danék?"

Wull tensed. He felt Mix's hand on his arm.

"My father was the keep before me. . . ."

"And?" said Murdagh. "I reckon yer father was a big man with hair on his backside. An' what are you?"

"I'm the Riverkeep," said Wull, "an' I've plenty hair on my backside."

Mix groaned as Murdagh and his crew exploded in laughter.

"Have you? Isn't that a fine thing? An' yer a waterman who tends his gentle puddle and stays out o' harm's way. Good for you, cut-squirt. But don't you stan' there an' tell me yer a man o' the water who can look me in my clear eye just 'cause you can row a boat."

All eyes in the room were on Wull, except Murdagh's, who had returned his attention to the fruit.

"Be gettin' yerself out o' here," he growled, "while ye've still got the legs to carry you."

Color burned on Wull's face. "The Danék's a treacherous—" he began.

"*Is* it?" said Murdagh, whirling round and pointing the blade of his knife under Wull's chin, his crutch falling noisily over, the fruit bouncing away on the floor. Murdagh's rotten breath was sharp in Wull's eyes and, close to, he saw that the surface of the old sailor's hidden, bloodied eyeball was pulled tight by scar tissue.

"Let me tell you, hairy-backside cut-squirt, that yer wee pond an' yer *rowboat* mean nothin' to me or mine," said Murdagh. "*There* ye have a backyard to make pretty; out here ye'll hear the whistle o' hell comin' an' spend endless days wrestlin' broken waters an' waves the size o' churches. On the sea, on the *real* sea, a man o' the water stands against storms that could gut his boat like a fish an' send him rag-dolled into the deep, an' he does so without blinkin' or lettin' fear take him. He sleeps standin' up wi' his muscles an' bones screamin' for ungranted mercy till his dreams and his wakin' thoughts become a single, painful howl. A *real* man o' the water sails toward empty skies knowin' that in a thousand miles he'll not pass a hearthstone or find a soft place to lay his head an' he does so in a boat that's no more'n a feather in a gale.

"*You* sit in yer boathouse, watchin' the same trees and the same skyline, chuckin' scraps to the seulas an' thinkin' yersel' threatened because once yer safely tucked up behind iron bars an' locked doors an ursa might shuffle past. Ye've never felt through the skin o' yer feet that eternal war below, where all things prey on all others an' would eat you in a heartbeat were ye to but dip yer toe into their freezing hell. *You* think ye've a tough time fillin' lamps wi' whale oil, but ye've never killed such a beast yerself, chased one down in a tiny, delicate boat, then torn its flesh under yer blade, dragged it aboard, flensed its skin, an' boiled its flesh in stinkin' try-pots for days to *make* the oil for lightin' up cozy houses . . . like yours."

The knife broke Wull's skin.

"An' let me tell you, cut-squirt keep . . ."

"Wulliam," said Wull, meeting his stare.

Murdagh smiled appreciatively. "Wulliam Cut-Squirt," he said, licking his teeth. He used his empty hand to lift the flap of skin over his injured eye. "Let me tell you, little man, that the real sea'll take from you every ounce o' fortitude and deal you such blows . . . fatal to the last degree o' fatality."

Wull watched as Murdagh blinked, the passage of the torn lid over his split eyeball painful and slow.

"I need to kill the mormorach, sir," said Wull. "I've brought good harpoons and good rope for its catchin', an' I've no fear of it. It's not a question of just wantin' to—I need jus' one part of it to cure my pappa. The money you can have for all I care."

Murdagh kept his knife in place and shifted in his seat.

"That's fair kind o' you, offerin' to share a bounty ye've no hope of catchin'. If ye think ye're goin' after some *fish* who'll roll over for a tickled belly and let ye whisk him into yer little boat, then ye'll be dead in a day. So, ye've *harpoons?* Ha! Might as well tickle an ursa's lad with a feather."

His men laughed, and Wull felt the sizzle of embarrassment burning on his cheeks. His shoulders swelled.

"I's been huntin' the world's seas for longer than you've been squattin' on privies," said Murdagh, warming to his theme, "so let me tell you jus' how this is goin' to go for you, with those little pointy sticks you could barely lift. Most land-walkin' animals has in their veins some valves so that when they's wounded, their blood stops spurtin', an' they can get away an' survive. Not so with the whale—the whale 'in't got no valves anywhere in 'im, so when he's pierced even by so small a point as a harpoon . . ."

Wull felt a trickle of blood run down his neck and onto his chest.

"A deadly drain starts in his whole system. Then he dives, deeper and deeper, tryin' to live and flee the harpoons, blades bein' thrown hard by men wi' sturdy hands an' sure hearts. But what he dun't know's that the drain o' his blood pours out even quicker in the pressure o' the deep, an' the life jus' floods out o' him in great red waves. But there's so much blood in 'im, an' so many are the little fountains of it inside his grand bulk, that he bleeds for hours, hoverin' there in the dark o' the water while Gilt waits above, ropes fastened on the barbs o' the little harpoons, which is all's needed to break so great a creature.

"Even wi' an ursa, I'm told, though I's never hunted on land an' don't much care for the notion, there's weak spots: little nooks an' crannies in its hide that a decent marksman might find one time in ten, an' if he fancies 'is chances the ursa's there for the takin'.

"But the mormorach 'in't got no soft points: his hide can't be breached by normal barbs such as ye'll find on the end o' yer pointy sticks, an' even if ye can manage to cut him, his leaks stop the second they touches water. He's got gills so's he never needs to surface for breath, he's stronger than a hundred men, stronger than any ship or any wind or any number of gods you cares to call on for help. He'll grow, bigger an' bigger without stoppin' so long as he's got enough to eat, an' his jaws could smash through the transom of a keep's bäta like it was a floatin' wafer. Today I had 'im on the ropes, hurtin' an' blind, jus' where I wanted 'im, an' he jumped up regardless and took one o' my masts from me—cut me with the spines o' his tail, too."

Murdagh shifted in his seat and showed Wull the bandages, wetly blotched with claret, on his right arm.

"Gilt's had worse'n that," said Murdagh, slow-blinking his damaged eye, "an' he can take it. But you's not got any idea what you's wantin' to face, Wulliam Cut-Squirt, an' for all the gumption you's shown comin' here I's not impressed, 'cause front like that'll jus' get you killed."

Wull formed a reply, but felt the swollen warmth of his cut cheek and the impassive stares of Murdagh's crew and bit it back.

"All I want is his name," Murdagh carried on, "an' his skull for my prow; what value might be in his flesh is mine, but I got little enough int'rest in that. My crew can have the bounty, an' I 'spect they's no plans to share it with any other, least not some cut-squirt keep who shows up wi' a hard-luck tale an' a bad attitude," said Murdagh. "Now—leave."

He found the fruit on the floor, kicked it toward himself with the tip of his whalebone leg, and lifted it, resuming the work of his knife at its husk while Mix dragged Wull from the tavern and onto the freezing, cobbled ground of the market.

"Let me go!" he said, wriggling in her grip.

"Why?" she said. "So you can go back an' make a bigger fool o' yourself?"

"I wasn't . . . he's—"

"He's a mean old man whose head's full o' the sea, an' goin' back in 'in't goin' to change his mind, is it? All it'll do is get you another scar for your cheek."

Wull sagged in her grip. "How did you get so strong?" he said. "I thought you were a tiny little girl?"

"When it suits me," said Mix, releasing him.

They turned and started the slippery walk back to the guesthouse.

"Now what will you do?" she said.

"I don't know. Take the bäta, I s'pose."

"But Mrs. Vihv said—"

"I know what she said! But what's my choice? Row it back an' watch Pappa die quietly on the way? What did I come here for if not to go out for it?"

"But *you'll* die," said Mix. "You think Paps wants that to happen in tryin' to save him?"

"I don't know what he wants anymore," said Wull, rounding the corner and spying the guesthouse through the mist.

"Yes, you do," said Mix quietly.

Mrs. Vihv burst through the door. "You're there!" she said. "I've been worried out my box here! He's gone!"

"What? Who's gone?" said Wull, his guts collapsing. "My pappa?"

"No! The babby! Bonn! He jumped up and ran off an' she's near to—"

"But Pappa's all right?" said Wull.

"Bonn's alive?" said Mix.

"What?" said Mrs. Vihv. "What d'you mean he's alive?"

"Wulliam! Mix!" said Remedie, bursting into the street. Her eyes were frantic, her skin pale. "Bonn is gone! He's *gone!*"

"What's this 'bout the babby bein' alive?" said Mrs. Vihv.

"Nothing, Mrs. Vihv, thank you, we'll go an' look for him now. I'm sure it's all right," said Wull, leading the landlady by the arm toward her front door.

"Strange things's happ'nin' of late," she said. "It's that thing an' its magic! I swear I saw one o' my sand frogs twitchin' in its jar the other day. . . ."

"We'll be back soon," said Wull, pulling the door closed. "Keep an eye on Pappa for me, please. When did he go?" he asked Remedie, turning.

"Moments ago. The landlady wouldn't believe me, at first; she held me back from going after him, and now he's gods know where. . . ."

"We'll find him," said Wull. "Don't worry. He can't have gone far."

Remedie snatched up his hand. "He's so strong, Wulliam," she said hurriedly. "Not like a flesh-child. He'll run without cease, and he's no need for food, save the sun and clean water. I must away now to have any chance!" She kissed Wull's forehead and held his face. "Take care of your father. Be brave."

As she set off, she pulled Mix into a firm hug, whispered in her ear, then ran into the green darkness beyond the houses.

Mix watched her go, then looked at Wull, eyes twinkling. "Bonn's *alive*," she said. "Boy, am I glad I snuck onto your boat. It would have been right borin' on that bradai skiff!"

"We need to find them," said Wull. "Remedie needs our help."

"No problem," said Mix. She pulled back her sleeve, exposing a thin wrist that was marked with pale, elegant lines near to the elbow. Close to, Wull saw that they were husked and rough, like bark.

"What are you doing?" he said.

"Ssh," said Mix, grinning. She reached for his hand, linking their fingers together.

Wull watched the skin of her free hand change, becoming looser, almost jagged. "Mix? What did you steal?" he said, knowing the answer by the feeling that surged through his arm.

"This," whispered Mix, and closed her eyes.

Wull watched as she pushed her free hand into the wet ground and felt, through her skin, the moment it dissolved and broke like wave-battered sand. He felt her consciousness disappear, her senses taking over his mind as she began to see, to *really* see, the forest: she saw, and Wull saw, the breeze—not as it moved their bodies and tugged their hair, but as it played on the white leaves of trees, waved stiff grasses in the clearings, and toppled crumbs of earth; together they felt the slow, constant stirring of the soil, a great soup of roots and insects and worms and burrowing things turning over each other and moving the earth like breathing lungs; they felt the sudden, thrumming strike of fast mammalian heartbeats around them like little pools of light, the sonic tingle of the animals' frayed nerves playing through their bodies like hammer strikes on iron.

They felt each other's presence in the world, the weight of all their unique strengths and separate energies drawn to the other like water gathering in a rock pool. Wull felt Mix's heart thudding alongside his own, and knew in that moment that his heart beat in her chest.

And then they found what they'd been looking for: two sets of footsteps, running, one light and quick, the other farther back—frantic but sure.

Mix opened her eyes and smiled, drew back her hand, and rolled down her sleeves.

"What was that?" said Wull, once he'd recovered his breath. He found he couldn't look Mix in the eyes.

"How'd you think I found you in the woods before?" she

said. "Got pretty tricky when your heart slowed down in the cold—a real close one. An' it's how I know what's really happened to your paps."

Tears welled in Wull's eyes. "There's still some o' him left in there," he said. "I know it."

She nodded. "I know there is," she said. "Just enough. Remedie's already half a mile away. I need to go after them. She's goin' to need my help, I'm sure of it."

"Don't go," said Wull. "I mean, if Remedie needs help, then go, of course, I don't mean—"

"There's . . . people . . . lookin' for me, too—people that won't ever stop lookin'. I need to keep movin'.'"

"Because you stole that . . . thing by accident?"

She smiled. "I really didn't mean to, you know, I just . . ." She pulled back her sleeve, showing Wull the barklike markings on her skin. "The folk chasin' me, they don't care. It's theirs, this power. They's wantin' it back, an' they'll kill me, I know it—I've felt their thoughts through the world the way we felt Remedie an' Bonn jus' now. You don't need me here. You've got everythin' in your steady hand, Wulliam River-keep."

Mix lifted onto her tiptoes and kissed his cheek. Wull pressed his hand to where her lips had touched him and felt the green lightness of spring on his skin.

"I don't want you to go," he said, startling himself.

"I know."

"Will I see you again?"

"Count on it. Look after Paps."

Wull nodded.

"It's goin' to be all right," said Mix, then she turned and ran into the frosted shadows of the forest.

Wull watched until she disappeared, then headed for the guesthouse.

"Have you found him?" said Mrs. Vihv as he entered, dragging his feet. She was bent over the gut-splayed frog, a magnifying lens strapped to her head.

"Remedie's gone after him," said Wull. "Mix went after her."

"They've gone alone? All the gods, we'll have to send folk after them!"

"No," said Wull, stopping her by the arm and shaking his head. "They'll be fine. They're . . . very strong. They'll be fine on their own. I had to stay for Pappa."

Mrs. Vihv placed her hands on her hips and looked at him. "You're sure?" she said.

"Definitely," said Wull, thinking about what Mix had done.

"All right then. How'd you get on with the captain?"

"Badly. He told me where to go an' no mistake," said Wull. "I've never met anyone like him in my life."

Mrs. Vihv nodded and returned to the frog. "There's not many who have, the way I hear it. An' imagine—there's not even much o' him left. What must he have been as a younger man? You shudder to think."

"I felt sorry for him," said Wull.

Mrs. Vihv flashed him a look. "All o' us are worthy o' pity," she said, "even the worst behaved o' us. *Especially* the worst behaved, sometimes. Sit down then—your pappa's been asleep since you left, pretty much. Woke up an' ate some fish then nodded off. His . . . eyes, they're interestin', aren't they?"

Wull looked up from the armchair, his nose smoke-stung and his vision running in the acrid press of the room.

"What?" he said.

"I said your pappa's eyes are interestin'. How long have they looked like that?"

"Since he got sick," said Wull. "They . . . clouded up, an' he doesn't see so well now."

Mrs. Vihv gave him a prolonged stare. "An' you know why that is, don't you?" she said softly.

"No," said Wull. "He's ill, something in his mind, is all. This thing in the mormorach can cure him. It's why I need it. An' why I'm goin' after it even without Captain Murdagh an' his damn boat, an' it doesn't matter what you say to me!"

"All right, son, you know your own mind," said Mrs. Vihv. "It's jus' that . . . I've seen eyes like that before, once, before I came here, when I was still set up in the city an' payin' someone to fetch me samples from the coast. They were in a goat's head at the time, but it wasn't a goat was lookin' at me."

Wull kept his face turned away, looking at the flames.

"It was a bohdan," said Mrs. Vihv, "an' I only found out later how lucky I'd been. That's why his arms are tied, isn't it? An' why he's only eatin' fish."

"He's still in there!" said Wull. "He is! I see it sometimes and I hear him . . . jus' at the edge o' his voice I hear him!"

"All right," said Mrs. Vihv as Pappa, coughing and cursing, woke in his chair and started to mouth the sour crust of scales on his lips.

"It that speaks?" he said, looking around. "Untie the arms!"

"You need be careful o' this," said Mrs. Vihv. "I won't talk you out o' it because I can't imagine what you's been through to get him here, but be careful. It'd live inside you as quick as look at you—you've done right to keep his hands bound. There's no guarantee this creature'll cure 'im, though there's magic enough in it. But you need to understand it's not jus' a mind sickness your pappa's got. There's another creature livin' in 'im."

Wull nodded. "I know," he said, and the moment of saying it out loud fell from him like lead weights.

"Be up to bed now, an' sleep. There'll be bacon in the mornin'—burned's the only way I can make it so I hope your taste runs that way."

"Thanks," said Wull. He gathered Pappa under the arms and led him to the stairs.

"Sleep, it that speaks, stinking boy," said Pappa quietly.

"We can sleep now, Pappa," said Wull, and as he climbed the steps, holding the bones of Pappa's arms through his smock, he felt too the writhing, acid weight in his belly telling him that tomorrow would come sooner than he could ever prepare for it, and that it would decide his fate whether he was ready or not.

21

Canna Bay

Homunculus: literally, "little man." While the roots of this term are in the notion of preformation—of male seed each carrying a fully formed and tiny man (discredited: see Hertsökr, N.)—the term includes all forms of humanity created or built by any means other than the carrying of a fetus in the female womb, this including golems, revenants, and other reanimated forms. The homunculus displays outward signs of life but remains dead internally, possessing, in the words of J. H. Steele, "no circulatory, respiratory, or digestive function whatsoever." Homunculi are officially classified "unalive" however, rather than dead, owing to the theological complexity of their existence and their outward display of human physiology and function. There are frequent instances of their having demonstrated empathy, compassion—and even love.

—Encyclopedia Grandalia, University of Oracco Print House

Wull was awake long before the dawn burst its yolk over the horizon, sat up in bed with his aches fading into the background of his fear.

Beside him, in the other narrow bed, Pappa lay stiffly, his open mouth running spit, the jaw too wide, the tongue too long. Wull could feel the real Pappa inside, like the slipping grains of an hourglass—and he knew they would run out today.

Whatever happened, it would be today.

He climbed down the wobbling stairs as soon as he heard Mrs. Vihv at the breakfast plates, and sat in the cold, slow charcoal of the parlor while she pottered about, breaking eggs and apologizing to herself for cursing.

"MORNING! BREAKFAST IS—Oh, you're there, Wulliam. Good morning. I didn't hear you get up."

"I couldn't sleep," said Wull.

"That makes sense, right enough. I'd a bit of trouble myself, thinkin' o' you an' your pappa, and the young ladies havin' left in the night. Quite a thing, that wee babby takin' off like that. An' this mornin' all my specimens were bashin' themselves off their jars like they'd jus' been whisked out o' the sea. Strange things happ'nin', no doubt. Maybe it will do the trick for your pappa, right enough, this thing you say's inside the mormorach."

Wull nodded, lifted a shard of bacon to his mouth. "I hope so," he said.

"An' on that score, I heard a thing this mornin' from Mrs. Frame what does for Mr. Lockstop, somethin' that seems like right good luck for you—there's a shippin' clerk arrived late last night an' taken lodgin's down at the Brunswick Tavern. You mus' o' just missed him!"

Wull sucked carefully at the blood from the bacon-wound in his gum.

"What's a shipping clerk?" he said.

"Well, they sort o' make arrangements for the boats. Supplies, an' so on. An' *crew*. Seems you might find a way aboard Captain Murdagh's boat right enough!"

"Does it cost money?" said Wull, leaping to his feet.

"Often they takes a cut o' your cut, so to speak, but here, take this jus' in case."

Mrs. Vihv's hand went to her hair and withdrew a tightly rolled wad of ducat notes.

"Oh, I couldn't. . . ." said Wull, backing away. "That's your money. I couldn't take that from you. . . ."

"But I wants to give it you!" said Mrs. Vihv. "You can pay me back once you earn your way. Here, I'm makin' you take it." She pressed the money into Wull's reluctant hand.

"But why?" said Wull.

She shrugged.

"I spend most o' my time killin' frogs an' sea cucumbers an' urchins. It'd be nice to put some o' the proceeds to helpin' save your pappa."

Wull felt the corners of his eyes prickle. "I don't know how to thank you for this," he said.

"Don't. Jus' pay me back once you rake in the treasure!" said Mrs. Vihv. "I'll take care o' your pappa when he wakes up. Off you get to the tavern now."

Wull threw his arms around her waist and buried his face in her smock.

"Thank you!" he said. "Thank you, thank you, thank you!"

"Be off, ye daft sod," said Mrs. Vihv, laughing. "If you're not there quick enough, some other enterprisin' sort might take your place."

Wull ran upstairs, looked at Pappa, still grumbling in sleep, unmoved since he'd left. He slipped on his seula-gut shift and his coat; then, as he was forcing his feet into his big boots, he looked at the sack that held the mandrake and lifted it onto his shoulder. He wouldn't be able to do anything with it, but the thought of Mrs. Vihv finding it made him nervous. It was another strange thing, by all accounts, and he wasn't sure it would escape her questing scalpel.

"I'm goin' to kill the beast today, Pappa," he said. "I'll find a way onto that boat an' I'll kill it an' then you'll be better."

He leaned over and kissed Pappa's feverish brow, then ran down the stairs and sped into the ice-misted air of the coastal morning.

He ran through the foot-slipping streets gleaming like a

fresh catch under the moisture of the new day, and quickly found himself in the market square.

"If it isn't the long lad of las' night," said the barkeep as Wull barged into the Brunswick. The main drinking hall smelled of stale yeast and hay, and there were people still sleeping in corners and under tables. "If you've come back to try your luck wi' the captain, I'll start by tellin' you he 'in't even here."

"I know," said Wull. "I've come to see the clerk."

The barkeep waggled his eyebrows and chuckled.

"That'll be Mrs. Frame spreadin' gossip, I reckon, since she's the only one what's been by at this ungodly hour. Clerk's in room three, up the stairs an' to the left. I knows he's up 'cause I already gave 'im his breakfast. Runny eggs, he wanted, an' sliced water squash. Bit of a strange order, but I's served stranger."

Wull was already running up the stairs, taking them three at a time, his knees clacking together in stumbling enthusiasm.

"Quiet now!" shouted the barkeep. "I's other guests what's not even up yet!"

Wull slowed his feet with difficulty and knocked on the door of room three. When nothing happened, he knocked again, and was about to knock a third time when the door opened and a long, expressionless face peered down at him with eyes that were strainedly red and raw.

"Sir," said Wull, "I've been told you can get me to crew on Captain Murdagh's ship—I've got money, an' I'll happily pay you what you see fit from my share o' the catch if you could find a way to get me on it this mornin'. I have to go today, sir. I'm sorry to barge in on you like this so early in the mornin', but I have to go today!"

The clerk peered at him quizzically, took in the sack over his shoulder, then retreated to a desk in the corner.

"Sir?" said Wull. He stepped over the threshold. "Sir, I'll gladly pay you what you want. . . ."

But the clerk shook his head, flashed Wull a hungry smile, and began to write very quickly on a scrap of paper.

"I's not a great reader, sir," said Wull.

The clerk pushed the paper into his hand.

Wull read it slowly, taking care to untie the loops of frantic pen that splattered the parchment. He looked at the clerk's face then at the mandrake.

He thought of Pappa.

"Here," he said, handing over the sack. "We parted on bad terms, and I don't know if I'll ever see him again—but if I ever do, I'll bring him to you. Is that enough?"

Mr. Pent nodded and then rummaged in his coat. He handed Wull a small, brown lump, then recommenced his frantic scribbling.

The hills above Canna Bay were solid in their whiteness, snow-capped for months of the year, their immense height keeping the ice high out the reach of the coastline's salt. The only creatures happy to endure their privations were the hardy little tock ponies, their patched hides peeping through the drifts as they dug their tough noses into the cold to find the ungrowing scruff of grass below.

A small herd of them scattered at Tillinghast's approach. As he'd run through the night, the temporary bindings on his body had shaken loose, and he held chunks of himself in his hands, his fingers mashing the wet straw back into place. He looked down at the arc of little houses, saw the tufts of smoke and the bobbing craft—and the one seagoing ship, white in places with bone, sailing out into the open sea beyond the breakwater.

While his vision flickered, he grabbed at the apparitions before him: Clutterbuck, Wull, Mix, Remedie, all stepping out to catch him as he fell, small noises of pain escaping his lips. He saw the mandrake, too, full grown and ready to be given its freedom as he'd been given his, ready to enter the world and be counted among humankind.

Murky liquids were pressing through the gaps in Tillinghast's stitches as he swelled in painful, uncontrollable ways. He ground on, catching his balance on legs that bent like trees in a storm, and thought only of finding Wull, the boy's stubborn name like a drumbeat in his head.

Tillinghast wrapped his arms around his sagging bulk and whispered words to bring himself comfort.

The *Hellsong*

"Who're you then?" said Samjon.

Wull looked out over the *Hellsong*'s gunwale at the flashing wave wash and tightened his grip on the rigging. He'd never seen water from such a height, and was astonished to find his guts roiling queasily as the great ship smashed and leaped through the breakers, the gongs lowing mournfully as the hammers rolled on their surfaces.

"I'm Wull," he said, tightening his grip on the rigging, feeling himself smashed between sky and sea.

"I din't know we was takin' on new crew," said Samjon. "I might not be the youngest now. How old are you?"

Wull blinked at the unexpected question. "I'll be sixteen tomorrow," he said.

"Oh," said Samjon, "I'm still the youngest then. I'm Samjon. I'm the cabin boy."

"What's that?" said Wull.

"Skivvy, really. I do the jobs o' everyone else for half the pay an' all the kickings my backside can take."

"That doesn't sound good," said Wull.

"It's not," said Samjon cheerfully, "but I'll be the bo'sun's mate if I keeps up like this, then I'll get to kick someone *else's* backside." His eyes glittered at the prospect. "What d'you do?"

"I'm an . . . oarsman."

Samjon's brows furrowed. "We 'in't got any oars," he said.

"I know," said Wull. He tried to think of something to add, and settled for looking out to sea.

"All right," said Samjon. "How'd you manage to get onto the crew? I got on after cleanin' the captain's floors for a year an' because my aunt Ethel knew a woman who worked for a man what used to be on the crew of another boat what's captain knew Captain Murdagh."

"I went to a shipping agent," said Wull.

Samjon's eyes widened. "That's money, that is. How much did it cost?" he said.

Wull sighed. "Everythin'," he said, rolling the witch ball Pent had given him between his fingers.

"Swing those hammers!" shouted Murdagh, stamping onto the bridge and pointing his crutch at the crew. "Let's wake that beast up an' let him know he 'in't sunk us yet! He c'n take another mast today if he likes—we'll come back tomorrow an' beat the gongs some more until the meat shakes off 'is bones!"

The crew ran to the rails, knocking Samjon and Wull aside, and began to heave on the thick ropes that bound the hammers in place. The gongs set to ringing, a sky-splitting boom that moved inside Wull's head and hurt the soft parts of his ears.

Samjon gestured to him and they staggered away, the ship thudding heavily as they passed the breakwater and entered the wide sea, suddenly at the mercy of the waves, its ribs creaking audibly under the strain.

"What are they for?" shouted Wull.

"To confuse the beast!" shouted Samjon. "The captain says it hunts with sound an' so must we!"

"How can it . . ." started Wull, but the words stuck in his throat as the mormorach burst over the *Hellsong*, blocking the sun with its incredible bulk, water falling from it in sheets onto the deck. It wailed in agony through its arc, thrashing its trunk and splitting the rail, knocking one of the gongs and two crew into the water. Wull saw its head, the size of a carriage, the tusks as long as his arms, and the shimmering coils of muscle beneath scales the size of dinner plates.

The gongs stopped as men and women fell about, and Murdagh roared at them, stabbing his crutch as he spat and cursed.

"Gods," said Wull, the blood running to his feet. "It's . . . It's so huge. . . . It's bigger than the ship."

"Almost," said Samjon. "The captain says we'll all be rich once we've killed it."

"Start those hammers or it'll be the lash!" shouted Murdagh.

The gongs beat again, falling into a rhythm that sounded to Wull like the heartbeat of the earth. He clung to a tooth-studded cleat on the port side, away from the fresh, gaping wound wrought by the mormorach's tail, watching as the huge swathes of seawater darkened the timbers and drew from it a deep crimson, as though the ship were a living thing, bleeding under the strain.

Murdagh turned the sails to set her aback, settling in the open water just outside the port and dropping anchor.

"This is where he lives!" he shouted. "He's in that trench, an' he's filled with all *your* money! Let's bring 'im up!"

The gongs beat. Wull's ears trembled, his guts shaken by the wall of sound and the incredible sight of the beast—but the mormorach did not appear again.

"Are you all right?" said Samjon, sliding across the deck toward him.

Wull nodded. "I don't think I belong here," he said. "I've made a mistake. This isn't my boat."

"Well, you's here for a few hours now, 'less you c'n walk on water," chuckled Samjon, knees rolling with the shifting deck.

Wull heard the thud of Murdagh's bone leg on the stairs behind him.

"The cut-squirt! I told you what I thought o' you joinin' my crew!"

He grabbed Wull by the shoulder and dragged him to the side. "I hope you c'n swim, little river boy, an' in mighty choppy sea, too! You's gettin' none o' Gilt's prize!"

"I don't want your prize!" shouted Wull, wriggling free and knocking Murdagh's hand away. "I want the tiniest bit of it, an' I'll pay. I already paid to get here—you have to let me stay!"

"An' who've you gave money to? My crew? No *Hellsong* crew's goin' to take a bribe from you 'less they wants to split their own share. Is it you what's done this, boy?" said Murdagh, gesturing at Samjon.

"No!" said Samjon. "But I'll happily split my share, Cap'n, if it helps the ship."

"It would help the cut-squirt here," said Murdagh, drawing his dirk and running his tongue over his teeth, "but I's not in the business o' sharin' my ship wi' strangers an' liars."

"It's true!" said Wull. "I paid a man named Pent; he said he's found you crew before. He said you've worked together in the past an' I could trust 'im."

"I's never heard o' this Pent," said Murdagh, "an' I works wi' no other party. Man wants to work on my crew's got to earn it, not buy it."

Wull's heart fell into his stomach. Murdagh gave an ugly grunt.

"I'd say you's been swindled, cut-squirt," he said. "What'd you give 'im, exactly?"

"My friend," said Wull, his head spinning, picturing the little mandrake in Mr. Pent's hand, hearing himself giving Tillinghast up like he was trading pickerel.

He had handed him over: all so he could be here, all so he could save Pappa.

But Wull knew in his heart that Pappa wouldn't want to be saved for such a price.

Murdagh laughed. "An' isn't that a high fare to have paid to be thrown overboard?" he said.

"What?" said Wull.

"Cap'n, I's goin' to split my share. . . ." said Samjon.

"Get belowdecks, cabin boy! An' you heard me, cut-squirt: get off! Swim! Or you c'n stay an' be sliced into chunks. . . . The beast's sounded from the noise, an' a little bait in the water 'in't goin' to hurt Gilt's chances of drawin' him out. . . ."

"Cap'n!" said Samjon.

"It's all right," said Wull, touching his shoulder. "I don't belong here. The captain's right."

"You swimmin' then?"

Wull nodded, meeting Murdagh's red, twisted stare. "But I'm comin' back," he said, "in my own boat. I'll kill this thing myself, take what I need from it, an' sink its bones so it's lost. You'll get none o' your prize, Captain Murdagh, I'll make sure o' it."

"Gah!" shouted Murdagh, lunging at Wull, blade outstretched.

The mormorach returned.

It smashed into the side of the *Hellsong* with such force that they were scattered to the deck, the slick wood tilting as the creature pressed its strength against it. Then it yielded and the ship crashed back into the water, a huge wave sweeping over the crew.

Wull jumped to his feet, ran for the rail—and was stopped by the sharp points of Murdagh's fingers at his ankle.

"Ye little demon!" shouted the old sailor. "Ye've cursed my ship! I'll kill you!"

"Let me go!" shouted Wull, kicking backward.

"I'll kill you! I'll kill you!"

Wull kicked Murdagh's chin, drawing blood from his lips. Murdagh snarled and reached for his blade.

Wull saw how easily the old sailor would stab him, how free of conscience he would be in the moment. He felt through his coat the little lump Pent had given him and snatched it, throwing it straight into Murdagh's good eye.

The captain flinched and, with a huge effort, Wull booted his hand away, loosening his grip for the tiniest moment.

It was enough. He ran, struggling for purchase on the fast, lurching deck, and dropped into the water as the mormorach jumped free of the sea beside him, a gigantic train of muscle that reached the highest mast even as its tail left the water.

Wull landed with a thump that took his wind. He kicked off his boots and shrugged free of his coat, leaving them to sink into the icy sea.

"I'll kill you!" shouted Murdagh. "Get me a harpoon! An' don't stop wi' those hammers!"

The gongs picked up as Wull swam, their sound holding him through the water like a fist. He plowed on, the waves taking his momentum, taking in mouthfuls of sour seawater as he went.

The mormorach sped below him, the silent power whipping past in a second, throwing him up on its wave. Wull felt himself tiny and fragile, his soft abdomen exposed to whatever sharpness might lurk unseen below the black water. He knew with his instincts the limitlessness of the void beneath him, the stretching reach of the deep toward his small body and his desperately kicking legs.

The creature thundered past again, a flash of gray that seemed to fill the sea for that second, too fast even to see the details of its body or the features of its awful face.

"Swim, cut-squirt!" shouted Murdagh, distant now. "Swim!"

The tip of the breakwater was getting closer. In the still water of the Danék summer he could swim such a distance in half a minute; out here, on the wild sea, each wave pushed him back nearly as far as he'd come.

He heard the cries of the crew as the mormorach

launched at the *Hellsong* again, and swam harder, almost within reach of the rusting ladder on the breakwater's wall.

Then he felt the mormorach behind him.

It was still a way off, he knew, but its energy stabbed at his back like a whirlpool's point, every bit of its strength driving toward him.

As his fingertips made contact with the ladder he heard the hiss of its fins tearing the surface and the rush of water filling its opening mouth.

He heaved himself up onto the first rung, pulling his feet behind him. The mormorach halted sharply, sending a wall of water that knocked out Wull's air and struck his head against the breakwater's rock.

The beast streamed off, back to the *Hellsong*, from which the sound of the gongs was now muffled by distance.

Wull scrambled up the ladder. There was hot blood on his head where he'd struck the breakwater, and his steps seemed unweighted, loose. With tiny stones stabbing at his stockinged feet he ran past the statue of the woman, through the discarded anchors and the silent, beached craft of the port. Groups of townsfolk were gathered, talking and gawking at the battle between creature and ship. Wull scattered them like hens as he ran toward the Brunswick, past the protesting barkeep and through the door of room three.

"Wull?" said Tillinghast, bound to a chair. His voice was weak. "Gods above, get away!"

Wull ran over and held Tillinghast upright. His face was intact, but his body was spilling outward from crude bindings, his skin split like the rot-swollen bodies Wull and Pappa found after months in sun-drenched water. A crude, dull blade was stuck in his chest.

"Till! I'm so sorry. He wanted the mandrake to get me on the ship, an' I thought I had to so I could save Pappa, but it's not right. I'm sorry. . . ."

"You shouldn't've come here. He only wanted me, an' I'm finished now. You shouldn't've—"

"How did you even find him?"

"Chewin' that rosy rubbish? Once I remembered what I was lookin' for, it was easy." Tillinghast looked at the ground. "I's not proud o' this, but I's got a florist's nose."

The door clicked shut. Wull turned to see Mr. Pent, grinning with spit on his chin, turning the key and dropping it into his pocket.

"I jus' want to take him away," said Wull. "You've got the mandrake, an' that's what you wanted, an' you've got my money too, so jus' let us go."

Pent laughed. He lifted the tight roll of money Wull had handed him that morning, threw it into the fire, then pointed at Tillinghast.

"You only want him?"

Pent nodded.

"Why?"

Pent looked thoughtful, then flexed his hands in a gesture of maddened strangulation.

"I's got no idea what you's sayin'." Tillinghast sighed. "Mibbe if you explained it through the wonder of song?"

Pent pointed at Tillinghast and shrugged.

"I'm takin' him with me," said Wull, his anger rising. "He's a pain an' he's rude, but he's my friend. An' look at him, he's ruined. Let me take him."

Pent shook his head.

"I'm takin' him!" said Wull.

"Wull," said Tillinghast, "jus' go!"

"No!" said Wull, and he rushed at Pent, head down, knocking him backward against the wall. Before Pent threw him off, Wull felt all the pieces of tinkling metal under the black coat, all the little blades and trinkets of violence neatly aligned like books on a shelf.

Pent tossed him to the floor and stamped after him. Tillinghast tried to rise but fumbled—Pent struck him across the mouth and kicked the table aside as Wull darted backward on the floor. As Pent came at him Wull rose and charged again, butting his stomach and swinging wild punches at his sides.

Pent drove a knee into his windpipe and pushed him to the ground. Spots flashed in Wull's vision, and he coughed, tasting blood.

"Wull . . . I's sorry," said Tillinghast. "It's my fault. I told 'im you needed to get on a ship. . . . I's sorry. . . . I'd've turned me in an' all."

He tried to stand again but slumped backward, broken and defeated.

Pent hunkered down, a thin knife held loosely in his hand. He smiled again and held it to the back of Wull's skull.

Wull felt his skin tear, and thought of Pappa, of his courage and his strength.

"No!" he shouted, rising with all his might—knocking Pent's hand aside and pushing his ribs.

The big man laughed, stepped away, raised the knife, and prepared to drive its point into Wull's brain . . . when his heel caught the corner of his coat. The fabric twisted as he fell, bunching the sharp, cruel, tinkling things beneath him into a fist of steel.

Pent wheezed as the blades sliced into his back, through the cage of his ribs and into his heart. He coughed violently, spraying flecks of bright blood onto Wull's face.

Wull fell backward, kicking away from Pent's agonized wriggle, the empty mouth hissing wordless curses and cries as the floor around him turned vividly red.

Then he was still, his last sound a tiny gasp that seemed to Wull like a whispered "please."

"Wull!" shouted Tillinghast. "Are you all right?"

Wull nodded, looking at Pent's twitching body, the pool of blood moving toward him.

"I'm fine," he said, sagging, "I'm sorry I gave him the mandrake. I'm so sorry."

"'S fine," said Tillinghast. "I'd've done the same. Course that's what makes me such a wretched git, an' is the kind o' behavior from which I's now repented. You did well facin' up to that blaggard, mind."

Wull lifted the knife from Pent's hand and cut the bonds at Tillinghast's wrists.

"Let's go," he said.

"You need to help me," said Tillinghast. "I's mibbe savable like this but no good for much else."

Wull lifted him into a hug, and they held each other a moment.

"Let me go, soft lad," said Tillinghast. "Where we goin' anyways?"

"To get Pappa, an' then we're goin' after the mormorach."

"I thought you'd gave up on it?"

"Only on catchin' it with Murdagh," said Wull.

"Who's Murdagh?" said Tillinghast.

"The captain of the only huntin' ship left, the one I traded you to get on. But he tried to kill me. We need to go on the bäta, on my boat. That's how this ends."

"*He* tried to kill you an' all?" said Tillinghast. "You's havin' some Wednesday."

Wull retrieved the key from Pent's pocket and led them through the corridors and out the back door, through the long grasses and broken glass of the yard and into the cobbled lane to the rear of the market.

Tillinghast was heavy on his shoulder, almost incapable of carrying his own weight, and Wull felt the bones of his back popping under the strain as they moved slowly down the hill toward Mrs. Vihv's.

"Wait here," he said.

"No trouble," said Tillinghast, slumped like compost on the ground. "But if a decent bit o' skirt comes by, I'm chasin' it."

"What happened to you?" said Mrs. Vihv as he entered. "Where's your shoes?"

"Nothin'. I'm fine. How's Pappa?"

Mrs. Vihv pulled her lips tight. "He's not good," she said, then she whispered, "It's takin' him," and touched Wull's face. "That's not nothin', my boy—you've blood in your hair. Din't you get on the ship?"

"Yes, no . . . I was on it, an' I had to leave. I'm takin' my boat. It's the only way I know how to do this."

"I said I wouldn't let—"

"I have to!" said Wull. "Pappa's dyin' in front o' my eyes. An' I can do this—I know I can! This is my river!"

Mrs. Vihv stepped back from him, met his eyes, then threw up her hands.

"So be it," she said. "You know your own mind!"

Wull knelt down in front of Pappa. "Pappa, we're goin'

now," he said, shaking the slumbering form. "I'm goin' to fix you, an' then we can go home."

Pappa's eyes, slower than ever and milked into blindness, slipped open. "It that speaks?" he said.

"I'm here, Pappa. Are you hungry?"

"Sleep," said Pappa.

"Soon. Come on with me now. We'll make you better."

He pulled the skinny body to its feet, trying not to hurt him, trying to press Pappa's weight against his shoulder without hauling at his tender joints.

"See that you're careful," said Mrs. Vihv, holding the door for them.

"Thank you," said Wull. "We'll see you soon."

"An' how's the old man today?" said Tillinghast as they emerged.

"He's dying," said Wull. "We need to get out there."

"You're takin' me? What am I for? Ballast?"

"There might be some gland in this thing that'll help you an' all, Till. Jus' come on."

Wull, keeping Pappa on his left side, leaned down and scooped Tillinghast up with his right arm, their two weights balanced on his shoulders.

"Look at you, strong man," said Tillinghast.

"Jus' help me," said Wull through his teeth.

They inched along, step by heavy step. Tillinghast fell, spraying his messy limbs over the cobbles as Wull leaned down to catch him, Pappa grunting painfully in his grip.

Wull placed himself somewhere else, a hidden part of his mind he'd never been to before, away from the pain and the squeal of his body, the ache of his shoulders and his wrist and his face dissolving as he thought himself into the space of the river and felt the press of Pappa's weight at his side.

They came to the shore where the bäta sat, its eyes— to Wull, always hard, unsympathetic, and locked in with judgment—now seeming determined and ready.

He peered through the sun glare to see the *Hellsong*, its ringing cries of war now irregular thumps, still fighting the mormorach and down to its last sail, graygulls swirling around it like flies at a dying animal. She had moved back into the water of the port inside the protection of the break-water, and so, he saw as it thudded through the *Hellsong*'s keel, had the beast.

He laid Tillinghast on the beach as he helped Pappa into the bäta, running his hand over the gunwale as he did so. He all but lifted Tillinghast into the stern after him, the big body little more than a pile of damp straw in his hands.

Wull dribbled the last of the water into his burning mouth, head spinning, then tossed the pouch onto the bottom boards.

"Let's go," he whispered to the boat as he heaved it into the sea, wading after it and scrambling onto the center thwart.

He rowed through the waves, pushing through their punches and away from the coast, out into the water of the port.

The noise of the gongs grew louder as he approached, matched almost by the frenzy of the waves and the splashing of lost crew. As the mormorach surfaced again, it roared, smashing through the bone-trussed ribs of the ship and sending more men and women into the water.

"What you goin' to do?" Tillinghast said weakly. "You can't kill that thing. . . . 'S big as a castle."

Wull hefted a harpoon in both hands and stood on the tossing bäta.

"I can stick it," he said. "Pappa said these are good iron. If I stick it it'll bleed, an' if it bleeds it'll die."

"You can't stab this thing! Look at it! Look at you!"

"What else am I to do?" shouted Wull as the mormorach streamed past them and into the air. It smashed through the *Hellsong*'s remaining mast, sending it toppling like a felled oak to the water. The crew began to abandon ship, diving from the lurching decks into the water around the bäta.

"Untie the arms!" said Pappa.

Wull launched the harpoon. It hissed invisibly through the chopping surface, vanishing in an instant.

"See?" said Tillinghast. "You have to go back!"

"Is that you, cut-squirt?" shouted Murdagh from the *Hellsong*'s deck. "You back to face me?"

"I'm back to kill it!" shouted Wull. "You've had your chance—now it's my turn!"

He heaved another harpoon in his hands, saw the flash of gray below, and threw it as hard as he could. It sailed through the air, tipping as it reached the bulbous swell of the mormorach's back before bouncing off like a raindrop. The bäta rocked as the creature's trunk grazed its hull, a fissure appearing in the thin planking, a rib splitting with a sharp crack.

"Turn back!" shouted Tillinghast, water washing over him in white swoops of foam.

"I've got one left," said Wull, raising the last harpoon to his shoulder and sighting the mormorach approaching. "I've got one left. I can do it."

"Ye're not takin' my prize, demon!" shouted Murdagh, leaping down into the bäta on a length of rope, his sword swinging. "Gilt's been fishin' game on the seas since before you was a teat-suckin' babe, an' ye're not takin' this damn thing from me!"

He slashed wildly, sticking the blade in the gunwale and stumbling on his bone leg. Wull pushed him over and leaped back as Murdagh grabbed at his collar.

"Ye think to challenge me, boy? Is that it? This is *my* sea!" said Murdagh, licking his teeth.

"UNTIE THE ARMS!" shouted Pappa.

"I jus' want to save him!" said Wull, standing between

Murdagh and Pappa. "You can have the rest of it, I jus' need one tiny part!"

The mormorach streamed from the water beside them, twirling through the *Hellsong*'s falling sails and smashing apart the exposed keel in a hail of splinters.

"It's mine!" shouted Murdagh. "This thing is mine! This is my sea an' this is my beast an' I've not hunted for it these years to let it slip into the pink hands o' some cut-squirt *Riverkeep!*"

Wull roared, charging across the bucking bäta and barreling into Murdagh's chest, knocking them both to the floor. They wrestled, the wire of Murdagh's teak-strong frame getting the better of Wull too quickly, pressing him to the bottom boards and wrapping his rough hands around his neck.

"I'll kill you!" shouted Murdagh. "I'll kill you, and then I'll kill your damn pappa!"

"You'll not touch him!" shouted Wull.

"Wull . . ." said Tillinghast, his voice drowned by the crash of water.

Wull kicked the old sailor in the guts and rolled under the center thwart, ducking his head from Murdagh's slashing blade.

He grabbed the last harpoon and stood, swiping at Murdagh's stomach and jabbing him back to the bäta's stern. The mormorach swept around the bäta, its fast bulk rising and dropping the boat into the chopping waves and taking their balance, the tip of the tail swiping a chunk from its side.

Murdagh grinned at him.

"You think you's got what it takes to kill a man, cut-squirt?" he said. "Gilt's killed men, men who got in his way, men who tried to take what was his. Some o' them was fine sailors, good men, men o' the sea. I think o' them when I walk in their footsteps, but you, a bloody nuisance, a nothin'—you'll be no more thought of than a crushed bug."

"I'm the Riverkeep!" shouted Wull, his pulse throbbing in his ears. He slashed and stabbed at Murdagh, who parried and ducked, his balance momentarily failing him. "This isn't the sea—it's the Danék and it's mine! It's mine! I am *not* nothing—I'm the Riverkeep! *I* keep the river! *I* keep it!"

As he raised the harpoon to drive at Murdagh, the sword appeared from nowhere and knocked it aside, clattering the metal from his hands and into the waves. Murdagh stepped forward smartly and placed the sword's point on Wull's chest, just above his pounding heart.

Wull felt his skin break on it, felt the hot trickle of blood on his frozen skin.

"An' so into history," said Murdagh, smiling. "Good-bye, cut-squirt."

Wull met his eyes as the blade was drawn back, and reached out his hand to take hold of Pappa's shoulder. Murdagh drove the sword forward.

It sank into Tillinghast's body, the loose bundle of straw and skin appearing in front of Wull, taking the blade and drawing Murdagh toward him with arms that were little more than loose shapes.

"No!" shouted Murdagh. "No, get off me! Get back!"

Tillinghast, eyes closed in concentration, stretched his body around Murdagh's wiry frame, the bunches of straw wrapping wriggling arms and legs in a tight grip, pulling him so close that they seemed to be one man.

The great homunculus toppled slowly, exhaustedly, into the lashing waves, taking Murdagh with him in a howling scream.

"Till!" cried Wull.

"No! My sea!" shouted Murdagh before they vanished into silence.

"Tillinghast!" said Wull, running to the edge and pushing his face into the water. Through the freezing sting he saw their wriggling mass sinking slowly, saw the moment Murdagh's body emptied, his mouth left shouting at the surface in mute protest, watched as Tillinghast's last fragments of energy gave out and he burst apart, his limbs and muscles and straw drifting from Murdagh's corpse like a blossom from a tree, heading to the bottom in a slow, graceful spiral.

"Untie the arms, it that speaks," said Pappa softly. He

was piled on the floor of the bäta, spent and empty.

"Pappa," said Wull, kneeling with him in a tight hug, face pressed to the greasy, wet hair, tears at the corners of his eyes. "I can't do it, Pappa. That was the last harpoon. I'm sorry, I'm so sorry. I can't do it."

"Untie the arms," said Pappa again.

"I can't," said Wull.

He half stood, saw the waters around them filled with the frantic splashing of the *Hellsong*'s surviving crew.

"We need to save these people," he said. "There'll be room in the bäta. . . ."

Then he saw the mormorach, white razors slicing from its dorsal fins as it bore down on him with impossible speed, its silver bulk rising through the waves like the spear of a god.

"Oh, Pappa," he said, his strength giving out and his knees buckling. "I'm sorry, I'm so sorry—it's coming and I can't stop it! I couldn't save you! I'm sorry!"

He looked into Pappa's clouded eyes and sensed the bohdan inside looking back at him, felt his eyes connecting with the creature—then felt it look away.

"Wulliam," said Pappa, brown eyed again and with the faintest whisper of his old voice. "Untie my arms, my boy."

Wull felt his eyes fill, water tumbling down his cheeks, his chest crushed by the memories of the brown eyes' patience as they watched him learn his knots, cast his line after breamcod, the voice that told him stories, taught him to read—told him he was loved.

"Pappa," he said, "you *are* still with me."

"Just enough," whispered Pappa.

Wull loosed the bonds at Pappa's wrists and held the thin body to him, the mormorach's wash tilting the bäta as it drew closer. The mormorach roared.

And Wull knew then what it was. It was death; it was the power of the earth and the sky and the sea, the power of everything he couldn't control or fight. He hugged Pappa closer and shut his eyes.

Pappa's body emptied in his arms, what bulk remained vanishing under his hands like a cut sack as the mormorach broke the surface, crying out with a screech that split the sky. Wull drew back, watching helplessly as Pappa's empty skin fell into the waves' hissing white, and turned to find the mormorach stopped as it had jumped, its gigantic head lashing in pain as the bohdan took it from within. It fell back, gnashing, its mouth wider than Wull could have imagined; then its milky, clouded eyes opened, looked right into his before they snapped shut, and the enormous beast vanished with a thunderclap, drenching him and knocking the bäta on its beams.

Wull dived overboard, following Pappa, kicking down through water that was busy with the frantic legs of the *Hellsong*'s survivors scrambling to the little boat. He glimpsed Pappa's head and sank farther, his adrenaline already making a breathless panic inside him.

He swam down into void and the huge silence of deeper water, Pappa twirling away into the beyond.

Wull reached out his hand, brushing Pappa's fingertips before they were whipped away by the currents. He watched until his lungs were bursting as Pappa flowed downward, welcomed into the Danék's embrace, his body light and free, his expression finally one of comfort and peace, his eyes and mouth closed.

As he began to fade into the sightless depths, Wull was overwhelmed by a desire to follow, to wrap himself in Pappa's strong arms and sleep alongside him forever, away from everything, away from the pain that ripped at his body and his soul.

And then he remembered the people above, struggling and dying.

He let Pappa go, watched him vanish.

Then, with a huge effort, he kicked himself upward into the chaos of the port and the wails of the injured as they threw themselves across his bäta.

He swam over, climbed in, lifted someone gently from the center thwart onto the bottom boards, and took up the oars. They slotted neatly into the wounds worn by his journey, and he pulled them to his chest.

"Is everyone all right?" he said.

"We're fine, Wull," said Samjon, nursing a cut forehead. "But there's some folk left near the wreckage."

"Then let's help them," said Wull, heaving on the oars and turning the bäta toward the waving hands of the stranded and the helpless.

22

The Bäta

But, having said that, there really is nothing quite like spring's bloom along the Danék. No sooner have the first shoots wriggled through the moss than the dead, colorless world is born anew: wildflowers splash riots of crimson and lilac like painters' daubs; bony trees are suddenly rich with leaf and blossom. The world is restored by the Danék's spring, and we, the weary travelers, with it.

—Wheeldon Garfill, A Path Trod Well: Journeys of My Life

The water's chill was a wall of pain on his open eyes, but Wull swam deeper, easing his wind out in calm bubbles as he sank, gathering the loose floating things in his fists. His hands scattered crabs on the high rocks of the seabed and sent a wave along the massed ranks of anemones, their little red fingers vanishing in a slurp of panic.

He found a gray, heavy lump lodged in a little groove of stone and snatched it, shooing away a claw-picking pincrab before kicking to the surface again for a huge grateful breath and edging over to the bäta.

It sat patiently on the still water, the battered, bitten pieces of its ribs and frame still open and exposed, spotted by little tufts from the wood's fiber like growing grass.

One of its eyes, cracked by the mormorach's tail, hung out from the exposed ribs as though swollen. Wull pushed it back gently so that it looked forward again, easing the wood into place so it would hold together, at least until he could fix it properly.

He dropped his gatherings onto the bottom boards and pulled himself in, dragging his body over the transom and onto the center thwart, his eyes closed, more exhausted than he'd realized, colder in the coastal wind than he'd been below the waves.

He stood, looked around, his shirt freezing where it touched his skin. The first light of dawn was rhythmically pierced by the flare of the lighthouse, and the port was filled with fish craft of all sizes: little one-person dinghies; twin-sailed pot-boats hemmed with lobster buckets; wide deep-sea trawlers, many-sailed and many-crewed, all with teeming nets on their pulleys and voices raised in happy labor. The breakwater had caught the early-morning glow, framing the statue of the Mother, the fish tails in her basket visible all across Canna Bay.

Above the port, the village's white houses climbed toward the forest and the mountain. Wull stared through the mist at the dark, slow-swaying treetops.

"I wonder how Remedie an' Mix are gettin' on," he said.

"Oh, they'll be fine," said Tillinghast's head, propped on his neck like a rivermelon on a market stall. "There won't be many'd cross Miss Cantwell when she's got a face on."

"I hope you're right," said Wull, thinking back to what Mix had said before she'd run into the woods, and what they'd felt together.

"I am," said Tillinghast. "You's wastin' your time, by the way."

"An' how's that?" said Wull, stuffing the scraps of muscle and straw he'd recovered into a hessian sack.

"You's never goin' to find all my bits, that's how. I must be mostly halfway across the world by now. Which is nice, I s'pose. I's always wanted to travel a bit, so I's glad I is, even if it's jus' my bahookie that gets to do it."

"I found *that*," said Wull, shuddering. "It's already in here."

"I know. I was bein' funny. An' you's got all my arms an' legs an' everythin'. Mighty impressive. An' you got . . . y'know . . ."

"Yup," said Wull. "Gave me a right start."

Tillinghast grinned.

"I've found all o' you, I reckon," said Wull, stretching his muscles. "'S taken me two days."

"An' I appreciates it," said Tillinghast. He squinted out the corner of his eye at the sacks filled by his body, feet and hands sticking in a jumble from the tops. "But you's never goin' to be able to put me back together, that's what I mean."

"I stitched your hand pretty well."

"But most o' my herbs is gone 'cept the ones in my head, an' they's a big part of it."

Wull shook his head. "They're only a small part, an' we can learn 'em in books. There's no takin' away what you've got inside—even gettin' smashed apart din't take it away."

"That's true," said Tillinghast.

"You're a real man, Till, an' I can fix you," said Wull.

"Right you are," said Tillinghast. He scrunched his face. "My nose is itchy again."

Wull leaned over and scratched it.

"No, right inside it," said Tillinghast. "There's nothin' in there—don't worry. You've no idea what the tide does for your sinuses."

"One thing, though," said Wull, scratching harder. "If I hadn't come for you, you'd have been lyin' down there for a long time, awake an' waitin', right?"

"Sure," said Tillinghast. "I'd've been bobbin' around on the seabed forever, I reckon."

"That would've been terrible," said Wull, holding Tillinghast's gaze.

"But you came an' got me. An' when I was lyin' down there in the dark, I knew you would. It's almost borin' how predictable you are, young Master Keep."

"Glad to disappoint," said Wull. He stood and gathered the oars to him, sat on the center thwart and took a deep breath.

"How you feelin' now? 'Bout your pappa, I mean," said Tillinghast.

"That he's at peace," said Wull. He put his hand on his healing cut, felt the little pulse within. "I knew, really, what was happ'nin' once I read about that thing, the bohdan. But I knew too there was the tiniest bit o' him left in there beside it. An' there was. He can sleep in the river now, an' he saved me. That was all he ever wanted, really—me bein' safe."

He looked over the bäta's edge. The wind-pulled surface was oily with the discarded scraps of the trawlers and skiffs, and a hurtle of seulas was slipping among them—alternately fed and chased off by the shouting fishfolk. As the ripples of the bäta's frame spread out into the bay, Wull saw himself reflected: brown-skinned, tired, bruised, and scarred. But older, too, more like Pappa, and more like himself. "That reminds me," he said, reaching into the prow. "I found this washed up this mornin'."

He reached over and placed Tillinghast's hat on his head, tipping out sand on the way.

"You got it!" said Tillinghast, trying to look up at the brim. "Thanks, Wull." He sniffed. "It does half smell like fish though—you could've gave it a quick rinse."

"Next time, I promise."

"How's the mandrake?" asked Tillinghast.

Wull leaned over and peered into the sack.

"Big," he said.

"How big?"

"I don't know. Like a cat?"

"How big of a cat?"

"Quite big."

"Tha's good," said Tillinghast.

"Why d'you want it so badly? For money?"

"Gods, no!" said Tillinghast. "I's stolen so many things for money, but not her."

"Then what? What you goin' to do with it?"

"With *her*," said Tillinghast. "I's goin' to plant her. She'll be fine an' strong an' alive an' safe. An' she'll be mine."

Wull put the mandrake gently back in the prow. It was heavier than before, he realized—heavier than its size. "You ready to be goin'?" he said.

"Oh, sure, jus' let me get comfortable," said Tillinghast, stretching his face and batting his eyelids. "All right . . . go."

"You fancy givin' me a hand with the rowin'?" said Wull.

Tillinghast grinned. "You cheeky little blaggard. When you've put me back together I'll kick your backside."

"I might stitch you up back to front," said Wull. "You'll have to kick your own backside then." He smiled and started the oars, Tillinghast yielding to his deep, hearty guffaw.

As they laughed together, Wull sculled them out beyond the breakwater toward the mouth of the Danék, working a slow, easy rhythm that was so natural as to be barely felt, the strength of Pappa's hands on his guiding him toward the boathouse and his own safe corner of the world.

"Come on, little boat," he whispered to the bäta. "Let's go home."

Each stroke of the oars filled him with the river's slow strength, its eternal song moving through his arms and into his heart. He closed his eyes, feeling its currents rush through his veins, listening ever closer to its delicate voice; and there, on the very edge of it, he heard the split-glass whisper of winter's end, and the chattering buds of an early spring.

ACKNOWLEDGMENTS

To my wonderful parents, Ellice and Chris, whose support has been constant and inspiring. To my immediate family— Viv, Trev, Graeme, Kirsty, and Amelia—for all their love and tolerance of my scribbling through the years. To Julie, for reading every word and showing me how to lead my stories into the light and the warmth. To my brilliant friends, for being everything that they are ("Emile Heskey?"). To George Parsonage, who keeps the Clyde, for welcoming me into his home and telling me stories about life on the river (www.glasgowhumanesociety.com). To my agent, Molly Ker Hawn, who saw something in my early work to take me on, and whose vision sent me on the most unlikely path to publication. To the staff of Penguin and Viking: Amy Alward for first reading those four pages, the brilliant editorial teams, and especially my editors, Shannon Cullen and Sharyn November, for their guidance. To these great people, and everyone else whose contributions to my writing and my life have allowed me to realize this long-held dream—thank you.